INDIGO

Also by Clemens J. Setz

SONS AND PLANETS

THE FREQUENCIES

LOVE IN THE TIME OF THE MAHLSTADT CHILD

THE OSTRICH TRUMPET

INDIGO

A Novel

CLEMENS J. SETZ

TRANSLATED BY ROSS BENJAMIN

Liveright Publishing Corporation
A Division of W. W. Norton & Company
New York London

Originally published in German as INDIGO: Roman
Copyright © 2012 by Suhrkamp Verlag Berlin
Illustrations on pp 44 and 134 copyright © Wikimedia, Photo: Michel Mazeau. Illustration
on p 279 copyright © James Soc Nyun. All other illustrations from the author's collection or
Suhrkamp Verlag's archive.
Translation copyright © 2014 by Ross Benjamin
First American Edition 2014

For information about permission to reproduce selections from this book, write to Permissions,
Liveright Publishing Corporation, a division of W. W. Norton & Company, Inc.,
500 Fifth Avenue, New York, NY 10110

For information about special discounts for bulk purchases, please contact
W. W. Norton Special Sales at specialsales@wwnorton.com or 800-233-4830

Manufacturing by Courier Westford
Book design by Lovedog Studio
Production managers: Anna Oler

Library of Congress Cataloging-in-Publication Data

Setz, Clemens J., 1982– author.
[Indigo : roman. English]
Indigo : a novel / Clemens J. Setz ; translated by Ross Benjamin. — First American edition.
pages cm
ISBN 978-0-87140-268-4
I. Benjamin, Ross, translator. II. Title.
PT2721.E78153513 2014
833′.92—dc23
2014028510

Liveright Publishing Corporation, 500 Fifth Avenue, New York, N.Y. 10110
www.wwnorton.com

W. W. Norton & Company Ltd., Castle House, 75/76 Wells Street, London W1T 3QT

1 2 3 4 5 6 7 8 9 0

The land was so flat that you could
see to the horizon in every direction.
And the horizon was just about knee-high,
sometimes it was also up to my hip.

Magda T.

Eventually people will adapt against anything.

Dr. Otto Rudolph

It looks like we're getting closer
to the heart of this criminal artichoke.

Adam West as Batman

Raaba bei Graz, November 1, 2006

Dear Clemens Setz,

I assume you would like to know everything that happened after you lost consciousness. First we tried to lay you down on the sofa. But the sofa was too narrow, and our physical strength is, as you've seen, very limited, and so you rolled back onto the floor. That's how you got the wound over your right eye. Of course, we immediately put something on the injured spot (ice, wrapped in a dish towel), but your forehead swelled up quickly anyway. We had, to be honest, not expected you to slide so easily off the sofa. From your external appearance, we wouldn't have thought that even in a horizontal position your body's center of gravity is somewhere near your belly. After all, you're such a dainty, almost fragile-looking person! Be that as it may, when we saw the lump over your eye, we immediately decided to take you out of the zone and into another room.

You asked my husband and me about the difficulties we have to contend with since our decision to bring Robert back home—and now you've experienced those difficulties for yourself. Please be assured that we're very, very sorry about that, but I think that the situation has perhaps provided you insight you probably wouldn't have gained from a conversation alone. As a teacher at the institute, you might have been cut off from experiences like that.

We quickly carried you out of the room, because the lump looked really alarming, and you also hadn't responded to our attempts at resuscitation. In the kitchen your condition was clearly improving. You opened your eyes and let us sit you down on a chair, but then you suddenly keeled over again and began to sweat, and your left arm cramped, but, thank God, we were familiar with that, we've all felt that way before. Iceberg—that's what we call it. That feeling as if you were buried under tons of ice. We've all had to go through that. Of course, that's relatively easy to say now, because we've lived with it for a long time and developed a certain resistance, or at least know what to expect. But on an empty stomach—as in your case—it can certainly knock someone down.

Robert sends you his warm regards, by the way. At least I interpret his behavior along those lines. You never know with him. He probably won't be returning to the institute next year.

We drove you to the hospital. You were a little confused, but we had expected that too, because my father, for example, who visited us shortly after Robert's birth, couldn't speak right for a whole day, he slurred his words and babbled, and he was alternately hot and cold, and he had attacks of vertigo. At first we were worried that he might have suffered a stroke or something like that from shock, but he insisted on holding Robert anyway. There's a photo of that, taken from the yard through the window.

It's all in the head, Indigo nonsense, my father said. You know, the people of his generation and the way things were in those days, the low level of awareness in the general population, so . . . Okay, we also wanted to believe that it was all nothing. Nothing lasting, nothing that truly had to do with our child. Nothing real.

You take children by the hand, you touch them, my father said back then, and I just showed him my back, the scrapes I had from falling down so much at that time, the rash on the nape of my neck. I also showed him the burst blood vessel in my left eye. Back then I could still see a bit with that eye, and of course I didn't go to the doctor until it was too late, when the sight was already gone.

Herr Setz, we hope you're doing better. And we want to assure you that we don't harbor any prejudices against you—whatever the reason for the premature termination of your work at the institute might have been, we don't presume to judge. If you'd like, we can continue our conversation elsewhere. It goes without saying that our house remains open to you, and we welcome your visit, but my husband and I would also understand if you no longer want to expose yourself to what we have constantly had to deal with for almost fifteen years.

With our best regards,
Marianne Tätzel

University Hospital of Graz
Department of Trauma Surgery

Patient: Setz, Clemens Johann   Admitted
Date of Birth: November 15, 1982

Case History/Medical Report
Pt. entered ER accompanied by two self-described acquaintances.

Mental state: alert, clear, oriented, slowed. According to his escorts,
pt. lay unconscious on the floor for about 10 min. after accidental fall.
Beforehand pt. mentioned a bright flicker at rt. edge of visual field. After
collapse no layperson CPR was deemed necessary.
At time of hospitalization pt. not in life-threatening condition, car-
dioresp. system stable. Rt. frontal bruised tear and gaping, bleeding
occipital CLW. Several small hematomas on upper body. Pupils round,
medium width, isocoric, no facial paresis or hemiplegic symptoms. No
other neurol. abnormalities. Pain on percussion of skullcap. No nausea,
but slight disturbance of equilibrium. No other external signs of injury.
Joints have full active/passive range of motion, no pain.

Treatments
Frontal wound: cleaning with Octenisept, steri-strips. Suturing of occipital CLW with three stitches. Tetanus shot. Cranial CT scan ordered.
Results: No recent hemorrhage, fracture, space-occupying lesion, no
sign of recent territorial infarction.
Pt. discharged AMA. Informed of poss. complications and symptoms
resulting from fall. If general condition should worsen, pain should
occur, etc., pt. advised to proceed immediately to emergency room.

10/16/2006

Dr. Uhlheim

PART I

In a field
I am the absence
of field.

—*Mark Strand*

1.   The Nature of Distance

On June 21, 1919, the scuttling of the German Imperial High Seas Fleet took place at the British naval base Scapa Flow near the Scottish coast. The Treaty of Versailles, signed by Germany shortly beforehand, provided not only for the return of the skull of Chief Mkwawa to the British government, but also for the immediate surrender of all ships. But German Admiral Ludwig von Reuter chose to sink his ships rather than relinquish them to the British, whom he regarded as an uncultivated people. The warships have remained ever since on the seafloor at a depth of about one hundred and fifty feet. And that's fortunate for modern space travel, as high-grade steel salvaged on diving expeditions from the wrecks of these warships—which have been underwater for almost a hundred years now—is used in the manufacture of satellites, Geiger counters, and full-body scanners at airport security checkpoints. The rest of the steel in the world is—after Hiroshima, Chernobyl, and the numerous atomic bomb tests carried out in the earth's atmosphere—too radioactive to be used in the production of such highly sensitive instruments. Sufficiently uncontaminated steel is available only in Scapa Flow, at a depth of one hundred and fifty feet.

With this story begins the remarkable book *The Nature of Distance*, published in 2004, by the child psychologist and education theorist Monika Häusler-Zinnbret. On a Saturday in the summer of 2006 I visited her in her apartment in Graz's Geidorf District with its abundant villas. At that time I had already broken off my six-month internship as a mathematics tutor at the Helianau Institute. The principal of the institute, Dr. Rudolph, had warned me never again to set foot on the premises.

I sought out Frau Häusler-Zinnbret to ask her under what conditions, in her view, Indigo children live in Austria today, two years after the appearance of her influential book, which strikes hopeful notes in its opening lines. And whether she knew what the so-called "relocations" I had often witnessed uncomprehendingly during my internship were all about.

On the old front door with the three doorbells there was also an ornamental knocker, which looked as if it might once have been real—but then, on a hot day, it had simply fused with the darkly painted wood of the door and turned into an ear-shaped adornment above the heavy cast-iron handle. Next to the unusually magnificent house, in the little yard enclosed by a brass fence and a hedge veiled by many spider webs, stood a few quiet birches, aquatic-seeming and practically silver, and in front of a ground-level window I spotted a single sunflower, straining its head attentively upward as if listening to soft music, because it felt the morning sun coming around the next corner. It was a warm day, shortly before ten. The door was open. In the stairwell it was cool, and there was a faint smell of damp stone and old potatoes in the air.

A month or two earlier, I wouldn't have noticed any of that.

Before I went upstairs to the practice, I checked my pulse. It was normal.

Frau Häusler-Zinnbret kept me waiting for a long time outside her door. I had pushed the doorbell—under which her two last names were inscribed, linked by a wavy ≈ instead of a hyphen—several times, and, as so often in my life, marveled at the fact that female psychologists and education theorists always have double names. I heard her walking around in her apartment and moving furniture or other fairly large objects. When I at one point thought I detected her footsteps very close to the door, I rang again, in the hope of finally catching her attention. But the footsteps receded, and I stood in the stairwell and didn't know whether to go home.

I gave it another try and knocked.

A door behind me opened.

– Herr Setz?

I turned around and saw a woman's head looking out through the crack of the door.

–Yes, I said. Frau Häusler?

– Please come in. I'm in a . . . well, a transitional phase at the moment, as it were, please excuse the disorder . . . yeah . . .

Impressed and intimidated by the fact that her apartment apparently extended over the entire floor, I stopped right on the other side of the doorway and was only reminded by a clothes hanger that Frau Häusler-Zinnbret was holding out in front of my chest to take off my coat and shoes.

Frau Häusler-Zinnbret's physical appearance was impressive. She was fifty-six, but her face looked youthful, she was tall and slim, and wore her hair in a long braid down her back. Apart from her black boots, she was rather casually dressed that day, a knitted vest hung over her shoulders. When she spoke, she mostly looked over her glasses, only when she read something did she push them up a bit.

She led me into her office, one of three, she told me. Here she usually received her visitors—from all over the world, she added, and then flipped a switch on the wall that first lowered the blinds a bit and then raised them; a strangely hypnotic process, as if the room were blinking in slow motion. The morning sun entered the room. A sunbeam shining like cellophane crept across the floor, bent at the wall, and ran up to a large-scale abstract painting in which round forms vied with angular ones.

– Oh, dear, said the child psychologist. Did you hurt yourself?

–Yes, I said. A little accident. But nothing serious.

– Nothing serious, Frau Häusler-Zinnbret repeated with a nod, as if she had heard that excuse many times before. Tea? Or maybe coffee?

– Just tap water, please.

–Tap water? she asked, smiling to herself. Hm . . .

She brought me a glass that tasted strongly of dishwashing detergent, but I was still glad to have something to drink, for the walk from my apartment near Lendplatz to Frau Häusler-Zinnbret's had made me tired and thirsty. The night before, someone had dismantled my bicycle into its component parts. They had been left neatly in the yard that morning, the wheels, the frame, the handlebars, in an arrangement roughly corresponding to a quincunx pattern.

— So you're doing research for a book, is that right? she asked, when we had sat down at a small glass table.

Frau Häusler-Zinnbret took a fan out of a box that looked like an enlarged cigarette pack and unfolded it. She offered one to me too, but I declined.

— I don't know what it's going to be yet, I said. More of an article.

— The dark life of the I-kids, said Frau Häusler-Zinnbret, tapping with her forefinger a little *uh-huh* on the table. I nodded.

— And why that?

— Well, I said, the subject is, I mean, it's sort of in the air, so to speak . . .

The psychologist made a strange gesture as if she were waving a fly away from her face.

— Until recently you were still at the institute? she asked.

— Yes.

— You know, I'm acquainted with Dr. Rudolph, she said, fanning herself.

— I understand.

I was about to get up.

— No, said Frau Häusler-Zinnbret. Don't worry. I'm not one of his . . . Please, stay seated. Dr. Rudolph . . . I'd like to know what sort of impression he made on you, Herr Seitz.

Sounds of people on the stairs, an itch by my eye, a loose shoelace . . .

— A difficult person, I finally said.

— A fanatic.

— Yes, maybe.

— Did you live there, I mean, on the premises? Near the . . .

— No, I commuted.

— Commuted.

— Yes.

– Mm-hmm, said Frau Häusler-Zinnbret. That's better, isn't it? Because of . . .

There was a pause. Then she said:

– You know, the proximity to the I-children, or what does Dr. Rudolph call it now? Does he even have a name for it?

– No, he prefers—

– Oh, that damn idiot, Frau Häusler-Zinnbret said with a laugh, and then she added: Sorry. What was I saying? Oh, yes, the proximity to the dingos can change people. I mean, not only physically . . . but also their worldview. Does he still do those . . . those baths?

I was so astonished to hear someone use the word *dingo* that it took a while before I replied:

– Who?

– Dr. Rudolph.

– Baths? I don't know.

Frau Häusler-Zinnbret briefly pursed her lips, then smiled. The fan took over for her the task of shaking her head in disbelief.

– What baths do you mean? I asked.

– The bath in the crowd, she said.

– I never heard anything about that.

– Dr. Rudolph's personal Kneipp Cure. He has the little dingos surround him and bears the symptoms. For hours. He swears by it. But you must have seen that . . .

I shook my head.

– You noticed, though, that he's a fanatic?

– Yes, I said. I mean, he's structured his institute according to the mirror principle, that is, the teachers interact with each other no more than the students do. So that they know how the students feel.

– I can imagine one would get pretty lonely, said Frau Häusler-Zinnbret. But one would probably notice a few things too.

Was that a prompt?

– Yes, I said, trying not to let my confusion show. You do witness certain things, like, for ex—

– I used to really admire him, Frau Häusler-Zinnbret interrupted me. His work methods. And that absolute mastery of all techniques. He was lightning-quick, you know. Really lightning-quick. A virtuoso. But then I was with him once in one of his Viennese support groups, mainly kids with Down's syndrome, and a few other impairments too were there . . . Anyway, he played that game with them, musical chairs, but with the same number of chairs as participants. So completely pointless. And he recited some counting rhyme, and the, um . . . the kids ran in a circle and then, boom! They sat down. And then they looked at each other, as if to say: And what's the point of this? But Dr. Rudolph's theory was that no one should be excluded, especially not the slowest kid. No winners, no losers. Well, as I said, a fanatic. He always said there's no such thing as happy ends, only now and then fair ends.

– Fair ends, I said. Yes, that's right. He said that a lot.

– A lunatic, said Frau Häusler-Zinnbret.

The fan in her hand moved in agreement.

– He made it unambiguously clear to me, I said, that I'm no longer welcome at the institute.

– Aha, she said, and paused.

I felt the heat rising to my face. I took a sip of water and tried to undo the top button of my shirt. But it was already open.

– To come back to your actual question, said Frau Häusler-Zinnbret. It's been a while since I've dealt directly with a di . . . with one of those poor creatures. They are, thank God, rare . . . still relatively rare, yes . . . But that's not to say I don't remember well. You do have to ask me concrete questions, however, Herr Seitz, or else I can't tell you anything.

–Of course.

I took my notepad out of my pocket.

I had jotted down three questions. More hadn't occurred to me. I would like to claim that I knew from experience that you always learn more in an informal conversation than in a classic interview with prepared questions—but I had no experience at all.

– Yes, well, my first question would be . . . when did you first begin working with Indigo children?

It was apparent that Frau Häusler-Zinnbret was prepared for that question. She had undoubtedly been asked it hundreds of times, and in her look was a reproach: *You could have looked that up in other interviews with me, young man.* I took a sip of dishwashing detergent water and put my pen to the notepad, ready to take down all that might come.

– Well, she said, starting when the problem first became acute, of course. That was around '95 or early '96, when the first reports came out. You had already been born then, right? And as is always the case with things like that, there was all manner of uninformed chatter and journalistic chaos that relatively quickly became intolerable, at least to me and some others . . . and that's when I decided to do something. To shed some light on the matter.

I had taken notes. On the pad was written:

PROB. ACUTE 95/96, THEN Ǝ CHATTER. → DO SOMETHING ABOUT IT.

– Can you really read that later? Sorry I'm peeking . . .

From this or that word choice or foreign-sounding syllable, Frau Häusler-Zinnbret's German background could be heard. She was from Goslar, but had lived in Austria for more than thirty years.

– It's my cipher, I said. I always write in block letters.

– Is that so? And why? Isn't cursive simpler for quick note-taking?

– No, not for me. I've never been able to get used to it.

– Interesting.

Her nod was unmistakably that of a child psychologist, as if she had given up her original nod like a hard-to-understand dialect only late in life, perhaps during her studies, and had been working ever since on this new nod. And her forefinger again tapped *uh-huh*. No doubt she already had a name handy for this disorder, a particular form of dysgraphia, an antipathy to the continuous line, the child who would rather play with alphabet soup than with spaghetti . . .

– And you can reconstruct the conversation on the basis of those notes?

– Yes, it's like instant coffee, you take the powder, and then all you have to do is add some hot water and . . .

I broke off, because the comparison had failed.

– Um, Frau Häusler, I said. You mentioned that the *problem* first arose at that time. So was it perceived that way? As a problem?

– Well . . . certainly, what do you think? People were getting sick by the dozen, and didn't know why. Mothers vomiting over their baby's cradle. A big mess. Dizziness, diarrhea, rashes, down to permanent damage of all internal organs, those are serious symptoms, after all, which can't always be explained psychosomatically. Understandable that panic sets in, isn't it?

I nodded.

DIZZIN., DIARR., RASHES, DAMAGE ∀ ORGANS.

– And then the first voices piped up: Yes, the symptoms always occur only when I'm at home, only near my children, and so on.

When Frau Häusler-Zinnbret imitated those voices, she used a heavily exaggerated Austrian intonation. I had to laugh.

– But that's exactly how it was, she said. You definitely wouldn't have laughed if you'd been there. It was eerie.

– Yeah, I can imagine.

– And the people's hysteria. The way they walked around in the children's rooms with their Geiger counters and tore up the floorboards and inspected everything, really everything, but there was nothing. Nothing.

∀ INSPECTED APARTMENTS: RES. = ∅

– Except . . .

– Well, that last step was one nobody wanted to take, of course. People always forget: When they had to give the disease a name, they at first named it after the first child that had been demonstrably afflicted with it. Beringer disease . . . But the name disappeared very quickly from the medical literature, it never even reached collective consciousness. Then they called it Rochester syndrome or Rochester disease, those unimaginative cowards . . . but that didn't catch on

either, thank God. The objection was that such a name was discrim-
inatory, like the first name for AIDS. Do you know what AIDS was
called in the early eighties?

– No.

– GRID. Gay-related immune deficiency. Of course, no one
remembers that now. They're forgotten very quickly, such names.
Indigo, that name ultimately took root, strangely enough, even though
it's definitely the most ridiculous one of all. Totally absurd. Borrowed
from some esoteric self-help books. The kids aren't blue, after all, and
neither are the people who fall ill.

There was a brief pause, because I couldn't take notes quickly
enough.

– And when did you first work with one of those children? How
did that come about?

– Hm. At the time, I wasn't really interested in such family-encom-
passing problems, though that might sound narrow-minded today. But
back then, I mean, the late nineties, they were, so to speak, the second
seventies for developmental psychology. It was a crazy time.

NO FAM.-ENCOMP. PROBL., NARROW-MINDED, 90s=70s, CRAZY *t*

– But of course, Frau Häusler-Zinnbret went on, of course you
often can't just discount all that, I mean, that whole complex, school,
home life, temperament, learning environment, natural ability, how
does a kid turn out who has certain difficulties in school, perhaps
hemmed in by their personal environment, and so on. In any case, I
realized more and more clearly that I . . . Well, it would be best to give
you an example, okay? I enter a room, and some opera is blaring at
full blast from a stereo system, that alone is already really strange, and
the family's also completely hysterical, in tears, and I see the baby in its
crib and, my God, that was a sight, all right, that completely helpless
little face. Honestly and sincerely at a loss, and only two years old. But
already at its wit's end, so to speak.

I just nodded.

– And that time wasn't yet as hysterical as today. Back then you were still allowed to ask someone who was clutching his temples whether he had a headache. But nowadays, ugh! Impossible. Because right behind him there might . . . Oh, what a misery . . .

She laughed. And added:

– You know exactly what I mean, right?

I nodded uncertainly.

– How often have you made such a faux pas?

– A few times.

– Dr. Rudolph, Frau Häusler-Zinnbret said, shaking her head. I bet he even teaches his dog . . . Oh, never mind. It has no effect at all on animals, of course, apart from a few exceptions. Those cases are very rare, thank God. And they might even be completely normal statistical deviations. A monkey in a research institute, for example, it was, wait, I'll quickly look it up . . .

She stood up and went to her bookcase.

– I'll show you the picture, she murmured.

When she had found it, she held the open book toward me. The picture showed a monkey in a box. The face contorted with pain. I turned away, held a hand out defensively, and said:

– No, thank you, please don't.

She looked at me in surprise. Her right shoe made a little turn. Then I heard the book snap shut.

– What? You'd prefer if I didn't show you the picture, or—

– Yes, I said. I can't stand things like that.

– But you have to know what it looks like, if you're interested in these issues. It's not that bad, wait . . .

I held on to the seat of my chair. Julia had advised me in moments of sudden fear to focus all my attention on something from the past. As always, the white flight of steps came to my mind. Cloudless sky. Venus visible in broad daylight.

– Open your eyes, Frau Häusler-Zinnbret said gently. Everything is okay.

– I'm sorry, I said. I react really badly to things like that. Animals and such. When they . . . you know. It's a phobia of mine, so to speak.

A brief pause. Then she said:

– Phobia. I don't know whether that's the right word, Herr Setz. Are you sure you don't want to see the picture of the monkey? Shall I describe it for you, perhaps? The apparatus? Would that help?

– No, please . . .

I had to lean forward to breathe better.

– My goodness, said Frau Häusler-Zinnbret. No, then of course I won't bother you with it.

– Thank you, I said.

My face was hot, and I felt as if I were looking through a fish tank.

– Have you ever been in treatment for that? she asked in the kindest tone I had heard her use up to that point. I could recommend someone, if you . . .

– No, thank you.

– Really? I do think you should face up to it. Writing exercises, for example. Attempts to visualize what frightens you.

– I–in your book, I said, you compare . . . well . . . in the very beginning . . . you write that the children are like that sunken steel in . . .

A somewhat longer pause. I made an apologetic gesture.

– Yes, well, said Frau Häusler-Zinnbret, you must have read the old edition. I actually thought as much. But that doesn't matter, the mistake can easily be remedied.

She stood up and went to a shelf, took out a book, and brought it to me. When I opened it, I saw that the preface had been replaced by a new, much shorter one. And now there was a black-and-white picture of a baby in a crib. The baby, about two or three years old, stood upright and held on to the wooden bars with one hand. It was crying, but the face didn't look distraught, more curious and relieved, as if the person the baby had long been yearning for had finally come into the room.

– I took the picture, said Frau Häusler-Zinnbret. With a telephoto lens.

As she brought the picture closer to my face, she laid a hand on my back.

Tommy

Tommy Beringer was born on February 28, 1993, in Rochester, Minnesota. He was the third child of Julian Stork, an electrical engineer and computer scientist, and Roberta Beringer, who was just twenty-four years old at the time of Tommy's birth. She had had her first child at sixteen. The couple had moved from Sharon Springs, Kansas, to Rochester in the late eighties, both of them came from families with many children. Julian had graduated with honors from the University of Kansas School of Engineering and soon found a relatively well-paid job, which allowed Roberta to stay at home and take care of the children.

Shortly after Tommy's birth, Roberta became ill. It began with impaired balance and nausea that lasted days. Later came severe diarrhea and short-term disorientation. Because Roberta had had health problems after her first two births, she didn't think much of it and didn't go to the doctor. But shortly thereafter, her two sons Paul and Marcus became ill. And they had similar symptoms.

A doctor suspected a problem with diet. Another said that the symptoms might indicate allergic reactions to certain synthetic materials used in the construction of the apartment. When Julian too began to suffer from severe headaches and nausea, the family decided to move. They gave up their apartment and bought a small house, for which they had to take out a mortgage.

The symptoms didn't subside, they actually intensified. Soon Julian noticed that he felt better when he was at work and that his splitting headaches always set in when he had spent a few hours at home. On the weekend they plagued him all day.

A weeklong vacation on Roberta's parents' farm in Sharon Springs brought about no improvement worth mentioning. So it must have had something to do with diet after all. A macrobiotic regimen was tried, also a month of raw food. At the end of the month, Roberta had to be taken to the hospital one night with acute breathing difficulty. There she recovered fairly quickly from her symptoms. The doctors told her that she was perfectly healthy, but pointed out that early motherhood and the constantly intense nervous strain that taking care of three little kids naturally entailed for a young woman could often cause such symptoms of fatigue. They advised her to book a stay at a health spa and hire a part-time nanny.

– Does that mean I'm crazy? Roberta asked the doctors.

They assured her that she was completely fine. She was very tired and might have passed that on to her children. It would probably do her and her three sons good to have someone new in the household.

Julian didn't like the idea of a nanny. He was worried, and justifiably so, about the family's financial situation. After all, they had just bought this house here and were a long way from being able to regard it as their property. To hire a nanny was quite simply unfeasible, he said. But of course he understood that things could by no means go on as before. Every time he visited his well-rested wife, free of all maladies, in the hospital, he was struck by the difference. She was full of energy, played chess with Paul, who was eight or nine years old at the time, in the hospital lounge, and spoke with a louder voice than usual—indeed, she was even in a joking mood and bantered with the young doctors.

Julian continued to suffer from severe headaches, but these could be managed to some extent with painkillers. And in the meantime the children were doing a little better too. It was summer, Paul and Marcus played a lot during the day in the yard of the small house, and the older brother taught the younger how to ride a bike. But shortly after Roberta returned home, her symptoms reappeared. In autumn the whole family, with the exception of little Tommy, suffered from bloody diarrhea and rashes. To prevent him from becoming infected, they brought him to Sharon Springs to stay with his grandparents for a few weeks. The diarrhea afflicting the whole family got better immediately, and the other symptoms disappeared too, practically overnight.

When they received a call from Roberta's mother, Linda, after a few days, and she told them that they should probably come and get little Tommy, his parents were alarmed. Linda complained of diarrhea and vomiting and intense attacks of vertigo that would suddenly overcome her; this morning, she said, she had even passed out in the kitchen with a cup of hot cocoa. Think of what could have happened!

They picked up Tommy. In the car Julian felt sick, and he had to pull over to throw up. Afterward he began to have difficulties with motor skills. He couldn't turn the key in the ignition.

– It's the worst feeling in the world, he said later. When you're too weak to do anything, even the smallest thing, actually physically too weak. It's as if your own body had decided just to call it quits, to waste away.

And Roberta summed up the subsequent months and years as follows:

– No one can imagine the odyssey we've been through. If it weren't about the welfare of our children, I would have given up years ago.

The picture everyone associates with the name Tommy Beringer shows him as a baby. His disgusted and thus unusually adult-seeming facial expression and his mistrustfully tilted head might well account for the extraordinary popularity of the photo, which seems to have struck a nerve, so to speak, and adorns T-shirts, posters, album covers, and, in the form of a stencil image, graffiti walls all over the world.

The picture of the divided chamber has become equally famous. In the middle is a thick lead wall. To its left little Tommy Beringer is playing in a box full of colorful foam balls, while to its right the female test subject is hooked up to various medical devices measuring her skin resistance, heart rate, brain activity, and other bodily functions. The picture was taken by Australian photographer David J. Kerr during one of the numerous tests. With a telephoto lens. Because all pictures of Tommy shot at close range were either out of focus or looked as if the photographer's hands had been trembling violently.

The test subject had no idea which child was on the other side of the wall. It could be either an I-child or a completely ordinary child, she had been told. The young woman's face displayed skepticism toward the purported effect. After only half an hour, the project had to be aborted, because both the young woman and a doctor got sick.

Tommy was moved to an isolation ward, in which usually only radiation victims were treated. The whole ward was empty, Tommy cried often and was attended by a nurse who came hourly for no more than five minutes, fed and cleaned him and put the toys he had thrown on the floor back into the crib with him.

In 1999, when Tommy was six years old, the family, overwhelmed by the prospect of further tests and interview requests, immigrated to Canada. Julian divorced his wife in 2002 and has since moved back to Rochester. He doesn't like to talk about the past. In 2004 Roberta Beringer and her three sons became Canadian citizens. They lead very reclusive lives, don't participate in the worldwide debate about the Indigo phenomenon. Any attempt to locate Tommy Beringer is consistently blocked by his mother. He isn't enrolled at any school in the country, and a website with his name, on which now and then photos of a teenager on a bicycle and short, melodramatic texts about the universe and loneliness were posted, turned out to be a hoax by two college students from California.*

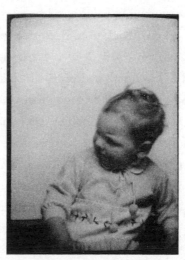

* The British band The Resurrection of Laura Palmer named their second studio album, *The Beringer Tree*, after the boy.

2. Robert Tätzel, Twenty-nine, Burnt-Out

They brought him the monkey in a wooden box. The box didn't look at all like lab or science equipment, it was dark and had a few lighter spots and traces of wear. It was hard to say what was normally kept in it.

Robert had set up the easel, the dabs of paint on the palette (he preferred a smaller one, for too much choice paralyzed him) looked like a rainbow designed by a planning committee. All the brushes were new, five minutes ago he had taken them out of their packaging. He loved the smell of virgin paintbrushes.

The picture he was going to paint would be on the small side. Thin paint on a thickly applied background. A thin paint will stick to a thick paint, Bob Ross (the other deep voice besides Adam West that was directly related to God) had said on the instructional iVD.

The monkey made a face as if he recognized Robert. He extended a wrinkly black hand toward him. When the hand was not taken, he brought it to his mouth and bit gently into it. The coordination of his arm movements apparently caused the monkey great difficulty. Particularly the left side of his body seemed impaired.

– What's wrong with him? Robert, without looking up from his canvas, asked the young lab technician who had brought the animal.

– He's not used anymore, the man answered.

The technician walked once around the box, laid his gloved hand on the monkey's back, and tilted him forward. Robert saw: The back of the monkey's head was shaved, and something that looked like a tiny faucet jutted out of the cranium, complete with shutoff valve and a damply glistening outlet.

– What's that for? asked Robert.

He tried to lend his voice the most emotional tone possible. That wasn't easy, but the focus on the preparation, the slight turns of the brush, which soaked up paint, helped him.

– An emergency exit, said the lab technician.

The brown of the forehead was exquisite, a rare nuance. To re-create it, to track it down among all the possible mixtures of paint on the palette, would definitely take up the next few minutes. After he had tried out several shades of brown, he realized what he was doing, and he looked at the technician, who was sitting, bored or lost or satisfied with himself or in anticipation of some major disaster, in the office chair.

– You don't have to . . . , said Robert.

And because he couldn't gauge the reaction to his words, he gestured to the canvas.

The lab technician tilted his head as if Robert had said something very interesting that he had to think about.

– He got used to us, the technician finally said. That's quite normal for primates. In general, they don't see any great difference between related species. Did you see the parade yesterday?

Robert dabbed a little bit of paint on his left hand. He gazed at the spot and tried to extrapolate what impression the paint would leave on the canvas.

– No, he said, without looking at the technician. I didn't.

– Totally insanity, Herr . . . ?

– Tätzel.

– Herr Tätzel. Yeah, so it was total insanity, I mean, we had to close the windows. The worst part was those horns. When a hundred people are blowing into those little things, it bursts your eardrums.

Robert decided to face the technician and simply stare at him. The time for that had come.

But the technician had rested his forehead against the back of the chair, in which he was sitting backward.

— Parades, the technician murmured into the back of the office chair. No one knows what they're supposed to be good for. And the faces of those people . . .

He shook his head, and even though the wasp waist of the chair back was between his legs, he crossed them. Robert always found it unbearable to be presented with the soles of another person's shoes. Most of the time it happened in exactly this way: Someone formed a sort of roof with his upper leg, a shinbone lectern. At that point he would have liked nothing more than to punch that person. Luckily, it was primarily men who sat like that, but he was now and then cursed with a glimpse of a woman's soles too. What a disgusting sight, the pavement-gray tread and the pieces of strangers' lives stuck to it, that horrible documentation of everywhere someone has been. Unbearable, those people. Truly sensitive people didn't have things like shoe soles at all, they showed them of their own accord no more than men would show the sticky underside of their penis.

He wiped a small mistake from the corner of the eye in the sketchily pale monkey face on the canvas in front of him. *We don't make mistakes, we have happy accidents.*

— Are you familiar with Bob Ross? he asked the technician.

— Uh, the painter?

— Yeah.

— Yeah, said the technician, I find it totally soothing, that show. I have some episodes on my iSocket.

— It always makes me aggressive, said Robert. But in a good way.

— And did you study art history too? asked the technician.

The *too* bothered Robert. Yes, he had tried it. Two semesters. And he hadn't liked it, okay? What business was that of this idiot nobody? He had to put down the brush and focus for a while on the monkey. His heartbeat slowed. *A thin paint will stick to a thick paint, Robin.*

———

– We have drawing classes here pretty often, said the technician. Most of the time they're in the conference room, everyone sits in a circle . . . But they don't usually ask for monkeys. More for the mice.

– With the ear on their back?

– What?

– Oh, I just . . . , said Robert. There was once this article in a magazine, which my biology teacher gave me at the time, about a hairless lab mouse with a human ear on its back.

– Ah, said the technician. The Vacanti mouse. That wasn't a human ear, that's a misunderstanding. That was just cartilage they grew there and they just molded it into this special form, so that . . .

– Art, said Robert.

– Yeah. In a way.

– Where might the mouse be now? asked Robert.

And he felt a slight twinge in his chest. So soon.

– They don't live long, said the technician.

– Where do you think the mouse is buried?

Another slight twinge, this time higher, just under the Adam's apple. There was a pause. The technician drummed his fingers a few times on his knees.

– And you're doing a whole series of these? he asked.

– Yes.

Painting sounds, brush on canvas. The softest scraping in the world. Like the scratching of clawless paws on a closed door.

– Hm, said the technician. Is it okay if I . . .

Robert looked up briefly to see what this was about. The technician was holding up a cigarette. Robert nodded. Relieved sounds of a lighter, deep drag, silence. Why is the smell of a freshly lit cigarette so good? Cigars are an entirely different matter. Principal Rudolph. As if someone were carrying around a factory chimney in his mouth.

– I have nothing against it, said Robert.

– Thanks.

Silence. The monkey had fallen asleep.

– And you're really doing a whole series of these, huh?

– Yes, said Robert.

– What will that look like?

– Excuse me?

– Ah, I don't want to bother you. But I was just wondering, will they all be animals?

– Mainly, yes.

– Crazy.

– Do you think so?

– Oh, I'm sorry, that sounded worse than I meant it. Honestly. Sorry.

Robert liked it when people put up their arms as if they were being held at gunpoint. That gesture helped him imagine what it would be like to actually fire a gun at them. The cloud of smoke, the recoil of the weapon, the suddenly bursting abdomen, the reverberation of the shot.

– You're just doing your job, Robert said in a conciliatory tone.

– Um, well . . . yeah, I guess . . .

Robert had to restrain himself. A small window in the technician's attention had opened. He could have played with him now. This attention window, he was familiar with it, felt the draft coming from it. Just one or two well-placed sentences, and the guy might even start to cry.

Maybe another time.

– Do you think it looks like him?

– What?

– The painting. Here, take a look.

Robert turned the canvas slightly to the side so that the technician only had to crane his neck. Just don't show too much, maintain control. The window was still open. The technician's features looked intimidated, like the face of a child asking an adult stranger the time or the way home.

– Mm-hmm, the technician said with a nod.

– Looks like him?

– Yeah.

– But not photorealistic, right? Because that's not the way I paint.

– Like a photo? No, I wouldn't say it looks like a photo.

– Wonderful, said Robert.

He enjoyed the growing unease the technician was exuding. It was like that extremely high, buzzing sound that turned-on TV screens made. When he had passed a whole wall of those devices for the first time at the age of twenty-one, it had almost knocked him over.

He wondered whether he should say something that would completely horrify the technician, but still condemn him to silent attention and inactivity, something strange and yet logical, something like: Don't you have the feeling that the sky outside has turned red? Or: Have you ever let God into your life? It was that simple. He didn't even have to look at the technician's face.

– What's his name?

– The monkey? Didi.

– Nice name, said Robert.

And he added in the dubbed German voice of Adam West:

– So you see, Robin, it's always important to give animals a name. For they are our friends.

They were silent for a while. Then the technician said:

– Hm, that's funny. Do you ever paint from photos?

From his more composed voice—the anxiety window was slowly closing—Robert could tell that he had finished smoking his cigarette. Nothing brings back self-confidence as quickly as the stubbing out of a cigarette, while the world turns on its axis and somewhere far away suns shrink into red dwarves.

– I've taken photographs, said Robert. Sometimes. But I've stopped ever since some psycho has been sending me his photos. It started a year or so ago. They just come in the mail. Always from a different sender, all made up, of course, nonexistent.

– Crazy, said the technician. What are the pictures of?

Like lightning Robert went through a catalogue of the uncanny: sexual acts between faceless creatures, close-ups of human skin, photos of his own apartment taken from impossible angles, photos of family

members who are long dead, photos of corpses on operating tables—
but then he told the truth after all:

— Oh, nothing special, just landscape photographs. But strangely
blurred, all the details fuzzy. You see only the general picture.

The technician made a hissing sound in acknowledgment, the
unarticulated version of *crazy*.

— The letters frighten my girlfriend, Robert murmured. Well, anyway, that . . .

He broke off and let the paintbrush speak its ancient whispering
idiom.

The wonderful inner peace, the first in a long while, dissipated immediately when he stepped out of the building. Twenty-nine years on
the planet and in all that time probably four hours altogether of perfect peace. During the years at Helianau, it had most likely been no
more than three minutes. Not counting sleep.

He had to carry the painting with some care to the car, but for the
last few paces that care was so hard to maintain that he would have
liked nothing better than to fling the painting like a Frisbee. The car
chirped cheerfully as it felt him getting closer.

When he was sitting at the steering wheel, he tousled his hair with
his fingers until he felt disheveled enough.

Then the car drove him home.

As always he rang his bell before unlocking the apartment door.
That way the soft echo of the motif consisting of three notes descending in a D-major chord received him like a welcoming melody.

Welcome, you burnt-out lightbulb . . . your apartment is ready for you.

He stood at the window and looked down into the courtyard. The
sky had become angry about something and now showed the earth
the grim gray back of its head. The blue had disappeared. A storm
announced itself. The white shirts hanging on the clotheslines in
the courtyard gesticulated excitedly and tried like nervous dogs to
break free from their bonds. The window shutters of the neighbor-

ing houses had come to life and began to knock, rattle, and squeal like prison inmates in adjacent solitary cells when the guard passes by; some were seized quickly from inside and subdued, others went on clattering grouchily or slammed shut with a bang, only to reopen shortly thereafter, slightly dazed and astonished that their pane had remained intact. On the old cobblestones (meanwhile endowed by the city council with a sort of landmark status, which was, however, nothing but a curse, because it forbade them from transplanting their exhausted medieval souls into new, fresh stones) the wind blew something around that looked like plastic utensils, pliable little knives, forks, and paper plates, accompanied by an agitated horde of fluttering napkins. Robert stood on tiptoe to take a look at his bike, which was probably not doing well in the approaching storm. He sensed the slowly inflating ball in his chest. With each breath the hollow space grew somewhat larger.

Some marmels with dull red, almost black snouts roamed around the garbage cans below.

Now he felt the first thunder, it was still inaudible, but the finer nerves of the buildings had caught it and passed it on. Robert began to feel aggressive. He had to turn away from the window—and instead went for the little bonsai tree on the kitchen table. *I shouldn't do this.* But the tree was so small, and besides, it was an insult to every eye trained in perspective, because no matter where it was in the room, it always appeared to be several hundred yards away, as if in that spot space had been bent and pulled into the distance with tweezers. A thing like that shouldn't even exist, he thought. And he also thought of the monkey, of its eyes, which had made him so calm, the little attempt at an emergency brake, but the monkey was painted, done, the peace was gone, and tons of water would soon fall from the sky, as heavy as studio rain in old silent films, liquid threads lashing wildly back and forth, capable of sweeping hats off bald human heads or knocking over sun umbrellas or within a few seconds turning whole façades into dark, shiny reflections of the street lighting.

Stop, stop.

Batman, I want to destroy this little tree. — Yes, you know, Robin, some-times we have to do what our inner voice tells us to.

Just at that moment, as he reached for the ridiculously tiny cup in which the Japanese miniature tree existed, the melody of the bell sounded, the descending major triad, and the apartment door imme-diately exerted the strong magnetism emanating from a still-invisible visitor.

— Yes, who is it?

— Hello, Herr Tätzel. I'm the mother of . . . of the . . .

— Oh, yeah, okay, said Robert.

He didn't invite his neighbor in, but rather stood pointedly in the doorway. Her name was Rabl, he didn't know her first name. Or her son's—even though he knew well that this was about him. A few days ago the kids who played in the courtyard had backed away from Rob-ert as he walked to his car and had shouted something at him. Okay, he hadn't really been angry about it. He hadn't even understood what they had said.

— Yes, said the woman, I wanted to apologize to you for my son.

— What did he do?

— Um . . . well, it's about last week . . . He confessed it to me only now, you know. And that's not the way I'm raising him, which is why I was appalled by it. By what he called you.

Called?

Robert opened the door a little wider. A representative object pricking up its ears.

— Um, I'd rather not repeat it, of course, I . . .

— No, said Robert, go ahead and say it, because I don't remember, honestly. I hear quite a lot of things. So what did he say?

— The *d*-word.

— Dingo?

His neighbor nodded.

— Okay, that's . . .

Robert searched for the right word. He couldn't think of anything.

– A-and . . . s . . . septic pig . . .

His neighbor's voice was barely audible. But Robert had understood.

– Fuck, he said, taking a step toward her out into the hallway.

– Oh, God, I shouldn't have said . . . I mean, repeated that, Herr Tätzel, I'm sorry, please, my son has no idea what those words mean. They just use them casually!

– Yes, said Robert. You should see what they do with the mongoloid from the yard next door!

The woman winced.

– You know, said Robert, feeling his heart begin to pound. The one with the big tongue with which he can . . . *llllm* . . . lick several stamps at once. Who laughs so much and always wants to hug everyone. They took turns punching him in the stomach. Your son was there too.

– What? I don't know who . . .

– The mongo—

– I don't know about any child with Down's syndrome, said Frau Rabl. My son was definitely not . . .

Her face was so furrowed that Robert became quite intoxicated by it. He was fond of such faces. He had once painted a portrait of a dog that looked just like that.

– Yes, you must know him, he said. Ask your son. He'll also tell you about his discovery, which he explained to me recently. Totally sick stuff, but also fascinating. If you punch a mo . . . person with Down's syndrome in the face, he will apologize to you as if he had done something wrong! Poor guy, picked on by everyone.

Robert made a vague punching gesture.

Frau Rabl now became completely flustered. Her face looked almost cubist. Robert gave her a brief wave goodbye and then closed the door.

He began to sing the "Rama Lama Ding Dong" song loudly, slurring the words, until he thought that Frau Rabl was out of earshot. Then he sat down on the balcony. It took a while for the shame to catch up with him. He could have kept running away from it, for by nature it moved with the speed of old memories. But it didn't matter. He had made his position clear.

Later he sat on the edge of the tub in the bathroom, the north wall of which he had had painted black a few years ago in memory of the Lichtenberg huts at Helianau, and considered what would be the most effective method to dispose of the stupid neighbor boy.

The problem was that he couldn't think clearly. Frau Rabl's visit had rattled him. *I'd probably feel better*, he told himself, *if I broke something*. He had already looked around for something. To no avail.

Of course, he could get those small containers of rat poison from the cellar, that would be the classic variation, so to speak. He played the scenario out in his head a few times and discovered that he felt no satisfaction at all. It wasn't that the kid wouldn't suffer enough, no, rat poison was really awful. It dissolved the stomach lining and you began to bleed like crazy and choked on your own blood and so on.

Maybe he should just frighten him, chase him around a little. But then the miserable homunculus would of course tell everyone about it. No, he had to find a final solution. *Final solution*, the term was forbidden, radioactive, you weren't allowed to think it, not in this context, it was disrespectful to use it this way, the millions of cold-bloodedly murdered . . . Robert stood up. His heart was pounding.

– Final solution, he said. Final solution to the neighbor boy question.

But the feeling in his chest was already gone. The allure of the forbidden phrase had become too weak. He sat down again on the edge of the bathtub.

My God, how ridiculous this was, he was sitting here uselessly on his butt, while that rat ran with impunity through the courtyard or the stairwell and experienced a carefree childhood. Maybe the mother had scolded him a little, that was quite possible, but definitely not too much, because she thought exactly the same as her wayward turd of a son.

Robert punched himself in the knee.

A natural disaster, he thought. You would have to unleash a natural disaster. A climactic event. Or climatic? The one was a sort of turning point, the other . . . What was it, *actic* or *atic*? . . . Damn gap. Indigo delay. The best thing would be, Robert told himself, sensing with a certain gratification how with this thought he crossed the borderline into insanity, the best thing would be to shoot himself directly in front of the neighbor boy. He gets a pistol or a rifle, then he goes into the courtyard and stands in front of the children. He aims at them and orders them all, except the dirty rat, to clear out at once. Then he says: Get on your knees, you little shit. And then he puts the barrel to his own chin and shows in the brief moment he has left a wild, cruel grin, the mouth wide open and the eyes two big white balls. And then he pulls the trigger, brain, gunpowder smoke, jawbone fragments, and teeth scatter in a red and black cloud through the courtyard and rain down into the child's future memory world, his whole life he will have to think back to this terrible moment, he will be in therapy for years, will turn back into the bed-wetter he once was, will react to every loud noise in school by cringing and suffering an epileptic fit, will then, after dropping out of school at the age of fourteen, never complete any vocational training, night classes are out of the question, because the now-eighteen-year-old can't go outside anymore after dark without having horrible panic attacks. On New Year's Eve, when the firecrackers and rockets go off, he hides in the bathtub with a mattress over him. He's unfit for normal family life, he becomes more and more addicted to alcohol, hangs around in parks during the day and tells everyone who stands still long enough about the brilliant future that was once open to him, in the abundantly tree-shaded, wind-sheltered inner courtyards of the neighborhood in which he spent his childhood, until he one day made a mistake, a grave, grave mistake.

It gave Robert a terrible scare when the door to the bathroom opened. He came within an inch of falling into the tub.

– What are you doing here? asked Cordula. Didn't you hear me?

– Are you already . . . Why are you home already . . . ?

Robert looked at his watch.

– Everything okay with you? asked Cordula. Should I leave you alone?

– No, no . . .

– Are you sure?

– Yeah, I was just . . . You know, that asshole down there, that fresh kid of Frau Rabl's, he said, well, that is, she rang the doorbell a little while ago and told me what he said, because she's just as stupid as her son, he said—

– Shh.

Cordula caught his head in her hands.

Robert froze. Canary cage over which a sheet is thrown.

– And that upset you? she said.

– You haven't heard what he said about me.

– Oh, he's just a kid.

– He said, upstairs lives a sep—

– No, Robert, said Cordula, squatting down in front of him.

At eye level. He was forced to look directly at her.

– I know, he's just some . . . But . . .

– Should I bring you a matchstick house, hm? To break? That will probably make you feel—

– No, I don't need that. Thanks.

– You sure?

– Yes.

– You know what? said Cordula. I got you something from the Chinese place on the way home. Do you want it?

– Why are you so late anyway?

– I had to finish the accounting. Angelika isn't there, and of course allowances are always made for her, and—

– Yeah, so did you study accounting too? asked Robert. I mean, you never even told me that. That's news to me. You have all sorts of things, but not a doctorate in accounting, as far as I know.

– Why are you so aggressive? she asked gently. Come see what I've brought for you.

———

In the corridor, between the kitchen and the living room, he grasped her by the arm.

– I have something for you too, he said. The painting that I . . . today I was . . .

– Oh, it's finished already!

He led her by the hand into the corner of his room, which always seemed to be dreaming of one day expanding into the whole room and transforming it into a real painting studio.

Outside the storm had passed, the lightning bolts had changed into distant flashes. A vain horizon, having itself photographed again and again. When no audible thunder followed lightning, Robert always felt compelled to clear his throat.

Cordula squatted in front of the painting of the monkey with the metal thing in the back of its head and looked up at it as if it were a stained-glass window in a church and she were contemplating the city, a familiar world in altered colors, behind it.

– What do you think? he asked.

Cordula turned around and looked into a different corner of the room.

– Is he real? she asked.

– What? Oh, you're asking if today . . . Yeah, today was the appointment at—

– Oh, God, she said with a shudder.

– What do you think of it?

– You know that I can't stand things like that, Robert, why do you show me these awful things?

– So you think it's bad?

– No, Robert, I don't think it's bad, I just think . . . Why do you always have to paint such horrible pictures? The poor animal . . . I . . . I think I'm going to be . . .

Her face looked a little like Frau Rabl's. Cubist distress. The way the eyebrows bent in the middle. Like snapped twigs.

– Oh, come on, said Robert.

And then:

– Oh, come on, this isn't believable . . .

She left the room, heading for a sink, any sink.

While she vomited, her hands wandered to the back of her neck, and she made a movement like someone trying to take a deep breath underwater. Then her legs gave way, and she collapsed on the floor. An attack, Robert registered it and tried to remember how long ago her last attack had been. A few seconds passed, then reality streamed back into his veins, he realized that he had to do something, he began to dial the ambulance, but at the second number Cordula stood up again, apologized softly, and went to her room. He followed her.

– Now, this really isn't believable, he repeated pleadingly.

3.   The Messmer Study

She still remembered well, said Frau Häusler-Zinnbret, how the phenomenon first came to her attention. She had read in a magazine
article that in Hungary after a long political to-and-fro (which finally
ended in a backward-looking fro) several homes for I-children were
closed due to flagrant deficiencies and some of the unemployed nurses
came to Austria to look for work here. She had then searched for
reports on those homes and eventually came across coverage from a
Belgian camera crew that had visited one of them. The conditions had
been indescribable. The children and their supervisors had been forced
to live side by side in the most cramped quarters, had suffered from
chronic fatigue, nausea, migraines, irritability, and extensive eczema.
The Hungarian name of the institution, *fertőző gyerekek otthona*, meant
home for infectious children. The term *Indigo* was not yet used at the time,
said Frau Häusler-Zinnbret. It came, like so much strange nomencla-
ture, from Germany. From there it spread in recent years all over the
world and replaced the name Beringer or Rochester syndrome. In
2002 a guest on a well-known talk show who called herself an angel-
seer and medium claimed that she could perceive people's aura. For
years, the woman explained, she had classified everyone according to
the traffic light system: Those with a red aura were unpleasant types,
quick-tempered, fussy, slow-witted; a yellow aura meant patience, caring, understanding; green meant silliness, wildness, sometimes laziness.
But for a few years she had been noticing here and there little blue
beings, children with an indigo-blue aura. The host asked her about
them, but the seer, who was dressed like a bat, shook her head and

declared that she couldn't for the life of her say what qualities that color represented, but she suspected it had to do with the coming of a new age, that of the fish. This connection was comprehensible to no one, and so the woman explained that these children might be more spiritual, intelligent beings who had come to earth to save the planet.

Then five children were presented to the woman, among whom she actually claimed to pick out one with a bluish tinge to his aura. Since no one else in the studio could see this color, of course, a second test was done: The woman was blindfolded, and the same children were presented to her again. This time the woman said that with no. 3 she felt a stabbing headache. Even though child no. 3 was not the same one she had originally identified, this experiment was somehow judged a success, at least the audience clapped enthusiastically for a long time, and a few magazines published articles on the strange bat woman.

In early 2003, when the—as Frau Häusler-Zinnbret put it—problem had become acute, people everywhere began speaking of Indigo children, even though this name was criticized in esoteric circles.

– The Messmer study particularly bothered them, said Frau Häusler-Zinnbret. Me too, to be honest. Probably all of us, or . . . well . . .

She put the fan down, picked up her book, and leafed through it. When she found the page she was looking for, she turned the book around and showed it to me. A diagram with various categories: self-esteem, interpersonal skills, group dynamic behavior, and so on, twenty-four items in all. And next to them an elegant bell curve, the helmet that nature wears to protect itself from anomalies.

– Yes, we were a little disappointed too. The pure steel of Scapa Flow, which remained untouched by world affairs, yeah, that didn't appear to be the case, unfortunately. Wishful thinking. I basically knew that already at the time I wrote it, but it's a great story and a good opening for a book, so . . . yeah, the study had a particularly negative effect on the parents' hopes, of course.

I began to copy the bell curve from the page into my notebook.

– Take it as a gift, okay?

Frau Häusler-Zinnbret gave the book a slight push toward me.

– That's really nice of you. Thank you very much.

– Pure selfishness. Otherwise you'd quote from the first edition, which really isn't up-to-date.

– Okay, I said. So was that study to blame for the failure of the school project for affected children that had been planned in Riegersdorf?

– The tunnel project. Well, that fell through due to many factors.

She picked up the fan again, moved her face back and forth in the gentle current of air. A wisp of hair fluttered behind her ear.

– Really? But the study appeared at around the same time, in late 2005. By that point, the building permits for the complex and the tunnel systems had already been issued, and the subsidies had been approved. Despite all that, nothing happened. Of course, you get conflicting information, but as far as I can gather, the Riegersdorf Indigo school project was called off, right?

– Yes, possibly. It's so easy to lose track.

My only real question thrust itself forward. It had waited long enough and wanted to be asked now. I let a moment of pre-explosive emptiness pass before I began to speak.

– One question, Frau Häusler. While I was working at the institute, some students moved away in the middle of the school year and afterward it was very difficult or impossible to—

– Yes?

– And once I saw one of the kids, a certain Max Schaufler, being picked up by a man. And he, that is, Max, he . . . well, he was dressed up as a chimney sweep. Like, with a sooty face and . . . I don't know, I asked Dr. Rudolph, of course, but he said only that he had been *relocated*. And that he was no longer tolerable for the institute.

– And?

A brief pause.

– Well, isn't that strange? I said. I mean, I've never seen anything like it before, it was really eerie, that getup.

– That's often done, she gently interjected. Wearing costumes helps children deal with a difficult situation. I assume that that was a traumatic moment for the d . . . for this, what was the name? Max? Well, for the student.

– Okay, but—

– You often see it in cemeteries, at funerals. A child with makeup on. Dressed up as a cat or . . . or wearing a funny hat. You see it often.

– All right, it's not so much the costume I'm wondering about, but more the fact that so many students at the institute were transferred or . . .

– Relocated?

– Yes.

– I can't tell you anything about that, Herr Setz. But I'll write down for you someone you could visit. The woman was once in treatment with me. After the birth of her son. Single mother. Inding . . . Indigo kid. Depressive. The whole package. She lives in southern Styria.

She reached for her electronic organizer and searched for the entry. Then she wrote all the information on a piece of paper. *Gudrun Stennitzer. Son: Christoph. Glockenhofweg 1, 8910 Gillingen.* Under that a cell phone number. Frau Häusler-Zinnbret continued to fan herself. Her face had begun to shine a little.

– I know, former patients' information, usually . . . (She made a movement as if she were waving away several flies.) But it's okay. She really likes to talk about the topic. She had her son home-schooled *because of it*. Because of the problem. Which is, of course, quite common in the di . . . in the community, as you can imagine.

– What problem? That of the relocations?

Fan movements, bobbing strands of hair. Then she exhaled and said softly, with a slight shake of her head:

– Chimney sweep, *ts* . . . But who knows, well, Frau Stennitzer will probably be happy if you visit her and mention her in your article. She likes to interact, you know. With other people and such. Does her good too, internally and externally.

– Okay. Thank you very much.

– Would you like another glass of water, Herr Setz?

– No, thanks. Just one last question.

She laughed.

– Sorry, she said. But you just grabbed your forehead like Columbo. When you said that. Hahaha.

– Have you ever heard of Ferenz?

She stopped moving the fan and held it next to her face as if she needed a third ear to understand what I wanted from her.

– Excuse me?

– The name. Ferenz.

– That's a game, she said. As far as I know.

A short pause.

– Yes, Frau Häusler-Zinnbret said again. A game.

– A game?

– Yes.

– Like musical chairs?

– Something like that.

The fan began to move slightly.

– Thank God I don't work with I-families anymore, said Frau Häusler-Zinnbret. All that's behind me.

– May I ask why you stopped?

She folded the fan and put it on the table in front of her.

– The mothers, she said. The mothers more than anything else. There's only so much of that you can take, you know. Those dark rings under the eyes, the crooked fingers, the matted and unwashed hair, those accusatory lips, which always tremble a little, burnt-out, burnt-out, and then the absurd notions they have . . . Well, all right, they can't help it, of course, they want their kids to do as well as other, normal kids. But you can stand those mothers for only so long. The way they sit there and talk about nothing but their exhaustion . . . and that suffering tone they always adopt, probably only women can do that.

She laughed.

– No, she added, I've also met enough young fathers who were a nervous wreck. But, of course, the kids themselves were too. That cold, distant . . . The way they endure everything, no matter what you do to them, that . . .

She looked again at my empty glass and asked a second time:

— You really wouldn't like another . . . ?

— No, thanks, I said. What else did you want to say about the I-kids?

— You've met them yourself.

— Well, only from a distance.

She laughed.

— I-kids, she repeated, that sounds so harmless . . . They have no compassion. I mean, the burnt-out cases, they can occasionally regenerate a little over time, but the others . . . drift farther and farther out in their space capsule.

She fell silent. I waited for her to go on.

— Well, it's nice, Frau Häusler-Zinnbret finally said, that you've actually read up on the subject a bit before you came to me. A lot of visitors don't, you know. But I receive them all, of course, without exception, unless they get really impertinent. I mean, really, truly impertinent. But that rarely happens, thank God.

She leaned forward and picked up the book she had offered me as a gift. From the side pocket of her knitted vest she pulled a pen. She opened to the first page.

— Shall I inscribe it for you . . . ?

Because I didn't know how to respond to that, I just nodded and closed my notebook. Frau Häusler-Zinnbret wrote a dedication, affixed a bold signature somewhat reminiscent of Spirograph designs, and then asked me the date.

— Today is the . . . ?

— Twenty-first.

She wrote the date, inexplicably blew on the page, and presented me with the gift.

— Thank you very much.

— As you can see, cursive has certain advantages, she said, gesturing to her signature. You should practice it. Half an hour or just ten minutes a day, it makes no difference, as long as you really do it every day.

— All right.

I stood up. We shook hands.

Frau Häusler-Zinnbret accompanied me to the door, this time it was the other one. Her apartment had, as I now realized, separate entrance and exit doors, like a supermarket or a hall of mirrors at a carnival.

Outside the sky was so blue that you could hear a pin drop in it.

Two Truths

After the conversation with the child psychologist I flipped a bit through the book she had given me, the new edition of her standard work. I had borrowed the out-of-date version from the university library. I had photocopied some interesting pages and put them in my red-checkered folder.

The new edition differed only slightly from the earlier one. The tone seemed in some places somewhat sterner, and there was an expanded appendix in which Frau Häusler-Zinnbret provided a sort of overview of her previous studies. In her typical vivid and illustrative style she writes:

A lone bust of Vladimir Ilyich Lenin stares into the polar night. The monument is located on the so-called southern pole of inaccessibility, the geographic point of the Antarctic farthest from the coastline (about 500 miles from the South Pole). A few buildings of a Soviet research station used to stand around the statue, now it is all by itself. It faces north, i.e., toward Moscow. The bust itself stands on the chimney of a hut now completely submerged in snow, in which a few ghosts of the past might still be living, bent in end-less discussion over antiquated world maps . . . As in the case of this lone bust, when we consider phenomena such as dingo pride *or the call for an* uncivilized solution *to the Indigo problem, we are always confronted with two competing truths. The evolutionary truth (the invisible, submerged foun-dation) has largely shaped the European cityscape: exclusion and custody of the sick, contagious, abnormal, etc. Similar to the way meerkats deal with a sick member of their species who might endanger the successful progress of the* clan, by joining forces to bite it to death or simply leaving it behind. Sick cats withdraw to die alone, because there's no other way to carry out this process anyhow. Evolutionary truth thus intends for some of the population to die in order to make possible the existence of the rest. Human truth (the visible head) says: Everyone must survive, or rather: Everyone has the right to survive. It's pointless to ask: Why? The question cannot be answered, except with auxiliaries like compassion and the avoidance of pain. The reason lies in our brain, which can identify with and empathize with everything, particularly the things it has to protect itself from: sickness, suffering, and death. It's a strange consequence of the evolutionary cultivation of our cognition, our capacity to have a nuanced sense of other existences, that a way of thinking emancipated from evolutionary logic has necessarily developed: human morality, which coincides in only a few points with evolutionary logic (e.g., in the isolation of people with highly infectious diseases, the containment of epidemics, etc.).

An anecdotal refrain of our time is that I-children lack that very ability to put themselves in others' shoes or have learned to suppress it. The evidence for that assumption might be everywhere, right under our noses, so to speak— and yet up to now no one has seen it, let alone managed to derive any benefit from it.

I bent over the page to better make out the tiny photo of the strange bust. An odd smell rose from the book. I inhaled carefully. Disinfectant.

The smell evoked a memory . . . The infirmary at the Helianau

Institute a few weeks ago. Minutes after my feigned fall outside Dr. Rudolph's open office door. *The horror, the horror.*

A warm spring day outside the windows. Inside the building the air is stuffy, large heavy casements that are never opened, in every nook and cranny the sharp smell of fresh lacquer and the aggressive floor-cleaning products that are apparently spread each weekend by a cleaning crew with breathing masks in the corridors of the three stories.

—Herr Setz? You fell down? Did you hurt yourself?

—No, it's just my head . . . Do you have something for a headache?

—You really don't look good. Come, sit down here. And look at me. You're very pale, do you know that?

—That's normal for me.

—You didn't get dizzy?

—Yes, outside my door, shortly after he left my office, said Dr. Rudolph, who had accompanied me to the infirmary.

—I'm sorry, I said.

—Well, he said, I have to go back. You're in good hands here.

He left the room.

—You really don't look good, the nurse said to me. And you're lucky I'm still here. I was actually planning to leave at eleven . . .

—You know what? I said. I'd like to ask you something—

—Please don't talk for a moment, she said, laying the back of her hand against my forehead.

I waited. Her eyes wandered to the ceiling.

—Well, she said, you have a slightly high temperature. Have you spent time in any *proximity*?

I tried to hold her gaze.

—That's what I wanted to talk to you about, I said. How often does it actually happen that someone comes to you, you know, *for that*?

She rolled her eyes again, shrugged.

—Oh, I don't know . . . hm. Hard to say.

Then she went to her medicine cabinet and reached for a box of pills.

– Has it ever happened?

She pressed a pill into her hand and gave it to me. It was pale gray and was reminiscent in form of a little zeppelin.

– What is this? I asked.

– Something for your headache.

– Might you have a glass of water for me?

She brought me one. I put the pill under my tongue, gulped down the glass, and waved goodbye to her.

In the corridor I spat out the pill and hid it in the soil of the puny climbing plant in its pot in front of one of the windows. Then I got my things from the teachers' lounge and walked to the train station. I ran into no one.

That was probably the moment I knew that I wouldn't return to the institute, even before the brief scuffle with Dr. Rudolph the next day.

Julia found me, when she came home from work, at my desk in a strangely agitated state. She brought with her, when she entered the room, a smell of convalescent bats and rats and asked me why I was home so early in the middle of the week. She at first mistook my agitation for anxiety and wanted to know whether I'd seen something awful again on television or in a picture in a book.

4.   Back Then, Robin

The nape of Cordula's neck, which she had in her panic scratched red, smelled like back then. He would never forget it. The three long weeks in the psychiatric clinic, the time *before* the medication, *before* the therapy, and *before* the evenings when they would watch a bloody action movie or an old kung fu drama together, in which Asians who were determined to do whatever it took caused the most varied manners of violent death.

Robert wore a T-shirt with the Batman symbol on it and lay behind his girlfriend, who breathed quietly. On the night table, the small iBall blinked at him. Robert gave it a dirty look, and the iBall lowered its lid.

He had noticed the smell immediately, back then, when he had visited her for the first time, three days after her admission (unconscious, her shoulder probably badly bruised from the fall)—that special psychiatric clinic smell. He had to admit: He found it interesting. A dog could undoubtedly have analyzed the smell as precisely as a music student an orchestral score: passionlessly cooked hospital food, meant to impart discipline and a pull-yourself-together-damn-it attitude, mixed with the sweat of anxiety sufferers, plastic straps and rubber feeding tubes, and finally the pills hurriedly and unnoticeably ground into powder—all this you were met with when you entered the building.

Cordula had been put in a room with three other women.

She was already feeling much better, she said. And it wasn't his fault (he had suggested the movie they were watching when it happened, *Tetsuo: The Iron Man*, a Japanese trash horror film in high-contrast, extremely attractive black-and-white), the attack had already announced itself over the past few days. An oppressive feeling here, a skipped heartbeat there, and sometimes difficulty breathing while watching certain scenes on television, for example, during the movie, in which people keep looking out the window of a very tall building, and down below those insect-sized cars are driving by, that was when everything in her contracted, but she didn't say anything because she thought it would pass, but this time it obviously didn't pass, hahah (when she was scared, her laughter always broke off before the last syllable), he must have been really worried, how long had she been lying there, defenseless, oh, I mean motionless, of course, is my face red?

— No, everything's fine, said Robert.

— Really, because I have the feeling that my face might be red, I mean, not like fleshy red, but really red, like it's been smeared with lipstick, that must be the effect of that thing there, oh, I feel so shitty, I'm so embarrassed, I'm sure it was a good movie, but I messed everything up once again, just as I always mess everything up, I—

— It's all right, Robert forced himself to say. The movie wasn't even that good, in my opinion. Artistically, I mean. Not really successful.

— No? Cordula asked.

It sounded so hopeful, as if a negative judgment of the Japanese movie held the key to her ultimate recovery.

Robert had noticed that at the foot of the three occupied beds in the room little Post-its were stuck, on which smiley faces were drawn. His practiced eye registered immediately that the faces were made by different hands. He checked whether a piece of paper was stuck to Cordula's bed frame too.

— That's for . . . when we . . . how we feel, said Cordula, and squirmed as if she had put on a too-tight skin this morning. I find it childish too, but that way they don't always have to ask us how we're doing.

For some reason Robert had to laugh. He tried to keep his face, which wanted to contort into a silly grimace, under control, turned away, went to the window and looked, his hands clasped behind his back, out at the parking lot or whatever that strangely bare area was supposed to be. Beyond it the woods. He remained standing that way for a while and made quiet throat noises.

– What's so funny? asked Cordula.

– Oh, nothing, Robert said quickly, turning around to face his girl-friend. It's just, I saw a hot air balloon out there.

– Really? Where?

– No, now it's descended behind the hill, said Robert. I was just imagining the people in the hot air balloon talking to each other, that's all. That was funny.

Cordula took a deep breath. Then a strand of hair fell in her face, and she caught it with a finger and held it under her nose.

She stood up and washed the strand of hair at the sink.

Robert hadn't noticed the sink until now. It was missing all the protruding elements that sinks usually have. The water came out of a seashell-like, edgeless opening over a photoelectric sensor. At night this technology, the invisible beam stretching across the room like a ghostly clothesline, must have frightened Cordula and the other women in the hospital room. Perhaps they even had to stick a Post-it over the photoelectric sensor. At the thought of that Robert again had to laugh. *Stop!* he admonished himself. *Just stop thinking.*

– Embarrassing, murmured Cordula, as she washed her hair strand under the running water.

– What's embarrassing? he asked.

– Oh, nothing, she said. Just smells like puke.

She checked the smell of the hair strand again. Her expression showed that she was fairly satisfied with it. Then she brushed the strand into her hair with her fingers and went back to the bed.

– The photoelectric sensor, said Robert, almost choking on the word.

Stop, you idiot!

– What?

– Oh, I just said, the . . . um . . . that thing there.

– Where?

He pointed to it.

– What is that? asked Cordula, and her voice vibrated with slight unease.

– Just a photoelectric sensor, said Robert, as reassuringly as he could. Nothing to worry about. But it goes across the room and directly over your bed into the wall. The beam, the infrared . . .

Cordula looked behind her at the wall. Then she shook her head.

– I feel weird from the medication. Why aren't they giving me Trittico again? I tolerated that much better back then. But it's not made anymore, they say. Why not? How can a drug that helps you suddenly be taken off the market? It's exactly the same with grocery items you like. You can be absolutely sure that in six months they'll disappear from the supermarket shelves. Always the same . . .

She shook her head more vigorously, and then came the tears. Robert wondered whether, as when someone goes into cardiac arrest on a TV medical drama, he should press the emergency button so that a hysterical team in white coats would come running into the room. Electroshock. One, two, three—clear!

But Cordula was only crying.

– I definitely wouldn't want to trade places with you, he said to her.

She stared at him, aghast. Weeping woman face.

– Why would you say something like that?

– Well, I just wouldn't want to trade places with you. I imagine it must be pretty awful, getting up early and . . . also those beds and the sink, which . . .

He went silent.

– Something's wrong with you, Robert. How can you say that to me? In this situation!

Shortly thereafter, he felt it. Maybe a consequence of the slight guilt Cordula's last words had planted in him. Worry. He was already sitting in the dark gold tram, but wanted nothing more than to turn around and stay by Cordula's side.

That was new.

Okay, he had to take a deep breath, figure out what this was about. Perhaps he had inhaled chemical dust on the clinic premises, which was now playing with his brain, pressing buttons, turning taps on and off, as on the backs of lab monkeys' heads . . . The thought of those monkeys did him good, he calmed down.

When it came down to it, it was only a feeling in the chest, he thought, nothing more. Your thoughts gained centrifugal force and you felt like a rubber band being painfully expanded. Your fingertips were unaffected by it, they could move completely freely, your toes too. He wiggled them a little. No, everything was normal. Only in his throat or just below it, in his chest, was that thing. When he stretched, it was particularly unpleasant, then something told him he should immediately collapse limply again.

I'm just going to get some clothes, Robert told himself.

And a moment later he wondered what the hell was the matter with him.

I'm just going to get some clothes? Who was he talking to, damn it? *I'm losing my mind. I'm a burnt-out lightbulb, which has lost its corona, and, my God, now this too.* He wiped his face with his hand and tried to focus on the feeling again. *Want to go back. Not home. Have to stay there.*

Stop, stop, stop! I'm just going to get some clothes!

When the tram stopped at Merangasse, the sign for a pastry shop happened to catch his eye. And when the tram began to move again, he realized that it had caught his worry too, dragging it out of him and away.

The smell of the old travel bag in which he was about to pack the clothing for Cordula reminded him of the black coat of tar on the outside of the Lichtenberg huts at Helianau. Robert pulled various items from Cordula's wardrobe without thinking much about whether they would make sense or look good as outfits. He also searched for a shower cap (the shower rooms in the clinic were not to be trusted with regard to the risk of infection), but he found nothing, only a small nest of fashionable sunglasses wintering here.

The open wardrobe, now it had another job, it was a supply cabinet, no longer a vanity case ... Open, yawning, it stood there, mirrored inside ...

What's the point of all this? thought Robert. *Why panic attacks?* He came across an old *Star Trek* shirt he had once bought for Cordula, a fruitless attempt to lure her into his universe. It showed the triumvirate Kirk, Spock, and McCoy against a red background. Hyperspace, he thought. Did the word even appear in the original series? Was it a *Star Trek* term? First episode, Cordula in Hyperspace.

I can understand your doubts, Robin, but sometimes you have to give a person space. – Holy electroconvulsive therapy, Batman, you're right!

On the tram heading back to the hospital he felt nothing. He sat between blocks of people and was safe. The iBall over the driver's cabin looked elsewhere. Robert caught himself giving a friendly nod to the sign for the pastry shop as he passed it. Maybe nothing but a memory was to blame for the irritation before. When he was taken out of Helianau to visit his uncle at the hospital. Okay, at the time they had, of course, shielded him well, in several respects. He could still remember that afternoon, when he had shouted to his friend Max (relocated in 2006, chimney sweeps bring good luck) in the yard at Helianau: My uncle is suffering from psychiatry! The usual Indigo educational impediments, particularly clear in linguistic expression, *you septic pig*. The famous delay. Dingo delay. And Felicitas Bärmann, the overachiever, had immediately corrected him. Half gesticulating, half yelling across the schoolyard. What had become of Felicitas? Did former Helianau students ever meet? Was there something like a reunion from which he was excluded? Maybe in an airplane hangar or on a soccer field, like back then for the class picture ...

Robert's uncle Johann had from his earliest youth been afflicted with a strange counting compulsion, which in later years decreased in range but increased in intensity. He stopped counting lamps, bathroom tiles, freckles on faces, or the windows of distant buildings, and was now obsessed exclusively with a single number, to which he had to add 1 every few hours. It had in the meantime become a six-digit number, and if you asked him what it was, he would fire it back at you, but then immediately add 1 and repeat, somewhat more softly, the new number. To have a rational conversation with him was impossible. He was interested solely in matters related to this number, such as the question of whether it might at present be a prime number again or display another interesting arithmetical quality—as at that memorable moment when it had been exactly 111111; Uncle Johann had supposedly run out of his room and had stood in the hallway in front of an open window and gratefully greeted the fresh new world and its glorious light, passionately blowing a kiss and somewhat awkwardly making the sign of the cross, which had caught the attention of one of the nurses and led to a rather unpleasant hallway conversation.

Any topic of conversation but this monster in his head, growing by a certain amount every day, every hour, was for his uncle uninteresting to a grotesque degree.

Yet he himself seemed not at all to suffer from the presence of the number-parasite the way those around him (who longed for ordinary communication with him) did, he maintained and cultivated the number like a flower bed. He had cared for it from infancy, through the very early stage of 5, 6, 7, then through the rapidly developing two-digit and three-digit, and finally even through the adolescent four-digit range, which it had also soon left behind. It could be claimed that the number was now gradually nearing mature adulthood. Every evening he entered it in a small notebook, which was meant only as a sort of summary of the day's events, not as a memory aid. For he never forgot the number itself, not even after seventeen hours of sleep under the influence of strong sedatives. It stayed in him.

Sometimes, when the number had an unremarkable phase ahead of it, the day would be a good one, then you could go for a walk with him or treat him to an ice cream in the quiet café just after the entrance to the clinic. He would sit on one of the plastic chairs, would be responsive and calm and even capable of making a joke. You could get along with him. Now and then you could tell from a silent nod that he had again added 1 and was now taking in the taste and the shape of the new number. If he licked his lips, you could assume that he was satisfied with it. But even if the number wasn't all he had hoped, he was never mad at the new number for that, it couldn't help its appearance or its behavior, it had just hatched, after all, and needed attention, just like any other number. Who knows, maybe it would ultimately reveal a few nice divisibility properties, hidden talents that had escaped him at first glance.

The fact that the number kept growing didn't bother him, for it went nicely step by step, he explained. Sure, if he suddenly added a three-digit number and so skipped hundreds of other stages of the number's development, then that would certainly throw some things off. That would be like starting a car in a too-high gear. But the way it was going now, each day about fifty steps, that was manageable, that didn't demand all too much of you. For he was quite well aware of the danger emanating from such a companion number. How easily people with less robust nerves than his might suspect in the numerical sequence a secret code or a message from the beyond or from other realms of heaven. It was perfectly clear to him that the number was only a number, no more and no less. He looked after it and dealt with it responsibly. He had never made a mistake, taken a counting step twice or reversed two digits within the number, no, the number was completely safe with him. Nothing could happen to it, even if some people claimed it would one day be taken away from him. He knew that this was not even possible, was in fact a contradiction in terms. In any case, he would continue to fulfill his care obligations toward this precious and vulnerable being, for he, Johann Rauber, was simply the only protector the number had in the whole world. Impossible to imagine what might happen to it without him.

Robert sat on a bench in front of the psychiatric clinic at the University Hospital of Graz. There was always something off about psychiatric institutions, that is, in architectural terms. Either they were as large and labyrinthine as a courthouse, or the architect had taken the metaphor of illness literally and applied it to the roof structure, or they were intimidating in the way the doors sprang open of their own accord, or they were, like this building here, hidden in the woods. All the other clinics could be reached by climbing a few steps from the final stop of tram line 7; from that point on everything was logical, even the signs made sense. Not so the psychiatric clinic. You had to walk down a dark and accursed path through the woods, and you then came upon a building in which you could not for the life of you imagine mentally ill people getting better. The view from the window every evening alone! All night long the trees talked about you with rustling gestures and read your thoughts.

At least here, just next to the parking lot, a beautiful, quiet tree grew, which seemed not to belong to the small patch of woods. Like an opera singer in front of the chorus it stood there, in the endlessly complex contortion that makes up a tree. Why did trees look like that anyway? They grew according to a simple principle, after all, straight line, divide, two straight lines, divide, four straight lines, and so on, where did those crazy angles come from? Possibly water veins, magnetic fields, or sunlight played a role. Or maybe, thought Robert, a tree was just terribly sentimental. Recently he had with some abhorrence looked at the famous picture by the photographer David Perlmann in an art magazine showing a tree in Pennsylvania that had, as it were, embraced a white single-family house from the side with its branches. First the branches had grown through the perpetually open kitchen window, then they had leaned up against the house's south wall, finally it had been the roof's turn. Within thirty years, in which a married couple had grown old in the house and hadn't bothered with anything that happened outside, the tree had merged with the house. The family that lived in it now had the burdensome tree, a danger to the stability of the roof, which had been built with very light materials, photographed before having it removed. There had, as the magazine reported, even been a sort of competition. David Perlmann's picture had won first prize, because the tree looked so sure of itself in it. And maybe that was the problem, thought Robert. A tree always wanted to embrace everything. It stands in the same spot for a hundred years and is overwhelmed every day by its affection for a few ducks in a pond, an intertwined couple on a park bench, a delightful, colorfully overflowing garbage can, or a mysteriously curved park lamp. When one of the creatures or things attracts its attention and the desire to embrace it becomes irresistible, the tree begins—slowly, of course, terribly slowly—to grow in its direction and to stretch out its branches toward it like arms. It's like in those well-known speed dreams, in which you can't move precisely when you're desperate to. If you give up, however, you sometimes even fly away—into the sky, always in the wrong direction. And the tree, as a result of its many minimal daily, hourly changes of direction in its growth over the years, has turned into a bizarrely distorted form.

Stupid tree.

And stupid clinic. One morning in it, and he was thinking completely retarded nonsense. *Stupid tree, suck a Frisbee, motherfucker!* To bring himself back down to earth, Robert recited a few forbidden, radioactive words: *filthy cunt, Jewish pig, degenerate, nigger.* Then he stood up.

No, these long hours with Cordula did him no good. He constantly had strange thoughts, as if they were being put in his head by a different, older brain, he felt remote-controlled. No wonder. And his clothing was always soaked in sweat, even though it was only seventy-two degrees. As after a sweat bath in the wretched yard at Helianau. The disgusting feeling of being the only one they could do it to. Because his I-space, his zone, his region went through those lunar phases in late puberty, waxing and waning, then even vanishing completely. What vileness.

And today, on this late summer day in 2021, after he had put away his freshly painted monkey portrait, he was very grateful to Cordula that it hadn't been a bad attack this time. She was sleeping. She was breathing normally. She was well adjusted.

THE HALDRESS OF BONNDORF

IN THE YEAR 1811 there lived in the city of Bonndorf, in the Danube District, a haldress named Beglau. She took great joy in her baby, to whom she had given birth a few weeks earlier. But then came the comet, which in autumn visited the sky over the earth and of which the kind reader has elsewhere heard.

During a midday meal at the Wounded Landlord Inn, the Family Friend was told that after the appearance of the comet in the vicinity of the moon a change had occurred with the haldress in Bonndorf. While the comet, like a holy evening prayer or like a priest when he roams the church and sprinkles the holy water, like a noble good friend of the earth who has a great longing for her, like a mischievously winking eye in the night firmament, remained there, people at times felt as if it wanted to say: I was once an earth too, like you, full of snowstorms and thunderclouds, full of hospitals and Rumfordian soup kitchens and churchyards. But my Judgment Day is over and has transfigured me into heavenly clarity, and I would like to come down to you, but I do not dare, because of the oath I have sworn, lest I become impure again from the blood of your battlefields. It had not said this, but it seemed so, for the closer it came, the more beautifully and brightly, joyfully and fondly it shone, and when it receded after a certain period of time measured in accordance with celestial principles, it became pale and gloomy, as if it were itself grieving deeply. The haldress Beglau in Bonndorf must have looked up at it often when she crossed the wellbridge in the evening on her way home, where her baby waited for her. The baby was still quite small, a little lump of living tissue in a cradle next to the stove. The more she stayed outside in the comet nights, as her occupation required, the odder the broad fluttering belt of the Milky Way and the other cosmic curio sets of the stargazers appeared to her. Like jugs and pots in a cupboard, those things up there seemed to her disorderly, and she had all sorts of fantasies, so that she soon acquired a rather strange reputation

in the area. Meanwhile, she began to fear her own baby. The people of Bonndorf heard about that too, and they sent the doctor to her, who examined her. Unable to find any causal change in her vessels, he took a look at the baby in the cradle. He was a fine boy, wrapped in clean white linen. And as the doctor now looked at the child, he was beset by a terrible headache, followed by pains in his body and a malaise of the soul more intense than anything he had experienced since his boyhood on a strict and bleak abbey estate. The haldress, meanwhile, complained of exactly the same ailments, and together they only barely made it out to the well and leaned there against its stone. Having recovered his breath, the doctor realized that his usual strength had returned.

The baby was subsequently named the *Comet Child* and grew up among caring nuns in a separate area.

Remember: It is fortunate that in certain cases we do not first send for the priest but instead for the doctor. Thus was the city of Bonndorf saved in the year of the comet 1811 from an arrival of the devil incarnate.

(FROM: Johann Peter Hebel, *The Calendar Stories: Complete Tales from the Rhineland Family Friend*, p. 334-335)

5. *In the Zone: Part 1*

By Clemens J. Setz[*]

Pension Tachler in Gillingen

Gillingen is a typical southern Styrian small town in the middle of hilly wine country and with a world-famous cable car, which is also touted as a tourist attraction by the neighboring town of Seelwand. It's part of those foothills that—as Elfriede Jelinek writes in her masterpiece *The Children of the Dead*—the mountain stuffs in its pants pockets.

When I arrived in Gillingen by train, pleasantly broken clouds hung in the evening sky over the town, the famous gondolas of the cable car hovered in the distance over the western slope of the mountain, and in the covered waiting area of the small train station I noticed to my great delight a man pushing an old-fashioned high-wheel bicycle out into the sun. I loitered a bit longer in front of the train station because I wanted to see the man climb onto his high-wheel bicycle and ride away on it. But he did nothing, he seemed to be waiting for something, looked at his watch, turned in all wind directions and stared. After about ten minutes I left in disappointment.

On the way to the hotel I called my girlfriend, Julia. She listened to my description and afterward asked whether the man had had a mustache. I said yes, even though I wasn't at all sure. Then we agreed that men with high-wheel bicycles must absolutely always have a

[*] Appeared, considerably abridged, in: *National Geographic* (German edition), January 2007.

mustache, and ended the conversation. I had almost reached Pension Tachler anyway.

The large building with the vacancy sign under the gable was in the immediate vicinity of a spacious tavern named Ernst'l. Written with chalk on a blackboard on the sidewalk was today's lunch menu: Pork schnitzel with fresh potatoes; ½ a fried chicken; boiled beef with sauerkraut.

The pension itself made a pleasant impression. Next to reception a large bird with a strikingly long beak perched in an open cage. A young woman sat in front of a computer and looked up.

– Good evening.

– Hello, I said. Clemens Setz. I reserved a room for two nights.

– Aha, yes . . . let me see . . . Yes, here.

She had found the entry on the calendar.

– Have you ever stayed with us before? she asked.

– No.

– Okay, then please fill this out.

She gave me the form, I entered the requested information, and signed it. While I was writing, I saw out of the corner of my eye the young woman grab her right breast and adjust it a little with a straightforward movement. I made a mistake on my own address and asked for a new form.

– It's all right, she said with an enchanting smile. Are you one of the ski lift people?

– Ski lift? No. I'm just here on a visit.

– I see, said the woman, apparently a bit disappointed. Well, anyway, there are so many people here because of the ski lift, yeah . . . It gets a bit weird after a while. But you're visiting someone, fine, fine . . .

She put the form in a drawer and looked for the room key. She found it under a small breakfast plate that someone had evidently left here in her workspace. With a sigh she placed the plate next to the cage, jolting the exotic bird out of its semiconscious state. It took a few steps sideways on its perch and eyed skeptically the strange world behind the bars.

– Room fourteen. That's on the second floor. The elevator is back there to your right.

– Thanks, I said. I have one more question.

– Go ahead.

– Do you know your way around here?

– Of course, she said with a nod. Where d'ya have to go?

– I wrote it down here . . . I have to go there tomorrow morning . . . One second . . .

I rummaged around in my coat pocket for the piece of paper, made the whole thing a bit more suspenseful by pretending not to find it right away, tried the one pocket, then the other. In reality I knew the address by heart and had even studied the satellite image on the Internet, but here, in this little town where everyone knew everyone, it would undoubtedly be revealing to find out how people felt about the Stennitzer family.

I pushed the piece of paper toward the young woman and focused on her face.

Stennitzer fam.
Glockenhofweg 1
8910 Gillingen

The woman's eyes went blank, then became alert, then she seemed to relax again. Information was being retrieved. *Maybe the name means nothing to her,* I thought. *Unlikely, but possible.* When she began to speak, I could tell that I had just turned into something scary in her eyes.

– So you're best off going out right here, outside the building, okay? Well, no, let me start over, you exit the building, okay? And then take a right, walk up the street until you get to the hill, and then take a left, so going up the whole time . . . uphill, that should actually . . .

She placed a hand on the key, pushed it toward me.

– Thank you, I said.

– They live pretty far out, she said.

It sounded a little like a warning, so I said:

– I'm sure I'll make it. What do you think?

– I'm sorry?

– I mean, walking there. That's doable, walking, right?

– Yeah, sure, it's all doable. At the very top of the hill. Just keep going uphill and . . .

I held her gaze and pretended I had to store the important information she had given me. When the bird in its cage made a rasping noise, the woman started violently.

– Thanks, I said, and went to the elevator.

While I waited, I looked over to the woman again. She extended a finger through the open cage door toward the bird, but it wasn't paying attention to her.

– Hey, you, I heard her saying softly. Got frightened, huh?

The key hung on a small piece of wood with the word *Jenga* on it. I imagined someone, frustrated after the collapse of his Jenga tower, throwing the blocks across the room and deciding to turn them all into key fobs.

The room was small and smelled minty.

The light switch in the bathroom activated, along with two flickering fluorescent tubes over the mirror, a vent, the sound of which was somewhat reminiscent of the buzz of leaf blowers in autumn. In the sink was a flower vase, half filled with water.

As always when I was alone in a hotel room in the evening, I turned on the television. Harmless voices, people, and events that had nothing to do with me made the room a bit warmer. Only then could I close the curtains without being seized by a slight panic in the face of my solitude.

I sat down in the broad armchair in front of the window and looked out into the area in the evening light. That feeling when you gaze from some distance at a landscape or a town in which you assume the presence of a particular person. The peculiar hue, like the quality, reminiscent of underwater photos, of television pictures from the seventies with their blending colors, their rounded corners, and the bright, unnaturally flickering orange into which ordinary sunlight is transformed. The certainty: *In one of these houses, on one of these streets.* Prominent architectural elements begin to beckon, dark spots send signals. Trees stand still as if for a group photo. Gillingen: a church spire, a few houses, a handful of shops. Wooded hills in the vicinity. So this was the hometown of Christoph Stennitzer, fourteen years old, profoundly affected by Indigo syndrome since the first year of his life. His mother owned a medium-sized paper mill, or rather, a few years earlier she had sold it in several steps, when Christoph's condition had been getting worse and worse.

Those were the words Gudrun Stennitzer had used in the e-mail she had sent me: *When C's condition was getting worse and worse.* Of course, Christoph was a healthy, outwardly inconspicuous kid. Once he had had the measles, another time a severe flu with mild pneumonia, as a result of which he had to be hospitalized for a week, but apart from that everything with him was fine. If you saw him in a video, you wouldn't notice the slightest difference from other children. The problem, the *condition*, lay elsewhere.

Christoph lived in his own roughly four-hundred-square-foot house, which had a bathroom and even—as I gathered from the photo attached to the e-mail—a satellite dish mounted on the roof. He had moved into it on his third birthday. *He was excited*, his mother had written me. *A little house of his own, just for him.*

After I had closed the curtains, the unpleasant hotel room feeling came after all and constricted my throat, so I focused for a few minutes on the images on the television and waited until it passed. Then I turned on the reading lamp over the nightstand next to the bed and sat in front of it. With the peaceful murmur of the television program, which was about the lives of reptiles in a Cologne zoo, in the background, I reviewed all my notes and organized them a bit for the next day. I was planning to go straight to the Stennitzers' after getting up.

We hadn't arranged an exact time. *We're always here, of course, where are we supposed to go.*

I had already noticed in Frau Stennitzer's first e-mail (which, like all the others, I had printed out and filed with my notes) the dramatic tone she tended to adopt every few lines, the tone of someone who hadn't spoken with anyone about her problems for a long time and assumed that she wouldn't be understood anymore anyway, now, after she had suffered for so long in obscurity. But perhaps there was something else behind it, for the Stennitzers, it seemed, did not at all live in isolation. Gudrun Stennitzer mentioned at several points her neighbor who often visited, and also a Dutch doctor who a year ago came every few months for his research.

I lay down on the bed and masturbated a bit to a telephone woman who begged to be called. She was cross-eyed, which for some reason made me feel very tender and protective toward her and made it difficult to think erotic thoughts. The woman looked dramatically to the left and right, shielding her eyes with her hand, but still the telephone didn't ring, while every few seconds an alarm with a rotating blue light went off in the studio and announced that the amount of money to be won had just gone up by two hundred euros.

When my compassion for her became too intense, I gave up and wrapped myself in the blanket. After I had found a station whose nighttime programming seemed harmless enough for me to let it watch over my sleep, I turned the volume down to the softest level, only a line away from complete soundlessness, and closed my eyes.

I usually slept best to *Space Night*, which was often shown late at night on BR-alpha, wonderfully hovering footage from orbit, the slowed-down dance of astronauts attached to their umbilical cords while they repaired solar receptors or readjusted antennae and under them continents floated and swirling clouds drifted across the Atlantic. But that channel wasn't available in the hotel, so I had to content myself with an N24 documentary on the making and loading of shipping containers.

Glockenhofweg 1

The next morning a man with glasses sat at reception. So I asked the same question again. I had to go here, please, I explained, and read from the crumpled piece of paper: Glockenhofweg 1, Stennitzer family . . .

On the screen behind the man a silent video clip of the band AC/DC was playing. The sweating guitarist Angus Young hopped across the stage like a limping bird, and his mouth looked like it was taking big gulps of air.

—Yeah, that's out there, the man said. But I can't recall right now . . .

— Roughly in what direction?

—Yeah, we can look at a map, if you want.

He turned around, closed the window with the hopping rock star, and opened Google Maps.

— So you've never been up there before? I asked.

He shook his head.

—You probably don't live here in the town.

—Yes, I do, he said. But I don't go up there. No reason for me to.

While the printer forced out the sheet of paper, we stood silently facing each other. I put the printout in my pocket, thanked him, and went into the breakfast room. When I returned to the entrance area, I saw that the man with the glasses and the young woman from the previous evening were sitting at reception and talking softly to each other.

The man, when he saw me coming, picked up the cage with the bird in it and put it on the floor. Then he disappeared through a back door, the woman stayed behind. She smiled at me as I passed her. The bird made a soft rasping noise.

Fortified by my breakfast, which had consisted of a glass of freshly squeezed orange juice, I walked up to the Stennitzer family's house. I was terribly nervous and, to bolster my courage a little, listened on my iPod first to "Sweet Home Alabama" by the Leningrad Cowboys, then to "Joyride" by Roxette, to the beginning of "Le Sacre du Prin-temps," conducted by Valery Gergiev, and finally to "Stop the Rock" by Apollo 440.

The spring in the stranger's step must have looked odd to the peo-ple who encountered me that sunny morning. And even more so the singing:

– *Shake my paranoia . . . can't stop the rock . . . shake my paranoia . . .*

This song always dispelled all melancholy or brooding thoughts and made me empty and receptive like a dry sponge—the ideal state for an interview. But that elation was soon clouded again by the impres-sion the people in the town made on me. They all seemed to me strangely elongated and excessively upright, like figures on a ceiling fresco, which can never entirely fill the space of the dome in which they live. Two-legged lizards. Perhaps my perception had something to do with my own compressed posture that morning, or perhaps with the mountain scenery, which was unfamiliar for my spatial sense. They weren't high mountains, more like hills, surrounding the town, but they were always there, awaited you at the end of every road and inti-mate side street, like creatures turned away from you, whose shoulders you have to study for a clue to their mood.

Frau Stennitzer was a small, pleasantly proportioned woman in her mid-forties. She had long hair, a pale face with deep, distinctive eye sockets, and a thin mouth that shone unusually red, like a diamond on a playing card. She greeted me at the gate to the yard on her property. She often spent whole days here outside, in the company of her plants, she said. In the house it was cool, the heat wasn't on yet. Not until September has really begun, Frau Stennitzer said. So I left my coat on.

I should have brought my scarf, I thought. The living room was particularly cold. But Frau Stennitzer seemed to be accustomed to the low temperature in her house. In addition to the cold, it struck me that the whole time I spent in the house the rattling of a washing machine could be heard. Every few minutes it took a short break, then it started again.

We sat down. Frau Stennitzer put both hands to her temples and made a few circling movements.

— Do you have . . . ? I asked.

— What? A headache? she asked.

— No, that's not what I meant.

— No, it's all right, she said. Please, you don't have to be careful around me in that regard.

— Okay.

— It's fine, she said. It's not like it's anything new.

A nervous laugh.

The room smelled strongly of air freshener. The bottle was on the floor next to the table, Febreze. Next to it another one. I also noticed a bottle on a shelf, but with a different label.

— Yeah, well, thank you very much for agreeing to speak with me.

— Oh, my God, said Frau Stennitzer, putting a hand on her collar-bone. Please, it's nothing. If it helps.

We were silent. I fished my notebook out of my pocket.

— Maybe you'd like to go right into the yard? The little house . . .

She said that like a weary museum guide who always has to show the visitors the *Mona Lisa* before anything else, even though hundreds of far more interesting paintings are hanging on the walls all around.

— Yeah, I'd like that. If your son won't—

— Oh, yeah, of course, it's fine. He's not in his room right now anyway.

— Then where is he?

Frau Stennitzer laughed, looked at her fingers folded in her lap, and then said:

— So you'd like to see his room, right?

— As I said, yes, if it doesn't bother him.

— Oh, well, he's not there, so . . .

— All right. But I meant: Only if he doesn't mind strangers entering his private space in his absence.

— I'm not a stranger. And you're with me, so it's okay, said Frau Stennitzer.

Whenever she finished a sentence, she pursed her lips a little and stuck out her chin, as if she had to give her lips and jaw muscles a rest from the arduous effort.

We stepped through the patio door into the yard. A few apple trees stood there, along with some hedges and charmingly overgrown bushes. Next to the fence that marked the property line was a small, conically piled mound of earth, the purpose of which I couldn't exactly determine from afar; maybe a work of garden art. The little house, as Frau Stennitzer had called it in her e-mail, was, it turned out, an actual small house.

We entered. Here too it smelled to an almost numbing degree of Febreze and something else, even bitterer, sharper.

An air mattress lay right behind the door to the first room, which was Christoph's bedroom.

Frau Stennitzer sighed and pushed the air mattress aside with the toe of her shoe.

What first caught my eye were the many books in the room: *Harry Potter*, other fantasy books, Terry Pratchett, but also, surprisingly, a thick biography of Frédéric Chopin. And a copy of Philip K. Dick's *Ubik*.

– Hey, I said. My favorite novel.

I pointed to the book. Frau Stennitzer sighed:

– Oh, really, yeah?

A half-gaping accordion. Several tennis rackets. A poster of Keanu Reeves in his *Matrix* outfit. A few medications on a table next to the bed. *Sviluppal*, I read on a bottle.

Frau Stennitzer laid the air mattress on the bed.

– No idea why it always has to lie around here, she said. But he can't be without it, he reinflates it every week. Sometimes that makes him dizzy. But he's fond of the air mattress. He learned to read on it, you know. Herr Baumherr from the APUIP recommended a private tutor for us back then. He was a really great young man. Passionate photographer, very cultivated, patient with Christoph and his peculiarities. Since then the mattress has always lain around here. He was illiterate for such a long time, you know. He refused to learn. He was a committed illiterate until he was about eight years old.

That phrase rattled me a bit. For a mother to speak that way about her child seemed unusual to me. The term *illiterate* is tinged with a certain horror, probably the reason that children released from a basement dungeon after years are always tested for their ability to read before anything else. A similarly horrifying atmosphere emanates only from openly asexual people and would-be suicides. They withdraw from our world, sit around, done with everything, waiting only for the opportunity to opt out again, to return to the peace they have tasted. But *committed*? The word made no sense at all. How could an eight-year-old boy be *committed* to his illiteracy?

In Christoph's bedroom were many toys, and everything was really neatly and lovingly arranged, a friendly dragon wallpaper pattern and completely dust-free corners. Such an immaculate room immediately evoked in me memories of that horrible room in which a five-year-old girl in Vienna had recently died of hunger and thirst. She hadn't even gnawed at the houseplants, even though they had been well within reach. The door had been locked, her parents out celebrating for several days and nights, and the first thing the officials actually discovered: no teeth marks anywhere. Neither in the wood of the doorframe nor on the peeling plaster of the walls nor on her own wrists—*nowhere*. The word haunted the newspapers for weeks. My girlfriend and I debated the question of what would be worse and grislier, teeth marks in all possible and impossible places or absolutely no teeth marks—and as stupid as it sounds, I don't even remember which position I took and which she took during this creepy debate, but I think that the absence of teeth marks ultimately won, and we talked and rolled around nervously in bed until late at night and then both deservedly had horrible nightmares. I seem to recall that at some point I even, in a nocturnally twisted and overtired way, became angry with the poor girl because she had died with such a terrible lack of resistance, as if in a tacit arrangement with the media and with people's sad hunger for sensation.

At the time Julia had said that something was wrong with my thoughts. They had become strange, were always straying to awful things, assumed gigantic, overwhelming proportions. I blamed it on the headaches and difficulties concentrating that I'd started having as a result of my work at the Helianau Institute.

– Everything all right? asked Frau Stennitzer.

–Yes, I said, letting go of my temples.

– If you have to go out for a little while, she said. (From her tone I could tell that these words had passed her lips hundreds of times before.)

– No, it's okay, I said. Oh, look . . .

On the windowsill of the room I noticed something that affected me strangely; I almost wished I hadn't seen it: binoculars. There were three pairs, two of them exactly the same type and a somewhat larger one. They reminded me of the nights during my childhood when, because there was a concert at the Orpheum concert hall across from my bedroom, I had to go to bed in a different room of the apartment and therefore often didn't sleep a wink until morning. It was my apartment, but the walls looked wrong at night, plus I heard the street, and cars were driving constantly as fan-shaped light-ghosts through the dark room. At some point, I received binoculars as a gift and spent the nights with—or better, in—them. They were especially useful when a school friend stayed overnight. Almost all night long we would patiently search the wall of the opposite house for interesting, sensational things. And since we rarely managed to find anything of the sort, we slipped gradually into invention, but without being aware *that* we were inventing things, which might have been the happiest and most relaxed state in which I had ever found myself.

From nights spent in the circular visual world of binoculars it's only a stone's throw to the purchase of a telescope. In the room through which Frau Stennitzer led me as if it were the conserved living space of a long-deceased famous person, there was one. I myself had never purchased one.

— Here's where he does his homework, that is, when he has some . . . And that's the intercom, it buzzes over in our kitchen and bedroom.

— Nice telescope, I said. Was it expensive?

— Pffff, uh, yeah, no idea, she said. My brother bought it for him back then. So you can assume it wasn't cheap. My brother's a pilot. Do you want to look through it?

— No, thanks.

I can remember only one time I looked through a telescope. It was several years ago in the house of a musician friend. For the first time in my life I viewed live the moon's surface, the incredibly sharp shadows of the crater rims, the gray swirls and ridgelines of the sandy surface. All gray on gray. Strange that most people, like Johannes Kepler in his famous dream narrative about the moon dwellers, imagined buildings and living things on that desolate, hostile rock, from which the sole comfort has for centuries been the mysterious face we can, with a little fantasy and fear, discern in it: an old man who has opened his mouth as if he were taking a deep breath after a strenuous march.

— I like to look through it, said Frau Stennitzer. I often come down here to Christoph's little house and then just sit here and . . .

She broke off as if what she had been about to say had been too private.

Basically, the man in the moon looked like Angus Young, I thought. Those half-open lips, that entranced . . . I realized that my mind was beginning to wander, my concentration was unraveling and becoming scattered among secondary things. So I took a deep breath, put a finger to the tip of my nose, and said:

— So where is Christoph, if you don't mind my asking?

— Yeah, he's . . . you know, it's complicated, we . . . we have a sort of agreement when it comes to visitors.

— To protect his privacy and such, I said.

— Yes, in a way.

– He doesn't like people coming here and asking him questions, sure, I'd feel the same way. But then where is he now, while we're in his room?

For a fleeting moment, Frau Stennitzer gave me a mistrustful look, as if she were grazed by the suspicion that she had apparently been wrong about me, then her face relaxed a little and she said:

– He can go anywhere. There's nothing stopping him.

– Ah, yes, of course, I said.

She stood there as if she were waiting for my next unpleasant question, then she reached for a few pieces of paper on her son's desk and held them out to me:

– Since very recently, Christoph has had a pen pal. They write each other regularly, you know. Demetrius Logan from Chicago.

– Excuse me? I asked.

She laughed.

– No, really, he actually exists. I checked. Pen pals, isn't that nice? I mean, that there's still such a thing nowadays.

The tone with which she said that was hard to interpret. I took the letter and said:

– Yeah, I think that's really great. I never had a pen pal.

– I don't even know why the two of them write each other letters, of all things. Usually Christoph writes e-mails, of course, just like everyone else. But this Demetrius . . . here's a photo of him.

A black boy, smiling, with a small fashionable hat on his head.

– He really exists, said Frau Stennitzer.

– Yes, I see that.

– In Chicago, said Frau Stennitzer. And the two of them write each other completely old-fashioned letters. Each week a letter arrives. From America. I always bring it here to the little house right away, without opening it first.

– I think that's wonderful. More people should do that. I mean, write old-fashioned letters.

– Hm, well. Yeah.

She took the sheets of paper back from me and placed them on her son's bed. I felt the need to get out of this stuffy building and return to the main house, so I stood near the bedroom door. But Frau Stennitzer sat down on the bed.

– The problem is, well, Demetrius is also . . .

– An I-kid?

She nodded.

– And that's the . . . uh, the crux of the whole matter. He can't come here, and Christoph can't fly to him, so . . . yeah, maybe this communication via objects you can touch is a sort of compensation for that.

– He can't travel?

– Of course not. Christoph in an airplane? How's that supposed to work? The pilots, the . . . Oh, never mind. A problem of range, like everything in our lives.

She made a sad, circular gesture with both arms.

– It was an awful day when I had to explain that to him. He didn't understand at all why he couldn't fly across the Atlantic. He went totally stir-crazy, and he . . . well, he simply imploded, there's no other way to put it. He raged, my God . . . Wouldn't sleep at all anymore. It was terrible, I lost fifteen pounds at the time. Not exactly what you'd call a happy ending, right?

– Well, I said, happy ends are rare. But it would definitely be nice if now and then there were (and I used, because it was really appropriate to the situation, Dr. Rudolph's favorite term) at least *fair ends*, wouldn't it?

I said that with a smile.

Frau Stennitzer winced and looked at me as if I had without warning spread out a frill-necked lizard's neck frill and hissed at her with a reptilian voice. Then she found her hands again, arranged them, left, right, as if they had gotten mixed up. And turned, half smiling, half keeping a careful eye on the space behind her, away from me.

After we had returned to the main house, I heard the front door open and close. But Frau Stennitzer acted as if nothing had happened, so I decided not to say anything either.

– Would you like something to drink? I have peach juice. Or wine, if you'd prefer . . .

– Peach juice sounds good.

No sooner had she set the glass on the table in front of me than I took a sip and then immediately drained the rest. I hadn't even noticed how parched I was. The dense air freshener atmosphere even affected my vocal cords. Every few seconds I had to clear my throat.

– So now that you've seen how we live here, would you like to . . .

– I have just a few questions . . .

– Go ahead, said Frau Stennitzer, collapsing into her armchair.

Frau Stennitzer had never married. Christoph's father, Peter, had abandoned her shortly after their son's birth. He hadn't contacted her since, and Frau Stennitzer didn't search for him either. She had managed very well alone so far, she said, her parents were here most of the time, reinforcements, as she called them.

– How did you meet Christoph's father?

– Oh, in the usual way. As people do. Do you want another peach juice? If you like it—

– No, thanks.

– But you had only one glass.

– Yeah, at the moment I'm satisfied.

– Good, okay, well . . . Yes, he abandoned me. It's not exactly a story of triumph. He said he was just going out for a few minutes to get cigarettes. Yeah, honestly. I know, to get cigarettes, I mean . . . Yes, he smoked. And he often went out in the evening to buy some . . . God, I was very naïve back then, but what was I supposed to have done?

She poured me another glass of peach juice. She spilled a little and wiped the liquid off the table with her palm, which she then rubbed on her pants with a weary, weak gesture. She seemed lost in thought.

How, I thought, do they do that, the men who say: Be right back, I'm just going to get some cigarettes—and from that point on it was as if the earth had swallowed them up? Perhaps they all ran aimlessly through the underground galleries that had been constructed for the large tunnel city, the *Giraffe* school project in Riegersdorf.

– He probably didn't even smoke, know what I mean?

I looked up.

– I beg your pardon?

– Well, said Frau Stennitzer, the way of the world. You rehearse and rehearse and then—boom, it's showtime. I wouldn't be surprised, in all honesty. If he had always just puffed. I wouldn't put it past him. Every week a dress rehearsal.

– Have you ever heard of those tunnel systems in—

– Yes, said Frau Stennitzer, of course. Sure, the thing in Riegersdorf. Yeah, they thought they'd really solve the problem from the ground up . . . Sort of out of sight, out of mind, right?

She took a big sip of peach juice from my glass.

I didn't return to Pension Tachler until evening. When I entered, I saw the young woman at reception pick up the cage with the bird in it with a hasty movement and (as the man with glasses had done in the morning) put it on the floor, as if she wanted to protect it from me. Her face was friendly, but she kept an eye on me.

– Good evening, I said.

She returned my greeting and withdrew into the back area of reception, among some boxes and cartons standing around there. She acted as if she were searching for something, and I don't know why, but at that moment I couldn't help taking a few steps toward her.

– Excuse me, I said. My hands are really cold, and my fingertips are practically numb. Might you touch them for a moment?

She backed farther away.

– Sorry? she said.

– My hands somehow . . . I don't know, maybe something didn't agree with me, an allergic reaction, or . . .

— Should I call an ambulance? she asked, but didn't come any closer.

— No, thanks, I said, withdrawing my hands. It's already getting a bit better. Probably just a circulatory problem. Hm, strange . . .

The young woman's face was pale.

On the way to the stairs I had trouble suppressing a grin. Only in the room did I begin to feel guilty. I called home and talked on the phone for a little while, then flipped through a few channels, skimmed my notes, and added a few things while I fought against the slight claustrophobia welling up in me.

First I tried to distract myself by searching the hotel room for hidden cameras and microphones.

— Ferenz, hello? I murmured as I searched. Calling Ferenz? Ferenz calling!

Then I checked the exact position of my suitcase's wheels and inspected its contents. I hadn't touched it since my arrival, and someone might have searched it in my absence. But everything was in its place, and I sat, breathing heavily, by the window and gazed into the night, which was adorned with a magnificent yellowish moon medal. Late at night came my salvation: a documentary about couples with Tourette's syndrome. A man and a woman sat on a couch, he had his arm around her and hissed insults at her, dirty slut, cunt, bitch, and her left hand kept wandering to his face and his neck and scratching him with her fingernails, until she intercepted it with her other hand and held on to it. We can basically never fight, the man said in answer to the interviewer's question. Every curse word that exists has taken on a different meaning for us. So we don't even know how to do it, to fight, haha. Afterward a few more scenes were shown from the couple's everyday life. While shopping, the man shouted nasty vulgarities at her while she threw things off a shelf and immediately picked them up again. People stopped, looked at the camera, then at the strange pair, and finally moved on. I was so excited that I bounced while sitting on my bed and clapped my hands.

Soothed by the wonderful documentary, I fell asleep, without a blanket, in my street clothes, but soon awoke, because I had again dreamed of frame no. 242 of the Zapruder film. That happened to me perhaps two or three times a year, usually when I was traveling, and it was always a terrible experience. It's the moment shortly after the first bullet hit President Kennedy in the neck. He is clutching with both hands at the wound, like someone trying to open a stuck zipper. And he looks to the side at his wife, who looks at him uneasily, but also kindly and helpfully: *Yes, what is it?* And he appears as if he wanted to say: *Here, I can't get this open, can you please help me?* And in an instant she will move closer to him and touch him and cry for help, until finally the second bullet hurtles down from the cosmos and tears off half the President's skull. But that explosive last impact is still many, many microseconds away. The universe remains at a standstill, held by the gaze of the fatally wounded man, whose voice probably fails, because he can no longer breathe, and he is actually already a dead man, who is trying to speak to a living woman, and the two of them are sitting in the backseat of a car, although they are in reality millions of miles apart; he is attempting to communicate with her, to explain to her what has happened, and she looks back at him understandingly and also somewhat worriedly.

In other variations of this dream, frame no. 242 appeared to me on a cereal box, another time I sat across from the two frozen figures in a train compartment. And then, about six months earlier, I was the salesman who had sold President Kennedy the stuck zipper, and I felt so ashamed of myself that I had trouble waking up from the dream.

6. Going to Get Cigarettes

They had been living together for three years. Since autumn Cordula had been well adjusted, that is, the medication had settled in her and set up a provisional but functional interim regime.

Robert had meanwhile put away in his wardrobe the portrait of the monkey that had so horrified Cordula. He took some pleasure in the idea that he had it at his disposal as a secret weapon, a last straw he could grasp at if all other means had been . . . He shook his head and drove away the strange thought. Straw?

When he passed the mirror that evening after brushing his teeth, he silently made monkey grimaces and scratched his armpits with his hands. Cordula had taken half a zolpidem, really just half a pill, which actually only made you very, very tired and not completely drugged, because that way she could convince herself that she was brave and could *in principle* get through the night without it. Besides, it had happened before that when she took, for example, two zolpidem tablets and fell into bed as if struck dead with a hammer, she couldn't get up the next day to go to work. Once, in the hospital, it had also come to pass that she had peed herself in the drugged night.

– How are you doing? he whispered (although, for some reason, he felt more like declaiming loudly in a Falstaffian manner).

– Hm, she said. Embarrassed. Always so fast, the trigger, the . . .

The half a zolpidem had worked. But you weren't even supposed to take the drug for panic attacks. In that case, Lexotanil or Xanor were more appropriate. Those strange medicine names, like magic spells from fantasy novels. As if they were invented by children.

– I wrapped the painting in a cloth and put it in my wardrobe. Just so you know where it is. You don't have to be afraid of it anymore.

When she didn't respond, he said (while playing in his head a scene from the Japanese movie *Tetsuo*, in which the insane man shoves a steel pipe into his thigh):

– The painting isn't that good anyway. Artistically, I mean. Not really successful.

Cordula nodded weakly. She seemed to be falling asleep.

– Do you know what I've been thinking about? he asked her loudly.

She looked up, was awake, but not really there. Then, perhaps out of politeness toward him, or perhaps out of a guilt that had from sheer exhaustion become loud and one-dimensional, she gathered up her consciousness, which had already been standing with its toes in the pleasant nonsense in which it got to dissolve each evening, and said:

– What?

Robert knew that it was his last chance to stop. Just say: Oh, nothing, we'll talk about it tomorrow, it can really wait until you're feeling better. Just say nothing more. Just say: You dealt really well with the anxiety attack this time, you know that? I'm proud of you. And you only needed half a zolpidem, really incredible.

He stood over an abyss and the thin rope on which he believed he had to balance cut into his toes.

He said:

– I think maybe I'll . . .

You can still turn back. Don't say it. Not at this moment.

– . . . go away for a while. To Gillingen or something, you know? See old acquaintances again. Check out the cable car. I haven't been there in a long time.

He sensed her drugged but not immobilized body stiffening, as if she were about to be pushed lengthwise, like a battering ram borne by several men, headfirst through a narrow opening. From a movement of the muscles on the back of her neck, the bright spot that could be seen well in the half-light of the room, he saw that she tried to swallow but was already too weak.

Should he wish that she hadn't heard his remark? But she had been awake, clearly awake, for God's sake, what was wrong with him! He stood up, made one or two monkey grimaces, then ran out of the room, sat down in front of the television, and had to hold his face in his hands so that the rats stayed in.

He felt as if he were about to explode—not spectacularly, however, with napalm majesty as in *Apocalypse Now*, but more like one of those firecrackers that made only hard, small explosions, which were more akin to the feeling of prepubescent erections, compact, anxious, enraged, confused.

I'd like to unfasten my arms and plant them in the earth.

Stop, stop, stop.

He turned on the television and put on headphones. Gillingen, he thought, that strange little town in southern Styria. On home shopping channels diamonds and bracelets were held up to the camera. The hand that turned the objects back and forth was extremely hairy. A report on container loading regulations at the port of Amsterdam. A game show with disabled people (blind person versus wheelchair user, Tourette's versus thalidomide). A documentary on a Norwegian Nazi named Hamsun to whom people made pilgrimages after the war and over whose garden fence they threw books. Robert tried to understand what it was actually about, but he couldn't concentrate, he continued flipping through channels, found horse racing and golf and Bilderbergers, a language course in business Chinese and a woman begging to be called. She was naked and her face might have been Pakistani, or maybe Indian, and he stared at her for a long time without thinking anything in particular.

Sunlight, as fresh as the air on a terrace full of tin watering cans, came through the window. The first day of theoretical freedom, thought Robert. He turned over and saw Cordula, she was lying bare-chested on her pillow, embracing him in her sleep. Her hair fell down her back, she breathed softly and regularly. Her spine, her shoulder blades. The gray half-light of the room on her flanks.

She did that on purpose, thought Robert. The past three nights she had slept with a pajama top on, *I freeze so easily, women's circulation is different from men's, a completely different system*, and it had been getting somewhat cool. The skin on her shoulders had that fine, dimply elasticity when it stretched over the round bones. Everything round is a mystery, precisely because it's round. You first grasped that when you tried to draw an apple. My God, the many hours wasted in still life drawing classes. Where the motionlessness of the students surpassed even the motionlessness of the fruit. The fruit at least rotted and began to smell, that was life, but the students . . . Not even when they had sat very close to Robert had they shown any reaction. He had never felt as naked as he had then, outside his zone for the first time.

He took a deep breath and for a brief moment smelled again the stuffy hot air inside his Lichtenberg hut at Helianau, and in there, in the still circle of light cast by the small reading lamp: the fruit bowl, the altar on which artists since Cézanne have sacrificed their talent and flagellated themselves. And all around him countless fruit flies, like a skin disease of the air.

With a heavy breath Cordula lifted her head. She looked around, saw Robert, and said:

– Oh.

He nodded at her.

Then he climbed on her, immediately her smell wafted toward him, her breath, which due to the sedative smelled stale and sour. Still, he felt the need to kiss her, but she lay there angularly and inhospitably, so he contented himself with sliding between her legs and pressing himself against her. She said nothing, but let him penetrate her, though only a few centimeters. She was not at all moist, so it would work only with great pain anyway. Robert stayed where he was. At the entrance, on the threshold. Another breath of stuffy hot air from the past.

I'm cruel, he thought. And for a moment the shadow of an image fell on him, like a bird flitting over a snow-covered landscape: the image of a disheveled rooster he carried in a crate through the snow, it seemed so remote from him and his situation, the animal had mean-while died, and nonetheless it was there, bright as the light at the end of a tunnel.

I'm cruel.

Usually Cordula had to go to the bathroom every morning shortly after waking up. Now she couldn't, and he was pressing against her, was perhaps pressing on her bladder. Cruel.

—Wait, she said softly and trustingly. You . . . can you . . .

She tried to shift him into a more pleasant position. On another day she would have pushed him away, called him an idiot and a mangy dog, and would have taken her time in the bathroom until his arousal had subsided. Then she would have marched naked through the room and might have asked what his plans were today. She had to go to work, of course, earn money, be normal, and so on, and he, what was he going to do, all day long? And that might lead to a little quarrel, a substitute for the aborted intimacy.

But today—nothing.

She moved back and forth as if her pelvis were nodding reassur-ingly, *Yes, yes, I understand, it's okay, everything's okay*—and he knew that he could now feel something like compassion. This time she was actu-ally frightened that he could leave forever. And that was what he was going to do too, first thing tomorrow. Today preparations, phone calls, tickets; tomorrow departure. She didn't want him to leave, and that was why she stayed still. Robert had respect for that attitude, for that consistency. *I'm cruel*, he thought again, and felt himself shrink, soften, slip out of her. She stroked his cheek with her hand.

Everything with her was actually fine. It wasn't her fault. She was kind, attentive. Her apartment was bright. She smelled wonderful, even her scalp and the always slightly sweaty patch of skin between her shoulder blades. And her dark blond hair was healthy and strong. She even sometimes let him try things out that he had seen in movies. She was patient. And even when she had headaches or migraines, she didn't blame him. She was well bred.

– I'm just going out for a few minutes, Robert said, standing up.
– Okay, said Cordula.
He left the room and stood there.

How do they do it, the men who say, I'm just going out for a few
minutes to get cigarettes, and then never resurface? They must be
out there, somewhere in the world they're all roaming around, those
hordes of cigarette refugees, they sit in cold hotel rooms, without a
passport, without a credit card, without much cash, and wait. For what?
Perhaps it's an ancient secret of the cigarette machines themselves, a
secret code you enter by pressing the buttons for various brands, and
then the box opens with a hissing hydraulic sound, revealing a passage into the underworld. From all the cities on earth, through the
openings on street corners and in the walls of public restrooms, the
men descend into the galleries, greet one another with a brief nod,
because they're not in the mood to speak, for far too long they have
been asked by their wives and children at home how they're doing
and where they're going and when they're coming back, and they
follow the glowing signs to the Great Underground Transit Station,
the secret hub for all those who want to escape their lives. Under the
large neon signs on which the logos of the cigarette companies glow,
they wait on vast platforms, each of them alone, each withdrawn into
himself, for further connections. Bearded figures in trench coats, with
caps and sunglasses. There are also young men among them, having
only just grown up and already impregnated a woman, they couldn't
endure that and are now here, frightened and shy, trembling in the
subway wind in the face of their uncertain future, their exile. Then
black underworld trains appear, lit only inside, which burrow through
the earth and bring the escapees to faraway cities, to Singapore, Saint
Petersburg, Cape Town, Los Angeles. In the cars it's as quiet as at truck
stops in the middle of the desert, the passengers don't talk much, some
perhaps murmur to themselves a little, while the others take apart
their cell phones or smash them with a hammer. Tracking chips of all
sorts disappear in sealable lead containers, which hang in each com-

partment. And there are also those who never take one of the trains and resurface in faraway cities of the globe with a false name and a new hairstyle, no, some get used to the coolness and the peculiar freshness of the air down there in the transit galleries, to the flickering neon light of the cigarette advertisements, to the McDonald's counters, which are run by blind people, and they sit down and think: *Tomorrow, tomorrow I'll take a train, and for this one night I'll just stay sitting here.* And then they fall asleep and, without realizing it, get through the famous *first night.* And after that they are free, they remain in the tunnel systems and improve them, expand them. It's important that they are there, for without them the tunnel systems and the artificial lighting and the trains wouldn't exist. All this didn't just grow in the earth, of course. All man-made, over centuries, like an underground ant city, starting with the first, unknown escapee, who scratched the wall next to the cigarette machine with his fingernails and wished the earth would swallow him up—he was followed by millions of lonely men, who wanted no more contact with their past and family and who dug their way into the earth with their bare hands or primitive tools they happened to pocket on their way out of their home, forever far from the domestic hearth—

– What are you thinking about?

From behind, Cordula put a finger on his head and ran it along the cranial suture, in improvised zigzags. Like the cartridge of a phonograph.

– Why do women always ask that? he replied.

Robert put on a T-shirt that said "Dingo Bait." The shirt had actually been a Christmas present for Cordula, but when she had unwrapped it, she had been horrified. He explained to her that it had been meant as a joke, that he had no problem with the term as long as it wasn't used pejoratively, and so on; for what must have been longer than an hour he had gone on and on to her, but she had remained unable to laugh about it. Then she had tried it on, had taken a few steps in it, and had torn it off again so quickly that her glasses flew off her face.

– Oh, Cordula . . .

– I don't want to wear it. What do you think my colleagues at the office will say if I walk around in that?

–You don't have to wear it to work, if there's nothing but humorless jerks there, but at least—

– Robert, I'm sorry.

And then, of course, came the trembling upper lip and the guilty look down at the floor, because it was Christmas, the holy time in which things always had to be wonderfully harmonious, and now she had rejected a present from him and so destroyed the Christmas peace, yes, those very thoughts were with certainty going through her stupid little head, thought Robert. He still remembered taking the T-shirt gently from her hand and putting it on himself.

In the meantime, he had several of them. Most of them were silly and had to do with Australia, such as, "I'm a father but I love my dingos." Or, "A dingo ate my government!" Or, very simple, "I need a dingo's breakfast." On the Internet you could also find some T-shirts that directly (and totally self-confidently!) referred to the Indigo topic, but they were all unbearably stupid.

At noon Willi and Elke were going to stop by. Robert had met Willi in Berlin. At every opportunity Willi mentioned that he had lived there for three years. Three years in Berlin. Really? Three years? Not just two? No, three. That number, connected with the vibrant metropolis in which every side street was steeped in history, formed the innermost core of his being. He had lived there with a woman who also came from Austria, and was deaf. She could read lips and speak indistinctly, but soon they communicated only in signs, a sort of doubly secret language, because their Salzburg sign dialect often met with incomprehension among deaf Germans, and people on the street with normal hearing understood nothing anyway. Willi's girlfriend had often been amused by the uselessly hanging arms and hands of hearing people, the way they carried them around listlessly as if they were broken windmill vanes, two burdensome appendages with which no one knew what to do apart from now and then pushing down door handles or hailing a taxi. Sometimes they had fun incorporating a curse or an obscene sign into everyday gestures, say, a harmless wave. But nothing of the deaf woman had remained in him, he didn't even like to mention her name, Ilona, the only thing that meant something to him was the number three in connection with Berlin. The more often you asked him about it, the brighter and more pleasant his day became.

A visit from Willi was always good, in his presence Robert was usually calm and relaxed . . . but nothing had grounded him recently as much as the monkey at the university medical lab. He could still feel it, the peace was like an arrival, like a—ah, he had to get up, go, move.

He went into the hall and dismantled an umbrella into its component parts.

He imagined a drill sergeant shouting at him to assemble the umbrella as fast as possible. Damn it, Private Tätzel! Why aren't you done with the umbrella yet! If this were the real thing, you'd be long dead, you miserable dingo!

Robert laughed.

Cordula found him on all fours, still occupied with dismantling the old umbrella. She greeted him, didn't ask what he was doing, but simply stepped carefully over him and the parts arranged in slightly staggered rows, roughly quincunx-like, and slipped into the kitchen, where she prepared snacks and drinks.

– Where did you put the white wine? she asked after a few minutes.

– In the sink, Robert said calmly.

– Ah, of course, didn't see it, she said.

– You know, Robin, Robert said in Adam West's German Batman voice, often we can't see the forest for the trees and sometimes we can't even see the tree for the branches. And even then birds are still perching on the tree and chirping.

To say anything more tender than that wasn't possible for him at the moment. Cordula understood and laughed at the joke.

———

A bit later Cordula, who had finished everything, came to Robert in the hall, who sat, more or less relaxed, in the middle of the parts.

– Everything okay with you two? she asked.

Even though the cheerful tone irritated Robert—he didn't like it when she was afraid of him—he answered softly:

– Yeah, everything's pretty much okay. I . . . I was just trying to repair it. It wouldn't open anymore, and . . .

– And? Did it work?

He shook his head.

– How are you doing, with . . . ?

– No aftershocks, said Cordula, sitting down next to him on the floor.

THE NEIGHBOR'S MELANCHOLY

Parrhasius, a painter of Athens, amongst those Olynthian captives Philip of Macedon brought home to sell, bought one very old man; and when he had him at Athens, put him to extreme torture and torment, the better by his example to express the pains and passions of his Prometheus, whom he was then about to paint. With an apparatus of his own design he unscrewed the eyes from the old man's face and placed him for days in fetters beside another captive, a young fellow in whose presence people tended to forfeit their sanity. It must have been something in the composition of this young man's humors that disrupted in a particular way the mental and physical equilibrium of other creatures. This phenomenon and other related symptoms are observed more often among young women than among young men. Hippocrates, Moschion, and those old *gynaeciorum scriptores* argue along these lines when they emphasize, *ob septum transversum violatum*, saith Mercatus, that is, that midriff or *diaphragma*, heart and brain are offended with those contradictory vapors arising from the foreign body. Those who stand in direct *proximitas* to the peculiarly composed body complain many times, saith Mercatus, of a great pain in their heads, about their hearts, and hypochondries, and so likewise in their breasts, which are often sore and dull,

322

not unlike closed flowers; sometimes, without forewarning, they are ready to swoon, their faces are inflamed, and red, they are dry, thirsty, suddenly hot, and feel confined even while standing in a vast landscape or under a starry night sky, are much troubled with superstitions and sleeplessness, &c. And from hence proceed *ferina deliramenta*, a brutish kind of dotage, often directed against family members, troublesome sleep, terrible dreams in the night of demonic visitations and feelings of a heavy weight even under the lightest covers, *subrusticus pudor et verecundia ignava*, a foolish kind of bashfulness to some, perverse conceits and opinions, dejection of the political mind, much discontent, preposterous judgment in quarrels over questions of compassion or religion. Each thing almost is tedious to them, they are apt to weep, and tremble, so long as that person with the strange composition of humors is near them. When he is removed from their vicinity, they suddenly feel better, they dance, are merry, and the diseases of the head and of judgment also gradually abate. And a lively feeling for their neighbor returns to them, because they can again regard themselves without danger or contradiction as such a one (*Proximus sum egomet mihi*, Terence, *Andria* 4, 1, 12).

(FROM: ROBERT BURTON, *The Anatomy of Melancholy, Bodily Causes Among People in Proximity*, p. 382–383)

7.   *In the Zone: Part 2*
By Clemens J. Setz[*]

The Head

The next morning I discovered in my hotel room a door that led
to a balcony. Pleasantly surprised, as if this access had grown from
the room overnight through my own dream efforts, I stepped out. It
smelled of the warm wood that had turned tar-black from years of
exposure to sunlight, and I stood before an unusually large and unusually beautiful watering can. Its tin head was stretched forward as if it
were on the lookout for something, and when I touched it, it let out a
high-pitched clang as if it had long been waiting for that release from
immobility. In contrast to watering cans made of plastic, ones made of
tin have an unmistakable character, a particular posture that resembles
a ballet dancer frozen mid-twirl in a photo. Their body is cylindrical
and stern, their surface usually rough and pleasantly recalcitrant toward
the skin of your palm. Fingernails break easily on it. Inside the watering can I discovered, when I held it up to the light, a system of white,
feathery spider webs, and I immediately went back into the room to
look for my cell phone and call Julia and tell her about my find. While
the phone rang, I stood next to the watering can and looked at it, the
phone rang three times, four times, then I quickly hung up, because
I realized how nonsensical what I was doing was. It was nothing, just
a watering can with a few spider webs in it, on a hotel room balcony
at Pension Tachler, in this town already buzzing sunnily away early in

[*] Appeared, considerably abridged, in: *National Geographic* (German edition),
February 2007.

the morning. The church steeple and the watering can were almost exactly the same color, I now noticed. I tried to take a photo with my cell phone of this remarkable correspondence, but it didn't work, the backlight plunged everything in the picture into midnight black.

The clatter of horse hooves could be heard at some distance when I stepped out of the pension, a wonderful, relaxing sound, as if the landscape were clearing its throat. Frau Stennitzer had announced that Christoph would speak with me briefly today. He was the reason for my visit, after all, and not, haha, she herself, she had said, yes, she knew, of course, how priorities were allocated in the world, in general . . .

The smell of air freshener, with which I was met already in the hall, was even more unbearable than the day before. I was about to ask whether a window could be opened, but Frau Stennitzer immediately led me into the living room. She had sweaty hands, and her cell phone hung on her belt in a flip-open case.

When I entered the living room and saw what was sitting there on the sofa, I dropped in shock my notebook and the muffin I had bought at the train station bakery on the way up here, and ran back into the hall. Only from the amused face of Frau Stennitzer, who followed me, holding up her palms reassuringly, did I realize that I must have screamed loudly. I heard laughter. Frau Stennitzer put a hand on my chest, then on my shoulder.

– You okay? she asked with a giggle. You got scared, heeheehee, you . . . did you really?

– What the hell is that?

She walked back into the living room with me, still giggling to herself.

– Ah, it's a mask, I said.

– Heeheeheehee, said Frau Stennitzer.

– And under it is . . . ?

– Yes, we prefer it this way, the mother said to the monster. Don't we?

The masked figure, which was apparently her son Christoph, stood up from the sofa and approached me. We shook hands. His was ice-cold. The huge, grotesque Easter Island head made of cardboard wobbled on his shoulders.

– Does it have a special meaning?

– He likes it this way. Right, Christoph?

A wobble that was probably supposed to be a nod.

– I really got scared, I said, picking up my things from the floor. The muffin, I immediately noticed, was completely flattened. Had I stepped on it when I had run out in shock? That wasn't very likely; at least I couldn't remember doing so. I took the muffin out of the paper bag. It looked like a run-over rodent.

– Heeheeheehee, Frau Stennitzer was still cackling.

I looked at the uncanny head. For an ordinary carnival mask it was too large, but that was quite possibly an optical illusion because it was being worn by a child. For his fourteen years, Christoph seemed rather small, he was thin, the skin on his arms was strikingly pale, and the tips of his feet when he walked were almost in snowplow position. Now, from up close, the head was no longer so frightening, I thought. The serious brow and the long distinctive nose that cast a sharp shadow even reminded me a little of the friendly face of John Updike.

We sat there for a little while like that, I speechless, mother and son in polite silence, surrounded by bright windows.

– Three minutes, Frau Stennitzer said softly.

She had learned to calculate it to the second, she explained, even for other people. That is: for strangers, like me. She knew exactly when it would be better for me to distance myself.

– Does his value change?

Frau Stennitzer shook her head silently, closing her eyes for a brief moment.

– Hello, Christoph. My name is Clemens. I'm writing an article on . . . Well, I wanted to ask how you're doing with it, I mean, to know . . .

My sentence broke apart in the middle, and both halves fell to the floor.

— Okay, said Christoph.

His voice was muffled by the mask.

—You are home-schooled, is that correct?

— Mm-hmm.

— I used to work in a boarding school where children like you live. Do you ever think that a school like that could—

Frau Stennitzer interrupted me:

— We've made an arrangement. He doesn't know the conditions there. How can he answer that?

— All right, then, I said. Sure, of course.

— I like reading comics, said Christoph.

— Oh, which ones?

— All different ones, he said. And wrestling.

—You like wrestling?

—Yeah.

— I haven't watched it in a long time.

Frau Stennitzer gestured to her watch. I felt nothing. She put her hands to her temples but went on smiling. Then she took a deep breath and cleared her throat. Christoph left the room.

What happens to Indigo children when they get older and finally grow up is a controversial question. A common view is that Beringer syndrome doesn't even exist and everything is only a matter of attitude. There's a well-known case in Australia of a now-twenty-year-old man named Ken S., who claims to have developed very intense Indigo symptoms as a child, which supposedly ultimately caused his parents to divorce and plunged his father into a deep and life-threatening depression. Currently he works in a call center and appears now and then on talk shows, where he likes to talk about how you can use positive thinking to distance yourself from your own fate. (During my own work at the Helianau Proximity Awareness and Learning Center in the Semmering region of Austria, I witnessed children's value gradually increase and their effects decrease. But even in those cases, the causalities were often not clear.)

Frau Stennitzer was, of course, familiar with such tales of *burnt-out cases*, and she sighed when I brought them up with her. Yes, sometimes it disappears in time or burns out, she said. Burnt-out I-kids are a fact. But:

– To be honest, none of that means the least bit to me. I mean, things like that always happen in Australia, far, far away . . . Next it's probably going to happen on the moon. But here, I mean, we see it, we live with it. It's not abating.

– Have you noticed no development at all?

– Apart from the fact that I'm getting used to . . .

– In the literature some cases are mentioned that—

– Yes, that's exactly the problem, they're always only mentioned, and the people being described are represented only by initials, and no one knows what it's actually all about, this secretiveness.

There was a pause, during which I politely closed my notebook to allow Frau Stennitzer to get really angry.

– I mean, I don't understand these people who write such nonsense, she said. They don't have to live with constant nausea and dizziness and with rashes and diarrhea, that's just a list of symptoms for them! It's nothing that affects their lives. It's always the same crap, everywhere! But as soon as anyone says it, it starts: Yeah, she's just burnt out, she's simply not the family type, must have to do with the emotional overload—no! You try living for twenty-four hours in the vicinity of this . . .

She put a knuckle to her upper lip to restrain herself. It worked.

– Sorry, she said. You probably don't want me to heap complaints on you.

I suppressed just in time the remark, *But that's actually why I came,* and only nodded in what I hoped was an understanding way.

– But do you wish it for Christoph?

– What?

Her look was sincerely at a loss.

– That it will get better when he grows up.

– No, I don't have any hopes in that regard, she said. In all honesty. I'm a realist.

The dry air in the room had made my voice hoarse again. I asked whether we could go out into the yard. Frau Stennitzer smiled.

– He's already gone, she said. It'll pass in a moment.

– No, it's more the air in here, I said.

– Okay, she said with a somewhat perplexed expression. Okay. Whatever you want.

The presence of the apple trees did me good, and a warm south wind blew around the house, which gave your body the sensation of growing lighter, letting itself be caught by the moving air. I noticed the conical mound of earth at the edge of the property and walked toward it. Frau Stennitzer followed me. When I was close enough, I asked what it was.

– Just an attempt, she said.

Then she mentioned, as if we had been speaking about it all along, that there are even specific funeral regulations for Indigo children. On private property they are permitted to be buried in ordinary graves, but in public cemeteries only in an urn, as ashes. Yet it had not even been settled with any certainty whether their harmful effects persist beyond death. All that struck me as extremely implausible, and I had a feeling that my host was pulling my leg. But Gudrun Stennitzer said it all as if she were talking about the weather. When I finally grasped that she meant it seriously, her story seemed to me like a terrible robbery. As if one of the two great tasks for which we're in the world were snatched from a person, namely, to participate in the delightful celebration given a dead body in the earth by all the microorganisms, which like ants carry away tiny pieces, digest and metabolize them, by the little worms and maggots, which dig their tunnels through the corpse. In an essay by the Czech writer and immunologist Miroslav Holub there is a description of these wonderful and monstrous processes. A rat falls into Holub's swimming pool, and before he can take it out, a passing neighbor runs home to get his gun and shoots at it, scattering the animal all over the place. And Holub, who, of all writers in the previous century—with the exception of Sebald and Kafka—is perhaps the one with the most strongly developed but also the most idiosyncratic capacity for empathy, goes on to describe what happens to the dead rat, to its blood cells, to the microscopic puzzle pieces of its body, the fluids and solids of which it consisted, he describes the transformations and chemical interactions that immediately begin— until, in the face of all the earth and blood and creatures, you have in the end completely forgotten the death of the rat. It's as helpful as it is disturbing to know that Holub's bread and butter for long years was the systematic torture and poisoning of lab animals. As an immunologist specializing in the combating and prevention of epidemics, he had to expose rodents specifically bred for the space-station-like life in the lab to the most horrible influences one can imagine, deadly pathogens and toxic substances, vaccines unexplored in their effects, and extreme temperatures. In an interview he once said that the poems he wrote in the evening usually arose in response to a workday spent with senseless cruelty to mice. How can we explain the fact that this man, who used his science fiction apparatuses to destroy one nude mouse after another in the most horrible ways conceivable, composed the most moving butterfly poem ever written (the competition is great!) and even renders the description of an anencephalic baby—lying shortly after birth with his empty, still slightly pulsating, baglike skull in a container in which he waits for death, which is somewhat late in coming—so tenderly that when you read it your breast inflates as if you were turning into the *Hindenburg* zeppelin itself—how in the world is something like that possible?

I don't know whether it was Gudrun Stennitzer's intention simply to leave me standing next to the little enclosure with the conical mound of earth. It's quite possible that she hadn't even thought about it, but had at some point simply gone back to the house, at a moment that seemed to her no more appropriate than any other. In any case, I now stood alone in the sun, drank in the buzzing of bees and various shades of green, and waited, looking several times in a row at my watch for a few minutes, until I was again to some extent composed and presentable, and then returned to the house. I admit that at that moment the sentence *I am in hell* went through my head, and for some reason, as I left behind the mysterious presence of the cone of earth, I couldn't help thinking of James Merrill's remarkable insight. NO SOULS CAME FROM HIROSHIMA U KNOW / EARTH WORE A STRANGE NEW ZONE OF ENERGY. In Chernobyl too, I thought, spirits of the dead were definitely nowhere to be found, not even in dreams. The radioactive ruins are too far away from us. They're metaphysically sterile, cleansed, *formatted*. When I reentered the kitchen, I saw Frau Stennitzer spreading on her forehead and neck a white cream from a small black can that looked like a container for a roll of film.

— Would you like some too? she asked. It helps.

Since I had no idea how to respond to that, I began to tell Frau Stennitzer about the preface to *The Nature of Distance*, the story of the sunken warships and the uncontaminated steel.

She nodded. Yes, she had heard about that. Quite often, to tell the truth. That had been the tiny sliver of hope back then that these children have some advantage, maybe even some spiritual abilities that others don't have, and so on.

She screwed the top on the can and wiped her fingers on her pants.

But of course the reality looked entirely different, she said. There were some gifted I-kids, but only in the area of reading skills.

— There are studies on that? I asked.

— Well, it's hardly surprising, said Frau Stennitzer. If wherever you go you always form the center of a restricted zone roughly ten yards in diameter, then you eventually begin to read books or amuse yourself with the computer. That's the way it works, not the other way around.

— Do you enter the zone regularly? Or do you consciously remain outside it?

Well, she said, she didn't actually see it as a zone that you can approach and with which there can be overlaps. She saw it more as a Ferris wheel. On a Ferris wheel there were different cars and the distance between the cars always stayed the same, they couldn't get closer to each other, the structure simply didn't permit that. And so you just went in a circle, the whole time, more or less separate from each other, every man for himself. If you had to use illustrative comparisons, Frau Stennitzer said, then at least use ones like that, not that sacredly sober magical steel on the sea floor! Incidentally, keeping one's distance was also healthy, in and of itself; in certain dances, for example, people didn't touch each other at all, she said, you just played with the other person's aura as if on a theremin, and in ballooning too it was well known that you were not supposed to get too close to another balloon floating in the ether, because then, oh, I don't know, those swirls of air or whatever it is. They were thermal phenomena of some sort, said Frau Stennitzer, but exactly what she had forgotten.

Without thinking, I told her about a duel I had recently read about. It took place in Paris in the early nineteenth century between two daring men, Monsieur de Grandpré and Monsieur Le Pique, for the favor of Mademoiselle Tirevit, a famous dancer. The rivals rose in two balloons about seven hundred yards over the Tuileries and took turns shooting at the skin of the opposing balloon. Grandpré won, Le Pique crashed with his balloon (and his second on board) into the roof of a building and died.

— He went out on the roof last spring, said Frau Stennitzer.

— And then Tirevit— I began. I'm sorry, what?

— Him. He climbed up.

— Your son?

She nodded.

Only now did I realize that my balloon anecdote wasn't germane to the subject at all.

— Yes. And then, when he was up there ... oh, it was an incredibly ... (she shaped with her hands an invisible snowball) ... an incredibly compact time back then, you know? As if you couldn't get out anymore, but only become more tightly ensnared in it, if you ... well ...

— Was he trying to do away with himself?

She shrugged:

— No one knows. Not even him, it seems. Later he said he just doesn't get out that much. Outdoors.

I said nothing.

– He climbed back down on his own, said Frau Stennitzer. Eventually. It's probably not all that surprising. The body gets tired. He came down, and we talked, all day long we talked . . . and I hugged him, even though he . . . well, even though, of course . . . oh, I don't know where all this is leading, you know? I mean, since last summer teenagers have been coming up from the town all the time and standing outside his window.

– They stand outside his window?

– Yeah, climb over our fence, you've seen it, anyone can get over it easily, with a bit of a running start.

– And then what do they do by his window?

– Hold out, she said, and her voice was now as distant as if it were coming from a space capsule. They *hold out*, stand there, in a circle. Sometimes even with a radio. And hold out.

– Hold out? I repeated stupidly.

– A dare.

The space capsule receded even farther.

– They drink beer from cans, which they then leave all over the yard, said Frau Stennitzer. They don't leave anything else behind.

– And what do they say when you chase them off?

– That's the problem, said Frau Stennitzer, looking up at the ceiling. They say, Okay, we'll leave, but this guy here at the window would like us to stay.

– Christoph?

– Yes, he . . . he sits by the window and talks with them. While they sweat and puke in the bushes, it's just so disgusting, I could slap him every time!

– So are they his friends?

– Fr—! No, they're . . . No, why would you say something like that?

– I'm sorry, but it sounds like they're kids who come to your son and . . . well, hang out with him.

– They're using him! They come just to see how long they can hold out in his presence. My God, I could slap him, every time, I swear to you, but I just can't bring myself to do it.

— To chase them off? I asked, because it was unclear to me what her remark was actually referring to.

— That's right, she said with her space capsule voice. This way he gets a bit of contact. But the fact that they're bad people who spend time with him only out of selfish motives? He doesn't grasp that. No, for that he's too . . . well, not worldly enough, I'd say.

— How could he be? she added bitterly.

And when I still said nothing, she snarled:

— Why can't they keep their distance, that riffraff?

I remembered having read that people who are overcome by altitude sickness on Mount Everest and can't go on are often not rescued. On high mountains people keep their distance from each other. Sometimes other alpinists climb past their confused and hallucinating colleagues sitting or lying in the snow and report on it afterward. David Sharp, who lay dying on Mount Everest in 2006 and begged for help, was passed by approximately forty mountain climbers. That image made me think of a well-known writer from my hometown, who hasn't published a book in years but is nonetheless invited to a reading now and then. Immediately after she has read her text, she usually apologizes to the audience with the explanation that she is a very busy author and rushes off, while the other authors who read with her (she is never invited anywhere alone, because probably no one would come) stay behind and grace their colleagues with their presence until the end of the event. Once, as chance would have it, I too had to leave early from one of those readings, which took place under the open sky. Then I saw her, remaining motionless at a great distance, practically invisible to the audience, her shoulders hunched and her summer dress hanging loosely from her body, as if she were standing on a seashore. She must have been standing there for over half an hour already, contemplating the sphere of her colleagues, from which she always took her leave almost as soon as she had entered it.

Interview with the Teenagers

In confusion I said goodbye to Frau Stennitzer and headed, I hoped, toward the hotel to take a rest. My thoughts were constantly wandering off, and I noticed everywhere things that appeared far more interesting to me than the actual reason for my stay in the town. I even managed to get lost in the few roads and side streets and several times I had to turn around at a wall that I had never seen before. I tried to reach my girlfriend, but at the moment I found myself in one of those spatial pauses for breath we call a dead zone; the cell phone was left all alone, stretched out its invisible feelers into the air, but reached no one with them.

It took a little while before I came to the main square of Gillingen. I looked at my watch and discovered that I had been marching through the town for almost forty-five minutes.

Then I saw them. Three young people, two of them bald, just as Frau Stennitzer had described them. They were coming out the door of the tavern, two older boys and a fifteen- or sixteen-year-old girl, who was probably supposed to represent the rurally appropriate version of Goth. The boys were almost a whole head taller than she was.

They stopped, looked at me briefly. Then they moved on. I followed them from a considerable distance, at a leisurely pace. A few times I had to stop and take a breather under cover of some sunlit house wall. To allay my sudden anxiety, which had grown imperceptibly during my meandering through the town, I played on my iPod "Monk's Mood" by Thelonious Monk in an endless loop and tried to breathe completely normally and evenly with the chords. Finally I caught up with the teenagers at a bridge. There were no more houses here, that happened fast in this area, an unmindful step and you're standing in a no-man's-land that you usually get to see only through train windows. Passionless and uninterested-looking grass growing at a slant from the ground, half-paved roads, and loads of strange equipment on the roadside, not yet nature, but no longer civilization.

– Excuse me, I called. May I ask you something?

No response. But they didn't run away, so I took that as an invitation.

– Hello, I said, as I approached. I'm not from around here, I'm just here on a visit. Do you know the Stennitzers, up there?

I gestured roughly in that direction.

– Shit, said one of the boys, throwing his shaved head back theatrically.

– Now it's really happened, said the other one.

– No, no, I said, raising a hand. Nothing has happened. I was just visiting there. And I was told that you're Christoph's only friends.

The girl grabbed the wrist of one of the boys and pulled on it gently.

– Everything's okay, I said. Christoph is doing fine.

– So, then, what is there to discuss? asked the other boy.

– Nothing at all, I just wanted to ask how—

– Oh, she shouldn't get so worked up all the time! the first one squawked at me. She's really starting to get on my nerves . . .

– Frau Stennitzer?

–Yeah, she shouldn't interfere.

A loud noise behind us. We got out of the way of the tractor, which drove over the bridge with a peculiar slowness that muddled your thoughts as in a fever dream. Light brown mud was stuck to the huge tires.

– May I ask something? What did you mean before by: Now it's really happened?

The skinhead laughed as if I had made an incredibly obscene joke. He slipped his hand under his shirt, formed there a sort of mouth through the material, and said:

– Omnomnomnom!

He snapped playfully at me and the girl. She laughed a little. Then the boy drew a pocketknife and flipped it open. I felt a tremendous urge to knock him out and then inscribe his compact bald head.

The boy tapped around on the pocketknife and I saw that it wasn't a knife at all but an MP3 player. I shook my head and took a deep breath. Country air. Tractor noises. *I'm in the here and now.*

Soft music could be heard. Cawing and screaming, accompanied by electric guitars and by drums being kicked through a room by a gigantic foot.

— Didn't mean anything, said the boy.

— How long have you known Christoph?

They laughed again. The girl clapped her hands.

— What's so funny?

— You're totally fried, right? the boy with the MP3 player asked.

— You mean from exhaustion?

They laughed again.

— With Christoph you can really listen to music, said the other boy, who up to that point hadn't talked much. Besides, with music it's okay. Right?

His friends agreed with him.

— It's easier with music? I asked.

My voice actually did sound somewhat funny. The teenagers slapped their thighs with laughter.

— Hold on, I'll turn up the volume. Poor guy, said the boy, pressing around on his MP3 player.

Although I was having trouble speaking at a normal speed, I explained to the teenagers that the thing with the music reminded me of a passage from the work of the great French entomologist Fabre, where he describes a peculiar superstition of Calabrian peasants, who believe that the poison of the tarantula causes wild convulsions of the limbs and irrepressible dancing mania among women. Music was regarded as the only remedy for this so-called *tarantism*, according to Fabre, I said. There were even special, particularly catchy melodies to which a clearly beneficial effect was ascribed, and those melodies were collected for centuries and provided on sheet music to every woman who was bitten by a spider.

The two bald boys snorted and nudged each other.

– Shit, said the less talkative of the two. He is royally roasted . . .

The girl looked somewhat embarrassed, not sure how I would react. But I laughed with them, in that bright, safe moment shortly before my departure from Gillingen, even though I had no idea anymore what we were laughing about or under what sign, plus or minus.

[RED-CHECKERED FOLDER]

§ 4. The Transference of Evil in Europe. The examples of the transference of evil hitherto adduced have been mostly drawn from the customs of savage or barbarous peoples. But similar attempts to shift the burden of disease, misfortune, and sin from one's self to another person have been common also among the civilized nations of Europe, both in ancient and modern times. A Roman cure for fever was to pare the patient's nails, and stick the parings with wax on a neighbor's door before sunrise; the fever then passed from the sick man to his neighbor. In the fourth century of our era Marcellus of Bordeaux writes of a man who could take the headache of another person into himself—Marcellus goes so far as to compare him with the Christian Savior, who performed a similar deed with the original sin of mankind. The man was paid with valuables by the parents of a stricken child; then the children or adolescents were left with him, in the next room. After a certain period of time had elapsed, they were free of maladies. When the man died, his fingernails and hair were removed from him, and both were much revered by the people of the area. The Jesuit priest Kircher mentions a monk in the Belgian monastery of Neutregen, in whose cell no one could stay for an extended stretch. Whoever spent a long time with him suffered pains in the head and limbs, joint rheumatism, and intense nausea. Authors such as Bellam even see in this a possible origin of the hermit movement. In the village of Llandegla in Wales there is a church dedicated to the virgin martyr St. Tecla, where such ill effects at a distance (as the Belgian monk exerted) are, or used to be, cured by being transferred to a fowl, in most cases a domestic chicken. The patient first washed his limbs in a sacred well hard by, dropped fourpence into it as an offering, walked thrice round the well with the fowl under his arm, and thrice repeated the Lord's prayer. Then the fowl was put back into the pen with other members of its species. If the bird, after a certain period of time, was attacked by the others and pecked and plucked by them, the sickness was supposed to have been transferred to it from the man or woman, who was now rid of the affliction. As late as 1855 the old parish clerk of the village remembered quite well to have seen the birds to which the ill effects at a distance had been transferred perching, scattered and far apart from one another, on the trees.

In some medieval medical manuals and also in a travel account by the captain of a British trading vessel to New Zealand, it is recommended to seek the proximity of certain exceptional people living on their own and usually in complete isolation. These people are usually themselves afflicted with the effects at a distance and prefer the company of bush and tree to exposure to the daily animosity in human settlements. In all these cases the antipathy seems to have developed gradually, the recoiling of their fellow men, inexplicable disgust that can be explained only by the magical interplay of dark powers. Very rare is a form of the ill effects at a distance that occurs shortly after birth. But in Cheshire there was a prescription even for this unusual case, which consisted in rubbing the head of the affected baby for three days with a piece of bacon and the soot of a chimney. Then, while the baby was still covered with the layer of fat, a hole was bored in an oak tree. The baby was washed, and the water containing the residues of soot and fat was brought to a boil and then poured into the tree. If the little patient had by its fifth month of life lost the ill effects, it was assumed that the tree had absorbed them. The tree was then avoided, and the fruits it yielded were regarded as bad. At Berkhampstead, in Hertfordshire, there were oak trees that over many decades were filled in this way with the ill physical effects of newborns as well as adults. Whoever built his house in the vicinity of these oak trees could be certain that in the next two or three generations he would be visited by misfortune.

(from: James George Frazer, *The Golden Bough*, Chapter LV, *On Ill Effects at a Distance*, § 4, p. 790-791)

8.   Holodeck

– Yeah, the supremacy of American culture and especially American television series, said Robert. All that's getting totally out of hand. For fifty years or so it's been getting out of hand. When I paint, I often see those waves, like on old TV sets.

– Out of hand, Elke repeated. Where does that phrase actually come from? Out of hand . . .

She held her own hands in front of her face and contemplated them as if they could reveal the answer to her. Willi reminded her how the two of them, in a stoned state, had discussed for over an hour whether the plural of still life was still lives or still lifes. They had seen on television a British painter who had actually said still lives. That had made Elke anxious, because she didn't like it when she had been saying something incorrectly for so many years. That was, she remarked, as if she were being retroactively stripped of the word.

– In the end I had no idea why that was so important to you, said Willi.

– You always say my English is perfect, Elke replied. And then I watch TV once, and boom!

– But you were high, said Willi.

– Yeah, you watched quite a lot of TV as a kid too, Cordula said to Robert, stroking his head.

Robert would have liked most to utter soothing Batman words of wisdom. Nothing in reality could compare to the bizarre inner light of those clever sayings. But then he swallowed them and said instead:

– Oh, I just mean, Wild West culture is quite simply getting out of hand; in every normal television series the screenwriters manage to smuggle in some sort of Wild West episode, someone takes a time machine and lands in the Wild West, or a brick falls on someone's head and he dreams he's in the Wild West, or he enters the holodeck and ends up in a Wild West story there, and the computer goes haywire and won't let him out of the holodeck anymore!

– Who? asked Elke.

– Worf and Alexander, said Robert.

– Wasn't that Picard? asked Cordula.

– Oh, give me a break with him! He has a French name and so seems European, sophisticated, and wise, but of course all from an American point of view, which makes the whole thing stupid and false. And he plays the flute.

– That's gay, said Willi.

– The holodeck, said Robert, that's one of those things too, of course, you can't touch holograms, and yet they perform operations on people, it's, well, it's—

– Hey, is it bad if I'm now totally lost? asked Elke.

– No, said Robert, it's not bad, but I don't understand how anyone can be lost, I'm talking about television series, not about art, so it has to mean something to you, doesn't it? The subject. I mean, in itself.

– Well . . .

– Take MacGyver. In one episode a flower pot falls on his head and he wakes up in the Wild West. They regard that as a logical plot development.

– More salad, anyone? asked Cordula.

Elke shook her head, her face as perplexed as that of an infant who feels pain for the first time.

– But you guys have eaten the salad from only one side, the cucumbers are here on the left and are still totally untouched.

– I'm sorry, said Elke.

– Oh, whatever, it was my fault, said Cordula. We should have turned the salad bowl more often while we were eating. Then that wouldn't have happened.

She took two forks and tossed the salad, mixing the cucumbers with the corn and beans.

– A flower pot, said Robert. Falls on his head, just like that.

– But wasn't that with King Arthur or something?

– What?

– When he woke up, said Cordula. I saw the episode back then too. The flower pot fell on his head, and he awakes and is in the time of King Arthur and performs miracles there.

– MacGyver?

– Yeah.

– No, definitely not.

Robert bent, without the others seeing it, the neck of a teaspoon.

– Yes, I'm sure, said Cordula, he performs various miracles there, because he has this enormous technical knowledge, of course, and he only barely survives his head injury, and in the end he returns from the Arthurian time to the present, that is, to the eighties or whenever the show was made.

– Now I'm confused, Robert admitted.

– But it's true, Elke said suddenly, again looking at her palms. You're right. These television series really do always include Wild West episodes. *Superman*, for example. In that one, it's a time machine's fault, I think, that they fall so far back and then they're there for quite some time too and can't get back to the future, even though that always really bothered me about the series, because: Here's someone who has superpowers, right? He can do anything, right? Absolutely anything— and then he has more problems than anyone, there's practically nothing at all he can do, because there's always kryptonite somewhere. Why tell this story at all? Here's Superman, and he has superpowers, but no, he actually doesn't have them after all, because everything is always made of kryptonite. That's crazy!

– Yeah, said Robert. Maybe it's also some sort of parable. For the historical situation back then.

– For . . . ?

– Well, Superman in German is *Übermensch*, right?

Elke nodded intently.

– Of course, she said.

– And of course they live in Metropolis, which is of course the name of that Fritz Lang film.

– Which Fritz Lang film?

– *Metropolis*, said Robert. And it's made by a German and it's about fantasies of omnipotence, about empires and so on.

– Hey, did you used to do nothing but watch TV, or what? Willi laughed, and Robert stared at him until Willi made an apologetic gesture and said: You know so many series that I watched as a kid, even though you were born only—

– And about the future, Cordula suddenly added. They have robots and such.

– This is starting to get weird, Elke said with a giggle, shifting around in her chair. You mean it's all just codes?

– Of course. Because . . . Hollywood was full of refugees and emigrants who had fled from the Nazis or ended up there due to historical circumstances in some other way, so . . . I assume they couldn't help . . . sort of . . . working in their own story.

– Sure, said Elke.

– But what I still don't get, said Cordula. Why is the holodeck not just a room full of holograms, but another world in which everything is as solid as in ours? Do the holograms even know that they're holograms? If not, then that would be freaky, in a way, wouldn't it? I mean, Picard often enters the holoca—oh, shit, the holodeck, and rides around on a horse in there. I mean—

– A woman who knows her *Star Trek*! said Willi, raising his wine glass.

– True, the thing with the holograms is unclear, said Robert. In the one episode only Data knows that they're in the hologram world, because he . . . well, he's a robot and has no human imagination like the others, and that's why he can—

– Wait, who?

– Data. No, means nothing to you?

– Mm-mm, Elke said, shaking her head.

She was too young. Only twenty.

– Data is a robot that looks like a human, except he's very pale, that is, his face is all pasty white. You've really never seen him?

– No, I don't think so.

– He has that white face, but he acts completely normal, like a human, he even has this emotion chip he can turn on and off . . . Or no, wait, he has that only later. At first he has no emotions at all.

– Awful, said Elke.

– Yes, but he has a brother who looks exactly like him. They're twins, and the brother is sort of the evil brother, you know? He looks the same, but he laughs nastily, and he has emotions and craves power, and he attacks Data and wants to kill him.

– Who?

– The brother.

– He wants to kill the brother?

– Yes, he wants to kill Data, because he has no emotions or . . . oh, I've forgotten what the reason is, probably the world isn't big enough for both of them, one of them has to go. But . . . God, where was I? . . . Right, once, in one episode, okay? The two of them are fighting each other, that is, the evil Data ties the good Data up and is going to give him emotions so that he becomes evil too, but he implants them in himself by mistake, and the two of them have switched places.

– Wait, I didn't follow that, said Elke.

– Me neither, Cordula said with a laugh.

– Okay, one more time, said Robert, forming two figures with his hands. Here's Data, my left hand, and here's the evil Data, my right hand. And the evil one comes to the good Data and ties him to a dentist's chair and infuses emotions into him, and suddenly the two of them are standing there, their places reversed, and this one here (left hand) says: Hey, suddenly I'm here, tied up, can't get out. And this one here (right hand) says: That's right, evil Data, you shouldn't have messed with me.

Cordula, Elke, and Willi burst out laughing and clapped their hands.

Robert had to restrain himself to keep from laughing too. His diaphragm cramped, and he urgently had to go to the bathroom. Always the same thing, damn it. The painful memory of that day in the classroom returned. The old biology teacher, Professor Ulrich, had stared at him and had then come closer, and from his face you could tell that he was inwardly *counting*. The zone countdown. Robert's laughter stuck in his throat. It's okay, he had said to the teacher. I have a weak bladder, everything's okay, it happens to me sometimes. The looks of his classmates sitting several yards away. Like stuck elevators.

Robert took a sip of his beer—and spat it all over his own shirt. He excused himself, stood up quickly, and walked out.

– Hey, Robert, said Willi, it's okay, you don't have to—

After some time Cordula came to him in his room. She approached carefully from behind. She cleared her throat so that he wouldn't be startled, then asked quite casually, as if it were about a newspaper subscription:

– Are you still taking your Sviluppal?

– Sviluppal, Robert said calmly.

He pressed his pillow against the wall the way you hold a framed painting to see if it will fit. Then he punched it.

– Ulipol, Trimco, Sviluppal. The names of medications always sound like they're from fantasy novels, he murmured, punching the pillow again.

Cordula took a step back. Robert sensed it, even though he wasn't looking at her—the first sign that he actually had to start taking that shit again. Warning level one.

– Would you like . . . me to bring you a fresh shirt?

Robert looked down at himself.

– It's not what you think, he said.

– Sure, okay, said Cordula, turning slightly to the side.

– Stop, said Robert.

– Doing what?

– Stop being afraid of me. That makes me totally nervous.

He heard a slapping sound and turned around.

– I just swatted a mosquito on my arm, Cordula said, holding up her arm. There.

– It's all right, said Robert. You don't have to . . .

Then he realized what he looked like. While guests were sitting in the next room, he was standing in his bedroom and holding his anger pillow in his hand. His anger pillow. Like a baby. He considered taking off all his clothes, just to change the channel, but then he decided against it. Cordula left the room and brought him a new shirt, which came fresh from the drying rack. The smell was almost too much for Robert. With his eyes closed, he put it on and then lay down on the bed.

When she sat down with him a bit later, he said:

– Gillingen. There's a world-famous cable car there, did you know that?

Cordula displayed a kind smile that struck him as bold and submissive at the same time. He looked at her silently and seriously, until she said:

– So when are you going there?

He turned to the wall.

– Hey, I have something for you here, look.

Robert grunted and then put the pillow over his face.

– Clemens Jo . . . what does that say? Jodokus . . .

She tapped the newspaper. The image came into focus.

– Clemens Johann Setz? Do you know him?

The pillow fell on the floor as Robert sat up.

– What?

– Does that name mean anything to you?

– He was my math teacher. Why?

– Here, look.

– Is he dead?

– No, he's here . . . Oh, see for yourself.

She gave Robert the newspaper. He enlarged the image with thumb and forefinger. The newspaper chirped. A smiling face appeared, bespectacled, greasy hair. Looked exactly the same as back then. Just a bit rounder. The eyes a tad more owlish. And the eyebrows still slowly growing together.

— Shit, said Robert, skimming the text.

Acquittal in a trial for the violent death of a man from Romania. Kept his dogs in a dungeon for years. Severe abuse. Death by slow flaying. Prime suspect Setz free as of today. The family of the victim, a small picture. People standing there sadly. In recent years mainly science fiction novels, a turn away from literature. Currently living as a freelance writer near—

— It says in the article that he worked at your school, Cordula began.

Robert interrupted her:

— You know what? They threw him out, because he was always coming to class drunk. You couldn't tell at all, but in hindsight that made perfect sense, he was always very nervous, never stuck to the subject, often just rambled on about this and that for hours . . .

— And now he's apparently been acquitted, said Cordula.

— He stripped off the damn skin of an animal abuser?

— No, actually, he—

— Fuck!

— He was acquitted today.

— Shit, he once visited us at home! said Robert. That was shortly after . . . But you know what? That was totally off, I mean, his behavior. He was totally gone, I mean, completely out of it. My parents invited him because he . . . oh, I don't know, he was such an odd duck . . .

Robert had fallen into an unpleasant cluster of memories. Jelly-fish nest.

— He was at your house in Raaba?

— At first my mother was worried that he would show up at our place completely drunk. And you know how allergic she is to something like that.

Cordula nodded:

— Oh, my, yes. New Year's Eve.

— Since 2007 has written articles, murmured Robert, who had

enlarged the teacher's biographical details in a little box and read them line by line. *National Geographic.* What the hell is that?

Cordula's face told him that he had once again run into his gap. General knowledge. Dingo delay.

– The skin, he said. Peeled off the damn skin! That's some sick shit right there!

– Well, it says here at least . . . , Cordula began again.

But then she gave up.

Robert read on.

The lines of the interview were scarcely more than rungs of a ladder he could hold on to with his eyes while his brain went its own way. He remembered that day in autumn of 2006, the forced politeness of his parents, the six minutes spent in accelerated conversation (at that time still: blessed 360 seconds).

He remembered the conversation and how senseless it had felt to address the visitor as Herr Professor. After all, he wasn't one anymore. Thrown out, drunk on duty. And then the crap he had talked! And now this! A brutal murderer, who was acquitted. Jesus, Mary, and Joseph.

Dogs, dogs—Robert's eyes widened. He saw the scene again before him. In his room, in the house in Raaba. The curtains closed. And the crazy teacher gave one of his incoherent monologues about who knows what:

I mean, there are a lot of people who can't go out, and of them you're still one of the luckiest, Robert. The others treated you badly. But you can go where you want. Abroad. Or onstage. You could become a performer, an artist. In 1999 a sword swallower in Bonn tried to swallow an umbrella. He accidentally pressed the button that opened the umbrella and died. A few years later a Canadian repeated the stunt and also died. And another sword swallower bowed to the clapping crowd after the act and in so doing suffered (Robert could still remember the peculiar shift in diction, probably the point when the previously memorized text took possession of the math teacher) *severe internal injuries. Another took a few steps and fell, with the sword in his throat, off the stage.*

Okay, Robert had had to laugh at that. It was funny. But why that freak had come around to that subject in the first place, no idea.

Just say when you have to go out for a little while, he had said.

A strong hint. Professor Setz didn't get it.

What's that? he asked, pointing to a small poster hanging in Robert's room directly over the bed.

That?

Yes.

A space dog.

The professor's face darkened.

Robert stood up from the bed.

Taken right in the satellite. Belka. The dog was totally high up back then, almost in the exosphere and . . . well, and that's when they took the picture, I think . . .

The math teacher took a step back and left the room without a word. *Hey*, thought Robert, *that wasn't six minutes. Pussy. Wimp.* He put on headphones and listened at full blast to Whitehouse, the album *Great White Death*, an absolute masterpiece. His consciousness dissolved in noise and screaming, became soft and permeable as a membrane . . .

What brought him back down to earth was his cell phone, which lit up briefly. A text message—from his mother, who was sitting in the next room! *Don't forget the casserole*, she wrote. For Chernobyl's sake! As if a strange day on which a strange person paid an extremely strange visit couldn't get even stranger. *But yeah, screw it, I'll eat the casserole. Whatever. Dance along in the absurd puppet theater.*

His mother had later come to him in his room and had told him that the wine hadn't agreed with the visitor. Probably relapse problems of the ex-alcoholic.

He even apologized to us, she had told Robert. For neglecting his duties as a teacher. But then he suddenly had to go, because he, well, you could tell from his eyes. He felt dizzy, he said. Anyway. How was the casserole? Did you like it?

What was that about with the cell phone? Am I nuclear waste now, which has to be handled by remote control from outside, or—

No, my dear, no, for God's sake, it was just, I couldn't let him out of my sight, because he . . . you know, I didn't want to tell you this, but your father and I, we had to . . . physically . . . escort him out, because he . . . well, you can imagine what...

PART II

In the beginning was repetition.

—*Jacques Derrida*

A cow was bereft of her calf. To console her the calf's skin
was taken, stuffed with straw, and then placed alongside
the cow. She commenced to lick the skin with maternal
devotion. During this process a particularly vigorous lick
caused part of the skin to give way and revealed the suc-
culent straw stuffing. The maternal instinct was at once
forgotten and the cow began to eat the straw, chewing it
with as much relish as ever she displayed when devour-
ing her ration in the byre.

—*Frank W. Lane,* Animal Wonderland

1.   Thesis

In late autumn of 2005 I finished my studies to become a teacher in mathematics and German literature with a thesis on so-called father-son problems in math education.

A father has two children. At least one of them is a son. What is the probability that the second child is also a son? The surprising answer is: 1:3. Not 1:2. And if we assume that the father has two children of whom at least one is a son—and the father shouts into the next room, at which point a small boy appears in the doorframe and says: Okay, I'm your son, and I'm completely fine—then what is the probability that the second child is also a son?

In my thesis I went into the history of these problems a bit, into the phenomenon of their great popularity in mathematics teaching methodology, into some selected examples, mostly from stochastic theory (variations of the famous Monty Hall problem) and the geometry of solar systems.

The thesis was highly praised by my professor. In a conversation I revealed to him that I was thinking of writing my dissertation on the same topic.

He leaned back a bit in his chair, crossed his legs, and said that this required a lot of thought, for a dissertation is an entirely different sort of project. In terms of length alone.

– You might repeat yourself, he said gently.

– Well, I said, I mean, I'll do my internship first, of course.

– Yeeeah, he said, sounding relieved. You still have some things to do before you can think about the next step in an academic sense. So where are you going to do it?

— What?

— Your internship.

— Oh, I haven't decided yet.

— You know, Herr Setz, I think I have an idea. A recommendation, so to speak.

2. Uncanny Valley

It was a snapshot printed in poster size of one of the two astronauts on the Sputnik 5 satellite. The dogs Belka and Strelka were shot into outer space on August 19, 1960. Unlike in the more famous case of the dog Laika, the animals landed a day later, quite distressed but nonetheless unharmed, on earth. After Strelka had puppies, one of them was presented as a gift to the daughter of then-President John F. Kennedy. Although the CIA explained emphatically to the president that this dog might contain mini-microphones hidden by the Soviets and therefore should be promptly killed, Kennedy let the animal live.

Robert was really excited when he showed Willi the picture. He hadn't looked at it for years, and it had taken some time before he had found it, rolled up, in a drawer.

– And they neutralized the mutt, so to speak? asked Willi.

He was relieved that his friend Robert had come back to the living room. It had often happened that he simply stayed away, buried in the black-painted corner of his room until the guests had gone home.

– No, they didn't, that's the point. Kennedy let his daughter keep it.

– Wuss. But the story is really . . . My God, the dog's face! Look!

He held the picture up to the women. Cordula looked away quickly.

– And that caused this Setz to lose it back then?

– Yeah. It immediately came back to me when I saw the article.

– Well, no wonder, said Willi. I mean, the whole thing already could have been predicted back then, huh?

Robert laughed:

– That he would skin an animal abuser fifteen years later?

– No, not directly. But you have to admit—

– But he was acquitted! Cordula said. Didn't you guys finish reading the article?

– Yeeeah, said Willi. Acquitted. But not innocent.

– That's unfair, said Cordula.

– I find it creepy, said Elke, hunching her shoulders.

– Well, the face of this dog here isn't creepy, is it?

He showed it to the women once again. Cordula looked away again.

– It's cuddly, that look. Things get really creepy only when the face almost looks like a human face. Then it's that valley, a phenomenon from the history of science . . . that . . . um . . .

Willi searched for the word. He made catching movements with his hands in the air in front of his face.

– Um, he said. De . . . du . . . uncanny! Uncanny valley!

– What's that supposed to be?

– Look, here, take this napkin. And draw baby faces on it.

Robert did so.

– Okay, said Willi. And now think of Data, okay?

– Of Data?

– Yes. *Star Trek.*

– Okay.

– He was played by a person who was only made up to look like a robot. Brent Spiner. These days he's fat and bald, advocates for wild bears. But at the time he was still a good-looking man. And they put silver makeup on him and did something with his eyes—and there was the robot.

– Okay, said Robert.

He was crumpling the paper napkin on which he had doodled the baby faces. It was worthless.

– That's one path you can take, okay? said Willi. You start with a human, in this case that actor, and alter him until he looks like something that is still close to a human, but actually isn't one anymore—a robot. That's the unproblematic, the simple path. But you can also take it from the other side, and that's when it gets problematic. For our psyche.

– In what way?

– What does this have to do with the crazy teacher? asked Elke.

– You start with something pixelated, Willi said to Robert, I don't know, some bad animation on a computer or in reality, a crude simulation of a human face. And you look at it and say to yourself, okay, that's supposed to represent a human, somehow, okay, I get it. But then— (Willi pointed with his forefinger directly at Elke's breasts)—then someone comes along, he has access to a really good computer. One with social skills, like an iSocket. And he creates for you a really good animation of a human face, with expressions and everything. And then someone else comes along, who manages to do it even better. And then the result is shown to a number of people. And what do you think the reaction was in most cases?

Robert pushed the paper ball that had previously been a napkin around on the table.

– No idea, he said. Maybe they were impressed, I don't know.

– They were horrified. They had panic attacks. Like the people in the nineteenth century who went running out of the theater when the train came toward—

– But they were naïve, said Elke.

– Sure, in the meantime we've gotten used to all sorts of things. But people were shaken, profoundly shaken. That's known as the uncanny valley. It extends from ninety-five to ninety-nine percent.

– Of what?

– Of a face. A human face.

– Aha, said Robert. You mean with skin and everything.

He made a skin-peeling gesture across his face and a grimace of pain.

– I think you guys are being unfair, said Cordula.

– Can't we talk about something else? asked Elke.

– This uncanny effect is always present with particularly realistic-seeming simulations, especially of babies. That's why I asked you before to draw a few babies.

– I've never done it, said Robert. Naked guys, no problem, but I've never seen a baby in a fruit basket, not in any drawing lesson.

He imagined it.

– Today you still sometimes see the uncanny valley with people who cross your path in a dream, said Willi. That quality of being off by a hair, that . . . no one can bear that. A human who was designed by another human, maybe it was that too, that religious element . . . but supposedly that wasn't the reason. It was probably more psycho-logical, know what I mean? We don't want to see something like that. Something that, from the other side, from the inorganic, approaches our side . . . so to speak . . .

The sentence hadn't quite turned out as he had intended, his hands made circling, nervous movements, as if he wanted to dispel the ruins of the botched syntax from the air in order to start over.

– Reborn babies, said Willi. You can order them. Look exactly like the babies you lost.

He looked around the room.

Cordula sighed:

– Yeah, I'll never understand that. Why women have those replicas made.

– Phantom pain, said Willi.

– Okay, I'm happy, said Robert.

Everyone looked at him.

– Yeah, because I'm lost, he said. I don't know what you guys are talking about.

– Lucky you, said Elke. It's really totally creepy.

– And my former math teacher is a brutal madman. Ha!

You know, Robin, people's attention is like a leaf in the wind, sometimes it flies this way, sometimes that way, and it lands somewhere on a pile of other leaves.

– I think the real problem is that robots don't *have to* look like humans, right? said Willi. But we do, for . . . evolutionary reasons, or else we'd go extinct, because we would no longer be able to, uh, reproduce, if we, well, that is, no woman would let us anywhere near her, of course, if we didn't look like human beings. But the robots, the robots don't have to look human, they survive even without our proportions and expressions and a pair of eyes and five fingers on each prehensile hand. That's why they appear so violated and surgically altered when they do look like us.

– But robots don't exist, Elke interjected.

– Sure they do.

– But not real robots, she said. Not the ones you're talking about, which walk around and can talk.

– Of course! There are even championships!

– But not really, Elke insisted.

– It depends what you mean by *really*, said Willi.

– You know what? said Robert. This is totally weird. I was lost in this conversation, and now I've suddenly found my bearings again and understand everything. Sort of retroactively. *That* is uncanny.

– Yeah, well, that's what you get for paying such close attention all the time, said Willi.

– Am *I* actually uncanny too? Robert suddenly asked, dead serious.

Willi looked as if someone had pinned a sheriff star directly to his eye.

Robert released him by grinning and firing with his fingers extended into a pistol a *Gotcha!* at Willi.

– Man, you are so . . .

– I am so convincing that I might be able to act on *Star Trek* one day, said Robert. As an energy field or something.

No one laughed.

– But not in the original episodes. Leave the Old Testament alone.

– And in the new ones?

– Depends which gospel. Picard and the others are sacrosanct, they would never accept you. But we might be able to find a place for you in the apocrypha, on *Deep Space Nine* or—

– Which was the one with that sexy old woman, Captain Janeway? asked Cordula.

– *Voyager!* said Willi, deeply impressed. Shit, do you even know how lucky you are that you have a girlfriend who knows her *Star Trek*?

Robert shrugged.

– But that was really awful crap, wasn't it? said Willi. There was that thing, my God, what was that, that creature, which looked like a dirty potato or a reptile, with those spots everywhere. Really disgusting. And that thing was married to some strange woman who was a member of a very rare species. And when she entered puberty, the holodeck medicine man had to massage her feet.

– What?

– Yeah, didn't you see it?

– No, I didn't . . . I mean, I was more into the classic episodes. *Deep Space Nine*, *Voyager*, and that other junk, those were, in my opinion, more like bootlegs. Cover versions.

Robert hoped that the word with *a* that Willi had used before had roughly that meaning. *The limits of our language are simply the limits of our world, Robin.*

– Hey, said Willi, I really didn't mean to upset you or anything before.

– It's okay, said Robert. Cordula managed to reactivate me a bit. With this sick shit.

He poked the newspaper, which flickered and then went out. He grasped at nothing, wretched, invisible thing, and shook it until it was back.

– Just like that time we talked about midi-chlorians.

– Han Solo shot first! said Willi.

– Absolutely! cried Robert, and they gave each other a high five. Elke laughed.

– Klingons, she said. What are Klingons, anyway?

– Wrong franchise, Willi said, shaking his head.

– But I mean, the actors, Elke insisted in an attempt to finally join in. Those were black people, right?

– Are you saying it was racist?

– I think she's right, said Robert.

– Fag, Willi said to him.

It was wonderful to spend time with Willi. In his presence Robert always felt safe. They became neither closer nor more distant. Constant conditions. Sometimes he even lapsed into the old gestures or wandered around the room as if he could still sense the edges of the old zone. He missed it a little. Imagine you cast a shadow your whole life and one day it grows thinner and shorter and more transparent until it is suddenly gone. Dissolved in the solar wind. In the particle stream. Or whatever.

– Oh, said Willi, Klingons are probably Mexicans with their faces painted dirty or something.

Robert couldn't help laughing and immediately put a hand on his belly. Better safe than sorry.

– Mexicans who bashed their foreheads against a wall.

– And doesn't Whoopi Goldberg come onto the *Enterprise* at one point, and she's from some strange planet where everyone gets totally old . . . ?

– Africa? said Willi.

Cordula rolled her eyes, tried to remain serious, and then laughed against her will.

– That's not funny, she protested.

– AIDS, said Robert.

She wanted to stop, but only laughed even more. Robert said:

– Flies on children. Bloody vomit. Civil war machetes, hacked-up faces.

When would she stop laughing?

He placed a hand on his uncontrollably giggling girlfriend's knee.

– You're such a jerk, you know that? said Cordula, who had calmed down.

– At least I don't flay my fellow human beings. What did he do with the skin? Make a cape?

You know, Robin, the bat cape is more than just a uniform. It's a calling.

– Ew!

Elke shuddered.

– I definitely have to read one of his books, murmured Robert.

– Will you guys stop already? Cordula said with a laugh. You're impossible!

He had an urge to take the small paper ball in which the little faces he had drawn were mixed like chocolate shavings in stracciatella ice cream and set it on fire. How beautiful a single cool, bluish flame in the middle of the kitchen table would be at this moment . . .

– Well, but you know what's really, I mean *really*, that is, in actual fact, uncanny? asked Willi. Forget flaying, forget the mutt in space. I just discovered something totally insane here.

He had the newspaper in his hand.

– Check it out, this thing here in the picture should look familiar to you . . . ?

The thing was obviously not the man with glasses and a serious face, the just-acquitted math teacher. He was looking directly into the camera. His gaze had something precociously owlish about it. But next to him, on the table, was a bottle. It wasn't clear what it contained. But on the label, a small dog's head could be seen.

– Doo . . . Robert said softly.

– He's got nerve! said Willi. But style too. That's what you'd call understatement.

– I feel sick, said Elke.

Willi seemed not to know whether to respond to that with a smiling or a compassionate face. He made both, which just looked ridiculous. Like a drunk clown.

– Glugluglug, said Robert, drinking out of his thumb. There you have it.

Willi studied the picture.

– You know what? You can't tell at all by looking at him.

– Yeah, he had that pretty well under control, said Robert. At least I assume so. Back then you couldn't tell either . . .

– After suffering an attack . . . reclusive . . . maintained his innocence to the last . . . devote himself completely to writing . . .

Willi's reading forefinger scanned the lines of the article.

– An attack? asked Cordula.

– It doesn't say here of what, murmured Willi.

– Like the virus that time whenever anyone beamed, said Robert, who wanted to change the subject for Elke. (Her face had gone pale.)

– Huh?

– That time when some error creeps into the beam system of the *Enterprise*, a sort of computer virus, and the people who are beamed all have a horrible attack after they've rematerialized.

– And what the hell is the white flight of steps about? asked Willi, who was reading a line in the article with his finger and hadn't caught any of what Robert had said.

– You know what? Maybe he really is innocent. Maybe we should—

– Maybe you should visit him? said Willi.

– Are you crazy? Haven't you read what he . . . And I'm supposed to go see him? He wouldn't even understand what I want from him. I mean, he has attacks and drinks and . . . peels . . .

– Robert, said Cordula.

– He doesn't look that way at all, said Elke, who had now ventured close to the photo too.

– What way?

– Well, you know. His eyes are somehow clear. Here, look.

– It's probably an old photo. Believe me, he definitely doesn't look like that anymore.

There was a pause. The newspaper became slightly darker and blurrier. Cordula tapped it.

– I wonder what can trigger a thing like that, she said. I mean, how it gets to that point. Does it build up gradually or . . .

– Why don't you just ask what you want to ask? Robert said angrily.

– What?

– You know what I mean.

– No, I—

– Oh, don't play innocent. You wanted to ask me, so ask. It's in your head and it wants out. No need to be ashamed. God knows I've heard worse things. Last week Frau Rabl was here and apologized to me for her filthy little piece-of-shit kid.

– Robert, I really don't know what you're talking about.

– Yeah, said Willi. I'm sure she didn't mean to . . .

– My God, it's really not that hard. Ask me. Go ahead. I can deal with it. Do you think that just because I don't have it anymore, it's gone? It probably never goes away completely. It's like a parachute I carry around with me my whole life. You know? Like those paratroopers who land on the ground and then drag the parachute along behind them like gigantic broken wings.

– Nice image, said Cordula.

– Yeah, I think so too, said Elke.

– My goodness, Robert said with a laugh, don't deflect. At least not so blatantly. I want you to ask me, please. In front of our friends. You see, I'm even begging you to.

– Robert . . .

– Should I fall down on my knees? Or . . .

– It's all right, she said.

She went to him. He hadn't even noticed that he had backed away into a corner of the room. She took his hands, which he held out in front of him, and guided them very gently back down.

—You don't have to shout like that, she said. I didn't mean to offend you.

— I want you to say it, said Robert.

Her face and her eyes were very close. That was a problem. Robert had to look down at the floor. *I have guests. I'm making a fool of myself in front of them.* She sensed his tension and let go of him, took a step back.

— I'd never say something like that, she said.

— No, Willi said softly.

—What would you never say?

She sighed.

— I'm sure, she said. You hear? I'm absolutely sure that it had nothing to do with his work back then. That's all I'm going to say about it.

What was the word for a female coward? Cowardess. You cowardly bitch. But that was too strong. Another hole in vocabulary discovered. And that at the age of twenty-nine. Indigo gap.

—With his work back then, said Robert. At the institute, you mean. Right? With us. In our proximity. In the zone—

— Robert, please. Please.

She had raised both hands. Conciliatory gesture. Back then, at Helianau, that was how they had greeted each other. You brace your hands against the air and press the invisible pillar between you and the other person. After a year or so, he could feel it, the resistance of the air. A gentle bulge, imaginary and pleasant, against the palm, always a few degrees warmer than the untouched surrounding air.

The fate of the girl M. reminded those of us who had been invited to the conference to an auspicious extent of the Arbre du Ténéré, the loneliest tree of all time. It was an umbrella thorn acacia in the middle of the Ténéré Desert in Niger. This acacia was the only tree in a 250-mile radius (making it literally closer to outer space than to the next tree) for probably more than two and a half centuries. It served for a long time as an important landmark for travelers and nomads; there was a well nearby. In 1973 a drunk Libyan man drove his truck into the tree and knocked it down. Today a small metal sculpture stands on the spot in its memory. The nearby well has since been contaminated.

HAUSLER — Z.
THE NATURE OF THE DISTANCE p. 13

3.   The Helianau Institute

I've often passed it on the train, this massive building that seems to grow directly out of a mountainside. This impression is strengthened by the trees surrounding the edifice and the ivy partly covering it. On sunny days, from a particular point, all the windows flash at once—as if an explosion were occurring inside.

I sat in an open compartment reading my favorite novel, *Kangaroo Notebook* by Kobo Abe, and listening to "Looking for Freedom" by David Hasselhoff in an endless loop. Across from me sat a man who had a mineral water bottle on the little table in front of him. On the numerous bends of the Semmering route the bottle wandered constantly from left to right on the table, and the man's gaze was so intent and fixed (instead of normal glasses he wore an old-fashioned pince-nez on his nose) that it seemed as if he were controlling the bottle's movements telepathically.

I was picked up at the Payerbach-Reichenau station. A mustached man with a circle drawn on his cheek with marker stepped out of a black VW bus and greeted me.

– You are Herr Setz?

– Yes, I said.

– Please.

He opened the side door of the VW bus and gestured to me to get in. I made myself comfortable on the bench seat among a heap of plastic bags. In the bags, as far as I could tell, were books and toys, as well as pieces of laundry. After a few minutes these objects began to give me an unpleasant feeling.

We drove down a winding road into the valley, a bit later the road ascended again and we reached the mountain ridge. The closer we came to the huge building with its flashing windows, the uneasier I became. At first I blamed this on the unpleasant effect the contents of the plastic bags had on me (I had the impression that the colorful laundry items were costumes for a carnival celebration), the stuffy air in the vehicle, and the centrifugal force shifting every few seconds from left to right on the curves.

Then we went more or less straight for a while, and the speed didn't seem as breakneck as before, and yet all of a sudden I felt violently ill, I reached forward and tapped the driver on the shoulder.

– Please, can you stop, I . . .

We exchanged a glance in the rearview mirror, from which, bizarrely enough, a small nail file dangled, and I could tell from the look in his eyes that he immediately understood. The interior of his vehicle was in danger. He slowed down, pulled over, and turned off the engine. I opened the side door, flung myself out of the VW bus, and bent over, because I thought I had to vomit.

The chauffeur walked once around the vehicle with calm, slow steps and stood in front of me.

– Nerves, he said.

I filled my lungs with the cool, oxygen-rich forest air. It did me good, and I felt a bit lighter. The nausea subsided, I straightened up.

– It's only nerves, the chauffeur repeated. In reality you can't feel anything at all from here. We're still at least a hundred yards away.

I wanted to explain to him that it had nothing to do with that, but the need to just stand there and breathe for another few seconds was greater, so I said nothing.

– You probably persuaded yourself, the man said with a calm voice, that you would soon be entering the zone. That happens to a lot of people.

He gave me a friendly pat on the shoulder.

A car passed us, heading up the forest road. A Mercedes. I watched it until it rounded a bend. Then I said to the driver:

– No, it wasn't that. I have . . . you know, I have a problem with huge buildings, that is, with institutes like this, sanatoriums or . . . yeah, basically with this style of architecture, I . . .

I was feeling a bit nauseous again. Leaning over, I rested my hands on my knees and took a deep breath.

– What kind of problem? he asked.

So I told him, standing on the side of the cool, shady forest road, that I had a strange phantom memory from my earliest childhood. But unlike other people who are quick to see that as evidence of a previous life, I believe that this memory was simply misfiled in my brain under *Experienced myself*, instead of being correctly filed under *Seen on television* or *Dreamed*. Mix-ups like that just happen.

– And the memory has to do with something like this?

He gestured to the large building complex, which actually looked even more awe-inspiring from up close than from the train window. Through the thin rows of trees you could, although it was only partly visible, get a sense of its monstrous proportions.

– Well, I don't know, I said. I remember a time I spent in a huge institute . . . and the boredom I felt when I waited all afternoon in the yard.

– Waited for what?

– For someone to pick me up. From the yard an uncanny, snow-white flight of steps leads up to the door . . . and behind it are hundreds of rooms, to the left and right, one door next to another, and at the far end a room where the doctor lives.

The chauffeur nodded.

I had never told anyone but my girlfriend this story. And now this man, whose name I didn't even know and who had a strange marker circle on his cheek. He lit a cigarette, took a deep, thoughtful drag, and looked into the sky.

– Well, he said, it happens. Stuff like that.

– The funny thing is that I of course have no conscious memory of the first three years of my life, I said. Like most people, I know what happened only as of the fourth or fifth year, before that everything is somehow . . .

I made a vague gesture with both hands.

– Mm-hmm, the chauffeur said with a nod, as if he had heard the same thing hundreds of times before.

– That's why I got agitated just now, I said.

– It's all right, he said. Happens to everyone.

I wondered what I would do if I discovered in the institute yard the flight of steps from my memory. Should I panic?

The chauffeur, who had noticed my unease, held out his cigarette pack to me. I gave a wave of my hand:

– No, thanks.

He put the pack in his pocket, took another deep drag from his cigarette. Then he said:

– You can walk the rest of the way if you'd like. I'll let the doorman know.

A bus waited in front of the main entrance in the sun. On the ground next to it stood a gas canister reminiscent of a muscular brown male torso. It was warm, there was a faint food smell in the air, and sparrows whirred and chirped in the cypress hedge to the right of the main entrance.

The chauffeur was waiting for me at the gate. He showed me the bell button, I pressed it. A voice answered, and the chauffeur bent down to the intercom and said:

– Yes, Herr Seitz for nine o'clock, please!

Then he waved goodbye to me. Behind me I heard him whistling, probably with relief. The gate buzzed and sprang open of its own accord.

I entered the building and found myself in a small anteroom; to the left was a booth as for ticket sales in a museum, to the right a tall closed portal. I approached the booth, in which I couldn't make out anyone, and looked inside. A head with a bread roll in its mouth appeared. Without taking the roll out of his mouth, the man smiled and greeted me with a nod. He gestured to a microphone protruding from the wall, through which I was to communicate with him.

– Hello! I shouted. My name is Setz! I have an appointment! At—

– Yes, great, came the voice from the loudspeaker next to the microphone. Welcome, um . . . hold on . . . one minute, okay?

He disappeared through a door in the back. I stayed where I was and stared at the bite marks in the roll, which now lay on the small desk. Next to it stood a thermos shaped like a cooling tower of a nuclear reactor, a laptop, and a thick *PONS* English-German dictionary. Behind the desk was a stack of boxes, next to it a fire extinguisher, on the wall hung a calendar with pictures of Elis dolls. I wondered whether I should take a few photos with my cell phone, but then I decided against it, because the room might be video-monitored.

After a while the doorman returned. He flipped a switch and the portal opened. Then he disappeared again into the back and stepped through the portal toward me. He held in his hand a small visitor's pass, which I hung around my neck.

– Do you have anything in your pockets like pepper spray, a taser, a knife . . .

– No.

– You have to leave your jacket here, please, I'll give you a coupon for it.

I took off my jacket and handed it to him. In exchange I got a small piece of paper with a number on it: 7/44.

Dr. Otto Rudolph, the principal of the Helianau Institute, is professor emeritus of education at the University of Klagenfurt. He is also patron of the charitable organization New Benjamenta devoted to the distribution of learning materials in underdeveloped countries. He has a firm handshake that conveys resolve.

When I saw him for the first time, he seemed to me like something that must originally have existed in a completely different form. His appearance was a bit too bright, and the contrast in his face was adjusted strangely. You had the urge to fiddle around with imaginary controls in order to change his color composition. Only his eyes were unremarkable, ordinary. A pale blue. As if his creator had made them first and for the construction of the rest had beckoned an apprentice.

—I'm glad you've come, Herr Setz, he said.

—It's my pleasure.

—You're lucky, said Dr. Rudolph. Professor Sievert is an old friend of mine.

—Ah, I didn't know that.

—Normally there's a waiting list for the institute. But in your case . . .

He made a jaunty fluttering gesture with both arms.

Right next to the main building a large tree grew at an angle from the earth, striving away from the structure. It looked like a limbo dancer trying to make it under the second floor.

At some distance I noticed a small striped cat sitting on a wooden stake like a motionless candle flame.

—Look, I said to Dr. Rudolph.

—What?

—A cat.

He nodded and kept going.

As we walked, I waved to the cat, which followed me with its eyes.

—The students here all have their space, said Dr. Rudolph. The space they need. If one of the children has to be transported, then we take this bus here.

—And then the child sits in the back row?

Dr. Rudolph gave a hint of a nod.

—It's not about subjecting the children to our understanding of proximity, but rather respecting their own. And that is, unfortunately, it must be said, truly possible only in institutes like this one here. Here they have a social structure they can rely on. A fabric in which they are embedded and . . . and it doesn't unravel with the first little irritation.

—So how much does it cost a year to stay here?

First Dr. Rudolph made a grimace as if he were disgusted by this question, but then he raised his hands and said:

– The basic fee the parents pay is twenty thousand euros a year.

– Twenty thousand?

– Sorry for laughing, said Dr. Rudolph. But it's a typical mathematician question. Haha. And on top of that come other special things, of course, such as zoom equipment. For dealing with everyday life.

– Would it be possible to see one of the classrooms?

– Of course. There are only three, by the way. But they are (he held up his glasses and looked at his watch) all occupied at the moment. At ten-thirty, though, Lecture Hall A will be free.

4.   Award Ceremony

The *M* on the cat's forehead had turned out particularly well. The rest was, well, *okay*, at best. The scars were pretty corny. The apparatus containing the animal was somewhat too foreshortened. And the wooden stake was too dark. A recurring mistake, unfortunately. But people seemed to like the painting. They saw all sorts of things in it. Sometimes women even burst into tears and clung to their own clothing.

This time he had worked with photographs. Or rather, not directly with photographs, but actually with stills from a movie. It was a documentary on a university in the United States, which was repeatedly mentioned in the media as a negative example. Eventually a student with a hidden camera had marched into the testing facility and had gathered over fourteen hours of video footage. The filmmakers, a married couple from Australia, had ultimately turned the fourteen hours into two. Interspersed with that material were interviews, one of them with the student. In it he explained how he had hidden the camera in his baseball cap, and then he elaborated a bit on his personal motivation for going through those rooms in the first place. Had he run into difficulties in his work? Had he been searched or at least asked what he was doing there? What exactly had he experienced? Robert had considered using a still of the young man for a painting too. But it wouldn't have been especially difficult, the colors he consisted of were all quite simple, and their interplay was no great challenge either, with the possible exception of the shirt. The cat that you saw at the 1:35:21 mark was certainly more difficult. And also the thing in its chest. Not particularly strong, but still.

The painting had even brought him something. State sponsorship award. Robert had told Willi first, and he had respectfully laughed at him on the phone, which had made Robert tremendously happy. Only then had he told Cordula. She had hugged him. The award ceremony was held in the lobby of a bank. Tuesday evening, seven o'clock. First came speeches by two older gentlemen.

The first man spoke of responsibility and art, the second of responsibility and society. He also referred to the crimes of the past. In the end he went into the subject of the future a little, which, as he said, was here in such numbers today, in the form of bearers of hope, and then took a step back from the lectern over which he had bent unusually far for the duration of his speech, as if he were giving it a chance to rest from the long ride together. Then the prizewinners in the individual categories were called up and went onstage. The prize for best stage design went to a stunningly gorgeous woman, and Robert forced himself not to stare at her incessantly.

Finally everyone was holding a champagne glass, and a billboard next to the entrance to the bank referred to a flute concerto that had taken place here the past week. The iBall at the entrance to the lobby blinked.

Behind their flipped-down visors made of safety glass, the bank counters looked serious and solemn. This year's prizewinners were arranged into groups of two and three and photographed from various angles. A man touched Robert on the shoulder to move him a bit closer to his colleagues, and Robert nearly hit him over the head with the certificate.

In the lobby of the bank hung a number of bad abstract paintings to which Robert clung in order to keep from panicking. They were the actual occupants of these premises. All night long they hung here, shapeless forms that no one wanted.

He took a few sips of the sparkling wine, which tasted like grapes that had gone insane, and began to repaint the pictures in his mind. A helpful gesture. The first painting he transposed into a contorted stick figure whose limbs appeared in different degrees of clarity or blurriness. The stick figure wore a hat, and from its face jutted a cigar or maybe even a chimney. Even though it had the unmistakable shape of a person, the depicted creature conveyed the impression of a primal form found in dreams in the somewhat too-bright corners of a church or in rooms in which the contrast was off.

– Congratulations, he heard a voice say behind him.

Robert feigned a bad fit of coughing. The invisible well-wisher withdrew.

The people at the celebration gradually got drunker and began to tell each other their secrets. Robert listened for a few minutes to a young woman who explained to him that she had finally made her peace with the world, after so many years, and that the resulting artwork was entitled *Men's True All Blood*. He nodded and asked what it depicted. The woman laughed as if he had made a joke. Robert imagined how she would look without eyebrows. Just a slight application of a soldering iron . . . And instead of eyebrows a scar line stitched with little *x*'s. Rampant keloid. He went to the buffet and took a piece of bread with cheese and half a grape and a dab of mayonnaise. A version of the *Jurassic Park* soundtrack played by a jazz trio now came from the speakers.

Robert looked at his watch.

It would still be impolite toward the organizers if he ducked out now. He hated these people, who had presented him with three thousand euros for a painting, for possessing such power over him. Almost like a remote control with which you could drive a car around in the neighboring apartment and make it crash into the walls.

The young woman from before approached him again. She had been outside for only a few minutes, she said. She looked somewhat frightened. Robert, who had a strong need to revel in something, asked her what had happened, she was acting strange. Oh, it was nothing, said the young woman, she had just wanted to go home, but outside small animals had been hopping around in the trees and so she had now come back into the bank lobby.

– Marmels?

– No, something else, said the woman.

– Oh, *those* animals, said Robert, nodding. Don't worry, they're here because of me.

The woman looked at him as if he had turned into a huge bull before her eyes. With a boys-are-stupid look she left him. Later, as the cluster of drunk people becoming more and more sentimental with the advancing hour threatened to close in on him, Robert produced a bubble around himself in which he could breathe by beginning to ramble on about contemporary art in itself, photography in particular, twin research (a subject plucked from thin air), and, of course, the old problem of chicken and egg, he also touched briefly on the Brussels legislation, even though he didn't know the first thing about it. It didn't matter at all, people listened to him. And they congratulated him again on the award. He thanked them and asked various people whether the lemurs were still sitting outside in the trees. Some gave him amused or questioning looks, some laughed, others nodded gravely.

Robert walked toward a bright restroom symbol at the end of a corridor. Here a fluorescent tube, probably years ago, had gone mad with loneliness. It flickered and buzzed an incomprehensible medley of Morse signals, an erratic eyelid twitch. It had waited so long for someone to finally stand under it, and now everything pent up in it burst out at once.

Robert was really relieved when he entered the restroom. It was a paradise. All the things you could vent your anger on here! Easily unscrewable knobs on the sink (unlike in the room in Cordula's psychiatric clinic!). And the door handle on the toilet stall was a bit loose. He touched it carefully and then delivered the coup de grâce. He held it in his hand, took a deep breath, closed his eyes, momentarily content, free. Then he emptied his bladder and, without washing his hands, returned to the lobby. He shook hands with as many people as possible, and when it was a strangely gaunt man's turn, Robert at first didn't even notice that the man spoke to him. Long sideburns adorned his open and attentive-looking face. The hair on his head had receded, only an atoll of gray, formerly black hair remained. The man was unusually thin, and the most striking thing was: He had no shoulders at all. If he had worn a black cape, he would have looked like a temaki roll.

– Batman, Robert replied to what the thin man had said to him.

He hoped that this had made his point clear enough.

– Nice to see you, said the man. Herr Tätzel.

– Uh, have we met?

– No, I wouldn't put it that way, said the man.

He had a peculiar accent, somehow French, but also something else, perhaps Romanian. Robert imagined how many thousands of molecules of his urine had just passed onto the hand of this joker.

– I'm afraid . . . , the man began, sighing.

Robert waited.

– I'm afraid I like your painting, said the man, stepping somewhat nearer to him.

– Ah, said Robert.

– I don't even know what to compare its effect on me to. Maybe the closest thing would be that . . . Are you familiar with the piece *Für Alina* by Arvo Pärt?

Robert shook his head.

– It's a very special piece, in my view. These days cultivated people no longer compose in melodies, in harmonies and so on. It's always structures, abstract forms . . . well, anyway. But the piece by Pärt is something else entirely, you don't even know where to begin . . .

– Ah, I see, said Robert, turning away.

The man grasped him by the shoulder. Robert's eyes widened. The thin man smiled, reached into his bag, and pressed a business card into his hand. There was no name on it. Just the name of a company: InterF.

Under it a mailing address in Belgium. E-mail: inter_f@apuip.eu.

– Pärt's music is just like your painting here. Of the cat. That stillness. You know, it's a piece for piano. And the left-hand accompaniment consists of only a B-minor triad, which is simply played up and down. Completely boring. And the right hand plays a similar melody. He hummed a brief snatch of it. And together they yield this absolute stillness. You can listen to the piece on the street, with headphones . . . and you're suddenly alone. Suddenly at peace. That electricity no longer in your bones, everywhere, you know what I mean?

Robert had the feeling that all the other guests had moved at least three feet away from the two of them. He would have liked most to reach out his arms toward them. The glass he was holding in his hand had begun to sweat.

— I think I do, he said. Hey, what was your name?

— After such a long time, finally a moment when the clock hands stand still, said the man. Or the Geiger counters. Or the sirens. Just stillness. That's an enormous achievement, you know? How did you do that?

— Um . . .

Robert raised his arms.

— I know, said the man. It's not easy to describe. The artistic process. But the peace you found there is like a special vintage. You can enjoy it only in small doses, not too much. You were a student, weren't you? At the institute?

— You mean at Helianau?

— At the Helianau Institute, exactly. It's in your bio.

— Hm.

— A burnt-out case, the man said into his champagne glass, as he brought it to his mouth.

— Excuse me?

— I said it turned out great. Your career, I mean. You know, I might have made your acquaintance sooner, Herr Tätzel. But then the parameters shifted, so to speak. Or rather, were shifted.

— What?

— The parameters according to which we exist. The circumstances.

— Did you teach at the institute?

A stupid question. Robert knew that the answer was no. He knew all the teachers, after all, and to keep the few names and faces in his head was really no great feat of memory.

— No, said the man. I was never really there.

— Aha.

— Would you mind if I asked a personal question?

— I can't say until I hear it.

— Well, then I'll give it a shot, with your permission. It's worth a try. You must have been in boarding school there, at the institute. I mean, you weren't one of the few students who commuted. That didn't happen so often, did it? But wait, that's not my question yet. My question is about daily life there and is, as mentioned, perhaps somewhat personal, but I hope you don't take offense at it. Have you ever played the zone game?

Robert held his gaze.

— You know about that?

— Well, yes, said the man, as if Robert had paid him a compliment.

Robert shook his head.

— No, I haven't.

— You really haven't? Because I thought . . . hm. Strange. I must have been starting from false assumptions.

The man took a sip of sparkling wine. As he did so, he touched his upper lip briefly with the knuckle of his forefinger. Piss, thought Robert. My piss.

— How's your mentor doing?

— Who?

— Your former math teacher, that, oh, what's his name, Seltz . . . Setz, right? Back then he . . .

The man made an odd gesture with his left hand, reminiscent of a police officer attempting gently but in awareness of his authority to drive back a crowd.

— I have nothing to do with him, said Robert.

– Oh, Herr Tätzel . . . (The man acted as if he were disappointed.) You don't have to pretend that . . . But okay, I understand, of course. But you must have been relieved to hear that he was acquitted, right?

– What's this about? Are you with the police?

The man laughed:

– No. It wasn't him anyway. I mean, the thing with that asshole they skinned.

– I really don't know what you want from me, said Robert.

And I'd now like to have my peace, he added in his head. The man poked a finger into his belly button. Robert immediately froze. He sensed that he wanted to cry for help, but at the same time he was stuck in a sort of tunnel. In a tunnel of heightened attention. The man's face came very close to his own, he smelled his breath, sparkling wine mixed with oil paint. As if he had licked the paintings.

– He visited me, did you know that? It was several years ago. He showed up, supposedly in search of, ah, I don't know, research for something. Which then never appeared, of course. He's written other things, the good man, since then. But I knew, of course, what his visit was actually about, Herr Tätzel. About you. Tell me, how did you get him to do it? I mean, I might, of course . . . ask Herr . . . Schaufler, I think, is the name, yes . . . Max Schaufler this question. How you did it, that is, what techniques of persuasion you used back then. So: How did you, I mean, you don't have to reveal any details to me about your . . . holy alliance so many years ago, Herr Tätzel—

Robert finally broke out of his paralyzing terror and threw his sparkling wine in the man's face. The man immediately began to laugh. People approached, Robert murmured an apology and rushed past them.

Robert made it home only with difficulty. When he finally arrived in his apartment, he couldn't have said what streets he had taken. Cordula greeted him and could tell from the look in his eyes that something was wrong with him. She was acquainted with it, it was her métier, ever since her childhood, so to speak. *Help, help,* thought Robert, and: *Look at what's happening to me, maybe it comes from contact with you—you, you . . .* His teeth chattered, he couldn't speak.

And Cordula—took a step back.

— Arvo Pärt, said Robert.

—What?

— Mmmh.

— What happened? Did someone make you angry? Wait, I'll bring you something, it'll make you feel better in no time . . .

Xanor, zolpidem, no, he didn't need anything like that, there was a reason he was this way, his state, but he still couldn't say anything. Just a moment, just a moment's patience.

Cordula returned and held a little farmhouse made of matchsticks in front of his face.

— Crush it, she said. It's okay. That's what I make them for.

Robert took the house in his hand.

— Don't know, he murmured.

— It's okay, Cordula repeated, making an encouraging gesture. Break it. That always makes you feel better. Eases the tension.

He had never before in his life bitten into wood, at least not matches. But as he chewed up the little house his girlfriend had built (maybe the bones of Arno Golch's fingers would have cracked and splintered the same way if he had bitten into them . . .) and noticed her surprised but still composed and motherly look, he gradually found his way back to a place in the solar system where his voice could be heard.

— Some guy accosted me, he said.

He chewed. Spat out the splinters of the anger house. Absently patted Cordula's shoulder and murmured a soft thanks.

— At the award ceremony?

— Was probably drunk. For all I know.

We have to be on guard, Robin, that we don't lie to ourselves. Man is a wolf to man.

— Did he . . . say something nasty . . . ? Like Frau Rabl's son?

Max Schaufler. How . . . ?

Robert wasn't good at crying. It wasn't his way. He knew lots of people who were really good at it, who could really cry you something, a whole story, an étude by Chopin, a social contract, a career leap. But he couldn't do it. Had never learned how. His face always just came apart, like continental drift, and the individual pieces did what they pleased.

– Oh, Robert, don't, that was just a . . . (a pause lasting a tenth of a second, because she didn't know, she had to guess) . . . a stupid, intolerant asshole who said something . . . No, don't cry, come . . .

5.   The Quincunx

On the soccer field the grass grew knee-high, it hadn't been mowed for quite some time. I asked the principal about it, and he only shrugged and said that in summer, in any case, games would be played here again. On the large meadow next to the playing field stood several trees that had just begun to bloom. A slight figure moved among them with strangely jagged and irregular steps. The principal stopped and told me to do the same. He shielded his eyes with both hands, then whistled by sticking two fingers in his mouth. The figure, a boy who was carrying something around with him that looked like an empty birdcage, responded with a similar whistle. In the principal's face was a certain strain, but also a genuine excitement, as if he were looking forward to the imminent encounter.

– Max! he shouted, beckoning the boy toward us.

– Is he . . . ?

The principal turned to me and nodded.

– Yes, he's from here. A really sweet boy. One we've pinned our hopes on! His parents are incredibly nice too. His father recently purchased a paper mill from . . . Yes, Max, hello!

– Good morning! shouted the boy, remaining at about ten yards' distance.

The principal approached him, the boy first backed away a little, then understood and extended his hand so that the principal could shake it.

– Come on over, he said, waving me closer. He doesn't bite, haha!

The boy named Max held out his hand to me, and when I took it, I noticed that it was ice-cold. Probably he was nervous.

– We'll stay a few minutes, the principal said with a kind smile in my direction. So, yes, Max, this is Herr Seitz, he is going to . . .

He made a gesture that was apparently supposed to signal that I should finish the sentence.

– I'm doing my teaching internship here.

The boy nodded. He put the empty birdcage down in the grass.

– Yes, the principal said enthusiastically. He will serve as Professor Ungar's replacement.

– Mm–hmm, said Max.

A tic yanked his hand up, and he held the back of it against his lips. Then he brushed three times in a row with exactly the same movement an imaginary strand of hair from his forehead.

I knew that I should ask something. How are you doing? Do you like living here? What problems are there in everyday life? How do the teachers behave toward you? Instead I said:

– Warm today, isn't it?

– Yeah, it's starting to get somewhat warmer again, said the principal. Max, you're on the way to . . . ?

– Main building.

– Yes, we were heading there too, yes . . . Great, great . . .

The whole time I couldn't help thinking: *I feel nothing. Nothing at all. A normal boy. A normal day. No effect. All in the head.*

Max nodded and again brushed the nonexistent strand aside.

– I think we'd better get going, then, said the principal, dabbing the sweat from his forehead with his sleeve. Was nice to run into you, Max. Ah, and . . . please tell Herr Mauritz to bring the keys up to me around six o'clock this evening. Because of the bus. And . . .

– Okay, said Max, backing away a few steps.

– Yes, and can you also tell him that the door to the yard still squeaks? He has to take a look at that. Today. Okay?

– Mm–hmm.

Max's backward movement appeared to happen unconsciously, it seemed like a natural reaction, like rubbing your palms together when you've decided something, or shifting from one foot to the other when you're waiting impatiently for something.

– All right, then, okay, said the principal, now taking a few steps back too.

Since I didn't want to remain standing alone in the middle, I followed him.

Max waved again and then marched in his jerky gait accompanied by occasional tics and twitches toward the main building.

– He notices, of course, when the effects set in. The children aren't stupid, when it comes to that. So a sort of etiquette develops, which you learn gradually. For that too it's good to be here at the institute.

Far away a bell rang. Shortly thereafter another student came across the field. He had the same choppy, jagged gait as Max and waved to us from some distance. The gestures were reminiscent of a fencer.

Dr. Rudolph waved back, I did the same. The boy, perhaps thirteen or fourteen years old, stopped, and I was about to start walking to greet him from up close, but Dr. Rudolph held me gently back. The boy also raised his palms in a polite stop gesture.

– New tutor! shouted the principal, pointing at me.

The boy bowed elegantly and then said something I could hear but couldn't immediately understand. He spoke at once quickly and slowly, like the live stream of an Internet video cutting in and out. On that day I encountered for the first time the strange mixed language of the institute children, an extremely fast system of hand signals probably approaching the differentiation of a sign language, combined with a somewhat loud, highly accentuated speech that unnaturally drew out certain syllables. It sounded as if they were articulating through a megaphone that produced a somewhat too-long echo. (Soon thereafter I saw in the dining hall of the institute a student who actually wore a small, light blue megaphone on a black leather strap around his neck.)

After the boy had moved on, the bell rang again and another child appeared.

—They come out one after another?

—There's an order, said Dr. Rudolph. An order . . .

His mind seemed to be elsewhere.

— Robert looked strange, he said. Did you notice his eye?

— No.

—Yeah, he said thoughtfully. It would be stupid if there had been another . . . You know what, I'm going to quickly . . . Just a moment, okay?

He pulled his cell phone out of his pocket and called someone. Because he took a few steps away from me, I couldn't understand what he was saying. I stood alone in my spot and didn't budge. Like a chess piece waiting to be moved. On its own it would never come up with the idea of leaving its square.

The dining hall was a strikingly low-ceilinged but large room. In it were long rows of tables, to which every few yards a chair was attached. You could slide the chairs along the tables like volume controls.

When the principal and I entered, several heads turned toward us. Dr. Rudolph went to a lectern pushed against the wall and flipped an intercom switch.

— Bon appétit, ladies and gentlemen! came from the loudspeakers mounted in every corner of the room.

— Bon appétit, the students replied.

We walked through the dining hall, past the eating noises of the students. I noticed: When the spoons struck the soup bowls, they made a bell-like high sound reminiscent of the soft ringing of a grazing herd of cows.

— And how many Indigo children are in a class? I asked.

Dr. Rudolph's eyes widened for a brief moment. Then he said calmly:

—We don't use the *I*-word here.

— Oh, I didn't know—

— No, we generally don't go so much by the perception of the outside world, but more by these young people's own concepts of environment and proximity, which they—

— Sorry, I said.

We turned through an open door into a corridor. Here some large-scale pictures hung on the wall. Dr. Rudolph wiped the sweat from his forehead. Then he said:

— Your math professor, Herr Sievert . . . He suggested you to me because you were, he says, a really dedicated student. You have discipline, he said.

— That's nice of him.

— Yes, and I always take such recommendations very seriously, you know. But I do have one question, Herr Sei . . . Setz, right?

— Yes.

— Herr Setz. The question is: Why are you interested in this institute in particular?

— Well, internships are . . . , I began.

Dr. Rudolph's eyebrows rose.

— I mean, it's an interesting challenge to work with young people who . . . who . . .

— So you're saying that it's very hard to get an internship these days. I'm sure that's true. And so you simply took what was offered to you.

— No!

— Please! Dr. Rudolph raised a hand. You don't have to . . . I don't expect at all that you enter an institute like this full of enthusiasm.

— I like to teach.

The principal smiled.

— As I tell all my teachers, he said, they are our future.

— We are?

— No, the children here.

— Oh, of course, sorry—

— I don't demand enthusiasm from my teachers. They also interact with one another less than in normal schools. All I demand, well, basically expect, is that they realize that these children are the future. They have to ask themselves again and again: What will they grow up to be?

—You mean, we teachers have to ask ourselves that.

—Yes, they, the teachers. Not they, the students. Also, when it burns out and disappears at the start of adulthood, which it doesn't always do, but it does in some cases, it's a backpack that you can't take off so easily. You must be familiar with Edison, right?

—The inventor.

—Yes. He was quite an extraordinary person. Hundreds of patents to his name. In the late nineteenth century he made one of the first talking dolls for children. In the 1880s! It was unfortunately a very scary creature that could say a few words with a tiny wax cylinder in its chest. And to change the cylinder, you had to open the upper body of the doll. So, pretty creepy. After it was played three or four times, the quality of the recording declined so steeply that the doll emitted only a horrible screech, like the faraway shouting of children. After a few months, production ceased, but that didn't discourage him, you know? Edison was never discouraged in his life. Where normal people have that little switch in them, that loss-of-motivation switch, he had nothing. He was fearless, really didn't flinch from anything. In 1903 he killed an elephant from the Coney Island amusement park, an animal named Topsy, by high-voltage electrocution, in order to prove that direct current was better and more efficient than Tesla's alternating current. The procedure was even filmed, he really thought of everything. Killing the elephant wasn't objectionable, because she had already been condemned to death by the zoo beforehand. For years the elephant's trainer had given her lit cigarettes to eat and . . . Everything okay?

—Yes, I just feel . . .

I took a deep breath.

—We're at a sufficient distance, Herr Setz. It's just nerves. Anyway . . . the elephant had a really brutal trainer who abused her for years, and then one day the elephant killed him. At the execution, fifteen hundred people were present and applauded when the elephant fell over. Fifteen hundred people. Well, in life there are rarely happy ends. But at least fair ends. She didn't have to suffer long. It was high-voltage electricity, after all, several thousand volts. Herr Setz?

—Yes?

—Would you like to sit down for a moment? Should we go back into the dining hall?

—No, it's okay, I'm just . . .

—Good, Dr. Rudolph said with a nod. What I'm trying to say: Edison had a special attitude, you know? He was, so to speak, *well adjusted.* For the development of the lightbulb he had to overcome one failed attempt after another, and none of those setbacks affected him in any way. On the contrary, the failed attempts probably even only spurred him on more. He was, at least in that regard, just like nature itself. Nature produced these children. And in a certain sense they are like lightbulbs. At some point, it burns out, they stop burning, the effects fade away. For most of them, in early adulthood. Although . . . there are conflicting schools of thought about that too, but anyway, the details don't really matter here. What's important is the broad, the long-term perspective. What leadership positions will these children one day assume? I often ask myself that.

Dr. Rudolph showed me a group photo hanging in a magnificent wooden frame on the wall in the narrow corridor outside the dining hall. In the photo were about fifteen to twenty young men on a soccer field. A few yards away hung a similar picture with young women. Both groups were arranged in a pattern known as a quincunx, something like this:

This design, which occurs everywhere in nature and art, had a very soothing and reassuring effect on me. The young men stood there like rows of trees, nothing could knock them over. The future belonged to them, no doubt about it. It was striking that the distance between them was always exactly the same, on top of that they were all wearing the same clothing, a white shirt with black pants, and the jacket—which presumably went with the pants—they had slung over their shoulders with their right hands. All were wearing white gloves. The photo seemed to have been taken on a hot summer day.

Graduating Class of 99 was inscribed on a silver plaque on the lower edge of the picture.

—Our hope is that soon the whole wall will be full of such photos, said the principal, smiling at me. All plastered with . . .

His face suddenly became serious again:

—You know, I still remember that day clearly, I was really incredibly proud, you know. I mean, all the work of the past years . . . and it is concentrated in this one moment. At the time we documented it for the ministry, with cameras and also an expert, who made a record of everything. It was important to us, we had been working for a long time toward that day.

Dr. Rudolph seemed to actually be very moved.

—A really nice picture, I said.

—We were able to choose from several, he said. Aerial views, close-ups. And so on. But this one here was really the best of all, it is . . . majestic.

He gently touched the picture's frame, as if it were hanging crooked by a fraction of a millimeter.

—Their distance from one another is impressive, I said. Always absolutely the same. As if measured with a ruler.

—That's the mathematician talking, the principal said with an appreciative smile. Yeeeah, that's the tragedy and also the triumph of the children, in a way. Their sense of their body is spherical, not . . . not like ours. Those are two entirely different topological spaces. And you have to be sensitive to that. They can accurately gauge distances down to a few centimeters. Some even dream about it, about distance measurements and so on. Me too, by the way, at least in the beginning, haha . . .

He shook his head as if he had just told an embarrassing anecdote.

—Are you still in contact with the students from back then?

His face brightened.

– Oh, yes, of course, yes, not in all cases, but I am, yes, yes, definitely . . .

– And are the boys and girls separated in class too, or . . .

– No, not in the classes. But here it was . . . more of an aesthetic decision to separate them. But I know what you mean, Herr Setz. We watch out for that too, of course, because there are, well, there are obviously always certain tendencies, especially at that age . . .

6.　Max

It had been shortly after the state ceremony. That's what they had jokingly called it at the time. A spring day with a pleasantly impatient atmosphere in the trees and a stiff, uncompromising wind in the morning, which at noon became somewhat more conciliatory, just in time for the federal president's visit.

To welcome you all here and in particular all the distinguished in the Proximity Awareness and Learning Center who always ask me what I think of our youth where the future of our country is actually happening already from the bottom of my heart to my esteemed colleague Dr. Otto Rudolph who in his tireless efforts and pave the way for the people of Austria to a better understanding of even the most remote ladies and gentlemen for your attention.

That was roughly how Robert remembered the speech. Apart from that, the moving images he could still retrieve from the event were not particularly varied. In a few years they would probably play in black-and-white. Altogether the visit hadn't lasted longer than an hour. In the middle of the yard the president stood at his lectern, accompanied by several people who, as you could tell from their body language, regarded themselves as invisible. And then there were also a few journalists, or maybe they were also from the institute, no idea. The students had been placed at some distance, at equal intervals, which was okay for Robert, but made people like Arno Golch or Hubert Stöhger sweat.

And then that strange image: the principal in front of the federal president. Despite the cool temperatures and the light wind he wore no coat, only his usual suit jacket. He looked so fat and happy in front of the president that the sight made Robert really nervous. How red could a person turn? At some point, the walls of the blood vessels would surely crack.

He would have liked nothing more than to run from his assigned place to the two men and ring them, the way you ring a bell. Certain people perhaps had no other purpose in the world than to be rung.

A pope, for example.

A pope's cassock looked just like a bell, and the aging little legs with the downy white old-man hair were the clapper. The Pummerin bell in Vienna, thought Robert. New Year's Eve TV broadcast. Live episode of *Musikantenstadl*, merriment gone crazy, like after a bloody battle, wandering blood-smeared people with helmets askew.

A battlefield full of bloody popes. Robert felt an exuberant electric shock in his chest when he recalled the potbellied, egg-plump figure of the head of the Catholic Church. A Humpty Dumpty nailed to the cross. The blessing hands and the vestments. Like a penguin from the nightmare of a gaudy fashion designer. A pope is called a pontiff, he thought, which according to television means bridge builder, so he deals with the building of bridges, and those bridges eventually reach him, and you can pick him up, plump fabric bell filled with an old man's body, and make him walk across the bridge like a windup soldier.

A pope always appears alone. There are never two of him.

A pope translates Rome and the whole globe back into Latin.

Robert had to cover his mouth with his hand.

A pope, in accordance with Catholic doctrine, swings with the other fist. A pope throws red balls of wool at the courtyard cats of Vatican City. A pope echoes for a long time after he has been rung in the deepest and stillest night of the year, Christmas, when the disabled Baby Jesus was born and immediately nailed to the cross, before his parents could request a wheelchair.

Don't start roaring!

The angel of self-control wears a bank robber sock over his face.

A pope is the front part of a queen bee, thought Robert, that is the size of a subway car. And this queen bee has two beady black eyes, which look out from the pope's palms. For what we call pope is only placed on the backside of the queen bee (where everything pumps and pulsates), just as the conical little Christmas angel is placed on the top of the Christmas tree. That's why the pope is always raising his hands in blessing, so that he can finally see something, with his beady stigmata eyes. A pope has much the same effect as Christmas tree ornaments on world affairs.

Robert looked around in search of help.

He had to share his stupid thoughts with someone. Or else he would blow his top. Implode and explode at the same time. Like those early Soviet reactors built in the Urals. Whole regions ravaged and the children into the five hundredth generation with hydrocephalus and deformed heart muscle. And mothers bring their children to the only man in the village who has a Geiger counter and ask him to measure them and are happy when he names a particularly high radiation value because they believe that the Geiger counter sucks the radiation from their children . . .

Not even the thought of this could temper his urge to laugh.

Radioactive children, radioactive children, radioactive children, he said over and over to himself, thinking of flaking skin and ash rain, but what he saw before his inner eye was only a big fat pope pumped full of royal jelly, leaning forward and roaring at the candles on his desk with his mouth gaping like a vacuum cleaner until they went out. And the Saint Nicholas hat fell off his head.

A pope without his hat is—a few ounces too light.

A pope is a salesman and goes from house to house, from earth to earth, and from dust to dust. A pope is named after another person—and always has a number.

What would it be like to press a pope very tightly against you, to feel his potbellied plumpness against your own breast?

Robert's laughter was no longer amused. Only painful. He had tears in his eyes.

Max Schaufler looked over to him, and something strange happened. He caught Robert's gaze, sick with the need to communicate, as if he knew exactly what was to be done. They gesticulated to each other silently how boring the event was. Max said that he had a new kung fu movie they could watch together. The prospect of a magnificently virtuoso Jackie Chan ballet actually managed to soothe Robert a little.

He sat relatively relaxed for the remainder of the event, until, right at the moment they were all supposed to stand up and give the eminent guest from Vienna their weary and uncoordinated applause, he suddenly wondered with an unusual intensity what Max had meant by that: *watch together*. Had he stolen the key to the projector room? Maybe he just wanted to lend him the DVD. Robert had lent him the movie version of *Batman* a week ago. *Shark-repellent bat spray*, the height of human ingenuity in 1966.

And then there was a knock at his door. Max stood there, his face shining as after a tennis match, and in his hand he held a few DVDs.

He asked whether he could come in.

Robert let him in, because he knew that Max would without doubt be the first to be overcome by dizziness, nausea, and all the rest.

Max was very excited. He didn't stay in the opposite corner of the room (out of politeness, Robert had moved immediately to the window), but stood next to him.

– I'm doing it, he said, I'm enduring it.

Robert saw the goose bumps on his forearms.

– Oh, come on, he said.

Robert knew that Max's number was very high. And his own—he didn't even know it anymore, something around 150, 160 seconds. Sometimes things seemed to be all right for much longer, that is, for a really long time . . . galaxies-drifting-by long . . . The reason they were constantly going for him. Termite in an ant nest.

And the worst thing about it was that he always enjoyed the first seconds, the way a cigarette that you lit up always smelled delicious, only later did the smoke become disgusting, and their hands also became disgusting, touching him everywhere, breaking through his thin layer of ice with their rough fingernails, Arno was the worst, his fingers were hairy, and he always stuck his fingers in Robert's mouth down to the little hairs and was cheered on . . .

– I'm enduring it! said Max.

It no longer sounded like autosuggestion, but rather like a genuine discovery. Now Robert's hair stood up too. Goose bumps down to under his wristwatch. He pulled the sleeve of his shirt over them.

Robert was reminded in an unpleasant way of his mother, who always said the same thing when she stayed in his proximity for a long time, and was always right: She really did endure everything. Disgusted, he withdrew to the normal distance, three to four yards, Max didn't protest, the glaring absurdity of their life under the sun he accepted as always, Robert wanted more than anything else to slap him, but then Max took off his T-shirt.

When there was another knock at the door and a moment later it opened, Max was more scared than Robert. Robert still had his clothes on.

Dr. Rudolph covered his face with a hand and politely took a step back.

– Schaufler, I saw that you . . . , he began.

– I'll be out of here in a second, said Max.

He looked at Robert with an imploring expression, as if he could conjure him away.

Then he put on his jeans and his shirt and left the room.

The door was closed, and Robert was alone. He put a hand to his forehead. No warmth, and no pain.

The next day they were both summoned to the small biology room.

It was an unpleasant-smelling room with an artificial skeleton (consisting of colored bones) in the corner. Stuffed birds, owl, raven, and a few others, all birds of prey, whose names Robert didn't know.

The biology teacher, Dr. Ulrich, wasn't there yet.

On the table at which they had sat down was an open magazine. Next to it a second one. *National Geographic.* On its cover was a frog with transparent legs.

Robert craned his neck in order to make out the picture in the other, the open magazine.

Goose bumps.

It was as if he were looking through the crack of a door into a strangely clean dream room, frightening and incomprehensible in its geometric purity. The picture wasn't beautiful, it was gruesome, it should have provoked horror in its viewer. It showed an earthworm. This earthworm was speared on a sort of wire and photographed by the lab assistant of the head scientist at the moment it formed with its body a curved question mark, the only gesture with which it could respond to what was being done to it. Treble clef, thought Robert.

The biology teacher was still taking his time. Max repeatedly sought Robert's gaze, but Robert kept brushing him aside like a bothersome insect.

Finally he could no longer resist and pulled the magazine over to him. The letters, immensely relieved to finally be allowed to make sense, glided along below him, but he didn't take in much, he incessantly had to stare at the short series of photos (all it would take to make it a comic strip were speech balloons) with which the worm experiment was documented. After the spearing with the wire apparently came (fig. 2) a brief pause in the process, perhaps somewhat more time had passed. In any case, the worm simply lay there.

Robert was still far too excited to focus on the meaning-giving mesh of unmoving text.

In the next picture the animal was freed from its instrument of torture. Robert imagined it: It fell on the sandy ground of a small box (fig. 3), which had already been blurrily discernible in the background of the first picture, and there began to crawl, slowly and carefully putting one body contraction in front of the other. Because its sense of balance had in all likelihood been damaged by the wire, it described a semicircle (fig. 4). Robert contemplated the image, overwhelmed with amazement. No person would ever have been able to radiate such peace after being put through the wringer to that extent. A wire implement pulled through the head, through the brain … But here was a creature that despite the horrible torture possessed absolutely no conception of revenge or self-defense. The animal simply crawled through the sand toward the hole in the ground from which it had been yanked some time ago. It wanted to return to the other members of its species, coil up in their presence, and react to chemical messengers. Perhaps it thought it had now been tormented enough, and simply put one whole-body coil step in front of the other, eventually it would arrive at its hole in the ground, and then only a few centimeters of familiar substance would separate it from its friends.

In his head Robert marched to the worm and picked it up. It took a while before its body noticed that it no longer had solid ground under it. It stopped moving onward and again coiled senselessly around itself, its head swung back and forth. The whole scene was of such heartrending senselessness that Robert had to laugh. Max made an astonished sound with his mouth. And then Robert noticed that the teacher had come in and had taken a seat. He quickly pushed the magazine with the worm story away from him, as if it had been holding on to him, and it slid almost a yard across the long, long table of the biology room, at which they, arranged in an equilateral triangle, sat.

Professor Ulrich didn't look angry or upset. On the contrary, he reached for his magazine, turned it around, seemed to skim the article, and then said:

– Right, huh?

In the days that followed Max seemed despondent and dejected, probably because there had been no punishment for his behavior, so no confirmation either that anything had ever happened. It occurred only rarely that their eyes met anywhere.

Soon thereafter Max was relocated. A car with international plates came and took him away. Robert had seen him as he (making noise with his clicker, which the teaching staff often jokingly called a leper clapper, *proximity awareness*) had passed his room, and a bit later as he stood bare-chested in the corner at his sink, his face looking in the mirror—and his hand spreading a sort of soot or black makeup on it. Next to him on a chair was a black tailcoat, as for a funeral or a piano concert. On the back of the chair balanced a dented top hat. Later Max had waved to them, with his soot-smeared paw, from the rear window of the car, where there were little stuffed animals stuck to the glass with suction cups. And that same morning the math teacher had burst into tears while reading an article about bees that had by chance been left in the lecture hall from the biology class. Freak. Robert still saw the scene so clearly before his eyes that the memory clenched his fist.

He looked for the business card of the man who had accosted him in the bank lobby: *inter_f@apuip.eu*. Then he tore it up and went into the next room to find something that he could break and repair before Cordula came home.

7. Romeo and Juliet at the Institute

There were, of course, some, well, how to phrase it, uh, Romeo and Juliet tendencies among the students, said Dr. Rudolph, that was also completely normal and to be expected, when the hormones reached a certain level in the individuals. And especially now, with summer approaching, he went on, the air was also saturated in that extraordinary way with substances that sort of rub your nose all day long in the existence of your own body. Pollen, flowers, and grass, the heat itself, which brought with it sweat and contamination of the pores and a *pervasive spread* of your own smell. It was absolutely normal that at this particular time especially intense feelings often developed in the young people. As an educator you always had to be cognizant of these circumstances, face them, as it were, with a steady eye, for nature had made provisions, in the truest sense. Yes, even the allergies afflicting so many of the institute children in these months were a constant reminder that you possessed a body, which, involuntarily and without concern for the desires and the will of its owner, reacted to its environment, interacted with it, took in molecules and then interpreted them falsely, yes, allergies of that sort were actually a very memorable symbol for all the other unpleasant effects a summer had on life in that age bracket and stage of development. And on top of that came, of course, the proximity problem and individually varying zone behavior, which quite frequently led to enormous nervous strain on the children, said Dr. Rudolph. He remembered in particular the case of Felix and Max, last year. Felix was now no longer at the institute, but at least was active in the spread of proximity awareness among the general public.

Dr. Rudolph repeated the sentence in a peculiar way, almost as if it were a mantra or a linguistic convention like hastening to add after the name of a deceased person *God rest his soul.*

And then, of course, there was Max, said Dr. Rudolph, that was a really unusual case, because no one could feel anything, at least not at first, he probably suffered from an extremely rare variety of proximity distortion.

— Sometimes scientific research grows out of its infancy too fast.

— Was that the same Max we just . . . ?

— Yeeeah, said Dr. Rudolph, nodding proudly.

— Aha.

— Felix has since been relocated, but with Max the problem is less a hormonal—

— I'm sorry, what do you mean by *relocated*? That he's been transferred to another school?

— Well, yes, said Dr. Rudolph. You could put it that way. You know, Herr Seitz, the world works a little differently for children with limited social options than it does for us. As I always say: There are no happy ends in such matters. But it isn't too much to ask for fair ends. Fair ends, you know?

I nodded.

— Fairends, repeated Dr. Rudolph, laughing. Fairends! You can always rely on that. That they come.

There seemed to be something agreeable for him in these words. Almost like a sweet memory he associated with them.

We again went down the narrow corridor toward the yard. When we stepped outside through the door, I saw at some distance from the building two teenagers talking with each other. Like two land surveyors they stood facing each other and gesticulated. Their voices couldn't be heard. The longer I observed them, the more uncertain I became what it was about the signs with which they supplemented oral communication that had such an unsettling effect. Then I realized that it must have been their gentleness. One gesture in particular, which each of them made at regular intervals, reminded me of the way adults would throw a bocce ball or another toy to me as a child: they would move their hand upward with scarcely any power—as if they wished the object wouldn't follow a parabolic trajectory at all—and release the ball into the planet's gravitational field, which would then take care of the rest, the path and the acceleration into my open hands.

The Zone Game

The most popular sports among the students of the institute were dodgeball, soccer, tennis. And once a month they walked to a nearby golf course and there whacked little chalk-white balls around a forty-acre area, but this service wasn't supported by all the parents, said Dr. Rudolph, at the moment only three children were active golfers. In the huge schoolyard there was also a ping-pong table, but someone had put a few stacked buckets on it. The somewhat smaller buckets in the somewhat larger ones, making a sort of tin ziggurat, the purpose of which I could not discern. A few coffee cups stood next to the tower on the table, which showed barely any signs of wear.

To witness the behavior of the children in the yard was really quite impressive, Dr. Rudolph said, but these days it didn't happen all too often. It wasn't the right time for it. In autumn, however, they all actually stood around constantly in the yard, God knows why. Their zone behavior underwent striking changes in autumn, their personal boundaries suddenly existed only to be gauged. Like wire models of molecules the students moved through the yard, always maintaining the distances between them, as if they were attached to steel connecting pipes. A human mobile. Sometimes just watching made you dizzy, said Dr. Rudolph. From his window he could contemplate the mystery practically all October, and it even reminded him of the starling flocks in Jutland in autumn, which he had seen once as a child, gigantic clouds of bird bodies moving over the land according to unknown principles, now swelling, now contracting, never touching one another in their morphogenetic field flight. Of course, the children could ultimately look back on a life spent with years of training for this special form of everyday movement art, and when you took that factor into account, the spectacle did seem quite a bit less mysterious. But still, said Dr. Rudolph, he always felt really strange when they moved back and forth in that way and talked with one another as if all this were completely normal. As if they had eyes in the back and front of their heads. Or feelers. Or a sort of spider web around them, and one of them needed merely to tug at one point for the others to know exactly where he had tugged. And never, with the trivial exception of bullying or a physical confrontation between two boys, did one of them get sick, no, that had never happened, not even an attack of vertigo, never did one of them run into a wall and so get pressed into another's zone, when that point was reached a new pattern simply formed. Truly remarkable and mind-boggling what situations human beings could come to terms with. And then that geometry also came out of it, which took your breath away. We could even live deep inside the earth, said Dr. Rudolph, in completely lightless circumstances, in areas with contaminated air and poisonous water, at polar stations in eternal ice, or in monasteries thousands of feet above sea level, where the oxygen content of the air was so low that everyone turned to God.

– Yes, eventually people will adapt against anything, said Dr. Rudolph.

And then these boys here, with their school uniforms, their fine shoes that always looked immaculate, and their expressive gestures. The preservation of the right distances. That moved him sometimes, he couldn't help it.

– The cluster has meanwhile also been used in the military and at management seminars, he said in a somewhat altered tone.

– What?

– The cluster, oh, right, I didn't mention that. That's our name for it.

– For the way the children stand around in the yard?

– Stand around, said Dr. Rudolph. You try to *stand around* in that way. You won't have a chance, your Venn diagram will constantly overlap with that of your neighbor. But for fields of activity in which teamwork is everything, or actually team *spirit*, the cluster is a very good exercise. We're the only authorized trainers in Austria.

I nodded respectfully.

– Yes, said Dr. Rudolph, this sensitivity to one another, this awareness of the tiniest nuances—though always from a distance—this can be extremely beneficial. Most extremely.

The Lichtenberg Huts

The yard behind the institute was not what I had feared. My childhood phantom memory of the uncanny snow-white flight of steps remained untouched. I had the feeling I had made a terrible fool of myself, and I would have liked nothing more than to go down to the chauffeur, chloroform him, and bury him somewhere so that he couldn't tell anyone about it, but then I was jolted out of my thoughts by something unusual: Farther away, where the tree-covered yard turned into a meadow, stood several little huts, which were all made of strikingly dark wood, jet-black in places. The distance between the individual huts had to be at least ten yards, Dr. Rudolph explained to me. So that there wouldn't be any overlaps. And everything was provided for, he said, beckoning me to follow him. As we approached the huts, I hesitated, and he noticed. He turned around to face me, laughed, and made a gallant gesture:

– At this time the Lichtenberg huts are empty.

– Lichtenberg huts?

He nodded.

– Why are they called that?

He dropped his chin to his chest, lowered his eyelids, and gave a hint of a head shake.

— I don't know, he said. That's always been what they've been called. The manufacturer?

Then he laughed again, clearly trying to cheer me up, and I obliged by smiling.

The door to the first hut was open, and I could take a look inside. My first impulse was to call Julia at work and tell her about the unusual sight. *It looks like a portable toilet,* I thought, *one of those old-fashioned ones that are outdoors behind farmhouses and in which you are seized by fear of rats shooting upward and in winter freeze to your own excrement—*

— Come on, let's go inside, said Dr. Rudolph. Here everything is still pretty much all right, presentable. Back there are Rudi Tschirner's and Mareike's stall . . . uh, Lichtenberg huts, we'd better not look at those. Difficult cases, you understand. Julius and Maurice are nothing in comparison.

I had always thought only people in novels smirked. An error.

— Does someone live here? I asked.

— Of course, he said. During the summer months it's really pleasant, and the distances can also be maintained only here, on grounds like these, you see, they go all the way out to where those poplars are, that's where they end.

I looked into the distance, but couldn't spot anything poplarlike. Only a few low trees. A brown hunting stand jutted like braces from the crown of a tree.

— Should I close the door or leave it open?

— It's okay, go ahead and close it, I said. I'm not claustrophobic.

— The light switch is here, said Dr. Rudolph, pressing it.

The first thing that struck me after Dr. Rudolph had closed the door was the extraordinary heat. It must have been over eighty-five degrees. All day the hut had loaded up with warmth, had stored solar energy, and now passed it on to me. The air was stuffy. There was dust everywhere. Only certain objects, which must have been used more often, were free of it.

On the inside a class schedule was stuck to the door. For each day three to four little boxes, in various colors. Next to it a key hung from a narrow board; the key fob was a small silver UFO. There were no windows. On the lightbulb, which dangled from the low ceiling of the hut, a black ring had been painted, probably with lacquer, dividing the light into two halves.

The cramped but curiously not-unpleasant room reminded me of an article I had read years ago in the weekend supplement to the *Krone* newspaper. It was about a young woman from Bavaria who was allergic to nearly everything. She lived, as the sloppily and unsympathetically written article never tired of emphasizing, in an empty room, all around everything was made of completely untreated wood (to which she was, of course, nonetheless slightly allergic), no plastics were permitted anywhere near her, not even bricks and concrete, because they immediately gave her horrible rashes and difficulty breathing. Three times a day she was brought a tray of food and medications, which she forced down in agony. The toilet was hidden behind a massive door, because the presence of the water in the tank was enough to endanger her life. I still remembered well the frustration I felt while reading this article several times. Another stone was always added to the heap, one terrible detail after another was disclosed, and eventually it just became funny, and I flung the weekend supplement into a corner. The description of the progressive development of her illness had driven me particularly crazy, a drama reminiscent of the stations of a cross: from the trailer at the edge of the woods through the wooden hut in the woods to the house made of clay in a colony specializing in this weird disease somewhere in Holland or Belgium—and still the young woman had once gone into a coma and nearly choked to death on her own vomit. So what do you do all day? asked the journalist. Nothing, answered the young woman. No clothes made of synthetic materials, no shampoo, no shower gel, etc. . . . I remembered these details, and although I had also tried that before, for a few weeks at least . . . (at the time I was a long-haired keyboardist in a heavy metal band) . . . I read, squealing loudly with enthusiasm, the article to my bandmates several times, and we eventually ended up in an absurd intoxication, and we improvised loudly, wildly, and dissonantly on this whole awful nonsense, on the flagrant senselessness of such a life and so on, on the filth, the shit, and the sensationalism in the final years of the twentieth century, and alas, no one thought of recording the whole thing on MiniDisc, which was an eternal shame, a terrible shame, just like the fact that I had never managed to this day to find out what had ultimately become of the young woman.

I had to sneeze.

Dr. Rudolph opened the door.

— No wonder, he said. The cleaning women never come in the huts. They stay in the main building. So far no argument has been able to change that.

8.   Animals

If you had a hand with a few thousand fingers, you could count the number of nerve cells in an earthworm on one hand. And if you now pick any cell in the earthworm brain, note its properties and surroundings, you will find exactly the same cell, with all those properties, in the brain of another worm of the same species. From this it follows that earthworms have isomorphic brains.

There is only one earthworm.

Robert knew he had waited his whole life for this information; it came from Professor Ulrich instead of a stern lecture or an explanatory talk or whatever. Max had, while the biology teacher spoke, dissolved into thin air next to him. Like a sugar cube in coffee. Professor Ulrich mentioned studies in the United States and Norway. He looked at the magazine and kept gesturing to the ceiling while he talked, as if an interesting documentary on the same subject were playing there.

Robert took the information with him to bed, snuggled up to it, and thought of the cruelly tortured worm with the wire in its head. Why did he become so calm and relaxed in the face of this image? And the fact that there was only one worm—why was that so much more comforting than all the prayers and religious maxims he had heard in his life? He thought of tomorrow, of the moment Golch and the others would drive him into a corner or . . . what do I know? . . . they had definitely hatched some plan. But the thought no longer had anything frightening or dreadful about it. He saw two worms crawling in the dust, two living tubes that took in substance from the front, transformed it into worm mass, and excreted it behind them. And each one exactly the same, with the same thoughts:

Me: I am here.

Me: I see it exactly the same way.

Me: I know.

Me: I'm not entirely sure where we are.

Me: We?

Me: I.

Me: I came from that direction.

Me: Not me.

Me: That can't be.

Me: Well, the direction is perhaps not the decisive factor.

Me: True.

Me: I'm afraid.

Me: Fear is relative.

Me: Fear is not relative.

Me: Yes, that's the problem.

Me: How many are we anyway?

Me: I am here.

Me: And how many . . . ?

Me: I don't know how to respond to that.

In the days that followed, Professor Ulrich repeatedly provided him with relevant material. With the story of Mike the chicken, who survived for a year and a half without a head, was fed by his owner with a dropper, and each morning, in a futile attempt to crow, squeezed air out of his open throat. With the story of the two-headed dog created by a Soviet scientist; of the transplanted head of a monkey that survived for several hours and asked for water by pushing out his upper lip in a gesture he had rehearsed beforehand for several hours with his trainer; of the mysterious species of sea cucumber whose cells don't age; of the peculiar coot that had been owned by a Russian noble and exclusively laid eggs with already-petrified, mummified chicks in them. With articles on bioluminescence, transparent skin, and immaculate conception (aphids). With the wonderful mating ritual of the anglerfish. Or with the history of coelacanths.

Robert had been unable to tell Cordula what had happened at the reception in the bank lobby. And she didn't ask him to.

She preferred to let him into her body and stroke him, comfort him, this strange, constantly high-strung being whom she loved, every movement of his hips was like the plunge of a needle sewing up a wound. She kissed him and tried to get him to close his eyes while kissing, which he usually couldn't do. And then she succeeded, and she felt the tension in his shoulder muscles.

— Gillingen, she whispered.

It was a word with which she could tickle him.

— The world-famous cable car . . .

She felt the gentle trembling of his body inside her, the reaction to the intimate word. And then they brought Robert's small diamond-shaped computer into the bed and watched silly videos while they continued to make love. Outside it was raining, the first real late autumn rain, which already produced snow-light in the city and brought no lightning or thunder but instead hours of freezing drizzle alternating with heavy gales in which thick raindrops flew around like pearls that had slipped off a string. In the past few weeks the transition had announced itself: cool, long evenings, wet-trodden foliage-brown smeared like marmalade across the sidewalks. October on the threshold of November.

What else could you do at this time, thought Cordula, but hide in each other? She pressed her lips to Robert's chest and left them there, feeling his accelerated heartbeat.

On the Internet porn sites they watched together it was also autumn. The predominant categories were mature, MILFs, and a few longingly sun-drenched outdoor scenes. The chat rooms were abandoned, barricaded with boards like ice-cream stands and pavilions in a park. The pop-ups on the free tube sites, which usually lured you with hysterical fervor to live cams subject to a charge in front of which naked girls spoke to invisible phantoms, now directed you to links that were as dead as a skater half-pipe in winter: a snow-white cul-de-sac, a blank page. The comments became monosyllabic, the duration of the clips automatically suggested by the website longer—greater distraction, warmer spots to hole up in when it was cold outside. (A few animated, cursor-sized leaves even wafted through the Google logo on Robert's home page.) For Robert the most pleasant clips were those in which not much happened. Where two people just lay on top of each other and moved back and forth a little. Everything else flustered him or made him so nervous that his arousal disappeared. New to the list of his discoveries were those videos characterized by the strange word *bukkake*. In them you always saw the same thing: a naked woman kneeling on the ground. And around her stood men who were themselves completely naked (except for their funny sneakers) and took turns ejaculating in her face. Because this process was rather static and apart from the discharge of seminal fluid not much happened, Robert found them pleasant. Cordula was amused by them, but couldn't really enjoy them. Robert himself actually couldn't watch these videos for too long, because after four or five loads the woman's face always looked like the melting face of the Nazi in *Indiana Jones: Raiders of the Lost Ark*. The effect was only heightened by the fact that the women in the video clips usually opened their mouths wide like chicks (which was probably supposed to be erotic), just as the screaming Nazi does when he is struck by the pillar of fire shooting out of the Ark of the Covenant. When the bukkake scene reached this point, the sight was nothing but horrifying, and the despair that hung in the cool season returned to him with full force.

Cordula asked him whether he wanted to watch something else. She was lying on her belly, he behind her, so she had to type in the new keyword.

– Type in, Robert panted. Type . . . Oh, wait, I think . . .

– You're already there?

— Oh, wait . . .

He slowed down, lowered his head onto hers.

— Think of something neutral, said Cordula. And just breathe deeply.

— Okay.

— What are you thinking about?

— Why do you want to know? he asked.

— No reason.

— I'm thinking about how it must feel to be acquitted even though you're guilty.

— Oh, no, Robert, not again . . .

— You wanted to know what I'm thinking about!

— Yes, but . . . why are you thinking about *that*, of all things, while we . . .

— No idea. Now you're thinking about it too.

— Yes, but that's your fault. I wouldn't have come up with it myself.

— *You* showed me the newspaper article.

— But only so you . . .

Robert moved back and forth inside her in slow motion. Cordula signaled with a movement of her hips that she wanted to turn over. He slid out of her and remained hovering over her in push-up position, like a human cage, within the narrow confines of which she had to move. Then she lay in the position of the Christian missionaries, and he came back into her, warm, hard, her tissue (it was a sexy word, when you thought it at the right moment, *tissue*) stretched, and she drew him closer to her.

— I don't want you to think about such awful things, she purred.

— He must have been happy, said Robert.

— I want you to enter me completely when you . . .

The sentence hadn't really turned out as she had intended, it sounded somewhat strange, but Robert was already too far away to pay attention to such little things. He was in the zone. Panting, eyes closed, mouth half open, on the verge of climax.

— I bet it was him. But the evidence . . .

He now thrust somewhat harder.

– I want you to forget everything around you, she whispered in his ear. I'm here, and you . . . and everything that happens out there, all those awful things . . . forget all that, just come inside me, touch me all the way inside . . .

She pressed her pelvis forward so that the tip of his cock penetrated to that place deep inside her that was otherwise never touched by anything, the keyhole of a secret door . . . Robert knew what she was thinking. She had to nurse back to health this injured, distressed animal, which trusted her and had come to her. After all, she was closer to him than anyone else, she knew the smell of every spot on his body, and she had swallowed his semen several times, the protein of which had meanwhile settled in her bones and teeth and helped keep her from breaking apart. She had always assured him that she didn't experience his orgasms as burdensome tasks with which she had to assist him, but rather they seemed to her more like a joyful overflow error of the universe, a glitch in the Matrix, like the double cat, a magical, regenerating, fortifying déjà vu, the repetition of which always meant a young, fresh new beginning, even if the whole thing, you had to admit, did look somewhat funny . . .

– Come, she said (as she had that time when she had taken his hand and pulled him along with his skates, in which he wobbled like a poorly anchored Christmas tree, across the ice). Right there . . . come . . .

– I bet it was him, Robert moaned in a voice dull and hollow with excitement.

José Miguel Moreira
THE FIRST THREE

The First Three—these are the first three years with María, his daughter. She was born in 1999 with Indigo syndrome. What made her case special: It was discovered only after three years had elapsed. Not that the symptoms didn't occur until then, on the contrary, but José's interaction with his daughter was so distant in the first three years that he simply didn't notice. María's mother, whom the little girl was named after, died of an infection shortly after giving birth.

This moving memoir is a passionate plea for more closeness and warmth in the parent-child relationship, a warning against neglecting early contact with your own progeny—and at the same time a praise of distance.

"I couldn't possibly have accomplished my work with the necessary energy. I would most likely have been hospitalized at regular intervals or would have had to go to a health spa. It's one of the awful paradoxes of my life that I was able to offer my daughter an orderly life only because in her early years I didn't want to give her the closeness and care she deserved."

9. Class F

Name	Age	I-Number (approx., in sec.)
Felicitas Bärmann	14	120
Arno Golch	16	0 (immediate)
Esther Reich	14	250
Maximilian Schaufler	16	1000+
Sarah Schittick	16	45
Hubert Stöhger	17	10
Robert Tätzel	14	60 (2002), 180 (2004)
Daniel Waldmüller	15	?
Hedwig Wobruch	17	666
Julius Zahlbruckner	14	50

Dr. Rudolph's remarks on the list:

Schaufler, a thousand seconds and even more. On good days you can spend whole hours in his vicinity without feeling anything. No idea what he's even doing here. Well, his parents are rich. Developers from Styria. And Waldmüller makes a secret of it. In his case some speak of four to five seconds, others of up to half an hour. Probably a puberty/identity thing. He needs his privacy. As if he didn't already have a whole truckload, oh, what am I saying, a whole amusement park full of it. In Wobruch's case the value might be closer to 600. But she's a Goth and in the process of discovering her identity, what do I know, so we humor her and accept her ridiculous value. It would be funny, of course, if it were correct. Maybe you'd like to test it with a stopwatch? Or maybe you'll find a volunteer in the class and make a social project out of it? Tätzel is a problem child. Parents relatively well off, but not so rich that you'd notice. Also rather reserved people, pleasant on the whole. Mother comes regularly to visit, father has never shown his face. Classic bullying target. Requires socially sensitive framework and treatment. Responds well to flip chart, brainstorming, poster making. When the usual suspects organize a spa bath with him, he usually doesn't come to class. Relatively predictable patterns in this regard.

Each lesson at the Proximity Awareness and Learning Center began with a review. After a week the students had become completely indifferent to the fact that they would have a new math teacher—or, as it was known here: math tutor—for the rest of the school year. They sat, evenly distributed, in the large lecture hall and looked down at me with blank faces.

Each day I wanted more than anything else to run away screaming when I saw those horrible faces in the morning.

I scrawled the contents of each lesson in my tiny block letters into the lens area of the projector. In the enormous enlargement on the white screen I realized for the first time how ridiculous this handwriting looked. The little letters looked like huts blown over by a storm, especially the *M*. The *I* usually leaned at a slant on its neighbor. I tried to write the mathematical symbols somewhat more clearly, but didn't always succeed.

– 'Scuse me? Can you write a bit bigger?

I had to look at my seating chart to figure out who had spoken to me. A pale female face in the highest row. She held little opera glasses up to her eyes, which made her feel incredibly elegant.

I was always glad to get out of the lecture hall again. In the heavy sunlight I would lean on the corner of a wall and recover from the unpleasant tension in my head.

On the doorframe of the teachers' exit someone had written in permanent marker: *A dingo ate my baby.*

Years ago I had heard about a mother who regularly had to vomit over her baby's cradle, usually directly onto the child. At the time I couldn't help laughing.

Now I could understand her.

The headaches weren't particularly bad, and I ascribed them more to the change of air and the one-hour train ride I had to take every morning to get to work. The compartments in the trains of Austria's national railroad had a peculiar inner climate, which rarely had anything to do with the prevailing temperature and air pressure conditions in reality. On top of that, I barely got around to eating anything all day. When the students headed to the dining hall, I had to set off, in order to be on the platform on time. Otherwise I would lose two whole hours.

Only once did I stay longer and eat lunch with the students. That day math class had been postponed to the afternoon for a change.

On the plate that the lunch lady, a woman named Leni who was invisible all day, kindly brought to me at the table were peas, carrots, a decent portion of dark yellow purée, and a trout, which was indifferent to everything. Its eyes were open, and its posture spoke plainly. I barely got down a bite. The unappetizing eating and slurping noises of the students and the unpleasantly buzzing air in the dining hall spoiled my appetite. So I went outside and filled my body with clean, sun-warmed air.

Later I got a coffee from the machine in the entrance hall. Black, without anything. A cup full of eye pupils.

The air in lecture hall A was stale and musty. There were no windows that could have been opened. On top of that, the room was overheated. From a fire extinguisher white foam dripped on the floor. I had planned several times to inform the janitor, Herr Mauritz, but had repeatedly forgotten.

– Good afternoon! I said to the students.

They just sat there. Eyes stuck in faces. Some of them chewed gum. A girl in the highest row lay on her open notebook and seemed to be asleep.

I sighed and sat down behind the teacher's desk. What was I doing here? Second-order curves. I closed my eyes for a moment, ran my hand over my temples—although that might have been impolite toward the students—and tried to imagine an approach to the subject. Second-order curves. Second-order curves. It was as if the textbook knowledge had been blown away. In my head was only an image of a flat cone. I took a deep breath, told myself that I had just had a cup of coffee and would definitely feel its effects in a moment, and stood up.

A few sheets of paper lying around on the teacher's desk caught my eye.

For R. T., was written on one of them. I turned it over. It was a photocopied article from a science magazine.

A picture showed a bee whose backside was destroyed. I read the caption. *Bees don't always die after they have used their stinger in defense. This bee lived for seven hours without its stinger.*

I felt dizzy, and I had to hold on to the blackboard behind me.

Another picture in the photocopied article showed the bee lying in a small white box, useless and according to its nature already long beyond death. Confused. Unmoored.

– Excuse me, I said, and ran out of the lecture hall.

I imagined the grass under me was a baby in a cradle. I retched a few times, but nothing came, only the taste of burnt coffee rose in my esophagus, mixed with stomach acid. All that fell in the grass were the drops that ran down my cheeks.

I turned around and was about to head back to the lecture hall. But then took a few steps backward. As if I were set wrong. Operated in reverse.

In the quiet, abandoned teachers' lounge I sat down in a corner and called Julia. It took a while for her to answer. In the background a high, chaotic squealing could be heard. Probably the crowing of the new rooster. Or the bats were fighting again. Intermittent rattling of cages.

– Ah, you're not home yet either? I asked.

– No, where are you?

– I have an afternoon session. For a change. But I felt sick.

– Assholes.

–Yeah. This is the strangest job imaginable.

– Mine is stranger, said Julia.

–The animal shelter? Well, I don't know . . .

– There they at least understand your language, she said. I have to learn a new one every time. That's difficult.

– How's the rooster doing?

– He's being nursed back to health. I think he likes me.

– Have you given him a name yet?

–Yes.

– So what is it?

– Mmmh, it's still too soon to reveal it. He still has to get used to it himself.

– Seriously, this internship is no fun at all.

– But there are no other jobs. You said so yourself.

–Yeah, why do we even exist? We're superfluous.

– Me too?

– No, I mean, we teachers. I should have become a rapper or graffiti artist.

– Or a bat.

–Yeah, exactly. How are they doing?

– Hm. Hard to say. They're somewhat introverted. They just close the curtains and don't let anyone near them. I'm something like the mediator.

I closed my eyes and waited for the tension headache to pass.

–You felt sick? asked Julia. Really sick?

– No, not really. It's all so absurd, these students, I mean, I don't even know what all this is about.

– No one knows.

– They sit here in this huge building, far away from one another, and hey, I didn't tell you yet, the birds here . . . or did I already mention it?

– No, what?

– The birds here are totally weird.

– In what way?

– Oh, I don't know . . . I'm losing my focus again. I feel it. As if someone were pulling a string out of my body.

– In what way are the birds weird?

– Who?

– Oh, never mind. You sound tired. Do you really have to stay?

– I switched with this guy, this Ulrich. Biology professor. Looks like Virginia Woolf. Exactly the same profile.

– Gross.

The teachers' lounge looked like the waiting area of a small provincial train station. Rounded benches made of old, experienced wood stood around in it. Brown was the predominant color. There was a cabinet with textbooks and educational materials, there was a globe, a multistory copying machine, and even some head-high potted plants.

– During the afternoon session, I said, in the lecture hall. I saw something awful.

– What was it?

– Something really awful.

– With animals?

– Yes.

– Real animals? Or in pictures?

– Pictures. Really horrible. In an article.

– Yeah, you sound pretty upset, she said. It's good that you called me right away, hold on, I'm just going to a different room . . . the cackling is pretty loud here.

– And those wretched statues, I said, they all noticed, of course, that I . . . Ah, I can't imagine how I'm supposed to stand this any longer. You should see them!

– Maybe you should write something.

– Why?

– No reason, to distract yourself. That has always worked well up to now.

– Yeah, but those gruesome pictures . . . I mean, there was a bee that . . .

I didn't go on.

– Don't think about that now, said Julia. You can go home now, can't you?

– Technically, yes. But the train doesn't depart for another . . .

I looked at my watch and made a disappointed noise intended to imply the unpleasant wait.

– Then sit down in the library or in the yard—

– I can't go in the yard, the lunatics roam around there, my God, I really have to make a video of *that* sometime and put it online . . . They even have a special name for it. For the way they move in the yard. A special name! Shit!

– Well, in the library, then, Julia said calmly. Sit down there and imagine . . . I don't know, what's going on inside them.

– Oh, God, seriously?

– Okay, then imagine, oh, I don't know, what could you . . .

– Exactly.

– Pick one of them. And imagine what he'll be like someday. What sort of life awaits him. And why he has to look at pictures like that.

– Who?

– Just pick one of them and imagine how he'll behave later on. *For R. T.*

– And when? How far in the future?

– I don't know. In a few years. Ten, twelve.

– In twelve years humanity won't even exist anymore.

– So then ten.

– At that point there's civil war. Everywhere.

– In every country?

– Yep.

– Hey, said Julia, I have to go back to work. My bats . . . Can we continue this talk at home?

– Okay.

10. The Rooster

In autumn the sunshine seems to have stubble.

The leaves fell in the courtyard of the old building on Glocken-turmgasse 20/21, the wooden stairs indoors, compressed and worn to a shine like old ink pads from countless footsteps, creaked under the temperature and pressure changes, the calendar grew thinner, the names of the months longer and more melancholy, then, eventually, you needed a scarf when you were out on the street, and from that point on there was no going back to the warmth of the summer.

Except in this way.

Robert lay next to Cordula and nestled in her armpit. The world-famous cable car in Gillingen, he thought, a gentle rocking over the landscape. Even though she had never spoken about it and didn't let it show, he knew that she often got a slight tension headache when he stayed that way for a long time, so he slid down a bit and laid his cheek on her warm flank. Incredible, how warm a woman's belly always was. He had often compared it with his own belly. As different as day and night.

He closed his eyes and thought of autumn at Helianau. The heating in the student apartments was always turned on only in mid-September. Beforehand you could turn the radiator valve as much as you wanted. All that came was a tentative, muffled hiss in the pipe, perhaps air, perhaps a residue of weary water that had waited there through the whole warm season to finally be used. A water residue in which, as if to make up for the long wait, little creatures had developed, hybrid forms of algae and tadpoles, which now moved through the pipes and bred there in a new way, not entirely comprehensible even to them, consisting of symbiosis and division; in the pipelines hidden in the walls (Robert saw the walls of his room at Helianau as clearly before his eyes as if they were part of a picture he had painted himself) they lived and flicked each other with their tongues in greeting, their pale green, semitransparent bodies pressed close together in the autumn cold (the shiny film of skin care cream on Max's upper body, Robert's hand reaching out toward it . . .) and so again bore new creatures, and over the years they wandered from one house to another, test-tube babies of all inoperative radiators, and they formed a huge, listening horde in the walls, fungal colonies taking in everything that was said in people's lives, houses, and rooms.

Who might have heard the screams of the skinned man? And what had he made of them? Robert opened his eyes and searched for the newspaper. He wanted to check whether other, more informative articles about the case had come out in the meantime.

In autumn the restlessness had always been the worst. Robert put on his pants and went into the kitchen to do a few karate chops in the air. Bruce Lee, he thought. He could focus all his body's energy, his chi, in one point in his hand, and then he only had to touch you gently with it, and your heart stopped. He could have used that back then, at Helianau, when it got cold. On the one hand, so that he didn't freeze all the time, on the other hand, so that he could at least win the zone game now and then.

That ridiculous, but okay, yeah, yeah, also pretty fun standing orgy and the sensation of the zone feelers coming into contact with the others, just like the bodies of the heating pipe creatures in their tiny primeval pools in the walls, that was really something . . . While they were being watched, they always played it slowly and chess-piece-like, of course, but when they were left alone, things got wild. Arno Golch was always the first to breach the order, he always got bored very quickly. My God, Arno, head of conception at PETROPA, oil field development, pioneering work, John Franklin. Or Sven Hedin, screw it, smeared shiny black like the penguins and kingfishers in the South Atlantic. Back then already. Always the first to break through.

Robert remembered that the first one to burst into the ordered crowd, seize another student, and drag him away was called Ference. Max had always claimed with abundant gestures (imitating with both hands waves of an oscillograph) that the word came from interference. The Ference always came unexpectedly, that was the point, and . . . yes, right, when he grabbed his immediate neighbor and hauled him away with him, then that was a hundred points or what do I know, a lot of points, anyway. The institute yard in autumn formed a grid with finite elements, and then that disrupting signal penetrated it, like the waves that surged on the façade of the World Trade Center after the plane had flown into it, that rearing-up of the inanimate glass front, the bursting, sighing . . . he had seen it in a documentary as a computer-animated model.

Robert had never been the Ference. Too sluggish, too slow, generally too-easy prey. Who would have thought that in the twelve years that had elapsed since graduation the world still hadn't ended? *But we're working on it*, he thought, as he passed the iBall in the hall. The iBall had closed its lid and didn't raise it as Robert crept past.

He found the newspaper on the bookshelf. It often lay there, unnoticed and nearly invisible. You could recognize it by a pale shadow it cast on the wall behind the books. He took the newspaper and started the article search. His search terms were: *setz clemens flayed man dogs.*

The entries were more or less copies of the article about the acquittal. Only the photos of the now-thirty-nine-year-old math teacher were different. In some he actually looked the way Robert remembered him. A face that without the eyebrows would have been nothing. Tired eyes. Thin-rimmed glasses. A strangely protruding Adam's apple. Crooked incisors. Receding hairline. Puppy belly, round as a ball, under a patterned vest.

One article mentioned that the family of the victim had announced that they would challenge the verdict by all available legal means. At the time of his death two years ago, the victim himself had been forty-five years old. The man left behind two daughters. His farm, on which he had kept the dogs, had been sold. His surname was nowhere mentioned. It was always: Franz F., born in Cluj (Klausenberg), Romania. Daughters born in Austria, dog breeding at first only a hobby, later his main job—damn, get to the point already. But the article ended without even mentioning the horrible crime.

Robert released the newspaper and sat down at his desk. Interf ... Ference game, in autumn ... Strange, formless thoughts. Max. What happened to him? And the man who had spoken to him, he had said that ... what word had he used? Role model, no, mentor, right ... skin peeled off ... Max Schaufler ... mentor ... Klausenberg ... burg ...

He tried to imagine stripping off the skin of a screaming, writhing man. Ideally the shoulderless, egg-shaped man in the bank lobby. How long did it take before the man lost consciousness? And how did that work with the blood loss? And where did you begin? At what points did the body have to be fastened, and by what means? Did it perhaps happen under general anesthesia?

And a guy like that taught me.

Okay, okay, he was acquitted and everything, but still. Someone who was now walking around out there had definitely skinned the man. That Romanian-born guy, who kept his dogs in a basement dungeon, or what was it again ... ? Robert looked around in the room for the newspaper, but it was probably hanging around on the balcony, for some reason it liked sunlight, good-for-nothing little feather-light thing with no memory.

Basement dungeon, the term might have come from a different memory. At home in Raaba there had been that odd animal ... That is, not at his parents' house, but in the neighbor's basement. A rooster. The cry of that rooster could be heard all year long, shifted forward by a tiny unit of time each day. The rooster was kept in a basement and possessed, as far as he had been able to tell, absolutely no concept of daylight. Of course, there was the inner clock with which nature had endowed him. It told him when the first rays of the sun, invisible to him, fell over the roofs outside, but for some reason this inner clock was not quite correctly set, perhaps the genes that were responsible for its operation came from a different millennium, when the days on earth lasted a few seconds longer, because the planet had not yet been exposed to the strong quakes influencing the tilt of the earth's axis. The rooster was, so to speak, fast. Which didn't change the fact that you could always hear him, he never missed a day; not even in the deepest winter, when day hardly ever really arrived outside, did anyone in the neighborhood have to do without his cry early in the morning. Even in the gloomy winter light that drove so many people in the suburbs into melancholy and awakened their abhorrence of their own family, that special mood when nothing more connects you to your own planet, even in the blue hours the cry of the rooster kept in the basement sounded as always, just as it did in summer. It gave the people on his street a certain sense of security. It got on some people's nerves, of course. They wished the rooster dead and released.

– Can I see him? Robert had repeatedly asked his mother.

Only two days at home, and the old bug had bitten him again: the need to see the ravaged creature. He would absolutely have to bring his sketchpad, but in a lightless basement he wouldn't achieve much anyway. If he didn't set eyes on him, he would probably have to torture a hedgehog or catch flies and slowly melt them in focused sunlight.

– What? How is that supposed to work?

Even in memory the voice of his mother was unpleasantly loud. He couldn't turn it down.

– Well, he's not invisible, is he? Robert said, and noticed that he was beginning to talk faster than was conducive to normal communication.

– No, he's not, but . . . he doesn't belong to me. How am I supposed to . . .

– I would really like to see him.

– Yes, but . . .

— Mommy.

— Don't look at me like that. I . . . Oh, my head, wait, I just need a minute to . . .

— Oh, come on, this isn't believable!

Robert stood in her way.

— Robert, please, his mother said wearily. I just have to recuperate for a minute.

— I want—

— Robert!

She pushed him aside, her hand on his shoulder. Then she was in the hallway. He thought of slamming the door, but that wouldn't have accomplished anything.

— Fine, next weekend, then! he shouted.

Arno Golch, whom Max's disappearance from the institute had made unusually aggressive, waved to Robert on the playing field. Then he approached, with huge strides; Robert ran away, but soon Golch had caught up with him.

— You motherfucker! he shouted at Robert, kicking him so that he fell to the ground.

Robert was immediately seized by a violent urge to gag, and an attack of vertigo so bad that he felt as if he were rotating on a vertical axis while standing on his head. Side of beef on a meat hook.

— You just had to open your damn mouth! said Golch.

— I . . . I don't know what you mean . . . oh, God . . .

Robert retched.

— Do you know what I wish? said Golch, kneeling down and putting his hand on Robert's neck. That he gets *you*, the Ference. That *he* gets his hands on you. What will you dress up as, hm?

Robert said nothing.

And then the air suddenly returned to his lungs, because Golch let go of him. The voice of an adult boomed across the playing field.

———

One day in winter the rooster had disappeared.

No one knew how he had escaped from the basement. Faint tracks in the snow suggested that he had gone about two hundred yards on his own feet and then must have been seized by a larger animal and dragged away. In any case, the prints of his claws disappeared at a certain point and didn't reappear. Perhaps the wind had blown away the animal's delicate tracks. People in the neighborhood cracked jokes about the overwhelmed rooster running through the daylight with its tongue hanging out, *ooohhh*, half stupid with astonishment over the brightness of the world, which his cells had always told him actually existed, and he hadn't been able to believe it . . . Robert's mother was eating lunch in her corner while Robert shoveled the thinly sliced potatoes into his mouth at the other end of the dining room, and she wasn't talking. He could tell that it was about that and not about some other subject that she wasn't saying a word. He grinned. His sketchpad was full. And before he had delivered the excited but not at all frightened-looking rooster to Konrad, who, despite the cold, had come from the next village with his moped and a wooden crate, happy about the gift for his father's farm (which his father might finally praise him for instead of just laughing at him all the time for the way his moped in certain lighting looked pink), and who promised to take good care of him, he had given him a name. He looked at his mother and said the name without moving his lips. He would never reveal it to her. He had not even revealed it to Konrad. No one in the world would ever learn it. No one deserved it, at least up to now.

11. The Meaning and Secret of Second-Order Curves

I opened my eyes. A will-o'-the-wisp wandered at the edge of my visual field. When I clenched my jaw, it disappeared, but it returned when I relaxed it.

– Mmh, you're awake, said Julia. I didn't want to wake you.

– What time is it?

– Four-thirty, I think.

I checked the alarm clock. She was right.

– Oh, God, I groaned.

– The new alarm clock is too small, said Julia.

I looked at the alarm clock.

– Really?

– Yeah, I can't make out the display.

– Shit, I have to get up soon, I said. Four-thirty, what sort of time is that supposed to be? I want most to set fire to everything . . .

– Like what?

– I want . . . oh, I don't know . . . The students stopped taking me seriously when I burst into tears in front of them. That was my death sentence. They're beasts. Do you know what they look like?

– Describe it to me.

I got up and pulled the curtain aside, which made the room a bit brighter. Then I turned on the light. Julia hid her glare-sensitive eyes behind her hands and waited until they had grown accustomed to the lighting.

– Imagine: Carnival booths. Okay?

–Yeah.

– Okay, carnival booths. And in one of them hang balloons. Balloons you're supposed to throw darts at. In all different colors. That's exactly what they look like.

– The students?

–Yeah.

– At the animal shelter I have a few blue rats, said Julia. No idea why someone has abandoned them. And another, it has a completely indefinable coat color. At least everyone is in total disagreement. Some say it's brown, but I think it has more of a green tinge. Others think it looks red. Did I tell you where we found it?

– No, please don't, I can't hear that now. I . . .

– Really? You used to always want to know how the animals are doing.

– Of course, I . . . It's just completely dragging me down at the moment. Everything's so weird at the institute. Dr. Rudolph mentioned relocations. I don't even know what that's about. But yesterday I saw a student from another class, who was in a sort of . . . ah, what was it . . . well, some sort of harlequin costume, like a clown . . .

– I hate clowns.

–Yeah, anyway, he was walking around in some costume, and later the chauffeur drove him away, probably down to the train station. Another time it was a chimney sweep a student was . . . Oh, never mind. That disgusting mountain atmosphere up there, that country air, the grass . . . even the grass is hostile. It just grows. It doesn't care about the people, buildings. Not like city grass. City grass is respectful. Like city pigeons. They've come to terms with us. But the grass there . . .

I stumbled around in one pants leg.

Julia got up too.

– But you know what? I said to her. Your advice helped.

–Which advice?

– To write. To imagine what those di . . . ah, kids would be like someday and so on.

– I told you to do that?

– Yeah.

On the platform of the Payerbach-Reichenau station, newspapers flew around. Lame paper birds, defenseless against the wind. All they had wanted was to sleep on the asphalt, now they were being thrown all over the place. A newspaper even fluttered along behind me for several yards, like a child begging, and I briefly considered adopting it and taking it with me, but then I left it there.

At a transformer building I spotted a small graffiti artwork. The face of a baby spray-painted in black-and-white stencil technique. His disgusted and thus unusually adult-seeming expression and his mistrustfully tilted head seemed to pass judgment on anyone who passed. I automatically lowered my eyes.

On the last stretch before the institute the path through the woods spun once around me. That happened to me almost every time. I stopped briefly and thought of a white flight of steps, a quiet image that anchored my thoughts. Sometimes it also helped to imagine a comet, an object standing still in the sky, which you could hold on to with your eyes.

In the teachers' lounge I drank a cup of green tea I got from the machine. I still had some time, so I took my red-checkered folder (a gift from my father for my fifteenth birthday) out of my backpack. A piece of reassuring reality among the unreal materials for math class.

So, where were we . . . stardate 2021 . . .

When I heard the deep voice behind me, I immediately raised my head, but couldn't cover the sheets of paper with my hand and push them back into the folder in time. Dr. Ulrich had seen something.

– Dirty stuff, he said with a laugh.

– No, I said. Not really.

Dr. Ulrich was an intolerable creature. He was a hunter and liked to entertain the students, as he said, with stories from the exciting life with a rifle. On top of that, he was always leaving his materials lying around in the lecture hall. His biology tests probably consisted of questions about the correct disembowelment of a deer or the preferred manufacturer of camouflage-patterned binoculars.

Whenever I saw him, I developed the fantasy of tying him up somewhere and then shooting at him. First with arrows, then with handguns, finally with an old-fashioned harquebus, with which the dodos on the island of Mauritius were exterminated in the seventeenth century. Or perhaps skinning him, painstakingly, as he did to rabbits and foxes.

— You look pale, said Dr. Ulrich.

— Yeah, the air here.

— I understand. It was no different for me the first year. But it gets better.

— Probably.

— No, not probably. Definitely. It will definitely get better. You shouldn't lose sight of that. The students get used to you, and after that things aren't so bad anymore.

— Okay.

Dr. Ulrich, apparently happy to have helped me, left, and I again sat alone in the huge conference room with its antiquated furniture. On the brown globe in the corner, the national borders of the world before 1799 were marked. It was a cheap reproduction, but the thick layer of dust made it appear old and genuine and intensified my feeling of sitting around in the past. Now and then I snapped my fingers or clicked my tongue to savor the majestic echo the room gave. I put away my little private writing project and pulled the math book out of my bag. The preparations for the midday period weren't very demanding, basically I would continue trying to explain the meaning and secret of conic sections, so-called second-order curves. I had of course noticed how uninterested the students' faces, distributed evenly through the auditorium, had looked during the last session, so I had thought about how to pique their interest and at the same time steer it toward certain mathematical questions. Recently a newspaper clipping had fallen into my hands about a man who had lived for twenty years with a twin appendage, a shrunken, shriveled copy of himself. The twin had sat just above his hip, his face was only half visible, the one eye always closed; not once in the twenty years had it opened. But the twin was supplied with blood, his heart beat—only in the course of the seven-hour operation that separated the two brothers had he stopped living. The article mentioned that the man, still in the hospital, had presented to the journalists there his long scar and had also for the first time in his life let his left arm hang loosely. His gait, the article said, had been tilted slightly to the side. When he walked down the corridor and onto the balcony of the hospital, where the cameras of course followed him, it looked as if he were bracing himself against the wind. The removed twin was reported to have lain, after his final seven hours had elapsed, peacefully before the surgeons with his eyes still closed. And that was when it was clearly visible for the first time that he had during his lifetime had the posture of a little man slipping feet-first through a hatch, similar to a cosmonaut boarding his spaceship, or perhaps like a stunt pilot stuck up to his torso in the tiny propeller plane with which he flies daring loop-the-loops, several hundred yards above the marveling audience, and turns over and over, like a restless sleeper at night, whose blanket keeps sliding away from him in the coldness of the room. Twenty years ago he had boarded this large body, genetically identical to him, and had traveled in it from place to place, they had been together on three continents, until July 22, 2005, the day of the big operation. What was relevant to the math lesson, however, was something else: The scar on the man's flank, where his twin had for so many years perched as if on a seat, was in its form a nearly perfect ellipse. Closed scars in the form of ellipses are a very interesting class of irregular scar formations, I had learned that during my studies in one of the introductory lectures on analytic geometry. Why this was the case and why a fractal scar formation would have probably had to be hell on earth, I had saved as questions for the class. It was possible that we wouldn't even get to it, but it was good to have a cushion.

When, after some time, I cast a glance out the window of the teachers' lounge, I saw in the yard a peculiar gathering. The usual zone game had turned into a sort of circle of sitting students. In the middle, one of them lay on his back. Then, after a while, he turned onto his side and vomited.

I stood up and ran out.

The students immediately dispersed when they saw me coming. I strode through their zones without letting anything show. They grumbled and cursed softly and walked away. Robert Tätzel lay in the grass. I touched him on his shoulder, he cringed and looked at me. I helped him up.

– What are you guys doing? I asked him.

His breath stank of alcohol.

– No idea, he said, taking a few steps back.

– What was that?

– How should I know! he shouted, wiping his mouth with his sleeve.

Then he took another few steps away from me. Dr. Rudolph's voice rang out from the steps.

– Tätzel!

He walked straight toward the boy. Robert automatically backed away until he touched the wall with his back.

– What did we agree, for Christ's sake? shouted Dr. Rudolph. Huh? What did we agree?

Robert nodded. Dr. Rudolph took a step back, exhaled indignantly, and gave the air in front of him a karate chop.

Then he seemed to return to reality, turned to me, and said:

– You will . . .

He gesticulated, but the sentence refused to be completed in that form. So he turned back to Robert and said:

– Herr Setz will help you. The telephone booth in the lobby. And this time tell your parents everything. Do you hear? Everything.

He looked at me as if he were expecting a nod. I gave him one. Robert looked down. For a brief moment I registered the unusual way I-kids wept—it looked incredibly theatrical. I had observed it on several occasions in recent weeks, but only now did I notice the commonalities. A feeling of satisfaction and fascinated coldness permeated me. *So you too*, I thought. Like the mask of a Roman histrion, the mouth eggplant-shaped, the eyebrows knitted. A Noh mask. I said:

– Come, now, it's all right. Let's go . . .

And I put a hand on an invisible shoulder, about twenty inches away from the real, still slightly shaking shoulder of the boy.

Robert Tätzel walked ahead, I followed him. Up to now I had never noticed a student lingering near the telephone booth in the main building. As far as I knew, all of them had cell phones anyway. Robert walked up the few steps from the yard into the building and then down the corridor that led to the central staircase, as if he were submitting to punishment. As if he were on the way to a bush from which he was to cut the switch with which he would a moment later be thrashed. I would have liked to ask Robert what the deal was with the telephone booth. But he walked so quietly and purposefully in front of me that I didn't dare to speak to him.

At the telephone booth he pulled out his wallet and took a card out of it. With a mild but despondent are-you-satisfied-now? look he held it out to me. I only nodded, confused.

He disappeared into the booth, stuck the card in the machine, and lifted the receiver. He clamped it between cheek and shoulder and dialed. An old rotary dial. Meanwhile he wiped the tears from his face with his sleeve. Ran his hand through his hair, punched, still silent, in slow motion a resistance in the air. Then he began to speak. And I noticed only at that point that you couldn't understand from outside what was said inside. That was all right, I thought. But I didn't know whether Dr. Rudolph . . . *Servile little creature*, I chided myself. And I turned away, not wanting to stand and gawk any longer in front of the transparent door of the telephone booth.

———

After about five minutes, Robert came out and held the telephone card out to me. I reached for it, but quickly withdrew my hand, and he returned to his usual distance, about three yards.

—You have no idea how this works, do you? he said.

I took my hands out of my pants pockets.

— Um, to be honest—

— *Tsss*, he said.

—What did your parents say? I asked.

He laughed.

— Okay, I said. Then I'll ask you something else. Relocations. How often do they happen anyway?

Robert's eyes widened, he looked around.

— I have no clue, he said.

—Why did they beat you up?

—They didn't beat me up.

— Okay, but why did they . . .

— I don't know, okay?

— It's all right, Robert, you don't have to raise your voice.

— Sorry.

He crossed his arms and looked to the side.

— Ah, there you are! said Dr. Rudolph. I just had to finish a phone call. Now I can deal with this. Thanks, Herr Setz, I'll take over from here.

— But— I said.

— Robert, thank Herr Setz for helping you.

—Thanks, said Robert, without looking at me.

—You're welcome. But I—

— Come with me for a second, Dr. Rudolph said to me, and took a short walk with me through the lobby.

—Those are just toughening games, he said. Basically harmless stuff. But it was right that you intervened. This time it was still a mild form. You know, the students' altered proximity understanding is also . . .

— And alcohol is always involved? I asked.

— Herr Setz, Dr. Rudolph said, grasping my shoulder. It's a nonhomogeneous class, in terms of age too. These things happen.

– The problem is that they realize that his zone . . . proximity understanding . . . that it's waning.

– It took Edison hundreds of tries to get his lightbulb right. How often do you think it burned out on him after a few minutes? The equilibrium hadn't been found yet.

–Yes, I said, but—

– And it takes nature time too, you have to come to terms with that. We can lament it, of course, that is, this individual development, but on the whole the picture is a positive one, because for some individuals born with it, it does last. Into old age.

Dr. Rudolph stood in front of me, and something was reflected in his glasses that looked like the ghost of a water jet, but I didn't want to turn around to check, and besides, he was already continuing to talk:

–You don't understand the point, Herr Setz. I mean, you're a gifted tutor in your subject. And the students like you, as far as I can judge.

Then Dr. Rudolph walked away with the student Tätzel.

And I followed them.

Not conspicuously. More like an actor in a detective film: You just focus on the camera trailing you from behind and don't think about the people you're supposed to shadow.

I positioned myself in front of the principal's office. What could happen to me if they discovered me here? I had a headache, but curiously it made me adventurous. The midday period had begun thirteen minutes ago, as a glance at my watch assured me. I shook my head and laughed as if the watch had made a joke.

I stood there and tried to keep my body completely still. I felt a little bit as if I were drunk. Champagne bubbles rose in my mind and gave everything a lively, dancing quality . . .

Fresh air streamed through an open window. I felt it pleasantly on my feet. I had forgotten to put on socks that morning.

– Ferenz, how are you doing? I heard Dr. Rudolph suddenly asking.

I held my breath. The door to the office was open a crack.

–Yes . . . yes . . . why, *biensûûûûr*, said the principal.

He was apparently on the phone.

Where was Robert? Was he sitting next to him while the principal shouted into the telephone?

– Yes, the problem . . . We just had an incident . . . Yes . . . I know that you guys thought of him, but he is waning . . . his zone . . . his prox . . . yes . . . yes . . . Oh, Ferenz, you old bastard! Hold on, I just need to . . . You can count on that, you'll get your happy end . . . One second . . .

I froze, the footsteps were approaching, hopefully he wouldn't look out the door. So I tore myself away and took a few steps toward the hallway window. There I saw Robert Tätzel, walking outside across the yard, stooped. He hung his head. In his hand he held a conical party hat . . . How had he so quickly . . . Had he passed me and I hadn't noticed, or . . . But then the principal's footsteps were directly behind me, he came out of the office, I heard it as loud and clear as if my shoulder blades had ears, probably he was holding the cordless phone on his cheek.

So I dropped to the floor, collapsed where I was.

– I'll call you back! I heard Dr. Rudolph's voice saying.

Then I was touched on my shoulder and spoken to. I let my eyes close and counted unhurriedly to ten before I opened them again and stammered that I had just felt terribly dizzy. That way I didn't have to look the principal, who kindly helped me to my feet, held me by the arm, and escorted me to the institute nurse, directly in the eye.

PART III

This was placed here on the fourth of June, 1897 Jubilee year, by the Plasterers working on the job hoping when this is found that the Plasterers Association may still be flourishing. Please let us know in the Other World when you get this, so as we can drink your Health.

—Time capsule message in a wall of the Tate Britain,
discovered by chance in 1985

When the first baby was born back then, life suddenly took on meaning, said Herbert Rauber, Marianne Tätzel's father. And now, when a grandchild, Robert, was there, death had taken on meaning for him too. For what else was the job of a grandfather or a grandmother but to die for a young person, similar to the way a piano teacher played a piece for a student? Note after note was made accessible to him, not only the little nuances and transitions but also the great unity of the melody were demonstrated, the meaning, the arrangement, the scope. You showed him that this existed, that this was part of every life: the breakdown into component parts. Someone who had four grandparents, said Herr Rauber, would also come to know four deaths. The four had to die so that he, the young, new one, could exist and so that he could go on being here. So they lived and died for him, to the best of their ability. They behaved kindly toward him, were usually more unconditional in their love for him than his parents were, their duties in his upbringing were, after all, only a game, an avuncular cheerfulness surrounded every conflict—and that was how they remained in his memory. And the grandchild learned at an early age (the only time when this realization was still bearable) that something like that was possible and necessary: a posterity in which the dead person goes on existing, is held up like a hand puppet, sewn together from the memory scraps of the people who knew him. Ideally you not only died for your grandchild, but at the same time showed him how this final act was not so bad, no reason for true despair. And that had to be the most noble and meaningful thing you could do in old age. On the day your first grandchild was born, you knew that you would in the future make an effort, yes, you would pull yourself together, to die well, without great fuss, as peacefully and painlessly as would be granted to you, as reconciled and sated with life and ripe as your own acting instinct would permit. People who had no grandchild to die for were to be pitied; for them there was no comfort. For they would die miserably in a vacuum, anxious, helpless, and beset from all sides by the feeling that they still had so much to do on this earth. To have no grandchild, said Herr Rauber, was the worst deficiency you could suffer as a human being. And the death of a grandchild was of all things that happen in the universe the most unnatural. It had also seemed to him a blatant wrong when he was told that Robert was to be part of that new school project.

He himself had a brother with, well, with a psychological impairment. Johann. He had always been totally opposed to any form of locking away. What had been done to his brother, even if with the most humanitarian intentions, remained incompatible with his view of the world, in which all of us turn together through life.

Herbert Rauber was seventy years old. His voice was unusually high, almost feminine. He exuded a great calm, which nearly drove me out of my mind. I sat in the Tätzel family's living room under a ceiling that was at least thirteen feet high, the central room of their pale blue villa in Raaba.

Raaba is not much more than a village caught on the south side of the city of Graz, fused with it like the male anglerfish with the considerably larger female. A long street, company parking lots with flagpoles lining it on both sides, that was the first impression I had of the place.

I had wondered whether it was advisable to show up at the Tätzel family's house so soon after my visit with Frau Stennitzer, which still inwardly preoccupied me. Julia said no. I went anyway. After my return from Gillingen I had sat at home in a sort of torpor and had tried to understand what had happened. Now and then I fell into a feverish sleep and dreamed of a sheep with a large gray human mask and a party hat. I had seen the party hat on the day I had accompanied Robert to the telephone booth. My last day at the institute. The institute nurse. In the brief tussle with Dr. Rudolph in the yard I hadn't sustained any injuries worth mentioning—apart from a black eye, a lucky hit by that fat man flailing his short arms. It had been the chauffeur who ultimately pulled us apart. I had dealt the principal a blow to the belly, and he doubled up and seemed to be waiting to see whether he had to vomit, while the chauffeur laid a hand on his back. But then he swallowed heavily and said softly that I was to leave the institute and the grounds immediately, or—

– Or what? You'll put me in a costume and have me taken away?

Dr. Rudolph showed no reaction. But the chauffeur seemed to be startled. He took his cap off and rested a hand on his hip. I gave him the finger. He took a step toward me. Dr. Rudolph held him back—students were standing in the yard, watching us. Like zombies in a horror film they came slowly closer, but then they stopped and spread out.

Some time later I sat with trembling hands in a train compartment and tried to reach Julia, but she didn't answer. I threw the cell phone across the compartment and afterward collected the pieces remorsefully and reassembled it. And all this just because of a few questions. *Party hat. Costumes. Relocations.* I had begun to stammer, and it must have been obvious how little I knew about the matter.

Then the serious mustache voice of Dr. Rudolph: I was too impatient, I was still adhering to old values. But it was necessary to adapt to the students' needs and refrain from applying to them your own ideas of closeness, daily routine, and so on. To illustrate his point, Dr. Rudolph told me a little story. He had read, he said, that in the fifties at a Soviet primate research station near the Abkhazian city of Sukhumi a wooden structure with a small rhesus monkey bound in a crucifixion pose had been moved into the sun each morning. The significance of this installation had been double, explained Dr. Rudolph: on the one hand a mockery of what was at the time still the all-dominating Christian faith in the Abkhazian population, which had been a thorn in the side of the Soviet rulers and which they tried to drive out by means of the grotesque monkey icon through a sort of shock therapy; on the other hand it had also been a demonstration of the new age and its medical technological possibilities, for: The monkey lacked a scalp, and from his bare cranial bones projected electrodes on wires. And now the failed paradigm shift, said Dr. Rudolph: visitors to the zoo that was part of the station had, as an observer described, passed the monkey rack and had furtively and hastily crossed themselves, all the time, *Herr Setz, are you listening?*

– Okay, you're doing that on purpose, aren't you, Rudolph?

– On purpose? Herr Setz, I don't know what you mean. And it's *Dr.* Ru—

The rest was tussling.

In Robert's room visitors could now stay for six minutes. Ever since he had left the institute, his interval had steadily increased, and his region was shrinking.

– Six minutes, I said appreciatively.

Despite his fifteen years, he looked astonishingly grown up. But not all parts of his body had participated with equal enthusiasm in the last growth spurt, which must have occurred only recently. Part of the shoulders was lagging behind, and the cranial bones too were still holding back a bit.

– I can endure it longer, of course, said Frau Tätzel. And these days it takes me only a very short time to recuperate.

– Morning, Herr Professor, Robert had said.

While I stood in his room, I kept an eye out for the party hat. But it was nowhere to be seen. Instead I spotted an unsettling poster on the wall, which showed a dog photographed in a space capsule. Robert and I exchanged a few words, then I went back to the living room.

– The tea is excellent, Frau Tätzel.

– I'm glad.

– And it really doesn't bother you if I take some notes? It's just for me, it simply helps me focus.

I held up my notebook.

– Go ahead.

– I find it very interesting, Frau Tätzel, that you've taken Robert home again. I was recently in Gillingen, visiting a woman who keeps her child at home—

– Aha, yes.

Frau Tätzel crossed her legs.

– And of course I would like to thank you for being so kind as to receive me. I'm sure that Dr. Rudolph—

Frau Tätzel raised her hand:

– No, no, Herr Setz. He didn't say anything about your departure.

Herr Rauber shook his head too.

– Even so, I wanted to tell you that it's very kind of you. I think a rumor is going around that I'm an alcoholic. At least that's what I was told. I'd just like to assure you that it's not true. I left the institute for other reasons.

– We don't judge, Herr Setz.

– That's nice of you. May I ask you a question?

– Certainly, said Herr Tätzel, who had been silent up to that point.

– Okay, I said. This might sound somewhat weird. But do you by any chance have a family member or a friend named Ferenz?

Frau Tätzel placed her teacup lopsidedly on the saucer and corrected the position with her thumb.

– No, she said.

– Are you sure? I might have been pronouncing it wrong.

Frau Tätzel leaned back. The smile had disappeared from her face, but had been replaced by something very similar.

– Sorry, I forgot to turn off my cell phone.

– It's all right, I said. Go ahead and let it—

But she had already taken it out of her pants pocket and was tapping around on it, then she flipped it shut and said again:

– Sorry.

– No problem at all. You know, a few strange things happened during my time at the institute.

– It's the same for everyone in the beginning, said Frau Tätzel.

Herr Tätzel uttered a soft:

– Mmmh.

I told them about the costumes and the zone game in the yard.

– That's normal at that age, said Frau Tätzel. You don't have kids, I assume, do you?

I shook my head.

– Lots of things change, said Herr Tätzel. When kids are there. Right, Herbert?

– Yeeeah, Herbert Rauber said with a nod.

– I can imagine.

– And with a kid like Robert, well, even more things change, said Frau Tätzel. Do you still remember the first car ride with him?

– Oh, hahaha! said Herr Tätzel.

Herr Rauber sighed.

– That's why I bought that out there, said Herr Tätzel. The pickup. Because of the bed. The first long car ride with Robert, that I'll never forget. Robert was sick, and we drove him to the hospital. He wouldn't stop crying, and his belly was rock-hard. We were worried, of course.

And he told me about the initial slight dizziness as he laid the screaming baby on the backseat. His son had lain there completely doubled up, and due to his caution, due to his sympathy, he had lost precious seconds.

– Because I knew, of course, I didn't have more than a few minutes. After that the dizziness would become more intense, and I might have to throw up. I underestimated the first attack of vertigo, because I . . . haha . . . I started swerving around when I was out of the garage, remember?

Frau Tätzel smiled and nodded, yes, she still remembered well.

– The lights got weird after a while, that is, they looked weird.

– The lights?

– Well, the lights of the other cars and the streetlamps and . . . Have you ever read Oliver Sacks?

– Yes.

– It was exactly like that.

– Could you maybe describe it in a bit more detail? I asked.

– Well, the poor blood flow to the brain is of course to blame, at least I assume so. It also causes the splitting headache and the numb spots on the face. It's a really horrible condition, you know? You feel cold and hot simultaneously, your teeth chatter and at the same time you want to tear your clothes off.

– Did you have that feeling right after you set off for the hospital?

– No, I knew well you have to use the first five to six minutes, so I floored the gas pedal.

He laughed again.

– Determined, Frau Tätzel said suddenly. There's no other word for it. A determined intervention.

Unfortunately, now he could no longer drive a car due to his poly-arthritis, said Herr Tätzel. So his wife had to learn how. In general she had, after overcoming the worst phase of her life, taken the oars in both hands, so to speak. The oars, Herr Tätzel repeated, forming with his arms a sort of dinosaur beak in front of his face.

His wife laughed and patted him twice on the knee.

Unlike in the rest of the rooms in the house, in the living room only a single, very bright lightbulb hung from the ceiling, and its light flickered a bit at irregular intervals. The frequency was high enough that you noticed the flicker only if you concentrated.

– May I ask what you mean by *worst phase of her life*?

– I was depressed for a long time, said Frau Tätzel.

Her father put his large, benevolent paw on her shoulder and gave it a brief squeeze.

– The thought that evening was coming was enough to totally drag me down. Now it's light out, but later it will get dark. Now all the shops are open, but later they'll be closed, and I won't be able to buy anything, I'll be hungry and maybe even thirsty, since I don't drink the water from the tap because the calcium taste makes me sick. Thoughts like those, all day long.

– And that was . . . because of . . . ?

I realized that I had put my foot in my mouth.

– No, she said. No. It had nothing to do with that. So-called depression has, contrary to popular opinion, absolutely nothing to do with grief, exhaustion, despondency, or disappointment. Quite the opposite. In depressive stages of life, sadness would even be desirable. Salvation. I don't know whether you can relate to this at all, but depression means first and foremost a complete lack of interest. Everything seems boring and stale, and the state of curiosity is as far in the past as . . . well, farther than your own birth, you can't even remember ever having been interested in anything . . .

She looked at her husband, but he was playing with a hair on the back of his hand and didn't give her any sign whether she should continue.

– Of course, she went on, even depressed people can get through daily life and communicate with other people, but . . . but it's a tightrope act, and it can end at any time. Eventually you wake up and realize that there's no point in moving anymore, that there's no point in eating or drinking anymore, and that there's no point in taking care of your own kids anymore. It constricts your throat, and you can speak only with a very soft voice. I always tried to make clear to other people at the time what an immense exertion of strength it was for me to sit with them at a table and talk somewhat coherently. Most of them didn't understand that. It's as if you had to walk around with massively heavy clothing or in a diving suit. You've already visited every corner of your own head once, know all experiences you're capable of inside out.

She laughed and again looked at her husband, who was still occupied with the back of his hand.

– Right? she said.

He looked up. First he looked at me, then his wife.

– Mm-hmm, he said. It was on the whole a very difficult time back then. But in the end you did learn how to drive a car. You should see her, how she drives now.

– Sometimes depressed people begin to hurt themselves. With a needle or a bent-open paper clip. But that too, they soon realize, is pointless. Whether you bleed or not makes no difference worth mentioning, but—

Now Herr Tätzel took her hand, and immediately she stopped speaking and seemed enormously relieved.

I had attentively taken notes and leafed again through the last few pages in the notebook. It struck me that my handwriting had become virtually illegible. It had always had that tendency, but this here was really bad. On the three or four pages I had covered with writing in the last half an hour was nothing but little senseless clouds of lines, as if someone had tried in the dark, hanging upside down from a branch, to draw Kanji characters with a pen between his teeth. It was all unusable, I could throw it away . . .

— Sorry, I said. I think I made a mistake, I . . .

I felt dizzy. On top of that I was having trouble breathing, which was probably due to my folded-up sitting position. I stood up from the armchair. My left foot was numb.

— Is everything all right with you?

Supposedly I answered that question: I put my shoes on the wrong feet. But I don't remember that.

— I think I'll get going, I said. I'm somewhat . . .

When I said that, Frau Tätzel, her husband, and her father left the room. I remained behind by myself, swaying. After a brief time, Herr Tätzel returned and gestured to me to follow him. He wanted to show me something before I left, something really beautiful.

We went outside, to the front of the well-kept yard. The fresh air did me good, and the dizziness vanished. From here you could look over several neighboring yards directly into the parking lot of a large insurance company housed in a silver twin building built in the form of binoculars, which was surrounded by flagpoles from which lengths of fabric hung with a Sunday slackness.

Herr Tätzel pointed to the family vehicle, the pickup, which he hadn't driven for three years.

— Isn't it beautiful? he asked.

— Um, yeah, I said, stepping closer.

— The bed, he said.

He pulled a remote control out of his pocket. His arthritic fingers had difficulty activating it.

— She, he said with a sideways nod toward the house, she doesn't know that I still have this here.

He pressed the button, and the top of the pickup lifted. Slowly the roof folded into a pleasantly soft accordion form that had a soothing effect on the state of your own elbow and knee joints. Finally it retracted all the way, down into the bed of the pickup. I had never seen anything like that before.

— Wonderful, isn't it? said Herr Tätzel. Would you like to look inside?

— Sure, I said with a shrug.

He opened the driver's side door for me and had me take a seat behind the steering wheel. Then he opened the rear door, sat down on the backseat, and pressed another button on the remote control, which made the gate from the yard to the street open. Slowly and solemnly the two metal sides of the gate moved apart, an inviting gesture.

— The key is in the ignition, said Herr Tätzel. Isn't it wonderful?

— Yes, I said, nodding into the rearview mirror.

His eyes had taken on a strange expression. He looked several times back at the house.

— You have a driver's license, right? he said.

— Well, yes, I said, but it's a funny thing. I passed the driving test back then, but that was six years ago, and since then—

— Please, he said.

— What?

— Please, you just have to drive out and then take a right. I'll tell you then what to do next, okay?

— I don't understand.

— I'm begging you, really. It . . . well, you've seen what the climate is like in there, right? I mean, I saw how you were taking notes. You must have noticed that too. I'm sure you didn't just take down our trivial chatter. You know what's going on, don't you?

— Herr Tätzel, I don't know what you want from me.

I was about to get out, but a bent claw shot forward and pushed down the lock. I moved the hand aside and unlocked it again.

— What's this about?

— It's nothing, please, said Herr Tätzel. It's, ah, wait, I began completely wrong, the problem is just that I, that we, in a way, are under time pressure, you know? I'd be happy to explain everything to you during the drive, but for that you have to start driving first, okay?

— Is this supposed to be an abduction, or what?

— Why, no, please, no, you have it all wrong, I'm not intending to in some way ... but please, listen for a second, okay? I'm begging you, I'm really begging you to start the engine and to drive out, please.

— Okay, but why?

I placed my finger on the ignition key.

— Why? My God, we don't have to discuss everything to death right now! Please, I ... I'm sorry, Herr Setz, I didn't mean to shout, but we're under some time pressure, at any moment—

— Is this about Robert?

— I have to get out of here, Herr Setz, please help me.

— But if you want to get away, why don't you take a taxi or go to the train station, or—

— Please, said Herr Tätzel, please, I'm not prepared to put up with this treatment for one more ... I have to get out of here, before the interfe ... You don't understand at all what's going on, do you? You really haven't grasped anything, have you? You were actually only taking down our small talk? How can you not notice that!

— What? Tell me.

I stepped on the clutch in the hope that I remembered correctly how to start a car, and was about to turn the key.

— What are you guys doing there? said a cheerful voice coming from the patio door.

Frau Tätzel approached us. She had one hand hidden behind her back. Herr Tätzel stepped, as quickly as his physical impairment permitted, out of the truck, backed away from her, put the remote control on the edge of an empty rain barrel standing next to the truck, and took a few steps toward the house with his head hanging. In profile he looked exactly like Robert when he had trudged with the party hat across the Helianau yard.

I got out of the pickup too.

– He's really in love with our truck, said Frau Tätzel.

Her hand came out from behind her back. She was holding a thick oven mitt.

When Herr Tätzel saw the oven mitt, he turned around to face me again and said:

– Oh, well, then we'd better go back to the living room, huh?

Again the unpleasant light in the living room. I was on the verge of offering to change the buzzing, flickering lightbulb for them. Now I also noticed the removed lampshade lying right next to the patio door on the floor. I had seen it before, but had mistaken it for a silly model UFO.

– I have to get going, I said.

– Too bad, said Frau Tätzel.

Something moved at the edge of my visual field. When I tried to look at it directly, it slipped away into some blind spot and didn't come back until I turned my eyes again to Frau Tätzel, to the tea set on the little table, to the cell phone in her one hand and the oven mitt in the other. The indefinable thing on my periphery was light-colored, it even flickered a little, but at the same time it was bodiless and resembled cellophane, like the shadow of a water jet on a white wall.

The room suddenly spun around me, and the floor flew toward me as if I had stepped into a trap snapping shut. Fluid ran from my mouth and nose, unbearably hot and sour, I closed my eyes and tried to gather my strength, then I was suddenly back on my feet, and someone was supporting me, no, was pinning my arms behind my back, the vomit dripped from my chin, I tried to lift my head and understand my situation, but it didn't work, my upper body was bent forward so that walking became harder and harder, soon I collapsed again, and something heavy that had been behind me fell on me and caused me tremendous pain. In panic I wanted to free myself from it, kicked my feet, but something hard struck my head, and there was a bright flash in the same place where the cellophane-like thing had been before.

For a moment it was calm, and I could open my eyes and even make something out, but I felt terribly dizzy, I tried to cling to the floor to keep myself from plunging into emptiness, I pressed both hands against my head so that it couldn't move a millimeter, but everything was still spinning, it was as if I were lying on one of those rotating disks to which you allow yourself to be strapped in order to have your own body's contours traced with trembling blades by a knife thrower. I must have cried for help, and eventually someone came into the room, a small creature wearing jeans, an Adidas T-shirt, and a large diving bell on its head. The creature stood over me and reached out toward me. Then it was pulled aside.

I awoke with a splitting headache in a passenger seat. I kept calm, because I knew neither where I was nor whether the people accompanying me were well disposed toward me. Only once I was in the emergency room at the hospital did my memory gradually return. When Herr and Frau Tätzel and a man with a thick white beard who looked vaguely familiar to me took leave of me and wished me all the best, I even remembered what was going on and why I was here. The name of the young doctor who attended to me was Uhlheim. That was also the first word I said to him.

— Yes, that's my name, he said.

His tone clearly revealed that he thought I was an idiot. Or someone who had hit his head.

A few minutes after my arrival in the emergency room I had to fight off an unbearably strong feeling of déjà vu. All the actions happening around me appeared to me as if choreographed and performed for the hundredth time.

When I was home again and lay on my back in my bed, I thought: Someone drank from my health, and the glass was clearly half empty . . . *Drink your Health.*

Dodo, my feline attachment figure, to whom I always crawled when I had a problem, sat there so compactly with curled-up paws that she looked like a little rocking horse.

I had accidentally stepped on her tail when I had staggered into the room. The impossibility of apologizing to an animal. She hissed, puffed up her fur, ran away, and looked at me aghast from a distance. She didn't possess the categories *accident, apology, reconciliation.* But even worse and more disturbing was the eerie way she accepted my unmotivated outburst of violence—for that was how she must have perceived my blunder—as if it were the most natural thing in the world. A minute later she had forgotten everything, cleaned her fur, and let me pet her, but the uneasy feeling remained that always set in when the distorting mirror of your own clumsiness presented you with what you might actually have been capable of.

Now she sat next to me on the bed. I curled up into an egg under the blanket. For a while the room continued to spin around me. When I closed my eyes, I had the sensation of rotating while standing on my head, like an acrobat hanging from his rope in the circus. Only when I kept completely still and preempted every millimeter-movement my head involuntarily tried to make did the universe stop spinning. I remembered that Vincent van Gogh was said to have suffered from a condition known as Ménière's disease, which regularly caused such extreme attacks of vertigo. From that perspective, the cosmic swirls in his famous night paintings also struck me as completely natural, the swarming gardens and the houses with the brightly shimmering façades rising at a slant from the earth, the blurred faces of the harvesters and the confusing surge of a wheat field at midday, what else should he have painted? . . . I tentatively opened my eyes, and the room was somewhat slanted, but completely at rest. I blinked a bit and moved my eyeballs back and forth. Nothing.

I sat up. Dodo lay next to me, now curled up into a peaceful cat ball, her chin cushioned on her paws. When she noticed that I was looking at her she opened her eyes and lifted her head. I winked at her. She winked back politely. Then we lay down again. I dreamed that I was in Belgium. Somewhere in the countryside, among several low, white buildings. Behind me, in the distance, was a bus that had brought me here. And at my feet was a grave, no larger than a balcony vegetable patch, adorned with a fist-sized stone. It was the grave of that mouse with the human ear on its back. *Finally I have found it*, I thought in the dream, and awoke, my face sticky with tears.

On the wall next to my bed hung a painting by Max Ernst, *The Angel of Hearth and Home*, the sight of which usually made me happy, wherever I encountered the mysterious creature with the horselike head dancing across a plain in ecstatic laughter. Now I couldn't look at it, because I couldn't help imagining a child at the institute putting on this costume and then being taken away.

In the afternoon Julia came from work. She brought with her the smell of rats, hay, and feathers. She sat down next to me on the bed and asked me how the conversation had gone. Since I didn't answer, but only shook my head, she reached for the little violet plastic dinosaur on the nightstand and made it hop across my chest.

When she saw my injuries, she was alarmed.

Later, when I could get up and walk around again, we took a short walk. The air in the whole district smelled slightly burnt, but not unpleasant. Possibly a barbecue was taking place somewhere.

I described for Julia some interesting graffiti far up on the wall of a high rise near Oeverseepark. There are few things in a city that are as aesthetically satisfying as graffiti in unreachable places. It takes the eye only a second, and it sees the winged creatures that produce this work; equipped with several arms, they swing themselves over the architectural elements, smoothly and at a dangerous angle, and the gaze of the viewer reconstructs their feats of climbing, reminiscent of Marvel superheroes, which are necessary to reach all those wonderful impossible spots: the cross bracing of the steel structure in the middle of a bridge; the projecting part of a building, far from all balconies; the inside of a tunnel that is in use twenty-four hours a day; or the outer wall of elevators—I remembered having read of a case like that once years ago. In the course of the alteration of a twenty-two-story building in Vienna, the elevator shaft was widened and the car replaced with a new, larger one. When the workers removed the old one, they saw that every centimeter on the outside of the metal box that usually floated up and down on its steel cable was covered with tags and spray-painted love scenes. Out of sheer helplessness, the workers reportedly had the old elevator car immediately disposed of.

Julia noticed that I was talking more slowly than usual.

— I can't see clearly anymore, I said. Everything has become difficult.

— In what way?

— My forehead feels funny, I said.

At home I sat down at my desk and organized the contents of the red-checkered folder a bit. I read in Norman Cohn's fascinating study *The Pursuit of the Millennium: Revolutionary Millenarians and Mystical Anarchists of the Middle Ages* about various rituals involving the exclusion of children, photocopied the relevant pages from the book, and placed them in the folder. In the German and Austrian countryside it was apparently custom until well into the eighteenth century to marry a chosen child couple symbolically on New Year's Day, Cohn wrote, to dress them in white fur and declare them untouchable for a week. No one was permitted to respond or react to them when he encountered them on the street, they were completely on their own, if they stole things, they weren't punished, and they were ignored even when they begged desperately to abandon the game. They were *ritualistically invisible,* as Cohn puts it. For that week these children, known as *Riedln* or *Riedser,* were also not to be let into anyone's house and had to acquire food and shelter themselves. (Most of the time, however, small packages of emergency provisions were left in a previously arranged place by their parents and close family members.) This custom was not regarded as punishment, for after the week spent in total social isolation the children were reaccepted into the village community in a solemn ceremony and rewarded with abundant gifts.

While I leafed through and sorted the excerpts and pieces of paper in the red-checkered folder, I listened to some of the 555 sonatas by Scarlatti on CD, which had been recorded in their entirety in the eighties by the American virtuoso Scott Ross, who could play the harpsichord more finely and majestically than anyone else. For him a trill was not merely a quick back-and-forth between two notes, but rather could express anything, the anxious trembling of a stuck joint, the threatening rattle of a rattlesnake, the grumble in the belly of a hungry person, the fluttering of a flag in the wind, the impatient pulsing of certain stars in the night sky.

PART IV

If I were perfect, I would believe everything I heard.

—William T. Vollmann, The Rainbow Stories

It seems that communication always tends to be in favor
of the receiver. It gathers around him as moths gather
around a flame.

—Charles A. Ferenz-Hollereith

1. The Easter Island Head

[GREEN FOLDER]

How wonderful is the solemn emptiness that permeates the weeks after the last sign of life from an incessant anonymous phone caller: He now breathes once again for himself alone, without anyone else hearing. Possibly he has died, as silently and secretly as an insect on a house wall, has folded up his six little legs and has expired. They have become rare, these callers, who a decade or so ago still numbered in the thousands. Nowadays there might be no more than a handful in all Europe, the last, basically precious representatives of their kind, who still rise now and then from their bed and drag themselves on all fours to the old rotary phone in the corner . . .

In the first weeks of the year 2007, I had been called so often by the unknown person, who had never wanted to say anything, that I started taking phone calls only when I recognized the number. When I saw Frau Stennitzer's name light up on my muted cell one day, I answered.

– Hello?

– Herr Setz? How are you? This is Gudrun Stennitzer.

– Good evening, Frau Stennitzer. Nice to hear from you.

– Yes, she said. Nice. Nice, I don't know. It's kind of you, anyway, to say my phone call is nice.

– Has something happened?

– I had a very silly thought, she said. I thought: *You haven't abandoned us, Herr Setz, have you?* Haha. I mean, because you stopped answering your phone. It can't be that you have bad memories of us, right? I heard that you went to Brussels—

– Who told you that?

– I don't remember . . . You know, I just wanted you to know that you're welcome to visit us anytime. That's a fact. That is to say: Our hospitality still stands, you know?

There was a brief pause.

– Thank you very much, I said.

– Oh, don't mention it, really, you know . . . This isn't actually relevant, but Christoph mentioned that he . . . he said he wishes you all the best. He said that, really.

– Oh, thank you very much. I hope he liked my articles.

– Oh, you're much too modest. Has that never occurred to you? You're always so defensive and . . . well, I'd already noticed that during your visit.

– Is that right? Well, yes, I might be a bit defensive sometimes, that might be true . . .

– We wanted to assure you, anyway, that we would be happy if you . . . Ah, what else can I say . . . ?

I was silent and waited.

– Everything is pretty much good with us, yeah, said Frau Stennitzer. But now we have a new problem, haaaa . . .

– What is it?

– Oh, it's not your fault, of course, Herr Setz, but . . . haaaa.

I waited.

– Those teenagers were here again, said Frau Stennitzer. And they . . . aahh, what's the best way to put it? . . . they interfered. Again. Now I have to think really carefully about the next steps.

– What did they do?

– Hm. You know, I'm wondering right now how you can ask that. I mean, you mentioned them in your article, didn't you?

– Yes, I did.

Frau Stennitzer paused. It sounded as if she were taking a drag from a cigarette. *Just going out for a few minutes to get cigarettes. Underground vaults.*

– When he came home afterward, Frau Stennitzer said with an embittered tone in her voice. With his wet hair and the chlorine smell everywhere, I just couldn't believe it! That was truly . . . it was unreal. On Kenny.

– On whom?

– Uncanny. Don't you know the word?

– Ah, yes, uncanny.

– Yes, that was really uncanny, said Frau Stennitzer. I immediately recognized him, of course, but he had changed so much on the whole, in his essence.

– So where had he been?

Again she paused, and seemed to be gathering all her energy for the unpleasant information she unfortunately had to impart:

– At a swimming pool.

– At a swimming pool? You mean, he was swimming.

– Uncanny, she said, and laughed sharply. You should have seen his face, Herr Setz! Christoph isn't usually like that.

Through the telephone I could hear her shaking her head. Perhaps she had even closed her eyes. And perhaps her head was resting on the back of a chair.

– Okay, Frau Stennitzer, I said, I'm afraid I have to go, but—

– They took him to a swimming pool!

– Yes, I got that.

– And you think nothing of it?

– They probably meant no harm.

She made a shocked noise and swallowed. As if a chance passerby had suddenly spat into her mouth.

– They didn't even know if he could swim, she said. That didn't matter to them at all. They care only about their . . . dares, their sweat cure, the ability to hold out, keep holding out, the zone . . . They learned it from their parents, no question, they learned it from their parents! For the façade deceives. They only look like neglected youth, with shaved heads or spiky hair, but in reality they're the kids of well-off people here. You can tell by their shoes. And I should know, because they've left their shoes often enough outside Christoph's little house!

– Okay, I said. That's probably true.

– Skipping school, listening to music, hanging around under the Zetschn Bridge, that's what they do all day, and when they come home, the gold Mastercard is waiting for them.

– Mm-hmm.

– I really don't know what they were thinking. To parade him in that way like a circus horse! And he, he puts up with everything! His air mattress . . . came back wet. It was lying outside his door in the grass and drying.

At that point she could have easily burst into tears. But she didn't. I heard only the cigarette-like sound again.

– But the air mattress is meant for water, I said.

– Excuse me?

– The air mattress is—

– He reads on it! It's his reading mattress! He couldn't read on it for a whole day, because it was wet.

– Frau Stennitzer?

– What?

– I think I have to hang up now, out there . . . people are waiting for me.

– Where?

– Here in my yard. Something is burning.

With that I hung up.

Julia entered the room.

– Do you know what your voice sounds like when you're lying? she asked.

She went to the window and opened it. Outside the sun shone.

– What?

– Like you swallowed a spoon.

– Swallowed a spoon.

– Yeah, imagine you're eating a yogurt, okay? And then you get too greedy and accidentally swallow the spoon along with it. But it gets stuck in your throat. Like in those X-ray images. You know? Where some weird Americans have swallowed impossible objects.

– That's what I sound like?

– Yeah. Haven't you ever noticed that?

– And what do you sound like when you're lying?

– What, you don't know?

– No.

– Men, said Julia, shaking her head.

The year 2007 had begun with other irritations as well. They almost always involved peculiar blots. On the house wall next to our balcony a huge fungal mark had formed that could be washed away neither by rain nor by the water we sprayed on it with the garden hose. It had a reddish color and gave off an unpleasant odor reminiscent of old potato cellars. That odor often penetrated to us in the apartment, especially in the kitchen, where I liked to work, so I left the house more often and spent time in various places where I wouldn't be disturbed or spoken to.

One day in March I sat in a small café near the large meat processing plant that dominates our district. It was already early evening, and I had nothing to do but wait patiently until a rather large tea stain on my pants had dried. If I stood up now, it would have looked as if I had had an embarrassing accident. After some time a man sat down at one of the other tables. A monocle hung from his vest, or maybe it was a pocket watch. He looked at me. At first I evaded his eyes, then I met them: *What is it?* The man nodded and pulled an edition of *National Geographic* out of his bag.

It was obviously the issue in which the second part of my article "In the Zone" had appeared. He turned page after page, now looked elsewhere, yawned pointedly and turned the page again, acted astonished, as if he had discovered something unusual. His posture changed, and his expression became serious and focused. Then he began to tear some pages out of the magazine. I stood up and was about to approach him. But before I could take the first step, he had already walked out of the café. I followed him, but he had disappeared.

For several minutes I stood, at a loss and intimidated, on the street under a lamp that remained dark despite the advanced hour.

Disconcerted, I returned home and immediately lay down in bed, but I couldn't fall asleep for a long time. At some point I drifted away in a sort of canoe that was partly a balcony. At night I was visited by a white animal with a large skull, sad and pensive-looking, which it dragged with difficulty but, as it seemed to me, without particular haste to the foot of my bed: one of those gigantic ornamental heads of stone with the narrowed eyes of someone weeping, a large geometrical nose, and a broad-lipped mouth, from which, as if in tacit admission of great helplessness or guilt, a single coarsely grooved incisor jutted. The animal stopped at the foot of my bed and began to grind its head on the creaking metal post. It made a strenuous effort, and soon it managed to separate the head from its torso. With a satisfied heavy breath the head fell on the floor. What remained of the animal was a white fur ball, without limbs or discernible entrances and exits, a white, thick-haired sack that moved back and forth in rhythmic contractions, as if it were still breathing. I touched it with the tip of my foot—and it suddenly let out bloodcurdling screams and wails, but after a few minutes it went silent again, and the two parts, which had now without doubt been entrusted to decay, lay lifeless at the foot of my bed: the stone head and the fur sack, both frozen in a sort of solemn meaninglessness. For fear that the spectacle might, if I paid attention to it any longer, repeat endlessly, I pulled the blanket over my head. When, about a minute later, dazed, with difficulty breathing, I tore it from my face, I was lying in total darkness. I groped around and grabbed hold of one of the plastic buttons that formed a row on one side of the blanket. The button was pleasantly cool, and as in the case of a stranger's earlobe, which, through a lucky chain of circumstances, you grab hold of for the duration of a blessed moment, it was very soothing to touch it. To reassure myself that everything, at least in rough outline, was still as I knew it, I moved my head back and forth on the pillow and noticed that it was soaked with sweat, so I sat up and turned it over. But when I picked up the pillow, I realized that, without knowing it, I had been lying all night on soft bog soil, only a thin sheet and the pillow separated me from mud and black, stagnant water.

I hadn't told Julia anything about that. The strange vision had not returned, and I didn't want to worry her. She was glad that I had begun to work at a normal school. I had only a half-time teaching commitment, and didn't have to get up as early as when I had been employed at the Helianau Institute.

The Factors That Must Be Taken into Account

Soon I received another call from Gudrun Stennitzer.

– Hey, she said.

– Oh, hello, Frau Stennitzer, I said. How are you doing?

– Well, yeah, where to begin, how am I doing, ah, yeah, how am I doing, anyway? Ah . . .

She seemed to be out of breath.

– How's Christoph? Has he recovered from . . . ?

A button on the telephone was pressed. *Tooot.*

– I actually wanted to tell you about that last time we spoke, said Frau Sten-

nitzer. Tell you about the changes that have . . . well . . . happened, one after
another, and everything . . . ah, yes, what else . . .

You could hear paper being crumpled up relatively close to the phone.

– Changes?

– Ah, yes, you must know how it is. *Panta rhei*, everything changes. Is always in
flux. Nothing remains the way you once fixed it in your mind. Christoph . . . well,
he coped relatively well with the outing. The mattress has of course been dry for
quite a while too, in the meantime. He's reading again now, thank God. And . . .
yeah, so he still remembers you well, of course. Your visit.

– I'm glad to hear it.

– Well, under the circumstances, he's doing . . . well, actually, no, of course not,
how should he be doing? You know, I really wanted to call you again, to make
contact, as it were, because I would otherwise feel so left alone, you know?

– Left alone in what way?

A heavy, impatient exhalation from Frau Stennitzer.

Then she said:

– The awful thing is that you're always wise only in hindsight. I assume you
know the feeling. That you're wiser afterward than beforehand. And those two
articles back then and everything, that was really, well . . . I certainly got wiser, I
definitely wanted to tell you that. By phone. If not face-to-face.

– Did you dislike the article? I asked. I sent you both parts back then. Okay, it was
shortened quite a bit afterward, and the pictures were added . . .

– Yeah, yeahyeahyeah, all that, yeah, sure, I know that, of course . . . sure . . . I just
wanted, so that no misunderstandings arise, I just wanted . . . all that didn't do
Christoph good, you know? He, I mean . . . he was already introverted before, but
the article and everything, that was, well . . . and then the swimming pool, that
was more symptomatic, you know? I mean, it was only an indoor pool, but still.

Another heavy exhalation. I sat down on the bed.

– Hold on, I'm going to switch to the headset, then we can talk better.

– Headset, no, not necessary, exclaimed Frau Stennitzer. I wanted anyway—

I pretended I didn't hear her anymore, took my time with the plugging in and
the finding of the correct angle between microphone and lips.

– Hello? I then said. I'm back. This way we can talk better.

– Yes, Frau Stennitzer said with a crumpled voice. I didn't want to bother you long. Christoph didn't cope well with the move, and then there was your article, and now the absence of his friends too—pshaw, he still calls those filthy skin-heads his friends, ridiculous . . .

– Wait, I said. I didn't really understand. Did you move?

– Yes, don't you remember? When you visited us? The boxes in the garage and everything, well, sure, you were there for only two days, in that case people see only what they have to see, I guess. For the job, haha.

– I really didn't notice. And Christoph's friends stopped coming, you say?

– Well, it's better that way. They should feel free to stay away.

– Tell me, Frau Stennitzer, have I maybe done something to upset you? I asked carefully. Because what you're saying sounds a little bit like—

– No, no, no, exclaimed Frau Stennitzer, and you sensed that somewhere in the world a fist was clenching. I didn't mean to suggest anything like . . . But the situation, the . . . events have simply been happening too fast since then. The fact that the move became necessary, after your article, that had obviously been foreseeable, and of course I had thought carefully about all that beforehand, or else I wouldn't have let you into my life, you understand.

She laughed. It was a deep, throaty laugh, which lacked any trace of relief.

– I'm sorry if my articles have had negative consequences, I said. So what exactly happened? Did the people in the town harass you—

– No, no, you misunderstand me, oh, I've really expressed myself wrong. It's just that for a while events have, in a way, been happening too fast, and that was simply too much for Christoph. But he doesn't mean it like that.

– What doesn't he mean like that?

– Well, I didn't want to bother you with that.

– You're not bothering me, Frau Stennitzer. Please tell me. What's the matter with Christoph?

– Well, she said, taking a big, crunching bite of an apple, so close to the phone that I could feel first the resistance and then the sensation of bursting apple skin in my own jaw. Well, his friends stopped coming after the visit to the swimming pool, and that threw him for a loop. It is, of course, also the stage in life when everything looks somehow dark. And there are of course always many factors that must be taken into account.

– Such as . . . ?

– Oh, well, testing limits, for example. That is, of course, a big part of that stage. Bitterly big.

She took another bite of the apple, and I had a sudden vision in which the apple stood red before my eyes. A red balloon right in front of Frau Stennitzer's face. The wrinkles around her mouth, which tauten when she bites.

– And what problems is he now having exactly?

– Well, she said, taking a deep breath. It's definitely not your fault. Your visit, back then. And the two articles. I wouldn't want you to think *that.*

– But what—

– Kids say a lot and of course also do a whole lot of things that they shouldn't do. In that respect they are like . . . like . . .

She seemed to be unable to think of any fitting comparison. Instead came another, somewhat softer apple bite.

– But that sounds very alarming, I said into the headset. So is he not doing okay?

– Everything heals. As I said, testing limits. Is a big part of that stage. And of course you can't disregard all the other factors either.

– Yes, you're probably right. But I still don't know—

– A man from the APUIP was here and took a look at him. Herr Baumherr recommended him to us.

– APUIP. That's that equal treatment organization?

– Well, they're sometimes portrayed that way. But they actually do more charitable things, like . . . You don't know Herr Baumherr?

– Not personally, no.

– He's from Vienna, Frau Stennitzer said, chewing the apple. And he really knows a lot about such cases. In the past he has overseen several relocations.

Somewhere, in a distant land, a needle was stuck in the eye of a voodoo doll with my facial features.

– Wait a second, Frau Stennitzer, he's done what?

She sighed.

– Christoph is doing really badly. He is . . . I mean, he tried . . . Aahhh . . . All this is really difficult, you know? I'm not asking for everything to come to a happy end for me, I mean, I'm not asking that of the world. Not after all I've been through. But the outcome should at least be fair . . . Yes, fair . . .

– Did Christoph try to do away with himself?

– As I said, Herr Setz, you shouldn't let it trouble you. I didn't want to bother you with this. So I'm going to . . .

She took a loud, cracking bite of the apple, sucked in the overflowing juice, apologized softly, and hung up.

A little plastic dinosaur hopped across my shoulder. Julia had linked arms with me, we walked along the late-winter streets of the district, and she played with the little animal. She jokingly called the plastic dinosaur my therapist.

– It's a strange world, I said. I don't understand anymore where . . . what . . . the poor boy has psychological problems, and she calls that strange guy from Vienna, that association for equality for . . . Oh, how should I know what they're for?

– You shouldn't get so caught up in this thing, Julia said, sliding the violet dino through her fingers. You've been away from the institute for a long time. You've written the two articles. Your constant headaches are better. And I'm happy that you're home more.

– I think there's something bad . . .

– What?

– I mean, they're doing some odd things, I don't know, I couldn't find out, for example, what relocations really are. Everyone uses the word as if it were completely normal, and then that weird tunnel project, and now the poor boy, I mean, you should have seen him, he had that huge cardboard mask on, when I visited them that time, that's not normal—

Julia took my hand.

– You're talking much too fast, she said. Your thoughts can't catch up.

– And then Ferenz.

– Who?

– I have no idea who he is. Or what. But back then I heard Dr. Rudolph on the telephone—

– The one who gave you the black eye?

– Yes, yes, but that doesn't matter. He was talking to him on the phone, and he mentioned that student whose parents . . .

The enormous mass of details to explain agglomerated in front of me, and I could no longer go on.

– None of that has to do with you.

– But then why does that woman call me and imply that it's my fault her son is doing badly?

– Because she's stupid.

– I don't know. There's something else. Maybe I should ask that guy, that Baumherr, from the APUIP in Vienna, I mean, he must know what this is all about. Frau Stennitzer told me on the phone that he was involved in relocations and that he—

– Clemens, not so fast. It's impossible to keep up!

We walked along silently side by side for a while. On a sewer grate, folded up and as if poised for a frog leap, was a lost glove. Light brown leather, little holes in the fingers.

– Look, I said.

Julia looked at the ground.

– There, I said, showing her the glove.

She approached it and touched it with the toe of her shoe.

– Poor thing, she said.

We walked on.

– Have you written any more?

– Of what?

– Of what I advised you to write. Your diversionary story. The one about the student who gets older and—

– Yeah, yeah, yeah, I said. Hey, you know what that graffiti thing over there says?

– What?

– Do your laundry.

– You're making that up.

– No, really, that's what it says. Do your laundry.

– Sure, said Julia.

– And that house there has a weathercock, which is actually an owl.

Julia took my arm again and pressed it tighter against her.

– Uh-huh, she said. And what does the owl look like?

– Like a weathercock, I said, and we laughed.

At the Kalvariengürtel underpass we found the second glove, the mirror image of the first. It lay in a similar position on the ground, next to a snow-filled public trash receptacle.

– Oh, said Julia, now we have to turn around and get the other one. Damn.
Silently we set off.

– The loneliness of gloves, I said.

– Clemens? Can you try something?

– What?

– Can you try to distance yourself a bit more from all this stuff?

– That's hard. Why don't you try to distance yourself from your animals?

– Okay. But don't go to Vienna to see this Baum person, all right? Call him first.
Like normal people do.

2.   You Have to Respect
the Wood, Robin

An unmistakable sign of the colder season: momentarily mistaking every speck of dust, every mark for a bug, for a sitting fly. Then the continual disappointment that it's nothing, only a paint spot or a crack in the plaster. Everywhere, on the outside of the building, the walls in the courtyard, but especially in the air, the little creatures were missing. Only memories provided comfort. Like the one of the time, while strolling on the institute grounds, on the way up to the so-called Preiner Meadow, he passed a swarming anthill and was suddenly filled with an intense solace in light of the thought that he would one day be scattered among many, many tiny insects.

Robert felt good, but strangely worn out. Exhausted. Like the damp bottom of a well shaft. He listened on his iPod to the new album by The Resurrection of Laura Palmer in an endless loop, while reading an American science fiction novel called *Nuclear Family Therapy* about a married couple, George and Jody, and their little daughter Danielle. Cordula had pressed it into his hand. *Here, read this. Might take your mind off things.* The family in the novel leaves the planet earth in a homemade rocket to find a new home on an asteroid. They simply couldn't stand it on earth anymore, especially the father, George, he had been in a boundary dispute with his neighbor for years. Besides, the earth is radioactively contaminated. The carping begins already during the launch, Jody chides George for firing the engines a few seconds early, and on the next fourteen pages there's nothing but quarreling. They land on the asteroid and build a house, which is likewise accompanied by constant fighting and yelling and the breaking of small, defenseless things. Danielle is usually completely calm, or perhaps in a sort of fear paralysis, but sometimes she joins in a conflict between her parents and screams inarticulately and shrilly. Then she is reprimanded sternly by both of them, told to stay out of things she doesn't understand. Eventually the beer runs out. The pantry is relatively small, and because Jody was responsible for the construction of the family rocket, George accuses her in a raised voice of doing it on purpose. Of course, she yells back, do you think I want to live with a drunk for the rest of my life? And so on, the next sixty pages are also filled with quarreling. Then George enters Danielle's room and wakes her up. He presses twenty units of earth money into her hand and says to her: Would you please get me a few crates of beer, dear? But Dad, says Danielle, it's already so late, and the earth is radioactive . . . Don't worry, George says with a trembling voice, it's not so bad if you stay in the zone for only a really short time, just quickly in and out, you can fire the rocket yourself, okay? And he swings the ignition key over her head.

Robert threw the book into a corner. With a heavy breath he stood up, yanked the earbuds out of his ears, and walked across the room, then he reached for the jeans that happened to be lying on the floor in front of him and began to pull and tug at them. Of course, the material was too tough, he couldn't tear it. He pulled for a while longer, until he ran out of strength, then he strode to Cordula.

— Why'd you give me such nonsense to read?

— Robert! Your face is all red. What happened?

— What happened? You gave me ridiculous trash to read, that's what happened!

— Don't shout like that. Did you dislike it?

Robert didn't know what to say. Maybe she was trying to drag him down. She sat completely calm on a kitchen chair next to the window, with one knee bent, smoking and looking out. In front of her was the ashtray he had given her as a gift. He saw himself taking the ashtray and beating her with it. But then he said:

– It's not funny at all.

– Really? Well, I found it pretty amusing. How far along are you? Have they met the extraterrestrial therapist yet?

Robert shook his head.

– I'm going to . . . , he said. You know.

He pointed to his mouth and formed thumb and forefinger into a pill.

– Okay, said Cordula, turning back to the view of the city.

Roofs, balconies, satellite dishes. Building cranes, clouds.

After Robert had taken a dose of Sviluppal, he stood at the window and waited for the effects. Little chemical puzzle pieces were at this moment spreading in his body and searching for a compatible neighbor, a docking station. In the courtyard nothing moved, most of the leaves had already fallen, and that hadn't made the world any prettier.

Near the bicycles Robert spotted Frau Rabl and her son. He recognized her by the jacket. It was the same one she had worn when she had rung his doorbell. It was always the same one. His neighbor stood directly in front of her son. In her hand she held a jar of jelly from which she took little tastes with a spoon and fed them to the boy. With some bites he screwed up his face as if the jelly were terribly sour, with others he looked completely normal, though it was always the same jar.

Robert was surprised how little hate he felt at that moment. He imagined someone going for the kid with an axe, but it felt totally wrong. Odd. In his head he even took the axe out of the shadowy figure's hand and drove him away with it. Strange.

When he opened the window, he heard the noise of a small parade, which must have been moving very nearby down one of the narrow, winding lanes of the district. Some high-pitched cheers wafted over to him at full volume. He quickly closed the window again.

That evening Willi and his new girlfriend came for a visit. Willi was fast when it came to the discarding of old girlfriends and the finding of new ones. With this one here, Magda, who was very pretty but not boring, he already had his problems. And he made no secret of them.

— But the worst! Willi snapped, raising a forefinger. The worst is when she, after she has gone to the bath . . . Do you have anything against my telling them, sweetie?

Magda, whose profile in Robert's head still occasionally merged with Elke's, made a couldn't-care-less-sweetie gesture with her shoulders. Willi laughed with relief and went on:

— So when she goes to the bathroom and . . . makes . . . okay? Well, I mean, when she's finished, okay? Then she stands up, of course, dabs herself (he imitated the female way of wiping with toilet paper the last drops of urine, as if it were a profoundly ridiculous idea to use paper when nature gave us underpants for that) and, well, then . . . (he chuckled because he had caught the hard-to-interpret look of his new girlfriend) . . . and then she comes out and asks whether I by any chance have to go too, because that way we can save water.

— What? said Cordula.

— Well, to save water and such. If both of us take a piss and flush only once, then— Don't look at me like that!

— But you ruin it when you tell it like *that*, said Magda. You make it sound as if I were forcing you. It's only an idea, to help the planet.

— By looking at what you've left behind every time I take a pee?

— Oh, you're such a rhinoceros, she said, giving him a respectful, overly cute poke with her forefinger.

Robert had to look away. His hand felt the underside of the table. He found a screw, pushed the sharp edge of the screw head, which stuck out a few millimeters, under his fingernail. What would it be like to inhale hundreds of tiny flies and choke to death on them? The inner buzzing, the beating of the wings . . .

— Water will become increasingly scarce on this planet in the next fifty years, said Magda. The next war will be over drinking water.

Cordula nodded gravely.

— But if I can't even go to the bathroom by myself anymore, said Willi, then the planet can fuck off.

Outside the window a V-2 rocket soundlessly hit the ground. Robert felt the explosion under his fingernail. He pulled the hand out from under the table and examined the wound. A little red shimmer.

– Besides, we can fight for water, said Willi. It's not really disappearing, as if it were being siphoned by aliens, but rather it's being polluted. She's right about that, of course.

– I don't think it's a bad idea at all, said Cordula. I mean, saving water. Whenever Robert takes a bath, I think: *My God, those tons of clean drinking water.* But we could bathe in the river too.

– Like in India, said Magda.

– In the Ganges? said Willi. My God, that filthy muck. Well, it's actually mainly a population control measure, that river. I mean, in India, where such a vast number of people live anyway, slums, one-armed children who play the flute, and how should I know what else, so they just invented that Hindu religion, where they don't go into a church like normal people but instead go into that river and pray there in the waves. And the river is full of *E. coli* bacteria and dead rats and so on.

– Ew, said Cordula.

– Why do you always have to suck the beauty out of everything? asked Magda.

Willi held up his hands.

– I find it bizarre, said Robert.

Everyone looked at him, happy that he was joining the conversation. Robert had to turn away again. But he went on:

– Yeah, I find it bizarre how many movies are produced every year in India.

– Oh, my God, Bollywood! said Willi.

How readily they pounced on his topic. Include him. The burnt-out dingo. He felt for the comforting, pain-giving screw, but could no longer find it.

– Everything always turns into a musical! said Willi. *Hamlet?* Musical. *Superman?* In the end they dance and sing. Even the life of Abraham Lincoln was made into a movie by them, and at one point there's a brawl between abolitionists and anti-abolitionists in a bar, and then they sing again and dance around a veiled woman ... India in general, a totally bizarre TV country. They had this show where some kid played Michael Jackson.

– An action series? asked Robert.

– No, a sort of talent show. And a kid danced like Michael Jackson. Totally gay.

– Hey! said Cordula.

Willie went on:

– But what I don't get: Why does a young guy dress up as a pedophile? I mean, that's creepy, in a way. It's a Möbius strip.

– That hasn't been proven, said Magda.

– Michael is alive, said Robert.

– That too, Willi agreed with him. Why does a boy dress up as a pedophile? Why not at least as Elvis?

– Because he's dead, said Robert.

– But he wasn't even ... , began Cordula. You guys always have to condemn everyone even though they didn't do it!

– True, like the flayer, my math teacher!

– What? asked Magda.

– Anyway, these Möbius strips make me totally sick, said Willi.

– You always talk such nonsense! said Magda.

She said it appreciatively.

– Snakes biting their own tails in general, said Willi. And besides, where does a kid like that get the idea to move in that way? A dance that has been dead for so many years. They should work in mines instead, break stones and such. Or beg—have you seen those drugged-out kids who roam around the city and beg in cafés? How should I know what they do, probably sniff glue. When they stand next to me, I swear, it comes up to here—(Willi indicated with a hand in front of his chest a rising water level)—and then I lose it. I become violently ill around those kids. I always look around automatically to check whether an iBall is hanging somewhere.

Robert laughed and gestured to the corner.

– Come on, you're mean! said Magda.

A second of silence.

– Oh, shit, said Willi. I'm always putting my foot in my mouth. My mistake.

Magda gave a pained laugh and stared at Robert.

– I'm not your mistake, Robert said to Willi. You can call me cupcake, but not mistake.

Willi laughed with relief.

– You craven bastard, said Robert. Shall we fight it out? Kung fu?

– I would totally humiliate you, sensei, said Willi, presenting the sides of his hands. I give you a one-punch KO Bruce Lee combination.

Robert stood up and did the typical Bruce Lee bow: stick-stiff, with tense chest muscles, accompanied by a high-pitched:

– Ooohhh.

Willi nudged Magda:

– Didn't I tell you? He's a natural talent, this guy.

Robert sat down again. His heart was beating as if he had just committed a bank robbery.

– I trained with Chuck Norris, he said. I can make people puke with my mere presence.

Magda's face became serious.

Willi laughed cautiously. Cordula was pale.

– Who's Chuck Norris? asked Magda.

– You're too young, said Willi.

You have to respect the wood, Robin, Robert told himself, imagining the side of his hand breaking through the material. A single precise chop. Bones and tendons and joint fluid.

– Classic kung fu movies are always about the suspension of gravity, said Willi.

Robert looked directly at Magda. Okay, she was Willi's new girlfriend. And she was really good-looking. Nineties wide-rimmed glasses, somewhat out of fashion, but the spider web thing over her chest looked good on her. Accentuated her breasts.

– Yes, said Robert. Those fidgety little Asians, they're like fish in a tank, aren't they? If they move fast enough, they might even be able to fly. You're right.

– Sounds exciting, said Magda.

Willi put a hand on her shoulder.

– There's also a shot like that in the classic Easterns by the Shaw Brothers. All before our birth, but still the most sublime thing you've ever seen. The backward leap. It's actually a shot of a fighter who is simply jumping in a majestic way (Robert raised his arms in an improvised dragon fight pose) down from an elevated area, but then it's played backward so that it looks like he's leaping up backward. That really does look like flying.

Magda smiled.

– You know, a piece of gum would look really good in your mouth, Robert said to her.

He felt Cordula touching him gently with her foot under the table.

– Careful with your foot, he said to her, then he turned to Magda: What kind of gum would you prefer? I mean, the choice of gum is really important, much more important than, for example, the choice of a tie or a certain hairstyle.

– I don't like gum, said Magda.

– No? That's really too bad, said Robert. I would have liked to see it.

– Ha, said Willi.

It sounded less like a laugh, more like the bark of a dog who registers that a stranger is approaching the gate to the yard.

– Yes, he knows all about old movies, said Cordula, gesturing to Robert. But try dragging him to a movie theater . . .

– Kung fu, said Robert. You have to respect the wood. Even if you have a thick, fat, dumb block of wood in front of you, and it looks at you so damn stupidly and even brought along its new, smaller wooden block friend, you still have to respect it and . . . well, yeah, respect it. That's the most you can do. The rest takes care of itself.

He did a karate chop on the table.

– Ah, he said. You see? I didn't respect this wood here enough.

Everyone was silent. Magda twisted her mouth a bit to one side, which might have been the hint of a smile.

– Oh, now everyone's looking at me, said Robert. I've made a fool of myself. But just don't take me seriously, I . . . I don't know myself what got into me just now. Sometimes that's just the way I am, gum, well, hahaha, it can't be helped, from time to time, you know—

Willi began to laugh. It was long overdue.

– Shit, there's nothing in the world funnier than Robert apologizing, he said. I might have been able to keep a straight face even longer, but my face muscles hurt.

Magda now laughed too.

Robert stood up and gave a hint of a bow. Then he walked once around the table and pulled a pack of gum from the inside pocket of his jacket, which lay on a chair next to the peacefully wobbling newspaper. He took out a piece of gum and threw it to Willi, who caught it and laughed even louder.

Cordula had placed both hands on the table. She wasn't looking at anyone.

Willi dropped the piece of gum on the table and pounded it with his fist until it was completely flat.

– Respect, the, gum! Like so . . .

Robert laughed. Then he said:

– Hey, Willi, why do you bring a different woman with you every time you come over here?

– Boo! Willi said, and looked at Magda.

She looked as if she had been caught, Robert thought.

– Did she want to see me, hm? he asked. Visit the dingo?

– Hey, now, hold on, said Willi, raising his hand.

– I didn't want to see anyone, said Magda, turning red.

– Ah, now I know where I've seen you before, Robert said to her. In one of those parades that are constantly going on!

It was silent.

– That's not a joking matter, said Willi.

– My God, are you serious today! Robert said with a laugh. Now respect the damn wood and the stupid gum already and be quiet.

– Hey, speaking of respect, said Willi. Your face is all red again, my dear friend. Don't laugh too much, or else . . . I mean, if you have to go to the bathroom, now would still be a chance. Later, who knows . . .

Magda cried out when Robert flung himself at Willi. She was knocked off her chair and fell under the table. Cordula tried to pull Robert away from Willi, but he developed crazy strength when he was angry and desperate.

– Stop, please! she begged him. Stop!

She somehow managed to squeeze herself between the two men. Robert punched her in the stomach.

and perhaps they are indeed, as FELIX ADAMSKI-SCHREBER (ADAMSKI-SCHREBER, 1993) asserts, a relic, salvaged into our epoch via invisible temporal channels, from older days of terrestrial mammals, when they were still completely determined by the topological contingencies of the surrounding terrain, bouncing off each other like billiard balls or inadvertently mating and spawning a new being. Like the infinite chessboard in the *Game of Life* by JOHN CONWAY they emerged and disappeared, guided, mourned, or spurred on by no one, like a swarming play of dots on a dead screen. And as always when such a relic from a distant past, in which things like love and family cohesion were still incomprehensible and careless errors, is found unscathed and unchanged in the present, we shudder in the face of this negation of all the millennia in which we have existed. A classic LOVECRAFTIAN point. As with the folding of an accordion, a million years are compressed, and the only thing that can be heard is a heavy sigh in the deep registers. ADAMSKI-SCHREBER's theory, which is shared by more and more people, calls to mind a passage found in the work of DR. LOREN EISELEY. It's the magically brief description of the so-called Snout, or coelacanth, a creature that illustrates the first step of evolution in the transition from the simple, life-giving element of water to the empty, life-threatening element of air:

On the oily surface of the pond, from time to time a snout thrust upward, took in air with a queer grunting inspiration, and swirled back to the bottom. The pond was doomed, the water was foul, and the oxygen almost gone, but the creature would not die. It could breathe air direct through a little accessory lung, and it could walk. In all that weird and lifeless landscape, it was the only thing that could. It walked rarely and under protest, but that was not surprising. The creature was a fish.

In the passage of days, the pond became a puddle, but the Snout survived. There was dew one dark night and a coolness in the empty stream bed. When the sun rose next morning the pond was an empty place of cracked mud, but the Snout did not lie there. He had gone. Down stream there were other ponds. He breathed air for a few hours and hobbled slowly along on the stumps of heavy fins. (EISELEY, 1957)

AND THEN, a few eons after that memorable day in the mud, they were found again, a living school of young coelacanths. Up to that point only petrified fossils had been found, and they were thought to have been extinct, part of the great mineral cuneiform script in which the life story of the planet was written for us. But in the mid–twentieth century, some people unexpectedly encountered off the East African coast some coelacanths, which were completely indistinguishable from the ancient fossils. Each fin, each vertebra corresponded to the image of their ancestors. And they were splashing around there in the shallow water off the coast, as if the three hundred million years since their first appearance on the planet had never elapsed.

In a similarly dramatic way, argues ADAMSKI-SCHREBER, the contemporary I-phenomenon negates the advancement and the accumulation of certain cultural achievements. In its essential points, his controversial thesis is consistent with the fact sheet of the RIEGERS-

83

3.   The Man with the Lightbulb Head

[GREEN FOLDER]

Charles Alistair Adam Ferenz-Hollereith, Jr., lived from 1946 to 2003. He was the son of Luisa Ferenzi and Adam Hollereith, who emigrated in the immediate aftermath of the Second World War from Switzerland to the United States. (The *i* in Luisa's surname was collected as a customs duty, so to speak, by an American official on their arrival.) He was born in Boston. Until his death from three strokes in relatively close succession, he was a White House advisor on safety and health issues, previously he had worked for several decades at the CIA. The photo on his Wikipedia page shows a man with a strangely lightbulb-shaped face, a quaint shock of hair that sprouts like a medieval helmet plume from the middle of his head, and a slightly perplexed-looking expression. Although the picture, according to the caption, was taken in 1963, it seems older, as if it came from another era. This impression of an existence slightly displaced in time and

history was in fact defining and characteristic of the life of Dr. Ferenz-Hollereith. Of many people it is said that they were ahead of their time. That definitely does not apply to Ferenz-Hollereith. He lived to a great extent in the past, was a man of the fifties through and through, a time that in the United States brought forth a joy in medical experimentation that was completely novel in style and character, yes, it's safe to say, an entirely new spirit began to waft at that time through the psychiatric clinics and military hospitals. This spirit wafted directly from the past into the present, basically it was a sort of whirlwind, which did not so much drive things further in a particular direction as it made them revolve around themselves, in ever narrowing orbits: the scenes of systematic destruction and murder discovered and documented in the concentration camps liberated by the Allied forces, the Nazi doctors later treated with awe and dread, who were brought to America and were there to do essentially only one thing, that is, to talk, report, describe, the mysterious pioneering spirit that flared up in experiments with darkness and sensory deprivation—a snowstorm of new ideas pulling at the edges of the psyche. From this emerged, somewhat belatedly, after a time lag, Charles Ferenz-Hollereith. He wrote his dissertation on Walter Freeman, and many regard this paper as an attempted rehabilitation of that controversial physician, who has gone down in history as father of the modern icepick lobotomy. Shortly after Ferenz-Hollereith began working at the CIA, he apparently specialized (at least according to Zone [1994] and Helman [2003], Helman even presents some documentary evidence) in examining outdated medical experiments for their scientific content, their usability, and perhaps even their repeatability. An example: In the forties and fifties, huge numbers of cats, dogs, and monkeys were fed LSD and observed coping with disorientation, rapidly increasing panic, and disturbed motor activity. Shortly thereafter, these experiments were repeated with human test subjects, mainly soldiers who had volunteered. Ferenz-Hollereith wondered—or, as Zone portrays it, received from his superiors the order to wonder—whether the original animal experiments could perhaps be used to clear up other matters of scientific dispute. In the original series of experiments, something might have been overlooked.

So much for the fruits of the three-hour phone call with Oliver Baumherr. During the conversation Julia came into the room several times. Once she put a hand on my shoulder from behind and left it there until I jerked forward because Herr Baumherr had been saying something incredibly interesting. When I turned around, she was no longer standing behind me. I heard the apartment door close.

As we were saying goodbye, Oliver Baumherr invited me to visit him in Vienna. He had read my articles back then with great interest.

Subway Wind

On the train to Vienna I listened for two hours to the wild *Studies for Player Piano* by Conlon Nancarrow, which really woke me up and gave me self-confidence. Then I took the U1 toward Karlsplatz. The subway announced itself by the characteristic tunnel wind, an oddly meaningless movement of air, which smells and tastes the same in all metropolises of the world. Years ago I had read in an article that the loose hair swept by the tunnel wind from the heads of the people waiting on the platform collects over the years in the tunnel, in the strangest and most inaccessible places, and now and then bursts forth again and rolls along as a gossamer phantom train in front of the real train. In the nineties, huge hairballs had to be removed from the London Underground, which would have hindered the smooth running of the trains, and during the inspections they had also discovered nests, large enough even for a curled-up person, which had presumably been built by tunnel rats inspired by the oversupply of soft and ideally supple nesting material to construct these baroque dwellings. An entrance to a disused side passage or safety tunnel had been clogged by a sort of spider web of interwoven human hair, and the workers almost hadn't managed to remove it. And then there had, of course, also been the homeless man named Fred, for several days his picture had filled the newspapers, a person residing for years in the galleries off the large connecting tunnel, who had made himself a cap out of the hair flying everywhere through the air. This had later been stolen from him by a journalist, it was said, and it actually resurfaced not long after in a dubious auction house, albeit described incorrectly or with intent to deceive as a healing artifact of an extinct nomadic tribe from Niger.

On the phone Julia was a bit disgusted by my improvised description of a gigantic hairball, which had flown through the tunnel, directly past us. But she also laughed and asked what shape it had been.

– Like the Apollo 11 lunar module, I said.

She advised me not to listen to so much Nancarrow when traveling, that crazy music just made me unnecessarily high. Before I could ask how she knew what I had been listening to, she hung up.

APUIP

The man who opened the door for me was quite small and seemed squat and compact in an almost moving way. Immediately I developed a strong urge to pick him up, carefully roll him, and push him through a circular opening; the skin of his face looked as if made to be touched.

Oliver Baumherr was chairman of an organization with a bizarre name: Association for the Peaceful Use of Indigo Potential. Often—to Baumherr's chagrin—the name was altered to Association for the Peaceful Use of Indigo Children, he told me. Yes, now that I heard it, I realized that I had come across that phrase before, somewhere, in a magazine article.

When I mentioned this memory to him, he pulled a sheet of paper toward himself and picked up a pen.

– What article was that?

– I don't remember.

– Was it by that wretched Häusler-Zinnbret?

– I'm sorry, I really can't recall.

– But you can check for me?

I had to think for a while about how to respond to that. It was clear that I had touched a sore spot.

– No, I don't think so. I wouldn't know where to look for it.

– Was it in print? In a book? Or on the Internet?

I shrugged.

– But people usually remember the medium at least. Because if it were in a book, for example, *I* could even name the author for you, for there aren't that many to choose from, I could—

– I don't remember. Really.

He seemed to return a bit to reality, only a single step separated him from the present situation: he and I, in his Vienna apartment, on Walfischgasse 12 in the first district. It was Monday, five o'clock in the evening. (In Graz I hadn't been able to get out of school early.) Oliver Baumherr had at first stood opposite me in a bathrobe, had immediately apologized for how he was dressed, and had disappeared for several minutes. He had come back in a tracksuit, as might be worn to go jogging. He had asked whether I would like tea, and I had said yes. But after twenty minutes of conversation, he had apparently forgotten the tea. I had trouble imagining the management of an association in the hands of this obviously disorganized man.

– When did you found your association? I asked, to steer the conversation in another direction.

He drummed the pen on the blank sheet of paper that lay between us, sucked air through his teeth, and leaned back.

– It's not easy, he said. For me. And for the others. You have to understand that, Herr Setz.

I nodded.

– You don't know what it's like when you're met with hostility from all sides because of a cause you've devoted yourself to. It's terrible what happens to them, you know? Absolutely terrible, awful, horrible, you can't . . . well, you can't even imagine it.

– To the I . . . to the children?

– Yes.

– What happens to them?

He put down his pen. He pursed his lips, then he said:

– You know, I hadn't expected you to ask about Ferenz on the phone. That's never happened to me before. You were at Helianau?

– Yes.

– For how long?

– I was actually supposed to be there for six months, but then I had a . . . falling-out with the principal there.

– Glad to hear it.

He nodded gravely as he said that.

– Ferenz is not simply a person, that is . . . to begin with, he was, of course. But

I told you about Dr. Ferenz-Hollereith to test your reaction. That's all. Nowadays it's more a principle. A principle that is upheld by several people. In their eyes Ferenz is something special. An artist, so to speak.

Oliver Baumherr licked his lips and looked up at the chandelier that hung over our heads.

– But he's dead now, isn't he?

– Not the principle. But the person Ferenz-Hollereith, he is dead. Well and truly dead.

– Is he actually the inventor of the so-called Hollereith treatment? I asked.

Oliver Baumherr clicked his tongue.

– Ah, total nonsense, the Hollereith treatment is a myth. Those sweat cures, with which you are toughened for ... what do I know, the financial world, life, toughness, a secret society, what do I know? Nonsense, Internet chatter. Just like those MKUltra projects in the United States, which basically only constitute a platform for schizophrenics and recognition-seekers, who imagine that the government trained them in their childhood to be murderers.

I waited for him to go on.

– You're not even protesting, he said.

– Should I be?

– But how long were you going to let me babble on like that?

– For a long time. And I would have taken everything down.

He laughed and clapped.

– Touché, touché, hahaha! Very good.

He rubbed his hands together and reflected. Then he laughed again and said:

– What would you have done if I had said the same thing about the Holocaust, that it's all just a myth, gas chambers never really existed, and so on?

– I probably also would have taken notes and ... and maybe asked whether I had understood you correctly.

– No, no, no, it doesn't work like that, he said. You can't do that, that's cowardly. You're not here to take notes, after all, a dictation machine could do that better than you. I can fill a MiniDisc with babble for you and send it to you. It doesn't work like that.

I didn't know how to respond.

– How do you feel now? he asked. Like a cornered rat?

– No. I think you're right. I probably would have protested eventually.

– Eventually! Ah, that's easy to say in hindsight, of course. But you were at Helianau. Didn't you take notice there of . . .

– Of?

– Sweat cures.

– Yes, that is, no, I didn't see it directly, but Frau Dr. Häusl—

– Ah, said Oliver Baumherr, not that name! Terrible!

– She mentioned it, anyway.

– Awful woman. Doesn't have the slightest idea.

– About what?

Oliver Baumherr shook his head, and I again felt like kneading his pleasant roundness. Then he said:

– Have you seen that video that is ubiquitous . . . of that elephant painting flowers?

– What? No.

– Well, you see some elephant, somewhere in Thailand. In a Thailand zoo, to be precise. It has a brush in its trunk and is painting a picture on a canvas with it. Of an elephant with a flower in its trunk. And then of a flower. And again a flower. Wait, I'll show it to you.

– I think I actually have seen it, I lied.

– Okay, but do you also know how that's done? Is this elephant all right, or is it tortured until it has mastered this trick? Everything okay?

– Oh . . . yeah, I just feel . . . a bit dizzy. The long train ride.

– Would you like a glass of water?

– Yes, please.

Oliver Baumherr got me a glass and put it down in front of me.

– What we know about the relocated children is more than what is known about this elephant. They are well treated. Relatively speaking, at least. They're provided for, they aren't tortured, they're merely planted in a particular group that is to be destabilized. What do I know, in a school, for example, which is located next to a strategically important building. Or in a prison camp. There they sit in a room next to the cells. The adjacent room itself is beautifully furnished. Their parents are nearby. Usually they even move with them.

I had to concentrate to keep from losing the thread. Headache, dizziness, heart palpitations.

– Ferenz-Hollereith didn't call it Indigo Potential. We coined that phrase. For him it was simply known as Human Potential. He thought in more general terms. But the Hollereith treatment, as it is understood today, is something else again.

– But what does that have to do . . . with elephants painting flowers? I asked.

– Art is basically always something terribly pitiless and cruel, said Oliver Baumherr. I personally am sick and tired of it. These people who take up residence in villas or castles and then work on, what do I know, creating interventions in public space or some crap like that, and at some point they come out of the villa, erect a ridiculous sculpture, and that was all they were capable of. Absurd. Art is almost always cruel and disgusting. I'm telling it like it is. And that's exactly how it is with the elephants in Thailand, they're not well treated, they're tortured, and what—

– Okay, but what, then, is the Hollereith treatment exactly?

I had pressed my hand against my ear, the other was still uncovered. But my second hand was ready to fly up too and cover it.

– . . . and what do they make the elephant draw? An elephant holding a flower in its trunk, a huge flower, which it will probably present to the people. And everyone is saying Ooohh and Aahhh and is moved to tears and applauds. But the choice of this motif, this flower picture, this choice is, when it comes to cynicism, for me on a par with *Arbeit macht frei* or *Jedem das Seine*.

He went silent, just tapped with his forefinger a few times on the desk.

– Is this now the moment when I should protest? I asked.

– No. But I'll give you something you should read.

He pulled a green folder out of a file cabinet. He opened it and showed me the contents. Newspaper clippings. Interspersed with handwritten pieces of paper. *The Relocation of Magda T.* was written on the title page.

– Read through it. Then you'll understand better what we're about. Can you be here again tomorrow at eight in the morning? Then I'll introduce you to my colleagues, and we . . . we've also prepared a little demonstration for you. As I said, I read your articles back then with great interest.

– Thank you very much.

– And please forgive me that I'm now going to be so impolite and kick you out. I'm expecting guests this evening.

———

In my hotel room I poured shampoo and shower gel over myself in the bathtub until I became grotesque to myself, like those horrible figures in porn movies who are covered with the ejaculate of dozens of men and crawl around blind and sticky on the floor.

With slippery fingers I called Julia. She answered, and I could tell by her voice that her hair was wet too. Such long, voluminous hair retains a lot of water and changes the feel of the body.

– Do you know what's weird? I asked.

– What?

– Bubbles.

– What do you mean?

– They're here for a while, float around. Like little spaceships, and then they burst.

– Dogs love bubbles.

– Dogs, yeah . . .

– Are you doing okay?

– I don't know.

– Are there people making you uneasy again?

– No, this time there's no one . . .

– Following you—

– No, they're not doing that, I mean . . . oh, I have no idea. I have these head-aches again all the time and can't focus.

– Probably labor pains.

– Yeah.

– I told you not to go to Vienna. To see that Baum guy.

– Baumherr. He wasn't very forthcoming. That is, he was more confusing. But he gave me something to read. About a relocation.

– About what?

– Relocation.

– Clemens, you're getting much too caught up in this thing. Tell me instead where you're blowing bubbles. In the hotel room?

– Oh, no, I've just been playing with the shampoo. Do people actually do that? I mean, normally? Play with shampoo?

– Of course. It's completely normal.

– That means everyone does it, right? Pours it over their face and then makes bubbles. Because, it does burn your eyes . . .

– Yes. It's completely normal. Everyone does it.

– And you're sure about that, huh?

– Absolutely sure.

– I never know things like that.

For a while neither of us said anything. I splashed in the water a bit.

– I find the idea of bubbles strange, I said.

– Really? In what way?

– Well, I mean, that air, which is confined in those balls, that clear boundary between inside and outside, that . . .

I faltered. Stepped out of the tub.

Bathwater ran from my penis as if I were peeing.

– What are you doing? asked Julia.

– Hold on, I just realized something . . . the boundary between inside and outside, like a bubble . . . I just have to . . . I just need to write something . . .

– Oh, is this now that moment like in *House* or *The Closer* or *Monk*, when he says something that has nothing to do with the case, and suddenly he stops midsentence, and his eyes wander in that funny way to the side, and he has the solution?

– Um . . . what?

– Now the music should actually come in, something with vibraphone or whatever the thing in the beginning of *American Beauty* is called.

– Hold on a second, or else I'll forget what occurred to me.

– Tell me, then I'll remember.

– Well, so . . . I don't know exactly . . . Ah, this constant stabbing in my head . . . I can never focus on a single thing.

– This is all that institute's fault!

– No. No, it's not that . . . Oh, damn, what was it, now? . . . I've forgotten . . .

– Bubbles. The space in the bubble. The clear boundary between inside and outside. That's what you were saying. Should I rewind again?

– No, I . . . ah, I have no idea . . . Damn it, it's gone . . .

4. Happy Accidents, Midi-chlorians

It wasn't hard to find out Clemens Setz's address. You only had to look it up in the telephone book. A house on the outskirts of the city. The newspaper article with the interview had revealed to Robert that his former teacher still lived in Graz.

And skinned other people, if he didn't like them.

After lunch Robert set off. Burnt out, burnt out, he murmured to himself in his head. *Gap-delay-deedoo . . .*

A robust, lush autumn day. Even the trams moved as if their mouths were full. And the crows in the park seemed to be taking complicated measurements in the meadows, hopped three times, looked around, hopped another three times. Zone game.

Robert enjoyed the certainty that he was of no consequence to these gray-black birds. For them he was as real as Han Solo or a person from the year 3000 was for him. He remembered his enormous excitement when Dr. Ulrich had told him that a person who had smeared himself with mosquito repellent was not wearing a sort of protective armor made of unpleasantly smelling substances that scared away the little insects, but rather that he simply became invisible to the mosquitoes.

He imagined himself stepping in front of the teacher and the man looking through him. A human window, suddenly standing at his door.

My God, this city, how small everything in it became in autumn, even the shopping street seemed to him shortened. On Herrengasse he walked past the small church with the stained-glass window that depicted Hitler and Mussolini, past a beggar woman who was having a never-ending epileptic fit, twenty-four hours long, sometimes some saliva even ran out of her mouth. Her cup was nearly empty, and Robert had the suspicion that she ate coins.

His former schoolmates had all moved north. To Vienna, every single one of them. Like balloons that, once released, automatically floated upward. And from what you heard, they had all successfully found their place in life, protectively armored as always, as windproof and weather-resistant as nano-anoraks, and were probably at this very second holding pointers against diagrams in their enlarged conference rooms or shouting at people on the phone who afterward thanked them many times for the call, or they were simply sitting around and becoming more successful from minute to minute. Max Schaufler had entered his parents' business. What a shock. Robert still received an invitation from him every spring to some celebration on the company premises. Even the signature on it was printed and exactly the same every year.

He had written the teacher's address on his hand. He had actually been surprised that the man was still alive. Not because of his age, for how old could he have been now, forty maybe, at most forty-five, in any case nothing world-shaking, but he had always radiated such an unpleasant energy, as if everything he did occurred under a mysterious compulsion. Even when he stood around silently, he appeared possessed. When he smiled, he looked like those people who hold a copy of the latest newspaper up to the camera so that their family members at home see that they're still alive. And he hadn't taught them anything either.

Once they had covered trigonometric problems. One example had been about a room in which a man lived. The size of the bed is such and such and that of the wardrobe such and such, and a water vein runs across the room, intersecting the bed and the wardrobe at a particular angle. Now the man, who of course would not like to lie on a water vein, because he doesn't want to get cancer in his spine overnight, is forced to move his bed so that it is in an area unaffected by the influence of the water vein. And now the optimal position of the bed and also the wardrobe was to be calculated (for the clothes too could store the evil energy of the underground water vein in themselves at night and pass it on to their wearer by day). The math teacher was actually supposed to explain to them how they should approach the example, but then the situation of this man had apparently amused him, and he had begun to ramble. Holding in his hand the tiny piece of chalk (he always wrote with that almost circular lump and on top of that in those baby block letters that no one could read), he paced in front of the blackboard, looked now and then into the distant faces of his students, and said that the death of the old man (the example had mentioned nothing about the age of the man) was, in a way, preprogrammed: For he moves his bed again and again, because two different mediums, dowsers with their wire Y's, perhaps even three, were there, and of course there are contradictory measurement results, and the old man doesn't know which to regard as more plausible, so he looks for a compromise, for there is an area, in the front left (he pointed to the blackboard), where the desk is, which is indicated by all three measurements as safe, and so the old man thinks, better safe than sorry, and pushes his bed through the room for whole afternoons, in between he collapses on it in exhaustion and rests, and on the third day, hahaha, the water-vein-sensitive old man has a heart attack while pushing the bed and remains lying in the middle of the room. And from above his posture is reminiscent of a climber on an almost vertical mountainside. (The teacher drew a stick figure sketch of the dead man. It looked like a grasshopper that had been crushed underfoot.)

Granted, they had laughed heartily at the story, but the math lessons had nonetheless always been impossible. The teacher had wasted far too much time with his weird digressions, and had then—yes, right, Robert remembered—also constantly complained of headaches, even though he had definitely been told how terribly insensitive that was toward the Helianau students. But for that very reason, because he made no secret of his frequently occurring headaches and attacks of vertigo and problems concentrating, some students had really liked him.

And the same guy had flayed a man alive. How the hell did you even do that? The screaming alone . . .

But he wasn't . : . , Cordula's voice said in his head. She hadn't been reachable since yesterday. Probably needed a bit of time to cool off. He had apologized to her and everything. All right, she had run out and had shouted, *Congratulations, way to go*—as if he had now finally managed to drive her away.

Okay, he had made a mistake.

But we don't make mistakes. We just have happy accidents.

Like his first time. It wasn't something he remembered fondly. He was nineteen, and—in his head—he still moved in the zone. What a warm, safe feeling that had been, at least now, in retrospect. He had made an appointment with a woman who cost sixty euros an hour, surcharges would be discussed only later, during.

Robert knew that he should actually be thinking about Cordula. But his thoughts were drawn into the past. The headwind of the present was simply too strong.

The woman had greeted him at the door to her apartment—that was what those little rooms had been called, which had posters of enlarged porn video cover images hanging on their doors. Robert entered the room and tried not to seem all too scared. The first thing he did was to hold out the money to the woman. She took it and stowed it in a wooden drawer. For some reason it was the sight of that drawer that relaxed Robert a little. It was a thing that also could have been found in fairy tales.

The woman spoke German only poorly, but with several clear gestures she communicated to him that he should demonstrate what he would like to do with her.

– Normal, said Robert.

Then he pointed to his mouth and to hers. She shook her head.

– But I can . . . , she said.

And acted out what she could do instead: spit in his mouth. The pantomime was very convincing, Robert understood immediately. Oddly, he even thought about this offer for a moment. Only after a while did he realize that it didn't appeal to him at all. Spitting in the mouth. Disgusting. He declined. Then he indicated an ordinary missionary position and moved back and forth.

The woman briefly put her hands to her temples, shook her head.

So soon, thought Robert.

He said nothing.

— How old? the woman asked, pointing to him.

— Nineteen.

He showed his ten fingers, then just nine. She nodded and conveyed to him, yeah, yeah, she had understood the first time. Then she helped him take his clothes off. Now and then a sort of moan escaped her, and she took a deep breath.

She didn't take his penis in her mouth, but instead only rubbed it on her face, on her unhealthily shiny cheek. Robert closed his eyes and tried to imagine something erotic.

— All right, said the woman, lying down.

She spread her legs, revealing the ugliest thing Robert had ever seen. It looked like modeling clay. Like a crumpled-up octopus, which had been stuffed into a narrow cave. Like the shadow profile of Alfred Hitchcock. Soft, drooping flaps of skin with something nose-like in the middle. And that was supposed to be the mystery of life? He looked away and lowered himself onto her, his penis had shrunken to the size of a shrimp. She reached through under his arms and began to knead him, while cooing in an irritatingly maternal way, a sound that you otherwise heard only in documentaries about an indigenous people, who always lay naked in the dust and once in a blue moon smeared themselves a bit with blood and feathers, those damn idiots, and let someone film them doing so, really great . . .

— Okay? the woman asked him.

Robert nodded with his eyes closed and dropped onto her entirely. He supported his weight a little with his arms, but not too much, he wanted to feel her chest under his, her labored breathing. In the room hung a sharp, slightly sour stench, which wasn't too strong but made him think the whole time that hundreds of men before him had left their traces, on the plush pillows, on the lampshade, behind the mirror, even under the woman's fingernails. Robert opened his eyes tentatively and looked into the face under him. She smiled, but you could see the strain in her. Below her temples were a few beads of sweat. Her neck was sweating too. Of all the parts of her face, the eyebrows spoke most plainly: They were, despite the friendly mask she maintained, severely knitted and moved incessantly.

She ran her hand over her forehead, massaged it briefly with circling movements. Robert felt himself getting hard.

She put a condom on him and let him penetrate her. Robert thought of the smooth, uncomplicated genitalia of a female statue. He thought of the sketches he had sometimes made of that place. But a turkey head kept intruding on his vision. A turkey head that shook so that the red, chafed-looking thing on its beak waggled.

He again shrank a bit inside her, but he managed nonetheless to keep his head enough above water with fantasies about Felicitas Bärmann strapped to wall bars with black ropes to be able to pound away at her for a few more minutes with his hip thrusts.

He focused on her eyes, for there was nothing wrong with them. Human eyes. Tiny, like an amber insect, his own figure was visible in them, his pale, moon-round face. But now the woman closed her eyes, and a hand wandered to her temple. She rubbed and rubbed and took deep breaths. Then she opened her eyes again, and Robert could tell from their brief oscillation (experts called this phenomenon *nystagmus*) that the room was spinning around her.

She stayed as she was. He had paid, she stuck it out.

Robert felt for the first time something like tenderness. Perhaps even love. He stroked her head, she was a bit startled by the touch, but smiled again, then her head sank back, and she moved it from side to side on the pillow. He could have told her now that this would most likely only make the spinning sensation worse, but he didn't. He just looked at her, studied the hint of an Adam's apple on her female throat.

He was now aroused. His hands touched her breasts.

– Ohh, she said.

It was the sound people make before they vomit.

But she didn't vomit. She let her client continue to pound away at her, withstood each thrust with her pelvis, and now and then even stroked his neck with her hand.

Robert came hard. Part of him wished the condom would burst. He thought of proposing marriage to her. He imagined trips to distant lands. He lay panting on her chest, she conveyed to him with gentle touches in particular places that she would like to get up. But he remained lying for a few more minutes, inhaled her sweaty, sticky smell, and whispered:

– Thank you, you damn animal, thank you, thank you, I love you, thank you, thank you . . .

Afterward he waited politely until the woman returned from the bathroom. He asked her name. She pointed to a poster on the wall. *Alicia* was printed on it. The woman named Alicia didn't look the least bit like her, but Robert nonetheless held out his hand and said:

– Nice to meet you, Alicia, I'm Arno. Arno Golch.

– Goll, the woman said with a nod.

It was strange to shake a prostitute's hand.

Robert took a twenty out of his wallet and gave it to her.

He would have liked to linger a bit longer over this gentle image of a simple transaction between two people, but something had leaped into his view: In a coffee shop across the street from the tram stop he saw—yes, that was clearly Willi's idiotic hat, the one with the tuft of chamois hair. Embarrassing, the way he always went around. Should he go in and speak to him? Would Willi go for him again, like yesterday? All crazy people. You had to be careful. He decided to walk inconspicuously by the little café.

Then Robert fell into a deep well shaft.

Cordula was sitting next to Willi.

There was no doubt: His girlfriend and Willi were sitting side by side at a table in the café. He was explaining something to her. And then he took her hand and explained to that hand the same thing again.

The walls of the well shaft turned red.

He turned around and headed back. Back—where? It didn't matter, just away from here. He almost would have jumped over the guardrail of the Kepler Bridge. He only barely managed to hold himself back. A girl with a wool cap passed him, and he had to put his hands in his pockets to keep from snatching the cap off her head and throwing it in the river.

Then he stopped, and the world rolled over him, as if he were being broken on the wheel. The primeval brass plaque of the sun hid in the gloomy haze of the city.

I know where you live, he thought. *You motherfucker. You filthy, goddamn motherfucker.* He meant Willi. He had to poison him. He had to plant a bomb in his apartment. He had to make him disappear. A bit of fighting, tussling, my God, he had been drunk, and besides, they had really provoked him! Had battered him like a dog. From all sides! As if he were a punching bag. Yes, Robert knows a lot about old kung fu movies.

He knew where Willi lived.

You shouldn't, said the voice in his head. *Calm down first.*

– You calm down, Batman! he shouted, and a man on a bike who was passing him gave him a stupid, wide-eyed look.

He rounded a corner, stopped, tried to breathe, but it didn't work. It felt as if someone had torn a cellophane wrapper from his body and he was naked underneath, raw and scarred. As if he were lying in the grass of the institute meadows, which stank of cow and fertilizer, and a hundred Golchs were sitting around him and sticking their fingers in every orifice of his body.

He headed toward Willi's apartment.

First he stepped in a pile of dog shit.

Even a journey of a thousand miles, Robin, begins with the first step.

As if in a trance he arrived half an hour later at Willi's, with jet lag, because his soul was still standing in front of the little café near the Kepler Bridge and staring at Cordula, who . . . Why with that kiss-ass, of all people? He should have strangled them both! Yesterday he had been strong enough!

Without knowing what he was planning, he walked up the stairs. He didn't run into anyone. He stood outside the door. An advertising catalogue lay on the doormat. What should he do? Kick in the frosted glass window and open the door from inside? Outwit the lock? Maybe the door was unlocked. If it was locked, he would turn around and beat Willi to death right in the café. Pummel his stupid face until the bones gave way. *It's your own fault*, he thought. *If you locked the door, you're dead. It's entirely up to you.* He stared at the door, at its handle, at its keyhole, at the doormat, as if to make clear to it the enormous significance of the imminent decision.

He pushed down the door handle.

The door didn't give way.

Damn! Robert made a hiss of despair.

He held his head with both hands, turned back and forth, what should he do, what should he—

—You goddamn piece of shit!

He gave the door a powerful kick. At first it appeared unimpressed. But then it suddenly cracked. Something small made of metal fell on the floor. Robert pushed tentatively with his hand against the wood.

He had to hold two fingers to his lips so that they didn't spring open and let out a cheer. With the foreign apartment he entered another dimension. The dimension of fantasy. He removed his shoes. This polite gesture gave him a perverse feeling of satisfaction. He would destroy everything here.

In the apartment it smelled like woman.

On a shelf he discovered several books by Elisabeth Kübler-Ross. He was astonished to find such obscene muck here. Also sci-fi, of course, filling half the bookcase, appreciatively he ran his hand along the spines, took out a volume and imagined this activating a mechanism in the wall, a platform turned and opened the way into the depths on two sliding poles. And you slid down them into the earth, into ridiculously labyrinthine dungeons, where animals and people waited in cages to have medical experiments performed on them. And Robert freed a rooster, which had gone half mad in its isolation, from its cage, and the man in the next cage, a swollen specimen of a human being, begged to be released too, pointed to his tongue that had been seared, and he got out a few scraps of human speech, which sounded as if someone were trying to speak Latin with a mouth full of stones, but Robert turned away from him and led the rooster by the hand (wing tip in palm) as with a child back the way he had come. Then he faced the problem of getting back up into the apartment via the sliding poles, and lost interest in his fantasy. He put the book—Samuel Delany's *Dhalgren*—back. He had read it years ago and understood scarcely a page of it. Something with two moons and a gigantic red sun and a city that was constantly changing. This here, however . . . Robert had discovered another book, which was more to his liking: *Boy Wonder*—the autobiography of Burt Ward. *You know, Robin, writing books is the key to world peace. If all people wrote their autobiography, then we would all understand one another.*

Willi had good taste, on the whole. (Robert bit his finger to suppress the need to shout.) Apart from the Swiss end-of-life companion, that intolerable woman with the never-changing questions, his books were quite all right.

The afternoon sun shone into the room, a reddish shine, which said: I know that you're here, you don't belong here.

Robert stood in front of the window and looked out. Ferenz, interference, he thought. Old stories that he no longer knew. The man at the award ceremony. Clemens Setz. Stripping off skin.

Hey, who the hell are you? said the bedroom when he entered it. Because the objects in this room seemed to be a bit hostile toward him, he closed the curtains. The same thing was done with certain birds of prey. If they were blindfolded, they became peaceful and were no longer afraid of the people planning to do incomprehensible things with them.

Robert looked around and reflected. He recalled the image of the two of them. Cordula's arm, which was around Willi's shoulder, and then that Eskimo kiss, the rubbing of noses. Noses ... He couldn't help thinking of bad smells, of the stench in the room with the whore, with whom he had played the mating game for the first time. His thought that residues and DNA samples could be found everywhere in the room, in tiny traces, on the bristles of the toothbrushes, in the knots of the curtain cord, on the dark blue and red plush pillows on the bed ...

He went back into the hall and got his shoes. A nice big glob of dog shit was stuck to one of the shoe soles. Robert breathed through his mouth. He brought the shoe into the kitchen and there put it on the table, on a newspaper. Then he looked for straws or something similar. Finally he found Japanese chopsticks, made not of wood, but of black, grooved plastic. He took them in his hand and checked the tip. He would have liked to have a brush now. Or a palette knife. He had seen Bob Ross episodes in which the master had painted a whole mountain landscape solely with the knife. *People will believe it's magic. So from all of us here: Happy painting. And God bless my friend.*

In a kitchen drawer he found a long-haired brush with which Willi probably spread sauce or egg on a roast.

Equipped with the two utensils, he got to work scratching a tiny portion of dog excrement off the sole and checking it for its consistency. The excrement had not dried and hardened, still stuck. Robert smeared the tip of the chopstick with a sample of the disgusting substance and left the kitchen. The furniture and objects looked at him with horror: *What the hell are you planning to do with that?*

First up were the door handles. The undersides. They were no more than homeopathic doses of dog excrement, which Willi—and whoever else might stay with him and bill and coo through the rooms with him—would receive in this way. *Midi-chlorians are a microscopic life-form, which swims around in your intestines, little Anakin, and lives with you in symbiosis.*

Next he went into the bathroom and spread some dog excrement on the rim of the toothbrush cup, a trace so fine that it was barely visible. *Why do I have to brush my teeth every day, Batman? — You know, Robin, proper oral hygiene is essential in our dealings with our fellow human beings.* When he sniffed it, he noticed that you almost couldn't smell it if you weren't expecting it and paying attention. He went back into the kitchen and loaded up the brush. Then he ran water into the kitchen sink and held the brush for a fraction of a second under it, not even all the way. He added a bit more shit. By now he could breathe through his nose again. He drew a few pale brown streaks across the newspaper, until the brushstroke became almost transparent.

Then he went into the bedroom, which lay unsuspectingly in semidarkness. Drawn curtains, a room with its eyes closed. He ran the brush along the underside of the pillows on the double bed—the nearly clear residual moisture was soaked up by the fabric of the pillowcase and, as far as he could tell, was absorbed without a trace.

Two hairs and some air, the master Bob Ross always called that.

Robert went back into the living room, to the books. *On Death and Dying.* The brush made its soothing sounds on the spine, then he moved on to the other books. Perhaps he would cure Willi's asthma in this way, who knows.

Suddenly there was a knock. The brush almost fell out of Robert's hand. He froze, listened.

But the knocking was only in the walls. Muffled, repeating. A neighbor was probably hanging a picture or putting up a shelf on the wall.

Robert replenished his supply one last time. The brush this time got a full, visible load. And he bored the chopstick deeper into the sole of his shoe, where under the hard-trodden layer somewhat softer, lighter-colored sludge was waiting. He dabbed the window handles and was about to paint the apartment door handle with it, when he realized just in time that he himself still had to touch it today. So he gave the final, once again somewhat paler stroke to the mouse of Willi's computer, which had a slightly brownish color anyway.

Satisfied, Robert headed home. Newspaper, chopsticks, and brush he had taken with him and thrown in a garbage can at some distance from Willi's apartment. While he walked, he checked the smell of his fingers. They smelled a bit sweaty, but otherwise everything was fine.

As if to cheer for him, a shop for children's toys showed him a smiling face as he passed.

Forever Young was written under the face.

On the way home he thought of the empty apartment. He knew what he was supposed to be feeling. Cordula was gone. She had packed, had stuffed all her clothes in the travel bag that smelled like the dark years of the bad panic attacks, and had walked past him. Be happy, she had said to him. You finally did it.

When he tried to be horrified by it, as he had this morning in the kitchen, there was nothing there, only the memory of how her belly had felt when he had—

He held the moment. Pause button. But still nothing came.

Confused, he went into a pizzeria on Jakominiplatz and ordered a Margherita to go. Then he carried the box home like a portfolio, oil dripped next to him onto the street, and he let it drip. When he opened the box, the cheese had slid completely to one side. Stroke pizza.

Outside, at dusk, only a few cars played tag in the street. He ate, went to the bathroom, thought about what it would be like to let a kid in a wheelchair hurtle down a steep street, and took a shower. Warm water. The vertigo-suppressing face of Alicia came to his mind again. His erection looked stupid and unhappy. He pressed the head of his penis against the white tiles of the shower, played a bit with the tiny fish mouth the urethral opening could be formed into. The kid in the wheelchair, hurtling downward, went faster and faster and crashed through a large windowpane, which was being carried across the street by two silent film extras in slow motion. Glass shards everywhere. The kid's ostomy bag whirled away and landed on the mailbox of a house (one of those American ones, on a long post, with a little red flag that is put up when letters have come).

He forced himself to think her name: Cordula. He said it aloud, water from the shower head ran into his mouth. He swallowed it, as if in punishment. *Why do I exist? I stand in the shower. I paint one or two pictures a year.*

He staggered as he stepped out of the shower and dried himself. Gentle rampage fantasies accompanied him in half sleep. A knife fight, as soft and springy as a pillow fight. The man without shoulders who had accosted him in the bank lobby approached him and handed him a new business card. To replace the old one, he whispered to Robert, who pushed him away with both hands in disgust and let himself fall from the taut tightrope into the gloomy circus ring of sleep, where other creatures awaited him.

The Mojave Phone Booth (1962[?]–2000) was the loneliest telephone booth of all time. It stood in the middle of the Mojave Desert, many miles from the nearest settlement or highway. In 1997 it became an Internet phenomenon, many fans called the phone booth, visited and painted it and recorded the conversations that came about from time to time when someone actually happened to pick up the phone in the middle of the desert. Eventually the phone booth was completely covered with graffiti. The constant demand on the phone line was regarded by the manufacturer, Pacific Bell, as a wrongful use of the telephone service, on top of that environmental activists were upset by the incessant ringing in the middle of the desert, which supposedly disrupted the daily routine of certain animal species. On May 17, 2000, it was removed and destroyed by Pacific Bell.

H. - ZINNBRET
THE NATURE OF DISTANCE
P. 16

5.   The Relocation of Magda T.

[GREEN FOLDER]

Rough, migraine-yellow headaches alternated with attacks of vertigo. And yet,
I told myself repeatedly, no one was anywhere near me. The cool water mixed
with slimy white shampoo had been unable to dispel the (not feverish, but more
atmospheric) heat from my head. Nor did the symptoms improve when I, wearing only a bathrobe, walked through the nocturnal corridors of the hotel and
stood in front of the snack machine to turn back and forth a little in the ice-cold
light of the soda cans and chocolate bars. I returned to the hotel room, lay down
in bed, and counted.

An hour and another hour . . .

On their return to the pasture, the sheep compare the numbers assigned them
tonight by the sleepless man in his bed: What number did you get? – Nineteen,
again. – Who is number one? Hey, number one! We have to know who the leader
is. Disappointed, grief-stricken mother animals whose children got only a three-
digit number, once again not among the first one hundred! There are even sheep
silently weeping to themselves who have today remained numberless. Most of
them hang their heads, dissatisfied with life. But they still go to him every evening, the sleepless man in his darkened chamber, who counts them to become
tired. They need it as much as he does. Ultimately they love the moment the
number hits them, in the middle of their woolly belly. It allows them to forget for
an instant that their quantity, like the days and nights of the sleeper, is finite.
Finally I got up, a body moving with day speed in the slowed nighttime. I felt like
a spaceship.

I took the documents that Oliver Baumherr had given me out of the green
folder and studied them. The Relocation of Magda T. I sorted the newspaper
clippings on the narrow hotel desk. In the oldest articles there were pictures of

a child whose face was covered with a black anonymity bar, then, in the more recent ones, that had been dispensed with: A thirteen-year-old girl. Braces smile. Bright, cheerful-looking eyes.

She's doing well now, said the first sentence of an article. It dated from May 5, 2001. It mentioned that the father, Theodor T., had moved with his daughter at some point in 1999. However, it didn't speak of moving, but rather of relocation. *The first use of this word*, I thought in the voice of the *Oxford English Dictionary*. The small family then lived with one of the girl's uncles, who was a guard in a prison on the German-Austrian border. During the day she often played in a room that was completely empty. On a later inspection of the prison, officials noticed a room that was furnished like a children's room. But Magda had never been in there, the article said, the room had been furnished solely for visits from children. Children of prisoners.

I had to reread the article. Somewhere there was a jump in the story. Somewhere my focus had been lost. I closed my eyes, tried to collect myself, despite the late hour. So: She moved, relocation, okay, and lived with an uncle, he was a prison guard, got it, but then . . . an empty room in which she had played. Or actually hadn't played . . . Was the room in the prison or . . . The article didn't reveal it. Inwardly cursing the writer of this confusing, sloppily written article (I imagined drawing a little circle on his cheek with a marker in punishment and then abandoning him to the angry crowd), I turned my attention to the next article.

Only once I had read the first lines—*The worst day of my life was the evening I was brought back. The best day was when I saw the man on the other side of the glass window bore his fingers into his own ears until blood came, then I knew that I was really something spe*—only once those lines had run emptily through my mind did I realize that my revenge fantasy about the writer of the first article had been totally nonsensical . . . a ring on the cheek, in marker or pen . . .

I noticed that my hand was lying on the high-speed Internet plug. I took it away, and it felt strange. For some reason the plug was ice-cold. A stabbing headache flared up briefly, but then immediately dissipated when I touched my forehead with my cold hand.

With the help of my forefinger, I read on. At one point there was mention of a prison breakout, then of abuse, which was, however, hard to prove. There was no pan-European legislation regarding I-effects in relation to prisoners. The name

Brussels came up. The keeping of a child in a separate room did not in itself constitute a demonstrable . . . A crime had therefore not necessarily . . . Before her ultimate liberation by . . . The sentences lay side by side, and each sentence peeked over its period at the next sentence, like a creature staring at a creature of a different kind and seeking to fathom its mystery.

Then I turned to the notes taken by Oliver Baumherr's colleagues.

On the basis of several disparate scraps, they had tried to reconstruct Magda T.'s long and agonizing journey. Not one of these Venn diagram bubbles gave the investigators the pleasure of overlapping with another. The only element common to all the fragments was Magda. She was there, saw, and experienced. And erased from memory what overburdened her consciousness.

Here a compilation of things and situations that Magda remembered (jotted down by hand on a single sheet of paper):

1) A plain somewhere in a very hot region and hours of walking in the sun. One foot in front of the other, meanwhile the constant jerk of the rope on her wrist. Someone was holding the rope, but who it was can no longer be said clearly. It's possible that he's wearing sunglasses. It's a sunny day. A warehouse with cars, many of them lying on their side, a white road that runs past the warehouse and from which a lot of dust whirls up when a truck drives on it. In general, a lot of trucks are on the road that day. So there's also a lot of dust. As soon as a dust cloud has settled, the next is already forming, everything is covered with it, hair, eyelashes, toes poking out of sandals. In a warehouse that she passes, several large, unfamiliar pieces of equipment are standing around. Workers in light orange coveralls walk back and forth among these pieces of equipment.

2) A whole day in a room with round frosted glass windows, there's nothing in it, not even a bucket. It takes a long time before she can bring herself to simply pee on the floor. When that's done, she feels sick from the smell, and she pounds with both fists on what she thinks is the door, but in the half-light it isn't easy to make out. There are a lot of peculiar joints in the walls, as if their parts were held together by rivets; corrugated metal debris perhaps, which had been gathered somewhere. That day she pounds until she runs out of strength.

3) An amusement park. Signs in a foreign language, on top of that there's the lack of glasses (the loss of which she can't remember, however; as of a certain point in time they are simply missing), an altogether blurry impression. A clatter-

ing roller coaster that seems to pass very closely by her head. Strange-smelling money in her hands and brief moments in which she's not sure whether she is being observed or accompanied by someone. Yet surprisingly clear memories of home, especially of the sled run behind the house and the empty rabbit hutch. 4) Many hours spent alone in a room in which there's a sink, and even a bucket standing in the corner. It is regularly taken out and replaced. Every morning it smells overpoweringly of lemon. In a small medicine cabinet hanging on the wall there's bandaging material but no scissors with which it could be cut from the roll. Here too the milky white portholes. Loud noises penetrate from outside. Mainly at night the screaming of a man, or perhaps of various men, can be heard. These screams are terrible, they can be heard for hours, they simply won't cease. Loud and crowing, like a rooster. She can still hear them to this day and, according to the record of the interrogation, even demonstrated them for the investigators. But aside from the note *Imitates screaming*, there is no information, no more detailed description.

Another piece of paper quoted Magda T. verbatim. Sources weren't provided. On the back of the paper was only a word written in pencil: *Arboretum*.

The land was so flat that you could see to the horizon in every direction. And the horizon was just about knee-high, sometimes it was also up to my hip.

And:

In my uncle's house there was a chest that I was incredibly fond of. It was made of dark wood and smelled wonderfully of old fabrics and shoes. It was empty, so I often lay down inside it in the evenings and let the lid fall shut over me. The lid was slightly warped and didn't close completely, a narrow crack of light always remained, leaving me enough air to breathe. Sometimes I fell asleep in the chest. Once, when I saw my uncle in the yard, I went to the window and shouted down to him. I wanted to know what used to be stored in the chest. He shouted up to me that he didn't remember. He himself had still been a small child, back then. What he meant by that sentence I've never understood. But I never asked him about it either.

Once she was visited at night by a white crocodile, which had been very polite. Another time a little fish with legs came to her and performed in the half-light of the cell several good-naturedly clumsy balancing tricks.

She had been able to laugh at that.

Asked what she wanted to be one day, Magda answered with a smile: An astronaut.

And sometimes a man with a pyramid head paced on the balcony at night and talked to himself.

(Compiled by O. Baumherr, C. Thiel, and P. Quandt.)

The last thing to be found in the green folder was a Polaroid of Magda T. from the year 2003. She is standing next to Oliver Baumherr and two other men, smiling at the camera. Her eyes are narrow slits, as if something were blinding her.

I awoke in the middle of the sheets of paper and articles spread out on the narrow desk. A small piece of paper was stuck to my saliva-wet lips. I removed it carefully and put it with the others. I looked at my watch: six-thirty. At eight I had the appointment with Oliver Baumherr and his colleagues.

While dressing, I tried, as before a test, to recite all the important facts about Magda T.'s relocation. But I got stuck on the man with the pyramid head. Had I really read that?

I searched in the papers for the passage, but couldn't find it.

In the hotel breakfast room, I drank a strong green tea and imagined it making me more and more alert and focused.

– Herr Setz, good morning. Did you sleep well?

– Yes, in a way. Hello—

I shook hands with the other two men standing next to Oliver Baumherr, and they introduced themselves. Christian. Paul. They were immediately on a first-name basis with me.

– So, Clemens, you're interested in Magda? asked Paul.

– No, Herr Setz wrote those two articles, you know—

– Oh, of course, yes.

The man named Paul nodded.

– Back then we reconstructed her picture, it wasn't hard, because the child had been gone for only a few years. And then Ferenz took care of the rest.

The green tea was having an effect.

– Ferenz? I asked. Where does he live?

– Oh, him, said Oliver Baumherr. He's in Brussels at the moment. Or at an unknown location. As the case may be.

– Is he a descendant of . . . ? I asked. Yesterday we talked about . . .

Oliver Baumherr and Christian Thiel exchanged a glance.

– As I said, Ferenz is more like a title. Old Hollereith was a sort of patron for the whole thing. The idea has remained the same.

– Okay.

– Come, we've prepared something for you, Herr Setz. A little demonstration.

Software

The most important factor was time, said Christian. In the question of where missing persons might be, what they looked like now, or what exactly might have happened to them, time played the most important role. Then he told me about a case that had occurred a few years ago. A Russian programmer named Aleksandr Archin, Christian said, had caused quite a stir with new software for simulated aging. His program had worked more reliably than most of the others on the market at that time, his algorithm had been top secret, and the hype in the scene had been accordingly intense. Then some people suddenly claimed that, although the program was very fast and provided results that seemed convincing at first glance in terms of the hypothetical appearance of the aged missing person, the success and recognition rate was at the same time strikingly low. According to Christian it had taken a long time for this vaguely denunciatory criticism to give way to a more concrete and also considerably more astonishing assessment: the aged images *resembled each other*. The people who first noticed it hadn't believed their eyes, Christian said, he himself had felt as if he had been living for months underwater or on the far side of the moon. A downright painful awakening from hypnosis. The images had clearly developed from the source pictures of the missing persons, but in the cheekbones, in the slightly upward-tapering curve of the lips, and above all in the converging eyebrows, the same pattern always emerged, which often had nothing to do with the original pictures. Of course, the solution to this mystery was soon found:

the photo of the Russian programmer himself. He had, as it were, programmed his own face into the morphing technology of his software, as a visual constant underlying everything, toward which every hypothetical aging process tended. When, say, a twelve-year-old girl, who had been missing for five years, was made older by the software, she received a second, foreign countenance: that of Aleksandr Archin.

– In itself a pretty virtuoso stunt, Paul interrupted Christian's story.

– Hm? said Christian.

– Well, to program that in, that's actually . . . well, in itself, actually . . .

– Yeah, yeah, yeah, but it's absolutely criminal, isn't it?

– Does anyone know why he did it? I asked.

– I don't know, said Paul, maybe he wanted to sabotage the work of people like us. I mean, there are a lot of people who have something against it.

– Well, said Christian, yeah, yeah, at the time all that was already . . . these explanations, they . . . really went around everywhere. That he wants to protect the past and so on. The anonymous horde of missing persons, who might still be living somewhere, unrecognized, under another name. That a number of people in hiding gave him money to copy himself in. Or that he actually works for various governments that are involved in organized human trafficking. All hard to say.

– But then why did he use his own face, I said, I mean, there would have been a hundred other options.

The men shrugged.

– Hard to say, said Christian.

– And it's also consistent with the structure of programs like that, Paul added, that you use some sort of constant face mask as a basis, some sort of default setting of the various pivot elements. Iris, chin dimple, root of the nose, hairline, cheekbones, et cetera.

– You don't really have any idea what all this means? Christian surmised with a laugh, gesturing to my notebook, which during the whole discussion had been open in front of me, while its pages had remained completely white.

To demonstrate to me how such a program worked, Christian wanted to confront his latest SimulAged software, which he had recently purchased, with the picture of a child who had disappeared almost eighty years ago.

The boy had lived until December 1927 in the Upper Austrian town of Kremsmünster. At a dance one day shortly before his seventh birthday, at which his
parents were also present, he had simply disappeared in the middle of a crowd.
The parents, quoted in a newspaper article, reported having seen him calmly
walking toward the bodies whirling wildly around one another. He had walked
in a rather straight line, as people do who see the ocean for the first time and,
as if remote-controlled, drawn by ancient magnetism, march toward the waves
breaking on the shore. And it had been really eerie to witness how the whirling
limbs of the dancers always only very narrowly missed him—and how he was
suddenly no longer there, concealed by music and movement and colorful
clothing. The father asked the band to stop playing for a moment, his son was
somewhere on the dance floor. The bandleader had responded to this request
with understanding and amusement, according to the article. They began
to look for him, but the boy was nowhere, more and more people joined the
search, they checked everywhere, under every table, they even examined the
boards of the dance floor to see if one of them might be loose. But they found
nothing. The boy remained missing. Several years later he was declared dead,
and an empty child's coffin, carried by two men instead of six, was lowered into
a grave. Christian Thiel had discovered the article with the blurry portrait photo
of the boy by chance in a collection of old newspapers. I stood next to him
while he scanned the picture. The soft sighs of the scanner were reminiscent
of the sound of elevator doors sliding apart in an exquisite hotel. The software,
for which Christian had forked out almost three thousand euros to be able to
provide it to his agency's desperate clients, grasping at any straw, took only a
few seconds to calculate the result. On the screen appeared the face of a very
old man. Christian tried out several hair and beard styles and ultimately chose a
thick full beard.

– Looks like Tolstoy, I said.

– Really?

– Yeah, in a way.

– I don't actually know what Tolstoy looks like, said Christian.

– The way people imagine God, I said.

Christian laughed. He printed out the picture and tacked it to the wall over his
desk.

– That could really be anyone, he finally said, after he had studied the face for a while. Old people somehow all look the same.

– Once this factor is under control, said Paul, then you move on to the next point and take a look at the known story. In this case we know, um, well . . . he simply walked toward a crowd and disappeared in it. Do you believe the story?

– Well, the first thing is always the story, Christian said with a shrug. You have to start from it, yeah . . . With Magda T. it was in the beginning also only a story.

– Hm, said Paul. If he wasn't trampled by the people, he might still be alive somewhere, living in an old people's home, without family members, almost ninety years old, blind, senile.

– Pfff, said Christian. There are countless people like that too.

– Yeah, said Paul, you're right.

He cast a glance at me, the sort of look that strangers waiting in front of closed elevator doors exchange.

– The software is really impressive, I commented. Amazing.

– Hm?

Christian turned around to face me. He looked at me as if I'd made an extremely unusual remark.

– The software works, I repeated. And even with such an old picture. That's amazing, isn't it?

– I think so too, said Paul. It was worth the money.

Christian said nothing, he only gave a brief nod and turned back to the print-ed-out picture on the wall.

– After such a long time, he said softly. Look at him.

– We could maybe give him glasses, said Paul. Or a hairstyle like Einstein. Or Beckett.

– Who? asked Christian.

– Samuel Beckett.

– I don't know what he looks like. Also like God?

– No, not so much, I said. He had very powerful hair. The whole energy of his appearance was concentrated in his shock of hair.

– *Ts*, said Christian.

Paul typed on the laptop and conjured onto the old face a thick cloud of untamed hair, snow-white and flickering. When he saw Christian looking over, he took a step back and gestured to the screen. Christian only smiled and looked back at the picture.

– You know what's really odd? Christian said after a while. I have the feeling that I've seen him before. Somewhere.

– Where? asked Paul.

– Don't know. But I could swear . . .

He came up very close to the old face and tapped with his forefinger on its forehead.

– Could we do another test run? I asked. Just so I can see how it works. Maybe one of you has a photo ID we could scan? Or we could take a webcam photo, or—

– No, said Christian. That's a rule we have, no fake cases, we . . . Wait, I just thought of something . . . The . . .

Paul held up his arms, as if to say: *I wouldn't have anything against it, but he said no. He's the boss.*

– Okay, then I'm going to go, I said. My train . . .

– Yeah, we should probably also get back to work, said Paul. Now you have an impression, right?

– If anything, said Christian, then . . .

It seemed to occur to him that what he had intended to say wasn't appropriate to the situation at all. He had no longer been paying any attention to us. A slight flush passed over his face, and he pretended to clear his throat.

– Yeah, we really should get back, he said. Well, Clemens, it was a pleasure.

Oliver Baumherr saw me to the door.

– Impressive, isn't it?

– Yes, I said.

– But you don't look impressed. You seem somewhat disappointed, Herr Setz.

– I'm just confused. I read those pages you gave me. Relocation . . . Now I under-stand the term. It just means to move. And . . .

– Not *just* to move, right?

– I mean, yeah, okay . . .

– You really do seem confused, Herr Setz. But you'll realize that I've given you something you can use later. Good luck. And I wish you continued success.

– Thank you.

– Here's your coat. Hold on, I'll help you into it.

As I walked through the midday hum of the city toward the train station, I thought about Tolstoy—not so much his work as his face—and tried to imagine what the world would look like if he had disappeared shortly before his seventh birthday, never to be seen again, instead of the boy from Kremsmünster. Somewhere in Russia, at a dance, of which there were certainly enough at all times and in every country in the world. The parents of the boy from Kremsmünster would have been able to watch their child grow up, would have spent solitary hours reading writers other than Tolstoy, and the boy would have become an adult, later an old man. Sons, daughters, grandchildren. Finally he would have died and been buried in an ordinary grave. And the world wouldn't have missed the never-written works of Tolstoy any more than it now missed the boy. Unsettled and intimidated by this realization, I stood around on the platform and regained my composure only when a few men with large musical instruments joined me. As we boarded, one of them asked me to help him with the double bass, which I did immediately, happy and relieved about the fat, hefty weight of the large case, adorned with various travel stickers, in my hands.

Only once the train was moving did I realize that I had left my favorite novel, Halldór Laxness's *Under the Glacier*, which I had brought with me specifically to read during the two-and-a-half-hour train ride back to Graz, in the hotel room. Confused, I put a hand on the windowpane, as if that might brake the train a little. Ever since I was a child, my sympathy with things and animals had been stronger than with people. Lost scarves wept all night in the darkness, a busted umbrella felt like a raven with broken wings and was inconsolable about the fact that it would never again feel the fresh rain on its stretched skin, a bee buzzing along the inside of a window longed for the air and the sun and the nearness of its colony, and a tree from whose crown an old Frisbee was shaken was sad about the loss of its toy or jewelry. At the same time I loved exploding buildings, soldiers falling in flames out of helicopters or riddled with machine gun fire, and I jumped up and down with joy in front of the television when a person in a kung fu movie—whether or not he deserved it—had his neck broken by the acrobatic attacks of his opponent and he lay on the ground wheezing and struggling for breath, and the victor positioned himself majestically in front of him one last time and bowed to him, as if he were greeting death itself, which invisibly entered the scene to collect its sacrificial offering. To this day it seems to me as if I had learned only yesterday to empathize with people and feel their pain and still had to get used to the unbearable brightness in which it bathed the world. My hand slid into the pocket of my coat. It touched plastic. I pulled out the unknown thing. The case of a radio play cassette. Bibi Blocksberg, the little witch. I opened it. Instead of a cassette, there was a slip of paper in it.

Ferenz

33, Rue de la Loi

Bruxelles

And a very long telephone number, followed by *cell*. Confused, I looked at the cassette case. On the face of the little witch Bibi Blocksberg someone had drawn a Hitler mustache. When the train entered a seconds-long tunnel, I was overcome by an unusually violent urge to gag. I stood up and walked through the cars a bit in the hope that the balancing games made necessary by the gentle curves and the rocking and shaking would distract my body a bit, give it something to do. To soothe myself I called Julia.

– Hello.

– Hello, are you already on the train?

– Yes, I . . . I just felt sick.

– Too much Nancarrow?

– No, but I think, ah, you're not going to like this . . . I think I'm going to go to Brussels next.

– Clemens, she said in a sad tone.

– No, no, I think I now have a better overview, though it's still pretty difficult . . . I was given a contact address.

– Maybe you'll change your mind if I tell you who just called here.

– Frau Stennitzer again?

– No.

Then Julia told me that an hour or so ago a friendly-sounding man had called and asked for me. He was from the publishing house Residenz Verlag, she said. He had read my *National Geographic* articles and wondered whether I might have written other things too, stories, longer manuscripts, whatever I would like to show, he was very interested.

– From Residenz Verlag? Really?

– Yes, said Julia.

– Wow, I said.

For a while, neither of us said anything.

– Bibi Blocksberg.

– What? asked Julia.

– Oh, nothing. Good news. Residenz Verlag. Really good.

To bring myself completely back down to earth, I told Julia that I had seen in front of the train station in Vienna a little dragonlike dog chasing some bubbles that a girl with a dripping wet dispenser in front of her face conjured in the air like three-dimensional Venn diagrams. When Julia asked what color the dragonlike dog had been and what picture the term *dragonlike* should actually call to her mind, the connection broke, and I held the cell phone in Geiger counter fashion in the air, in search of a residual signal, which was perhaps hiding in a corner, and even pressed it, before I abandoned the attempt, against the cold window in the aisle, into the breathless flickering of the tree trunks in the little wooded area shortly after Wiener Neustadt, through which the train was passing.

6.   Sons and Planets

The only source of light in the nocturnal room was a glass of milk. Robert had been awake for a few minutes, but didn't want to move. His head lay in a tangle of pillows and T-shirts as if in a dream mixer. Probably that was why he had dreamed such nonsense: about the settling of a Chinese man. A family lived on the bald head of the Chinese man, and all year long an oppressive, melancholy atmosphere prevailed there, as in the beginning of certain desert sci-fi movies, the mother planted watercress and potatoes, it rained often. And then the constant marital dispute between the parents: Why did we have to move here, of all places? It was your idea! No, yours!

Robert got up, examined the milk. It had developed a white skin. Like a little ice-skating rink. He broke through it with the nail of his forefinger.

Then he emptied the milk down the drain in the kitchen. He remembered vaguely how years ago, shortly after he and Cordula had become a couple, he had ejaculated into a glass of sparkling wine. She had helped him . . . a wet, ice-cold towel wrapped around her head, she had knelt in front of him . . . why the towel again? For the obvious reason . . . ? The image disappeared again, but what he remembered was that the sperm held up and twirled by the sparkling wine bubbles had been the shape of a seahorse. For a few moments a seahorse standing relatively still in the fizzy liquid. He had turned the glass back and forth, and one of them had then made the joke that their child, if they ever had one, would look like that. Like a little seahorse.

– But in their case the men have the young.

– Really?

– Yes, Cordula had said, the male seahorses don't just carry the young to full term, the way some other animal species do. No, they really get pregnant. With all that goes with it, before and after.

– Fuck!

– Yeah, exactly. And that was also the reason Kurt Cobain killed himself. Didn't you know that?

He had probably laughed at that.

– No, really, Cordula had said, burying a finger between his buttocks. Honestly, look it up in his journals. He was a total psycho. Birds for him were reincarnated old men with Tourette's syndrome. And every morning they scream at the world in their bird language, which usually only old men . . . wait, bend forward a little, that way I can . . .

Her middle finger. *Fuck.*

Robert realized that he was standing with a huge hard-on in front of the sink in the kitchen. It wasn't exactly the most pain-relieving sight in the world. His gaze shifted to the doorframe, the Mondrian on the wall, senseless cabinets.

Congratulations! Way to go! Her last words before she had left. Robert had the feeling that he had only imagined them. But they were there, in his head, in the corner where usually only memories were cold-stored.

Yes, you know, Robin . . . (The rest is silence.)

With his autumn jacket on he always looked enormously puffy. Like a penguin dressed up as a zookeeper. He went into the courtyard to break his bicycle. It was really a shame, but just now he had taken a brief look at it from the window and thought: *Yes, you.* It was a loss heavy enough to be able to assuage his despair, his guilt, his great misery.

In the yard he was seized, as so often, by the strong suspicion that the garbage men were trying, through the way they left the garbage cans at the front entrance after emptying them in the morning, to communicate something to the occupants of the building. A coded message about the state of the world. Today the cans were lined up as nicely as the slot machines in a casino.

Outside it was surprisingly warm. A fever relapse of the season.

When Robert stood in front of the bicycle, he had the sensation that it was staring at him from the side. Like a horse or a bird. *I know exactly what you're planning to do.* He would have liked best to spread a white sheet over the handlebars and then pound them with a large hammer. But he had neither hammer nor sheet, only a screwdriver and a pair of pincers.

Behind him he heard rattling. A plastic bucket full of clothespins was put down on the concrete floor of the courtyard. The rack on which the wet clothes and linens were hung was two heads taller than the short, stout woman. One warm autumn day, and this weird female thing went outside to pretend it was summer. Hanging the laundry in the yard.

– Hello, Herr Tätzel!

She shielded her face with her hands in a silly way as she turned to him. Okay, not so silly after all, a sunbeam shone directly on her. Apart from that the yard was in the shade.

– Good morning, he said.

– How are you doing?

He looked at his neighbor. In his hand was the screwdriver. He took a step forward, she smiled, the edge of the Great Bubble slid into emptiness, didn't catch the woman. Misjudged by a few yards anyway. He didn't even remember where his zone boundary had been, autumn and shadows, the voices of the other dingos, vegetables rolling adrift on the shady side of a mountain in the Semmering region.

– Sorry about last time, he said.

No, he hadn't said that aloud. He hadn't even thought it, so his mouth couldn't possibly—

– It's okay, she said.

A clothespin was held, its mouth opened, led like a tame piranha to the right spot, and there was allowed to bite. Frau Rabl performed these movements with a certain grace. Probably she was a single mother. Robert had never seen her with a man. The boy was also . . .

– How's your son?

Okay, I'm shutting off, he thought. *Do what you please, you bastard. You filthy dingo.*

– Thanks. He's fine. School has started again, thank God.

– Ah, yes.

– Where did you go to school, Herr Tätzel?

Robert opened his mouth. His brain had crossed its arms in an offended way over its chest and looked elsewhere. *Do what you please.*

– At Helianau, that's—

– Oh, said his neighbor. Of course, sorry.

– No, it's okay. I . . . you know, my girlfriend . . . she . . .

He made a gesture.

– Oh, dear, what happened?

– She left.

Why are you telling her this? His neighbor dropped the little colorful piranhas back in the bucket and approached him. She grasped him by the shoulder. *Why did you have to tell her that?* She was really a very short woman. And round as a ball, especially in her face. Robert felt her shape, the space she took up on earth, bulging gently against him. *Why are you such a pathetic idiot?*

– Hold on, let's go inside, she said. That's terrible.

He let her escort him into the building. Clearly a single mother. Careful steps. Happy to have company.

– So you were at the Helianau Institute, huh? I'd figured that you . . .

– Why?

– Well, because you . . . um . . .

– It's okay, he said. I'm just teasing.

– It's a terrible affair, don't you think?

– What?

– Well, the teacher from there. Who killed a man.

– Ah, yes.

— He was actually a teacher at Oeversee High School for years, but he never mentions that! It's always just: Helianau, Helianau. I think he blames that school for his crimes.

— Aha, said Robert.

He was beginning to like the woman.

— I'm sorry that I immediately sprang that on you, his neighbor said with a laugh. But I was pretty sure that you had been at that school.

She took a step toward him:

— Did you know him?

I just tried to visit him yesterday. Unannounced. Putting my own skin on the line, so to speak.

— No, said Robert.

— Oh, said the woman.

She seemed a bit disappointed.

— I know only that he writes books. And flayed—

— But they acquitted him! Didn't you read about it?

— Yes.

— Yeah, I think it's a scandal too. You don't just send people who do something like that back into society as if nothing had happened! The fact that a man like that dealt with children for years. Look, here!

She held a book out to Robert. He took it.

— I haven't read it yet. But of course I immediately bought it, you know. Because in an interview he has now claimed that the book contains a code. He wrote it back when he ... ah, what was it? ... he ... he claims that it somehow proves his innocence.

— This here?

— Yes. If you ask me, he's sick. Simply sick. Is talking for his life. Even more so now that he's free.

— What does the title mean?

— No idea. But the novel wasn't at all easy to get. Sold out everywhere, because of the case. The acquittal! It's a scandal, what kind of a world we live in. As a mother, I ... I don't even want to imagine what kind of a world my son will live in one day.

— So what is the book supposed to have to do with his innocence?

– No idea, some sort of code or something. But if you ask me, it's total nonsense, a sales gimmick. Ashes.

– Ashes?

– Well, yeah, ashes, she said.

And pointed to her forehead, as if a corresponding mark were there.

– What's it about?

– Oh, I have no idea. It's so muddled. A young man who kills himself, and then his father publishes a posthumous manuscript by his son. And this manuscript is at the end somehow bur ... no, that's a different one, oh, the book is totally ...

She took an apple, put it on her head, and made shooting movements with her forefinger (*p'tshoo, p'tshoo*) to illustrate her impression of the book. Then she laughed, and Robert laughed too. Yes, he liked the woman.

– Did that man actually find you the other day? she asked, still laughing.

– What man?

– A man, he was here ... in the courtyard, and he asked me whether I knew you, and I said—

– Hold on a second, a man? What did he look like?

– Oh, I don't know, like ... the head bald and about this tall and quite thin. Especially here at the shoulders. Did he find you?

Robert felt how rigid his face was. He couldn't make up his mind to move any muscle.

– Yes, he finally said.

– Great, said the woman. That sets my mind at ease. Because I didn't tell him where your apartment is. That annoyed him a bit, I think.

– Did the man ..., Robert began.

But then it occurred to him that he had just claimed that the man had visited him.

– Did the man ... for you, I mean, in your eyes, didn't he have a rather ... lightbulb-like head?

The woman laughed. Then she said:

– Yeah. I guess so. Didn't look at it that way, but ... yes.

– So it was round, in your view, really lightbulb-shaped?

– Heeheehee . . .

With the book in his hand he had run out of the apartment. Frau Rabl hadn't even protested or tried to hold him back. He ran across the street, passed a garbage can, but didn't throw the book in. The taxi stand was empty. It would most likely take only two or three minutes for the cars to return. But then it took fourteen minutes. In the city an augmented reality conference was taking place, and there were masses of foreign visitors staggering around in disorientation, getting lost in price tags visible only to them or in the thicket of tourist information bubbles floating around, who wanted to be picked up by all available taxis on various street corners of the city.

Robert waited on a bench under a tall tree, leafed through the teacher's book, and checked whether the first letters of the chapters perhaps yielded a sentence or at least an anagram.

Unnoticed by Robert, blackbirds were meanwhile flying out of the crown of the tree over him and plunging soundlessly into the nearby park, only to return immediately. They were bringing fresh twigs and threading them into the nest emerging not many yards above humanity, as if they were sewing up a wound in the tree.

In 1934 a photographer named Ferenz Balkin discovered near Meiringen in the Swiss Alps an interesting, strangely shaped tree stump. After he had pressed his camera's shutter release, the strange tree stump stood up and ran away. The animal was probably the Tatzelwurm, the last of its kind in that region. The Tatzelwurm remained native to Austria for several decades, at the start of exploratory drilling for the Semmering base tunnel several smaller specimens were flushed out and chased away. After all the Tatzelwurms were gone, many workers complained of intense, persistent headaches and attacks of vertigo, which considerably slowed the progress of the excavation.

HÄUSLER – Z.
THE NATURE OF DISTANCE
P. 43

7.   Rue de la Loi

[GREEN FOLDER]

A few days before my departure for Brussels I received a spam e-mail with the subject line: *Going Belge?* The sender was a certain Merwin Thompson. When I opened the message, it contained only the well-known pitch for erection medication: *Wanna penis stay hard up all the time? Satisfy your wifes inner pleasure infinity! This really works have shown studies all around the world! Absolutely Powerful Unique Incredibly Penis-strength!* And so on. I read the e-mail through several times, in search of hidden messages. I printed it out and then deleted it from my inbox.

When Julia entered the room, I hid the sheet of paper from her. I put it in the green folder with the other documents about Magda T. Now and then I nibbled at them, when I felt unobserved.

The simultaneous fluttering of all the rolling letters on the display board at the Frankfurt airport updating itself automatically every few minutes: like a sudden gust of wind in the leaves of a tree.

On the airplane from Frankfurt to Brussels I read my favorite book, *Miss Lonely-hearts* by Nathanael West, which successfully distracted me from the compulsion to constantly figure out how horizontal or slanted the airplane was now as it hung in the air. At some point the plane plunged into a dense cloud layer, a uniform gray, into which the wings jutted. At the end of the wing, slightly blurred by the dense cloud mist, a light blinked, as if in proof that somewhere another pulse was beating. Inside a cloud it was possible to imagine that you were driving along on the ground. I put the book down and stared out a little, *Directly under us is grass,* I thought, *earth and grass, that's why the movement is so bumpy. A bumpy alpine meadow.* I couldn't help thinking of the article about Magda T. and tried to picture her face, but then the kind God-face of Leo Tolstoy intruded. I was particularly bothered by the passage in which Magda says she would like to be an astronaut because she thought that was a profession she could pursue without difficulty. Yet the long-term psychological damage from missions in outer space was still largely uninvestigated. The only thing that was certain was that the number of astronauts who in old age had to contend with severe hallucinations and unusually rapid progressive dementia was alarmingly high. (A short stretch of wild turbulence shook us.) An American woman astronaut had driven cross-country nonstop in adult diapers to kidnap a rival. Another astronaut had become incapable overnight of setting foot in his own house, so he slept for over a year in a garbage can and ate cockroaches and mice that he, as he said, squeezed like mustard packets to consume them. Another astronaut fell shortly after his return from his first space walk into a mania and, in an attempt to climb the façade of a hundred-story high-rise, broke several vertebrae. And the head of a training program for chimpanzees that had been sent on various missions succumbed in the seventies to a religious delusion and had his disciples wall him alive into a bridge pier somewhere in Oregon. The profession probably held a particular attraction for the sort of people who had always had a tendency to subject themselves to extreme situations, but it was also possible that the effects of the physical distance from earth had actually been previously underestimated. On a Mars mission the earth is no longer perceptible to the naked eye, and who knows what new forms of panic are born at that moment. The landing in Brussels was rough, the cabin lights went out twice, and an old woman took out her rosary and began, soundlessly, thank God, to finger the beads.

I had developed a habit of thinking after every successful landing: In reality I've crashed, pain and chaos, death and descent into hell. But then I'm granted a second chance, permitted to return from the gray asphodel swamp, like a broken lamp I am carefully laid on the boat that brings me to the other shore, back into this world, there I'm given some time to recover my breath. Slowly and arduously I relearn all the skills that I forgot at one fell swoop, distinguishing left from right, doing mental arithmetic, speaking, recognizing people and faces, and reenter life exactly where I was torn out of it: The plane has landed, a miracle, and I'm really standing on the earth, the old, familiar ground, which I had actually lost forever. Even as colorless a being as the secretary at Oeversee High School, to whom I had complained about how bad my stomach flu was, which meant I would probably have to stay home this week, seemed to me at that moment a true miracle, a gift from heaven.

I had such thoughts as I took a taxi to my hotel, and then I thought: Despite that uplifting, wonderful fantasy, which can sweeten your whole day, it would be incredibly funny if on the return flight I crashed in actuality and not only in an imaginary parallel world, if I had through my fantasy made that disaster palatable for fate, had raised the irony ante on the game table, as it were . . . And already I was panicking.

I was not even capable of retracing the fatal train of thought in order to retroactively correct it. I told the taxi driver to stop, paid, and looked for a little café, that almost always worked, the darker the café, the stronger the effect, shortly after entering you feel pleasantly bodiless . . . Soon I was doing somewhat better, and to round it all off, I ordered a number of childish things like a large soda and a couple scoops of ice cream with whipped cream (which I hoped would come with a fan-shaped cone and a little glitter umbrella, the wooden handle of which I would lick off first).

I pulled the green folder out of my backpack and read indiscriminately from the documents compiled by Oliver Baumherr and his colleagues.

I found especially funny an article mentioning that the two abductors who eventually took Magda away from her father and her uncle to bring her home apparently must have been heavily under the influence of drugs, so that they didn't blame the symptoms on the presence of the Indigo child in the backseat, but rather on the effects of the narcotic. Smart. They let Magda T. out somewhere near a psychiatric clinic, drove away in the car, and left no further traces. She had climbed a white flight of steps into the large building and had there told the first person she encountered who she was and where she lived. That hadn't worked right away, however, because the man had been quite slow on the uptake. He had just stared at her and shaken his head.

Then another man had come and had led her away from the first man. This second man had been considerably more receptive and understanding. He had asked her name, her address, the names of her parents, her birthday, her favorite ice-cream flavor, the name of her pillow, the exact age of her fingernails. They grew back completely every few weeks, he said, even if you pulled them off entirely—that was very painful, but you could be sure that they would eventually come back, as nice and long as before. She had not been able to answer all the man's questions, so she had asked him to take her to a telephone. The man had laughed and said it was *obviously prohibited* for them to use the phone, that only gave you radiation in your skull and a satellite loaded you up with electricity from outer space so that you would lie incapacitated in bed for several days, your head as big as the room and your hands as small as the red sulfuric heads of matches.

At some point she had been pulled away from this man too, finally people had listened to her and suddenly everything had happened very fast, a telephone had even been available, and they had called various agencies for her. After half an hour with the kind and understanding people she had been left alone again and after a while the understanding bearded man had returned, who had worn a white gown, and had said he felt somewhat nauseous and dizzy, he probably had an upset stomach from the *wretched muck they serve you here*.

Although I didn't entirely understand what exactly had happened and what I had just read, I had to laugh heartily.

To quell the excitement before the meeting with Herr Ferenz, I listened to a few songs by the British band Faithless on my iPod: "Mass Destruction," "Insomnia," and "Bombs."

Besides, I was in the city in which Europe was made. Here you could distract yourself for at least a few hours. I looked at the little peeing man, the city's greatest attraction. A dense crowd of tourists surrounded the tiny sculpture. An Italian woman had burst into tears out of sheer amazement and was photographing it fervently from all sides.

When I returned to the hotel, the man at reception said that someone had dropped something off for me.

– Voilà, he said softly, as he handed it to me.

A Jenga block. Somewhat scuffed, but still clearly recognizable.

– Merci, I said.

With the voice on the telephone I had arranged a meeting place near my hotel. In a small green and brown park full of ravens I waited for someone to approach me. I held the Jenga block out in front of me, clearly visible to anyone passing by. The large birds with their completely black, eyeless-seeming heads stalked morosely across the meadow and rooted around with their beaks between the blades of grass for food. At some distance stood a steel structure that obviously claimed to be art, and thus seemed so completely disengaged and dissociated from all present and future problems of the Brussels population that it was almost offensive.

– Jenga.

Herr Ferenz was a peculiar figure. Long sideburns adorned his face, although the hair on his head had already thinned considerably. He was strikingly thin, and had little more shoulders than an egg. When he laughed, his expression had something quietly content and open like that of a sloth.

On the way out of the park we crossed a meadow on which a large oak chest stood, next to it two men wearing silvery colorful stage clothing as if for a magic show leaned against a tree and smoked cigarettes. Three stone steps led us from the green space down to the sidewalk of the Avenue des Azalées. We followed it southward and eventually entered a small restaurant, in which Herr Ferenz was greeted with a bow.

– Thank you for making time, I said.

Herr Ferenz only nodded.

– You have to excuse my German, he said. It's rusty.

He spoke with a very slight accent, which sounded Eastern European.

– How did you get the name Ferenz?

– Oh, he said. On the black market.

He laughed.

– There's a black market for everything. Even names. Even appearances. A gigantic one. A monstrous one. But the problem is never the production in itself. That is, no one knows the formula. How it works. You understand? A proper, a functioning name.

I let the cream of pumpkin soup drip from my spoon back into the bowl, put the spoon down, and looked at him. His facial expression changed, became softer, more compassionate. He shook his head and said:

– Terrible, isn't it?

I nodded.

– But that's just how people are, he said, stuck a fork coiled with spaghetti in his mouth, chewed. Mmm . . . mm . . . They simply see their fellow human beings as tools . . . mm . . . Some tools stand around ready to harvest, you only have to stuff them into a van at the right time and drive away with them. Others you first have to plant, such as . . . let's say you need a little . . . a name for an experiment, then it hardly makes sense to locate this name somewhere, to memorize the times of day when it's attainable, that is, when a controlled extraction can take place and so on. No. It would be much easier if you simply paid a woman from Eastern Europe who is unintentionally pregnant with a name, so that you can have her name. The name isn't registered anywhere, so it won't be missed, if it—

I raised a finger.

– A question, I said. What exactly are you telling me here?

He laughed. Then he said:

– The world is a sick place. It does no good to stick your fingers in your ears and say *mimimimi.*

– Okay, I said.

He propped both elbows on the table, rested his chin on his fists, and looked at me. For three, perhaps four seconds.

– You're not naïve, he said in a tone as if he wanted to declare, *Check!* You know exactly what I mean. For most people the world is a . . . *un hypermarché du bricolage.* A DIY superstore. Shelves, shelves, shelves everywhere, and every single one full of tools that you can use until they break. Just think of animals. As soon as we discover a new animal, the first thing we're interested in is the question of whether we can eat it. And with us it's exactly the same. When a baby is born, people start thinking: *What might it be good for? In what way might it serve me?*

After the meal, during which I mainly had to tell Herr Ferenz about Oliver Baumherr, how he was doing, how he treated his colleagues, we went to his apartment. He led me up the Kunstberg to a building with a small shop on the ground floor that had abstract bird sculptures and hats in its display window. Little sculptures and hats, only these two things were sold there, at extremely high prices. The bird sculptures seemed archaic and could have stood next to many-armed god statuettes and erotic carvings on Dr. Freud's desk on Berggasse in Vienna, while the hats floated ownerless through his dreams and meant all sorts of things, anxieties about the future or geometrically impressive family constellations, or whatever, there was no salvation from interpretation, no more than there was an emergency exit from history.

Herr Ferenz's apartment was on the third floor. The air there was astonishingly fresh, as if the windows had never been closed in the last twenty years. Every-where stood small statues in the style of North American indigenous people. Masks hung on the walls or were stacked on the floor. Ronald Reagan was among them, Michael Jackson and Saddam Hussein and a number of other classic bank robber masks. A few colorful party hats stood, one inside the other like plastic cups in the supermarket, in the form of a slightly bent ziggurat on a workbench. On a desk leaned a calendar with pictures of Elis dolls. Each week a new picture. In today's space someone had written in large block letters:

ARRIVÉ!!!
C.S.—9:00.

C.S.—that had to be me, Clemens Setz. Strange, I thought, at nine o'clock I was just on the way to Frankfurt. I hadn't arrived in Brussels until around noon. And the three exclamation points . . .

On the wall next to the desk hung a few very impressive black-and-white photographs, which had presumably been taken with extremely long exposure times. The view of a city, a soccer stadium, a classroom. One of the pictures was signed with a wide *V.*

– Beautiful, aren't they?

– The pictures? Interesting, yes.

– That's a special technique, which . . . yeah, it would probably be too complicated to explain it now.

There was a pause.

– Oliver Baumherr showed me documents about Magda T.

Ferenz laughed. He had the Jenga block in his hand, though I couldn't remember having given him mine back. I checked my pockets. They were empty.

– Magda, yes, dear Magda, said Ferenz. I was the one who . . .

He ended the sentence with a rolling gesture of his right hand.

– You know . . . Herr Setz, right?

– Yes.

– Not Seitz?

– No.

– Okay. Herr Setz. When you called, I thought, *Olivier is sending me a gift.* But that's not the case. You really don't have the slightest . . . ? No, tell me: Why are you here?

– Well, I worked at the Helianau Institute.

– Mm-hmm, Ferenz said with a nod.

– And I noticed that students disappeared. They were taken away, and the name . . . your name kept coming up.

– That's what happens when you buy your name in a DIY superstore, said Ferenz.

– After that, I did some research and wrote an article about a single mother in Gillingen, I even brought the article along for you, and I visited the family of one of my former students, and at their home everything was really weird, I had an attack there.

It took a while for Ferenz to respond. Then he said:

– Seriously?

– What?

– Oh, never mind. Now you're here, right? And a friend of Olivier's is a friend of mine. Unfortunately, the reverse isn't true.

He leaned against the workbench, gave me, it seemed to me, a pitying look, and began to speak.

– If you give people the chance to do something they're too ashamed to do on their own, you always trigger an avalanche. In 1739 Thomas Coram established the Foundling Hospital in London. At the time it was the first care facility for abandoned children. Before that there was nothing. If a mother wanted to get rid of her baby, she took it and . . . (Herr Ferenz pantomimed it.) But the Foundling Hospital had only four hundred beds, and the rush of mothers who wanted to give up their babies was tremendous, well, you have to imagine: really tremendous, incredible, barely manageable. So all the mothers had to participate in a lottery. A container with balls. The mother reaches into it blindly. If she draws a white ball, the child is accepted, a red ball means waiting list, a black ball rejection. In many attics in England these black balls could still be found well into the twentieth century, mostly wrapped in some cloth so that they weren't recognizable at first glance. The old disgrace.

Pause. I said nothing.

– There are so many parents, said Herr Ferenz, who want to get rid of them, most often, for some reason, in Scandinavia. Last year there were eleven.

– Eleven children?

– Many parents take a close look at the new owners first, it's, well, it's terrible.

He left the workbench and walked through the room. Then he picked up one of the big-nosed masks and, with a weary sigh, put it next to his bed. The mask was probably supposed to portray a hippopotamus. It was stone-gray and plastered with a great number of shiny strips. In some places a few headlines of the newspaper that had been used to make the papier-mâché shone through from under the gray paint.

– Yes, that's terrible, I said.

– And there's nothing at all that can be done about it, said Herr Ferenz, picking
up the mask and putting it on.

He tapped it with his knuckles as if he wanted to check it for weak spots. Then
he took it off again, shook his head, and sat down.

– It all proceeds by way of friends and relatives, by way of families, he murmured. That's the great niche that no one ever gets close to. And if a family
would like to immigrate to Brazil or Argentina . . . together, you understand?
Hand in hand? Then you can't prevent them from doing that either. Ah,
putain . . .

He had turned the mask around and discovered something in it. With his little
finger he took it out. It was a residue of reddish paint, as if from lipstick. Herr
Ferenz moistened his thumb and wiped the remaining mark from the inside of
the mask with it.

The oh-God-what-the-hell-am-I-doing-here? feeling set in.

But that was nothing, said Herr Ferenz, he had once worked on the case of a
mother, an Albanian woman, who had sold her children to a pimp. The pimp, who
was distantly related to her, took the two kids one night. One of the two kids,
due to lack of oxygen during birth, was mentally disabled, couldn't speak, and
had difficulties with spatial coordination, and on account of those impairments
the mother had been promised a particularly high price for the child. So she had
the two of them (four and seven years old) picked up, and waited for the money.
But it didn't come, for weeks the mother waited in vain for the agreed-upon
high sum. So she went to the police and reported the pimp. But not for child
abduction or human trafficking, no, she sued him because he didn't pay his debts
with her. And that was how the whole thing first got out. And then, in court, the
woman wept and said: I made a mistake. Yes, he, Ferenz, had with his own . . . but
what, what— Herr Ferenz waited until I removed my hands from my ears.

– What's the matter? he asked.

– Nothing, I said, that's just automatic . . . when something makes me angry.

– Did you hear what I said?

– Yes, every word.

– Well, and then recently I heard about this incident, an unusual occurrence in
one of those long lines for a baby hatch in Brooklyn, a woman was standing
there—

– Whoa, whoa, whoa, hold on, one second!

I had actually waved my hands. Herr Ferenz looked at me with an amused expression in his eyes. He put the mask on the workbench.

– What?

– In line for the baby hatch? I asked.

– Yes.

– Isn't that a bit . . .

– In-your-face? Yes, of course, totally. Anyway, it was a few years ago, and there was this line, and you know how it is, like at the airport, you wait and wait, one woman behind another, and some have these little blue frozen bundles in their hands and wonder why it's not moving, others have come with a stroller because they at least tried it for a while, you understand, purchase of a stroller, ekseterah—

The French intonation of the et cetera brought me back to reality. For a moment I had accepted the invitation of the horror story and had imagined the situation.

– But that didn't really happen!

– Not here, said Herr Ferenz, shaking his head. In Brooklyn. But . . . well, anyway, these women are standing there in line, and some time has passed, and the night is also cold, always in winter, most babies end up in the hatch . . . um, most babies end up in the hatch in winter, ah, German word order, the faster I speak, I make more . . . the more mistakes—I—make, haha, but this is nothing, you should hear my Flemish, it's absolute crap, even though I hear it every day—

– You're joking, right?

– No, I can't speak Flemish, it's enough to drive you crazy. Where was I with the story? It . . . ah, yes, the night is quite cold, one of those nasty nights when really everything freezes, even makeup or superglue or the hands of a clock, and why isn't it moving, up front, the women begin to ask, first one, then the others, in Brooklyn a few years ago, a night like other nights, icy cold, and then suddenly someone answers, Yeah, because she's taking so long there in front, she still wants to say goodbye, and the others reply: Yeah, she should have thought about that sooner, this is already my third time here, and I've never said goodbye, that doesn't even occur to me, to let a bastard like that make me feel guilty, and so on, just the way it is in Brooklyn in wintertime. And then suddenly a woman in the line attracts attention, she doesn't have a baby at all. She's just standing there, in her winter clothes, and is, so to speak, childless. She's waiting, all by herself, and it of course quickly becomes clear to the others that she's not with anyone, she's not a companion or something. So they speak to her, What are you doing in our line, why are you standing here, if you don't even want to give up a baby? The woman doesn't answer, pretends she's deaf. When the others move forward a few feet, she moves forward a few feet too, but she does no more than that, she doesn't respond at all to the other women in line for the hatch. In the hatch line without a hatchling, you might say, hahaha.

He actually laughed.

During that brief breather it occurred to me to pay attention to my facial muscles. I seized the marionette strings, which had slipped out of my grasp, pulled them tight, and my mouth closed.

– And the woman ignores everyone who speaks to her, she turns her head away and doesn't answer, doesn't respond, the others look at her to see whether she might be pregnant, for some women also come to the baby hatch in Brooklyn to give birth astride it, as it were, it happens from time to time that idiots like that get in the line.

– Naaaa, stop, stop, stop! I cried. This is—

– It's almost over, the story. Anyway, the woman inches forward in the line, the others follow her, and she is standing in front of the baby hatch, and now everyone is really very, very curious about what she is going to put into it. Will it be a bucket with a face on it, like those crazy women from the suburbs always carry around with them, God knows why, or will it be a gift, for that happens now and then too, or money in an envelope or baby clothes in those depressing colors that baby clothes for some reason always have to be, you know, those depressing autumn colors, that dark red and that blue. Or what will it be? That's what the women in line are wondering. And then the woman without a baby is finally next, and she steps in front of the hatch, the automatic opening is activated, the motion sensor detected her, so she isn't a figment of their imagination or the appearance of an angel that has come among the poor lost souls, but a woman of flesh and blood. And what do you think she puts in the baby hatch?

– What?

Herr Ferenz took a step back and shook his head. As he did so, he laughed, as if at some childishness.

– We could go to a new club, to Getuige X-1. Just opened a few months ago. There's actually not much going on there yet, but . . .

– No, thanks, I said. I'd rather go back to the . . . But what was in the baby hatch?

Herr Ferenz laughed:

– I like you better this way, Herr Setz. You should see your face now. Open for anything.

8. Skin

The alprazolam always made him pleasantly dazed, his head a wreck-
ing ball swinging back and forth, constantly in search of something
it could smash into. He had taken half a pill to quell the enormous
excitement. Now he felt guilty, because he had over the years stolen so
much of Cordula's medication and hidden it in his room. A real little
pharmacy. Meanwhile she had always trusted that there was exactly
the same number of pills as she remembered. She was well adjusted.
Actually the most admirable thing there is, thought Robert distractedly, watching from his shaky head-spaceship as he floated through
the streets. The composure with which you tolerate the bad music in
a taxi. You determine where it goes, so you patiently tolerate the crap
from the nineties that is played on the ride there.

Stop the rock . . . can't stop the rock . . .

When they arrived in the area where Clemens Setz lived, he saw
through the taxi window three airplanes on the reddening evening
horizon, leaving very short vapor trails behind them. Like three com-
ets. The image reminded him of illustrations to science fiction stories
from the thirties, the holy era before *Star Trek*: the tiny spaceship and
satellite swarm in the background, in the atmosphere of the planet,
while in the foreground larger vehicles move, in which the main
characters of the story sit in shiny full-body suits.

Robert wore his "Dingo Bait" shirt and his coat over it. Even though
it was a warm day, he was getting cold. Definitely the sedative. When
he stepped out of the taxi, he was even freezing. He zipped his coat,
but the zipper got stuck halfway up, like a tiny elevator. He tugged at

it, tripped and almost fell over a sleeping beggar. In a pastry shop not far from the teacher's address, Robert bought a bottle of mineral water. The iBall in the pastry shop wobbled strangely in a circle.

He still felt cold, so he decided to run the next few blocks. It wasn't far, and besides, he now wanted to get everything over with as quickly as possible. When he stopped after a few steps because the bottle had fallen out of his coat pocket and he had to get it out from under a car, he noticed that at some distance behind him a man was standing on the sidewalk, breathing heavily, as if he had been running too, his hands resting on his knees, looking at him.

Robert wiped the mineral water bottle off on his coat, put it in his pocket, and walked on slowly.

He turned around. The man was still standing there.

Robert walked a bit faster, it wasn't much farther, he walked with his head turned slightly to the side so that he could hear any suspicious noise, not much farther, it had to be right up there—but then there were suddenly footsteps, faster than his, approaching him from behind. He turned around and saw the man. He was running with a hobble, but he was running. Toward him. And in his hand he was holding a bouquet of long-stemmed flowers.

When he started to run, Robert's bottle fell on the sidewalk again, but this time he didn't stop, but just kept running. He looked around briefly, saw that his pursuer had picked up the bottle and held it up. Shit. Robert ducked behind a tobacco kiosk. He looked around the corner. The man seemed to again be completely out of breath, he stood there, his mouth wide open, and began moving again only after he had rested a little and his chest rose and sank less dramatically than before. He was quite an old man. How ridiculous to be followed by such an old, out-of-shape guy.

Robert ventured out from behind the tobacco kiosk, and when he looked around he saw that the old man was moving again too on the opposite side of the street. However, he now seemed not to notice him, he was looking somewhere else entirely. Robert quickened his pace and tried at the same time to seem invisible, but then the man suddenly crossed the street. Robert jumped over the fluttering barrier tape of a construction site, a cyclopean camera eye on the brow of a large truck winked at him, he ran past a fence behind which a barking dog accompanied him a few yards, as if it were shouting after him to stay the course. Ridiculous, ridiculous, he thought in the double rhythm of his footsteps. Why was someone running after him? Ultimately he could simply stop and ask the man what he wanted. Probably the old man would then simply run past him, as if Robert were an advertising pillar. He looked back over his shoulder and saw the man with the bouquet of flowers at the end of the street. He couldn't tell whether the man was looking at him; in any case, he started running again, Robert too. Shit, shit, shit. And that stupid song was also stuck in his head, *stop the rock*, and it transformed into *the funk soul brother*, all that same nineties dance music crap, those endless repetitions.

He had shaken off the man.

Panting, he tried to orient himself. He pulled his cell phone out of his pocket, saw on the display that an iBall was right around the corner. Before he stepped in front of it, he adjusted his clothing and checked his hair in the mirror of a dark car window.

On the doorbell nameplate was written, in scrawly block letters, "SETZ." Robert rang, an ascending melody, from some opera, Cordula had sometimes played it in her pillow. A woman opened the door.

—Yes?

—Yes, hello, said Robert. I was looking for Herr Setz.

— Oh, well . . . My husband isn't well.

— I've come all the way from—

— He can't receive any visitors at the moment.

— But . . . it would be very important to me to see him. I've brought a book too, here.

He took the book he had borrowed from Frau Rabl out of his pocket and held it out to the woman. She leaned forward to decipher the cover.

– Are you a journalist? she asked.

– No. A former student of his.

– Ah, I see. From Oeversee. What year?

– No, from Helianau.

The woman's pretty face hardened, but then relaxed again right away.

– Come in, she said softly.

On the chest of drawers right next to the door, hats were stacked in increasing size into a tower, in accordance with the apparently steadily growing head of their owner over the years.

Robert took off his shoes.

A cat was sleeping on a windowsill and lifted its head as the stranger passed.

The woman knocked on a door. Behind it something fell at the same moment on the floor, and a man's cursing could be heard.

In the math teacher's room was an old overhead projector, like an ostrich robot sleeping while sitting.

– Hello, said Robert.

– Hello, replied the man.

Robert recognized him immediately. The teacher, however, clearly didn't have the faintest idea who was standing in front of him.

– How can I help you? he asked, confused, looking at his wife.

– My name is Robert Tätzel, Herr Setz. Do you remember?

The man's face fell as if he had suffered a bilateral stroke.

– Yes, he said. I do, of course. How are you? What are you doing these days, Herr Tätzel?

The fact that the teacher addressed him as Herr Tätzel confused Robert. He tried to focus on the phrases with which he intended to explain why he had come. But all he saw when he looked into himself was a glass of milk from which a peculiar gleam of light emanated. Cordula. And the unpleasant man in the bank lobby. Then he realized that the teacher had asked him about his career. He pulled out of the inside pocket of his coat a few postcards on which he had

had some of his paintings printed, among them the prizewinning painting entitled *M*.

The teacher held them up in front of his face with interest.

Then he recoiled and looked for his wife, seeking help. He took off his glasses and pretended to keep looking at the paintings. But Robert could tell from his eyes that he was looking through the postcards. His focus was set to a distant point.

– Very interesting, said the teacher. And what brings you to me, Herr Tätzel?

Robert took the postcards from him and put them back in his pocket.

He had noticed that the math teacher's hands were trembling.

– Yes, I didn't want to bother you, said Robert. After you've been through so much. I mean, I want to say right at the outset that I was always convinced of your innocence. I also brought something along ... for signing ...

He held up the book. The teacher put his glasses back on. He shook his head.

– I can't concentrate, he murmured.

He felt around on himself as if he were searching for a lighter.

– My glasses, my glasses ...

His wife came up to him and showed him that the glasses were in the middle of his face.

– Ah, he said.

– Did you hear? his wife asked him gently. He would like you to sign his book.

The man raised his head.

– What?

– I ... , said Robert, blindly pulling from the fish pond the first phrase he caught hold of, I recently received a prize. For a painting.

Then he simply ran out of breath. He breathed in, out, this room had a peculiar atmosphere. It had been stupid to come here.

– Yes, so, what now?

– Everything will be fine, the woman said, stroking his head.

– Has he read my books? asked the teacher.

The woman gave Robert a questioning look.

He nodded.

– Well! Oh!

That seemed to make the teacher happy.

– I wanted to talk to you about . . .

– And now you would like to do something for me?

– Um, well, Herr Setz, said Robert, I've actually come to ask you something. I was recently at an award ceremony, and a man approached me there, and he said that he knows you. And that you had something to do with, um, what do I know . . .

– I don't know, the teacher said to his wife.

She put a hand on his shoulder. Robert's mind began to flutter. He looked into the teacher's face, which was overwhelmed by the situation, and searched for a word with which he could get through to him. He found it.

– Ferenz, he said. Interference. Does that name mean anything to you?

During the silence, which lasted nearly a minute, all that could be heard in the room was the buzzing of several mosquitoes. That was what a dentist's drill would sound like, thought Robert, if it had a soul.

– Okay, said the teacher, in a totally changed voice.

His face also no longer looked confused.

– How long have you been back? he asked Robert.

– What?

– Well, how long . . . ?

– I don't know what you mean.

– That is, you haven't just returned from . . . ?

– No.

– Oh, God, said the man. Oh, thank goodness.

The teacher laughed and shook his head. He put his hand to his mouth.

– Robert Tätzel, he said. I wouldn't have thought that you . . . And your zone, so it really is . . . ?

Robert made a tabula rasa gesture with both hands. The teacher nodded. He reached into his pants pocket.

Robert was afraid that he was about to slip him, like a bellboy who has lugged a heavy suitcase to the twelfth floor, a crumpled bill. But it was something else. Slowly and deliberately his former teacher placed an old telephone card in his hand. On the back of it someone had drawn a little party hat.

Thank you, Robert wanted to say, and he imagined the slightly distracted tone of his voice. But he said nothing. The card lay in his palm, he nodded and put it in his pocket. An unexpectedly relaxed feeling suffused him. He was suddenly totally at peace. Just like that time on the tram when the sign for a pastry shop had caught his eye. The clock hands of the world stopped between two seconds. Dead calm.

– Yes, all right, then, said the woman.

– Can you show him out, Julia? the teacher asked his wife with a soft voice.

He seemed suddenly very tired. With an exaggerated-seeming sigh he flopped down in his armchair. It was clearly acting, just like his confusion earlier. When Robert, disappointed with the short, unsatisfying meeting, left the room, the teacher briefly raised his hand. He returned the gesture.

Robert registered a trembling in the eyes of Setz's wife. Nystagmus. He thought of Alicia, but that couldn't be it, she didn't seem to be dizzy. So he asked her:

– Pardon my asking, but . . . what's the matter with your eyes?

– Oh, no one really knows, said the woman.

– And . . . can you see me?

She looked at him, reached out her arm, and her forefinger pointed to the middle of his face. Robert backed away.

– There, said the woman.

– What?

– There's your nose.

Robert laughed so that she would take her finger away.

– You know, you shouldn't upset him. You should see him when he . . . talks about the past, about his time at that horrible institute . . . Sorry. He collects these articles about . . . oh, what do I know, about all sorts of things, torture, really awful things are in them. He can't even look at them anymore. Puts them away in a folder. But I think your visit made him happy.

– Yes, I had actually wanted to ask him . . .

The woman had turned away from him slightly, as if she wanted to go back into the room. But then she reached out her hand again and put it on something invisible directly in front of her. Robert exhaled as heavily as if someone had given him a forceful push from behind. He got goose bumps.

– There, the woman said softly.

Her hand ran along the old contour.

– Blue, she said, shaking her head, as if someone had made a stupid remark. I've never understood why people always say: blue . . . indigo blue.

Robert didn't budge and followed the path of her hand. It was the most pleasant thing he had experienced recently. His chest seemed to widen, and he breathed twice as much air as usual. To suddenly feel it again, after such a long time . . .

– You can trust me, he said.

His own voice seemed to come from a muffled sound source in the middle of the room. The woman's hand slowly sank. And then she clutched her head and massaged her temples. The universal migraine gesture.

– There are books, said the woman, he can barely even touch them anymore. If he has to put them on a new shelf, because the old one is full, it looks like he has back pains. He walks like a tyrannosaurus. All bent forward.

She took a step toward the door. Robert noticed that she was about to bump into the dresser with her hip, and he held her back by the shoulder.

– Watch out, he said.

– Thanks, she said, and pretended to sneeze.

At the same moment the door to the study opened, and the teacher stood in front of him. He held some folders in his hand.

– All right, he said. Thanks for waiting. You can come in. Everything is ready.

Robert looked at the woman, then the teacher, the apartment door.

– Please, said the teacher, pointing the way into another room, which was somewhat farther back, in the more poorly lit interior of the apartment.

– It's a peculiar network, said the math teacher, and his voice was hoarse and longed for him to clear his throat, but he didn't. It seems not to matter at all who this person actually is. The name stays the same, only the spaceship in which the name sits is always a different one. Or no, spaceship is actually the wrong image. Yeah, what was I going to say . . . You know, my concentration isn't the best. Anyway, yeah, it's . . .

The acoustic equivalent of old tree bark. Robert didn't know what the man was talking about, but he was so preoccupied with listening to this voice longing for a throat-clearing that he didn't really mind.

– A peculiar network, in any case. It's unknown how long it's existed. The funny thing about it is that the name doesn't seem to change, only the man who bears it. He's like a new body module for the same idea. Ah, I didn't express that well. Mm-rrhm!

Finally! thought Robert. The throat-clearing, the release. The teacher's voice was clear again.

– I met him, you know.

Robert wanted to ask, Whom? And what the hell is this all about? But the teacher went on:

– And I'd like . . . Well, yes, here . . .

He handed Robert a green and a red-checkered folder.

– Pedestrian light system, said Setz. Green: Go. Red: No-go.

In the folders were photocopies, printouts, and a great number of handwritten pieces of paper. Robert blinked, the writing was tiny, all capital letters, pressed close together. Like a minimalist carpet pattern. From a certain distance they might as well have been zeroes and ones.

– There are people, said the teacher, they inscribe a coin and spend it, what do I know, in a bar, for example, somewhere, and then look at every coin they come across very closely, to see whether it might have come back to them. As you can see, I've signed every piece of paper here. Here (he leafed through them) . . . here . . . you see?

– Yes.

– And, well . . .

The woman entered the room and touched her husband on the head. The head had grown considerably rounder, Robert thought, since back then. Well, okay, in the lecture hall at Helianau he had actually always seen him only from above.

– For me? he asked.

It wasn't entirely clear to him what he was supposed to do with all these pieces of paper.

– In the green folder, began the math teacher.

– Clemens?

He turned around to face his wife.

– Look, I have something for you here, she said.

She placed it in his hand, and he looked at it, smiled gratefully, and put it in his mouth. With his hand he made a grasping movement and looked around. The woman gave him a glass of water. He emptied it in one gulp. Then he winked at her, gestured to Robert as if to say, We got him, and even nudged Robert with his elbow and laughed.

– Such a little rascal, said the woman.

Robert nodded politely.

– Doesn't he look like an owl? said the woman, stroking his face with both hands. Here, this part here, it keeps getting rounder, and this hair here, he has a cowlick there, it always sticks out. And in the eye of the hair tornado . . . appears the bald spot. Do you like bald spots?

– Um, Robert said with a shrug. No idea.

– I like them, said the teacher, again forming a grasping claw hand.

– Okay, said Robert. So, thanks for this here . . .

Just get out of here.

– Why did you write that on your T-shirt? the teacher suddenly asked.

– Hm?

Robert looked down at himself.

– Oh, that, he said, well, I don't know.

– I see.

– A statement, I suppose.

– What does it say? asked the woman, leaning forward.

– Can you make it out, Julia? asked Setz.

– Nnn . . . The writing isn't easy to read . . . Din . . .

– Dingo Bait.

The woman made a surprised face.

– Let me see! she said, pulling Robert closer to her by the T-shirt with both hands.

– *Ts*, she said. You're an odd duck. You should actually get along well with my husband.

– Ah, yes, said Robert. We do get along . . . very well . . .

– I once visited his family, that must be fifteen years ago now, said Clemens Setz.

– Oh, that was you? asked the woman.

– I assume your relationship with your family isn't the best?

– No, said Robert. It's not.

– Thank God, said the teacher.

He pointed, as if in proof of his assertion, to the folders in Robert's hand.

– Yes, as I mentioned, some people also mark the coin with a notch on the side.

– Oh, are you telling him your coin story? said the woman. You know, he really did that once a long time ago. In Paris.

Robert looked up.

– In Paris, that was on a day when we were on our way some-where . . . Where were we when it poured so terribly?

– Um, said her husband. We fled into the Virgin Megastore, as soaking wet as otters after a meal.

– You and your comparisons, said the woman.

– And the people there, those weird Parisians, looked at us as if we were crazy, even though we were only wet. As if they had never seen a wet human being before. My God, we were really drenched to the . . . that was something, hahaha, that was something.

He clapped his hands.

– Doesn't he look like an owl when he laughs like that? asked the woman, again stroking his head.

The teacher found that so funny that he slapped Robert's knee instead of his own. Robert winced a little, clenched his teeth, and smiled amiably. He had an urge to break small things.

– And the coin?

– What?

– The coin, said Robert. The one you marked and spent. Did it ever come back to you?

Setz gave his wife a look that meant, Isn't he funny? Then he again patted Robert on the knee. He took off his glasses, cleaned them, and said, in a somewhat altered tone:

– Read it. You'll see, it's a very, very peculiar network, the whole thing . . . And let me say something else. I'm happy that you're here, Herr Tätzel. I mean, here. Not elsewhere. It could have been otherwise. Maybe my effort paid off.

When Robert stepped out of the taxi and crossed the street, he had to put a hand on his Adam's apple, because he had the sensation that the air he was breathing was coming out at that point in the neck without permission. As if his breathing were doubled, had an echo, so to speak. He couldn't swallow, at least his mouth didn't want to, his chest was also narrower than usual.

Even though he debated silently for several minutes with the supervisory authority in his head, which advised him strongly against doing something stupid in this state, as he passed a pleasantly colorful graffiti wall near the Kepler Bridge (on which a rat dressed in drag was painted, holding a long Saint Nicholas staff in its paw), he stopped a passerby and asked him to hold the telephone card for a moment and then give it back to him. No, no, just hold it first, you don't have to do anything— But the man recoiled from the strange offer and hurried away. Robert tried it a few yards farther on with a young woman who was walking with a stroller. In the stroller lay a baby with bluish, almost translucent skin. Like a fish dressed up as a baby. He explained to the frightened-looking woman what to do. And she did it, but she looked so intimidated and braced for disaster that the soothing effect wouldn't set in again. Annoyed, Robert took the telephone card out of her hand and walked on.

In his apartment the heating had switched off, and he left his coat on. One warm autumn day was all it took for the iBall, like his neighbor, to think it was the middle of summer. Wretched, poorly designed thing. Robert put the green and the red-checkered folders on the bed. He planned to stay awake a long time and study everything. But then he simply fell over from exhaustion, wriggled out of his coat while lying down, and slept for several hours, and in his dream a golden tuba was the only being who understood his language, which for some reason made him so sad that he awoke around three o'clock in the morning with tears in his eyes.

At that time I first heard of the experiments by Dr. Harry Harlow. He was, it seemed to me, a doctor who was interested above all else in pain and suffering. In the sixties he performed various isolation experiments with rhesus monkeys. He compared, for example, a monkey who had grown up motherless with another monkey who had lived with his mother, locking each of them in a solitary cell, in which the little monkeys had nothing but food and a place to sleep. He kept them confined there for a year. Afterward he released them and examined them. Both monkeys showed clear symptoms of psychotic behavior, were scarcely capable of interaction, and soon died. Harlow repeated the same experiment again and again, until he finally achieved the result that confirmed his thesis: Even a happy childhood doesn't offer complete protection from depression—an insight that had been known to the human race since the beginning of time and had never been called into question by anyone. I was quite upset when I read this story and had persistent hiccups for several days. I called the boarding school late in the evening, but I was told the girls were sleeping already and shouldn't be disturbed. Only if it were an emergency, they said, would it be possible. – No, no, I replied, it wasn't an emergency. And hung up.

(Moreira, *The First Three*, p. 44)

9.   Getuige X-1, Rue des Minimes

[GREEN FOLDER]

– No reason to be ashamed, Herr Ferenz said the next morning. It's in our nature.

– What do you mean?

– We're Europeans. We're capable of torturing people if that will make our headache better. I think something's wrong with us. Probably our genes. Hard to say what exactly went awry, or when. But maybe it was all the plagues we survived. We were the first to live in cities that were so filthy that soon a whole range of completely new diseases arose. Bacteria, viruses. We bred them, so to speak, in us, died of them in huge numbers, and only a few of us remained. And they then dragged the plagues into the New World, and the people over there nearly died out. That's how simple it was back then. But something's wrong with us, we're not quite right in the world. We don't fit in, nature is of no consequence to us. Maybe it's we who are the descendants of aliens—and not the Asians, as current theories claim.

– Asians? What theory—

– And that more robust body of our remote ancestors, whoever they were, has a *défaut du matériel*, so to speak. Hardware error. Our thoughts take strange paths. That results in a great deal of art. Yes, subversive art too, of course. But we would probably even sink a whole continent in the sea just to be a little bit less lonely. We like to hear people scream, for example. Don't you like to hear people scream?

– Me? No, I don't know . . . Definitely not, no.

– Where are you from, may I ask?

– I really don't understand what you're trying to tell me.

– Okay, said Herr Ferenz, raising his hand. It's fine. I didn't want to . . . But you're familiar with Dürer's angel, right?

– Angel . . . No, I don't know.

– But of course you're familiar with it, it's a famous image, the angel, who sits among all sorts of objects and rests her chin on her hand.

– *Melencolia?*

– Yes. What would the angel do if she saw a man burning behind her? Or she sees on the horizon a man broken on the wheel, who is hanging between the spokes while vultures gnaw away at him? Or one of those cat sacrifices in the Middle Ages, where a live cat was . . . um . . . sewn into—

– Aaah, I said. Please don't.

Herr Ferenz laughed.

– Hold on, he said. I'm going to send this soon to Olivier in Bécs . . . May I show it to you?

– What is it?

– The consequences of a relocation, said Ferenz.

The mere fact that it was an old VHS cassette lent the whole thing a menacing air: No one had transferred the tape in all these years.

First only white stripes flickered, then the figure of a sitting child suddenly fell from above onto the screen. Over it floated the time code of a video camera counting minutes, seconds, and tenths of a second in white digits.

Herr Ferenz pressed pause. Shaky and blurred at the edges, dissolving in spectral colors like the toxic rainbows in oil puddles, the video image froze.

– Is everything all right? he asked.

– With me? Yes.

– *Vous saignez du nez*, he said with a smile.

I put my hand to my nose. A red dot on my finger.

– Thanks, I said, and attended to my nosebleed.

It was over right away, hardly worth mentioning.

The Lufthansa napkin I had pocketed yesterday on the plane absorbed a few red stains.

The head of the girl on the screen meanwhile jerked steadily downward, as if the creature captured on magnetic tape knew that it was trapped in a frozen image, but still absolutely had to try to escape. The pixels of the television screen gradually turned into grains of sand that vibrations caused to trickle down. The VCR was so old that it took energy and effort for it to hold the frozen image. Soon it would slip out of its grasp. The shaking and flickering increased, the colors at the edges became more psychedelic . . .

Herr Ferenz pressed play.

The suddenly restarting movement of the tape brought back three-dimensional space, I staggered a step forward.

– *Ça va?*

– I'm okay, I said.

A girl of about seven or eight sat in a somewhat strange posture on a chair. She squirmed this way and that, bent over her knees. Then I realized: The child was tied up.

– Okay, shut it off, I said, turning away.

– But . . .

– No, I can't watch this. It's too awful.

– Yes, it's awful, Herr Ferenz said softly. But you must know what kind of planet you've lived on for . . . for how many years?

– Huh?

– How old are you?

– Twenty-five.

– Well, then you know. But you see, here, nothing happens to the girl. She's just tie . . . tied . . . she's just stuck here, you see?

– Yes. Please, turn it off.

– But why?

– Because I can't stand it. It's horrible. Herr Ferenz pressed stop. The dark screen was such a blessing that I could take a deep breath and close my eyes for a moment.

– You don't want to see what happens?

– Can I sit down for a minute . . . ?

– *Mais oui, bien sûr* . . . Here.

He took a stack of old magazines off an armchair. I sat down and leaned my head back.

– Describe to me what happens, I said. I want to know, but I can't watch it.

– Why do you want me to tell you?

– It's . . . well, it's easier that way. I can't watch that girl be tortured.

– She isn't tortured.

– But she's tied up!

– Yes, but . . .

– That's torture! Who ties a child to a chair, in some . . . prison or wherever that was taped . . . It's sick, I mean, it's . . . Please, I can't watch something like that. And because he was still staring at me blankly, I added in French, the language that must have affected him more deeply than German:

– *C'est atroce.*

He nodded, put the remote control on the small table. Then he cleared his throat, waited a little while, and said:

– But you still want me to tell you?

– Well, I said, I have to know what happens.

– But how will you know that my version is true? If you don't see it with your own eyes, then you'll never be able to be certain. What if I leave something out? Or I don't remember all the details?

I couldn't look him directly in the eyes. On my knees I discovered smears of a white, powdery substance. Perhaps from a wall, crumbling plaster.

– I think you should watch it.

– I'm sorry, I can't.

When we were back on the street, Herr Ferenz spoke softly to me. He said he would like to do something nice for me. Some gesture. A favor. To make amends, so to speak. He hadn't meant to frighten me, he had thought that was why I had come to him. To see.

The sky was cloudy, the air smelled like just-fallen rain on asphalt. He could take me, Herr Ferenz offered, to parties where you had to sign confidentiality agreements to get in. Then he slapped me on the shoulder and laughed. He was just kidding.

Then he brought me to the club with the Flemish name Getuige X-1. It was a gloomy cellar, sparsely filled at this time of day (late morning). A sort of bouncer eyed us, but didn't budge.

The curtain went up, and a figure stepped onto the stage. To swinging Benny Goodman jazz it began to dance. Its legs looked normally developed, the face was that of a roughly thirty-year-old man. But where the upper body should be was almost nothing, just a shrunken stalk, similar to a thick neck. After the short dance performance, a man with a top hat came onstage, grabbed the figure by the neck, and carried it away, while it kept moving with an indifferent face. There was restrained applause. A brief whistle rang out. I had leaned far forward to see how the trick worked. Herr Ferenz touched me on the shoulder:

– Okay, he said, I can tell you're worried. So I'd like to tell you . . . um, the following story: A mother, okay? Let's imagine a mother who knows that her existence is vital to her children. She is a single mother and has no one, no social support network. Okay. Her own well-being, her mental and physical health, are very important to her, because her children's lives depend on her. She is not permitted to be sick a single day of the year, or else chaos would break out. So she watches herself very closely, tends toward hypochondria, excessive cleanliness. One day an old acquaintance gets in touch, who once felt slighted and humiliated by her and now wants to take revenge on her. He threatens her, berates her. The mother, of course, automatically equates a threat to herself with a threat to her children, right? So she takes a paradoxical approach to the threat: She sends her children ahead, even leaves them alone with the unpredictable man. Because, as she tells herself, the children's chances of survival are considerably higher than hers, the man has no quarrel with the children. At most he could regard them as representatives for her, and even in that case there's still the possibility that he would take revenge on them only symbolically. Their wounds would definitely heal, whereas she would run the risk of being permanently damaged or even obliterated, if she came near the dangerous man. Prize question: Is the woman acting out of selfishness or not?

– What?

– Where did I lose you? Ferenz asked in a kind tone.

– Nowhere, I . . . Maybe we can go outside for a minute?

– *Sì, certo*, said Ferenz. It's in the back of the building anyway.

I followed him down a corridor that led past a kitchen, then came the bathrooms (stick figure man and rocket woman), finally we stepped through a door into an inner courtyard. On the opposite wall I saw two entrances, each with intercom and number pad. Between them a narrow metal door, on which a caution-electricity sign had been put up: a jagged arrow hitting a thickheaded stick figure in the belly. Herr Ferenz unlocked this door with a key that hung from a small silver UFO. Stairs leading up. The legs of a man standing on a higher step could be seen. He came down several steps until he was at street level.

He smiled when he recognized Ferenz, and greeted us. I raised my hand, because I was suddenly afraid to let the stranger hear my voice.

– *Combien?* asked Ferenz.

The man opened his hand and showed: five.

– *Et sur le toit?*

Two fingers disappeared.

Herr Ferenz nodded.

Then he climbed the extremely narrow staircase. I followed him. The man turned away from me pointedly as I squeezed past him. When my face was for a brief moment very close to his, he even shielded his eyes with a hand.

– We'll go right up to the roof, said Herr Ferenz.

Having arrived on the roof, I had the sensation of being really close to the cloudy Brussels sky. It was astonishingly warm up here. In a corner sat three men. Cameras or something similar dangled around their necks. As I came closer to them, I realized that they were breathing masks.

The men were playing cards. On the floor next to them were three beer bottles. Blanche de Bruxelles. At some distance from them a few large toy cars stood around, dirty and faded from wind and rain. A little excavator, about the size of a rat, was missing all four tires. A police car lay on its side, as if after an accident.

– Taking a break, said Herr Ferenz, gesturing to the men.

They waved to him.

We went back into the narrow stairwell.

– What is this here? I asked.

– *Traitement sudorifique*, said Herr Ferenz.

– What does that mean?

– *Cure de transpiration.*

I saw what Ferenz meant. The man on the stairs was sweating quite profusely. He seemed to take no notice of us standing two steps above him and talking about him. His head was freshly shorn like that of a novice monk. On the back of his shirt a huge V-shaped sweat stain soaked through.

– Ah, fuck you, he said softly, and a shudder ran through his body.

He extended his arm and touched the wall with junkie-like crooked fingers. As if it were burning hot, he recoiled, brought the fingers quickly to his mouth, and sucked on them. I made an attempt to touch the wall myself. An ordinary, cool wall.

– *Voulez vous lui donner un coup de pied?*

– What?

– Would you like to kick him?

– Why would I do that?

Herr Ferenz descended a step and touched the man gently on the head. The man winced and writhed as if he had been dealt a brutal blow. Then Herr Ferenz drew his arm back and punched him with all his might in the shoulder. The man seemed not even to notice the second blow, but instead kept moaning while holding the spot on his head, which clearly hurt a lot.

– That's the new delivery. There, behind the wall. Arrived yesterday morning. The early bird gets the worm. And I picked this out for him. Here.

Herr Ferenz showed me a little toy model of a cable car, still in the original packaging.

– Come back tomorrow, he said. Then we'll go in. In the tank.

In the hotel I lay in the bathtub and poured warm water with my cupped hand over my head. One scoop after another. After a while Julia called me and asked what was the matter. Without bothering to ask why and how she knew that something was wrong, I told her about the horrifying conversation with Ferenz, the bizarre stairwell, the model cable car in its original packaging, the video, and was concluding with a description of the impressive steel structure with the ravens yesterday in the park, when Julia interrupted me and said, at home an hour or so ago a somewhat distraught-sounding woman had called, whom she had at first not even understood.

Gudrun Stennitzer.

– Okay, I'll call her right back.

– Yes, do that.

– I'll be home the day after tomorrow, I murmured, before I said goodbye to Julia. I called the number. Roaming charges, I thought wearily.

– Hello?

– Frau Stennitzer, how are you doing?

– Oh, Herr Setz! Thanks for calling back. I hope I'm not interrupting anything important.

– No, at the moment I'm in . . . Oh, never mind. What can I do for you?

– Are you sure that I'm not bothering you? Are you out at the moment? Or in another country?

– No, everything's okay, I'm at home.

– Are you sure?

– Yes, I'm sure.

– Okay, she said. At home. Yes, well . . . I just wanted to tell you that everything went smoothly.

– What are you referring to?

– Oh, Herr Setz, she said with a giggle, as if I had made a joke. Well, you can certainly imagine what a transfer like that means for a young person like Christoph. He's inwardly so peculiar, you know. He's not like other people, he's more like a landscape, I mean, deep inside, sometimes he seems to me like one of those warehouses big companies have, you know, IKEA or something like that, those vast buildings along some streets that all lead out of the city, built-up areas, where you find no sense of security, no point of reference, except maybe a few grassy strips, you know? Like those little green islands between parking spots. But apart from that . . . just cavernous buildings and dirty wet steel and industrial waste on forklifts and so on, like in the opening sequence of that terrible, gloomy Russian science fiction movie, my God, I saw it once years ago, and since then I've always been afraid I'll suddenly stumble into it again one night while channel-surfing. I usually change the channel immediately when I come across a black-and-white movie and don't immediately recognize the actors.

I again poured water over my head. As I did so, I had to lift the cell phone a bit, so that it wouldn't get wet. The characterization of Christoph's inner life had flustered me. Once again I had the sensation of having heard a prepared statement, like that of a bought witness in court. And a sentence from Josef Winkler's first novel crossed my mind: I am devoid of people. The moment when a being actually ceases to feel inhabited and populated by others, and that frightening point in history when it became clear to people that they didn't bear homunculi within them, that the man doesn't implant in the woman microscopic copies of himself in his seminal fluid, which then grow with their limbs in constant proportions.

What must this sudden realization have felt like, that we're inhabited by aliens, bacterial cultures and skin mites, which feed on dead flakes and cells and, like faithful janitors or groundskeepers, roam around all day on a tiny area of skin, which is probably not much larger than a postage stamp, and do their mechanical grazing work? I thought of the debate in Swift's *Gulliver*, in which scholars of the court of Brobdingnag, the land of the giants, debate whether this little person they have found in a field is a sort of automaton, a piece of clockwork without a soul, which has been taught language, or actually a human being. If I remembered correctly, despite Gulliver's ability to interact intelligently with the scholars, it was only by the measurement of his limbs that the matter of dispute was decided in his favor. I looked at my foamy hand, from which drops of water fell. And hadn't the doctor Sir Thomas Browne in the seventeenth century mentioned in a treatise his strange shudder when, while dissecting a brain, he discovered a convolution that—similarly to how the man in the moon has been perceived for centuries—was even without much imagination reminiscent of a tiny human figure, a sort of secret, no-longer-needed construction manual for the whole, which lay dead before him on the operating table? He must have wondered whether his brain didn't also contain a form like that, which at that moment performed exactly the same movements (the cutting, the severing of tissue, the holding, turning, and studying in the light) as he did, and perhaps for this incredible feat it required in turn a smaller version of itself, and so on and so on into eternity, a fractal process as with Benoît Mandelbrot's holy set, which after a long, long deep zoom through the fringes of its valleys and lakes and islands shimmering in various colors keeps presenting itself to us, wonderfully preserved in its tininess and identical with the whole, an infinite series continuable in both directions.

– Hello? Are you still there?

I looked up. In the steamed-up bathroom mirror someone had left a message in finger writing. But it was too blurred and too misted over to remain readable. Magic slate.

– Yes, I said. What? Um, it's only water. Keeps the brain alert.

Frau Stennitzer made a noise as if she were sucking on a cigarette. Then she coughed and said:

– Yeah, water is necessary for . . . But Herr Setz, am I really not bothering you?

– No, I said, I'm just in the bathtub at the moment . . . I like to take baths, you know.

– Ah, I see. Yes. Of course. You're in the bathtub. Well, then I don't want to—

– No, you're not bothering me. You were just about to tell me about your son, and then I . . . I was distracted for a minute.

The water I was constantly pouring over my forehead made the headache a little better, but when Frau Stennitzer began to speak, it came back. A sun that was waiting behind the mountain ridge and could suddenly rise at any moment. I closed my eyes and tried to focus. I saw fractal swirls, the seahorse valley. Males who get pregnant and release tiny copies of themselves into the world. Sons, planets.

– Yes, well, said Frau Stennitzer, that's why I'm calling. Christoph says hello, he really bears no grudge against you, Herr Setz. And the articles, well, that was quite a while back, right? Yeah, and . . . I just wanted to tell you that you're always welcome to visit me and that you don't have to worry. True, I don't want to skirt the issue, Christoph has had his problems with the transfer, of course, he is reaching that age, after all, but I think, despite everything, it wouldn't be fair if I hadn't tried it, right?

– Yes, I said.

I didn't have the faintest idea what she was talking about.

– You know, recently he has often gone for long walks. And then I've kept telling myself that I don't need to worry, that he's doing fine, wherever he has retrea— wherever he is. He likes nature a lot. And the few visits to the swimming pool back then, I mean, okay, that was probably simply a sort of retreat. I hope I'm not boring you, Herr Setz?

– Excuse me? I was just . . .

I splashed a bit in my bathwater.

– Well, I certainly don't want to bore you, Herr Setz, the last thing I'd want would be to rob you of your precious time, which you must need for . . . for writing and researching and whatever you do when you're working on your next—

– Hey, may I ask you something?

– Go ahead.

– It's a bit unpleasant for me to ask you, of all . . . I mean, this isn't meant to sound offensive, now, but . . . do you by any chance know a good remedy for headaches? I mean, you must, of course, have . . .

– Have experience with that?

– Oh, this is really stupid, I'm sorry.

– No, Herr Setz, not at all. It's not stupid at all. I have in fact tried some things. What sort of headache is it, then? With dizziness?

– Yes. A little bit.

– And what's the dizziness like? More spinning or just a feeling of disorientation . . . or is it a more deep-seated dizziness, less in your sense of balance and more in your core, in a way? I'm sure you know what I mean.

– More the first kind.

– Just spinning?

– Yes, when I lean back. Plus this splitting headache.

– And you're alone?

There was a pause. She hadn't asked this question in a different tone than all the others. Objectively interested. A woman who knew what she was talking about.

– So for *that*, Herr Setz . . . well, for *that* . . . there's nothing. Nothing that springs to mind. Besides painkillers. A massive amount of painkillers. But they usually don't make the symptoms go away.

– Okay, I said.

– A massive amount of painkillers. One after another, stacked into a pyramid. But be sure to leave sufficient intervals between the individual pills. Or else there could be a misunderstanding in your body.

– Thanks. I'll try—

– Something else occurs to me. A change of locale, maybe? That also does good sometimes. Go north. The nights are more pleasant there. I can't do that, unfortunately. I always have to stay here.

– Residenz Verlag, I said softly.

– Pardon me? asked Frau Stennitzer.

– I said, Re . . . Oh, I'm sorry, something just crossed my mind. A little disrupting signal, so to speak, an interf . . . um, you know what I . . .

– Yes, you make a confused impression, Herr Setz, she said, and hung up without saying goodbye.

10. A Peculiar Network

Robert felt as if he had drunk thick syrup through his eyes. To cool off, he stared at a harmless stain on the wall. A mark that had nothing to do with him and the rest of the human world.

He had read through the contents of the folders almost in their entirety.

Magda T., peaceful use of Indigo potential, Oliver Baumherr, Ferenz.

Even when he closed his eyes, the terms stood before him—the same effect that set in when you stood in front of the magnificent empty iSocket on Annenstrasse, in the middle of the night, when up in the sky only few stars and down on the earth only few lights were scattered about.

The telephone book seemed pleasantly surprised that, after so many years of total disregard, he was consulting it for the second time in a few days. It chirped softly and continuously while he searched for the name.

Hofrat Prim. Univ-Prof. Dr. Otto Rudolph.

Robert couldn't help laughing. He imagined biting off the title jutting out over the man's name like a protruding cellophane wrapper. Like when you take a candy cane out of the wrapper and nibble it down to a small stump, and then you put the stump back in the wrapper. Or like a much-too-long foreskin.

Robert slammed his fist down on the floor. The telephone book chirped and recoiled a little.

In his room he looked for the most *Matrix*-like coat he could find in the wardrobe. And sunglasses. It was an overcast day, but whatever. *It's 106 miles to Chicago, Robin, we got a full tank of gas, half a pack of cigarettes, it's dark, and we're wearing sunglasses.* He briefly thought about taking his Darth Vader helmet with him, but he left it in the wardrobe.

When he stepped onto the street, it was just beginning to rain.

On his way he ran into a festive parade made up of twenty to thirty people, who squeezed through a narrow side street. He saw the people equipped with horns and colorful flags from some distance. They were coming toward him. He immediately turned around, ran out of the side street, and for the rest of the way stuck to main roads.

The doorman wrote down Robert's name very carefully, and the iBall over him in the little booth looked frightened and paranoid, like an animal kept too long in a cage. Robert waved to it. No reaction.

A phone call was made, intercoms were spoken into. A little key was even in proper James Bond final boss fashion stuck into a lock on the desk and turned. Then he was let through.

Dr. Rudolph had grown quite old. But he greeted Robert warmly and with genuine surprise. He immediately asked him what he was doing these days, but then corrected himself right away, he had of course, obviously, heard about the award, the prize for the painting, oh, that was really wonderful, to become aware from time to time of the late fruits of his efforts. The institute was, since Riegersdorf had *totally taken off*, unfortunately a thing of the past, but still, he was always happy to hear from his former protégés.

– But please, please, come in, Herr Tätzel.

Robert stepped inside the room and looked around. If he had been wearing augmentors, the room would most likely have exploded into a sea of blossoms made up of price tags. It would probably look like a butterfly house during mating season.

– I thought I'd stop by.

– Yes, oh, that's really very nice of you, Robert . . . Herr Tätzel, sorry, I'm mixing up the time periods.

The old principal laughed. He seemed honestly moved.

– Have you heard, asked Robert, also smiling, about Setz?

The joy remained in Dr. Rudolph's face, but it required some load-bearing wrinkles.

– Ah, he said. Yes, a tragic affair. I'm glad that he didn't stay with us. Well, all right, now he's free. They couldn't prove anything. But the signs were there. The circumstances. The clues.

– He claims that he met someone in Brussels. A man named Ferenz. And I remember that at the institute—

– Would you like some coffee, young man?

– No, thanks. I—

– Are you sure? I can ask Adelir to make you one.

The principal put his hand to his neck and pressed. A cow-eyed man with a dark beard immediately appeared.

– We'd like some coffee.

The cow-eyed man nodded and disappeared again.

– I can't recall the details, what it was like, back then, said Robert. That's why I've come to you.

– That's why, I see, the principal repeated distractedly.

– My memory is a little blurry. I never understood why I spent that one semester at home. Everyone had a sort of wait-and-see attitude . . . And then suddenly everything was completely back to normal. Back to school, graduation . . .

Robert shook his head and tried to look confused.

– Well, I . . . (Dr. Rudolph again put his hand to his neck.) I don't know either. It was a long time ago.

– And now I've read that account by Setz of his visit to Brussels, and it's . . . it reminds me of some things, also that stuff about Magda T., I don't know what it is. But you can probably help me.

All titles had fallen away from the principal. His face was pale. He looked as if he would have liked nothing more than to merge with the carpet.

– Setz? But he was never in Brussels. Not that I'm aware of. He had enough to do in rehab clinics and so on. You understand.

Robert caught himself nodding. He turned away and bored a finger into the grainy plaster of the wall. Rough surface, fingernails, goose bumps.

– Where'd you get all this from? asked Dr. Rudolph. Is that murderer now writing his wretched articles again?

– I visited him, said Robert.

– What?

– I visited him. He even still remembered me.

– For God's sake, Robert, that's . . . Sorry, Herr Tätzel.

– It's okay. You can call me—

– But that's dangerous! That person, he's . . . he's not normal. He . . . oh, you have to understand what it was like back then. We still knew so little about it. And your number was steadily increasing. Back then such changes simply . . . caught us off guard, you understand?

Robert closed his eyes. He stood there like that for a while, then he opened his eyes and took a little figure off a bookshelf. A little plastic deer. He looked at Dr. Rudolph, smiled, and stuck the figure in his mouth. He let two seconds pass, then he took it out again, wiped it off on his sleeve, and put it back.

– That's all really wonderful, he said, approaching Dr. Rudolph.

– What? Well, I—

The principal's hand wandered to his neck.

– Wonderful, all great, said Robert. I have to shake your hand. You've dispelled my doubts.

– I'm glad, but . . . what exactly did you mean when you said you visited him? He doesn't receive any visitors, as far as I know, or . . .

– He was actually very nice.

– My goodness. Well, then you probably got lucky. You have to be careful. He most likely still has contacts.

– Only reading caused him difficulties.

– Reading, I see, yes, the principal said, confused.

Robert didn't know why he had said that. Reading. How had he come up with that? He would have liked more than anything else to take off his boots and fling them across the room. Or to bite into Dr. Rudolph's head, into that round human head, which had become even more lightbulb-like in old age, just a little bite into the forehead, where the aging skin formed that brain-like intestine thing.

He shook to get rid of the thought.

— How are your parents? asked Dr. Rudolph.

— Fantastic, said Robert, spreading his arms as if he wanted to embrace the former principal.

The man took a step back, but then came closer again, as if he were correcting an extremely impolite gesture. Robert grabbed his forehead:

— I have a bit of a headache, he said. Do you know what that's like?

— Yes, I think so. And you're also really wet, Herr Tätzel, you must have been caught in the rain.

— Oh, yeah, the rain.

— You should have taken an umbrella.

— An umbrella. That's a fantastic idea, Herr Principal.

Dr. Rudolph's face looked like a snapshot. The eyelids drooped, the mouth was half open. If he had looked in the mirror at that moment, he probably would have been frightened and would have immediately corrected his facial expression.

Robert was silent.

The raindrops pattered against the windowpanes, irregular and closely spaced as the clicks of a Geiger counter. At times they were reminiscent of a drumroll, at other times they eased to the nervous clatter of fingernails on a table.

11. The Walk

The light on this early summer day was hazy, moist, and vibrating. Like a nystagmus of the sun ball. The whole area, the whole district was filled with a Van
Gogh surge in the bushes and shrubs, making everything slightly vertiginous,
the clouds drifted heavily and thickly across the sky, like stencils being slid over
the image of an overhead projector, the wind awoke every few minutes from
uneasy dreams and swept over everything as if it wanted to wipe the slate clean,
forget everything, soccer balls and plastic bags left behind by their owners lay on
a meadow, and over the bare walls of the high-rises near the park drifted cloud
shadows, which alternated with a briefly gleaming glaze of sunlight.

– Xenopathic people? asked Julia.
– Yes, that's what they called it, during that sweat cure, it was on the roof, and
someone said: I'm half xenopathic! Wow, great . . . Do we feel anything? No. Say
Indigo, you idiot! Xenopathic, stupid goddamn word! You're an Indigo, a digger!
And then they all laughed.
– I don't understand, said Julia, you're talking so incoherently. And so fast. Come
on, let's walk this way.
We turned onto a path that ran along the pond. On a meadow a few teenagers
were playing soccer with an old black hat.
– But it's wrong, isn't it?
– What?
– The word *xenopathic*, I said. It doesn't mean that I make other people sick. It
means that I get sick from strangers.
Julia took my hand and stuck it in her coat pocket. My fingers bumped into her
bubble dispenser and a crumpled tissue.
– You stray so easily from the subject, she said.

– Yeah, I said. I probably have a way of speaking stuck in my head from the people in Brussels. I mean, we were in that bar, or no, it was a club, with a weird Flemish name, no idea, X-1 or something, and everyone was talking so fast there, the chatter . . .

– It's worse than usual, said Julia.

She was right. The evening before I had sat down and after long abstinence tried once again to do some mathematics, but my eyes kept slipping away from the curved set braces, the paper full of group theory blurred before my eyes, and the symbols performed a strange masquerade, a dance in a vacuum.

– Have you actually sent anything to Residenz Verlag yet?

– What?

– You know, to the friendly editor who called. I told you. I wrote down his name for you. He said he would be happy . . .

– Um, I don't know, I said, but . . . you know, those teenagers have no right to behave like that, I mean, look at the T-shirt that one over there is wearing.

The teenagers were several yards away, and Julia didn't even look, but instead tilted her head a bit so that I could tell her the answer:

– Dingo Rat.

– Hm, weird, said Julia.

I looked briefly into the sky, and the sun was a spinning wind wheel shimmering above the high-rises. A white, temperatureless pain pierced my head.

The label was doubly and triply unfair, I said to Julia, because it had been proven that rats were the most remarkable creatures on the whole planet, even more fascinating than the immortal jellyfish *Turritopsis nutricula* or that mysterious species of sea cucumber whose cells stop aging at a certain point in their development. Rats, I said, were organized according to an infinitely complex social hierarchy, so multilayered and rich with nuances that it naturally struck us human observers in most instances as a chaotic swarm, a senselessly teeming mass. The opposite was the case, every rat had in its head a precise image of the entire rat population to which it belonged, and when one died, its place in the larger whole shifted by a microscopic unit down or up, left or right, as the case might be, the rat population in the subterranean worlds of cities, in the sewers or subway shafts, was comparable to a school of fish held together by enigmatic, probably ancient lines of communication, the density and the connective element of water were merely replaced among them by something that was not yet known to us, possibly one of those morphic field things, I said, but since those were a pure article of faith, we of course couldn't believe in them.

– Maybe we have to imagine it like that zone game, have I ever told you about that?

Julia linked arms with me and said:

– Tell me more about rats instead.

– Rats, okay. Let's talk about rats. Rats are more important.

– Go ahead.

– Well, they exist in that in-between area that divides bedrock and earth's crust from modern civilization, and of course a few people live there too, mostly homeless people, and it depends, of course, on the particular city whether they can really live there or just go there to die. I once saw a report about people in disused tunnels. There were a few creepy things in it, for example, someone lay for a whole month with a deep wound somewhere underground where it was damp and muddy, and then, when he thought he could get up again, he had grown together with some sort of pipe that came out of the ground or something.

– Yeah, *or something*.

– I'm not making this up! You can check, the film must be publicly accessible, if it was on television, I assume . . . Anyway, they did this interview with him, it was totally sick, because . . . they interviewed him while he's there with his head on the ground and so on, that was so perverse that I had to change the channel. Well, anyway, as for rats, they have this infinitely ramified and intricate social system, okay? And it's so tightly woven that they sense precisely when another rat, say, one that occupies a higher position, is in trouble or when it has self-doubt or has gotten lost. But they don't help it, because they're not human beings, after all, right? For them the whole social thing works differently. Well, and . . . they have this structure and . . . and that's not all, though, because the network, it's so fine that they often even include inanimate objects, as symbolic fellow creatures, honorary rats, so to speak. Those could be objects that are important for the preservation of the population as a whole, a dripping heating

pipe in a shaft, for example, or the sun, or what do I know, the grate of a venti-
lation shaft through which a particularly large number of cigarettes always fall.
Things like that. In general, rats always think only in total populations, never just
in families or clans or packs. They're egoists anyway, of course. That's easy to
understand too, in terms of game theory, because . . . um . . . take, for example, a
business in the human world, okay? For example, a company that produces only
weapons and, what do I know, sells terrible nerve gas grenades to some other
dubious companies and nothing but irresponsible crap like that, but every
individual in the business, every human being is a really nice, friendly citizen,
who wants only to pay for his children's university education, who is content
sitting in the garden with a cigar in his mouth in the evening after his work
is done or rearranging the stones in his garden so that, seen from above, they
form a geometric message, or sitting in front of the computer and watching
harmless movies with weeping women. Completely normal people, men and
women, nice and affable, even reasonable. And that goes all the way up to the
top, only with different accessories and in luxury apartments, but . . . where
was I? Rats, they—

– Read me some graffiti, said Julia.

We were passing the wall at the far end of the park, which was updated regularly by its stewards armed with spray cans.

– There's not much new, I said.

– No Banksy rat or anything . . . ?

– Yes, of course, up there.

I pointed to a spot that was much too far away for Julia to make anything out.

– There it is, I said.

– Describe it to me.

– It has glasses on, I said.

– And?

We walked on slowly.

– It's balancing across a rope. With one of those tightrope walker sticks in its
paws. And looks like a rat and . . .

– And is anything written there?

I reflected.

– No, I said. Not a word.

– Your voice is completely back to normal, said Julia. Come on, let's go this way. I actually did feel a little more focused than before. More clearheaded.

A dog was going for a walk in the park with its owner. The leash was wound several times around the man's hand.

– Rats, I said, are completely different from dogs.

– Really? In what way?

– Well, dogs have been bred by us, in painstaking work from generation to generation. But what was actually the point of the slow breeding of the canine species? Guarding property boundaries and flocks of sheep, man's playmate, well, all right . . . The result is this strange love machine that worships its master . . . Maybe that was the plan too, to create an animal with which we could communicate. A sentimental companion to make the loneliness of our own species seem less complete, less unbroken and absolute . . .

I noticed that my voice had again taken on a life of its own, and paused, focusing on the brown-trodden gravel on the park path.

– Yes, that must be what's behind the friendship between man and dog that's lasted thousands of years, I said. Every temperament, every shape of the human heart is reflected in a particular breed of dog. The dog is a creature that we can actually prefer to other people, you know? That gradually, over the many, many generations in which it was kept in human company, learned to feel emotions similar to ours, separation anxiety, what do I know, obsessive-compulsive disorder, fear of death, hysteria, none of that is unknown to the dog, probably even anorexia and bulimia, a dog . . . a dog can succumb just as easily to one of those conditions as its owner. But it's still not in the same boat as us, that's why we can look at it without horror, without our deep-rooted need to destroy every simulacrum.

– Mmmh, Julia said, holding my arm somewhat tighter.

– But look at this life they lead, I said, gesturing to the small dog bustling about among the bushes. You live with large figures uttering incomprehensible sounds who are in command of food, toys, and your chances of running around outside. You wander all around for hours alone with them and suddenly you discover at the end of a promenade or on the other side of the street someone who speaks the same language, who has a tail and ears, who would even like to approach and present himself—and then you're yanked back by a rope, forbidden to move one centimeter toward the other. And with time that forceful jerk is transferred to your mind, you feel it inwardly when you see a fellow member of your species, and eventually there's nothing but enemies, each with its own restricted-zone radius around it, and when . . . and when these radii then, then intersect, you panic, pull and pull and bark and have to be calmed down.

Julia's hand on my cheek was cool.

– Banksy rat, I said softly. Banksy rat.

– Yes, describe it to me again, she said.

12. The Most Intolerable Thing
in the World

— Forget her! The most intolerable thing in the world is pretty women, said the teacher, waving his hands in the air as if he wanted to dispel an unpleasant smell. I'm telling you, the most intolerable thing in the whole wide world is women who are so pretty that all men turn into slobbering, floundering, undignified idiots, who are constantly trying to make the women laugh with their foolish clowning and writing sonnets or rock ballads for them. No, at some point that has to end! If you ask me.

The math teacher grasped Robert by the shoulders and shook him gently.

— If you ask me, he went on, men should pay absolutely no attention to any of the pretty girls of this world for several years. Yes, indeed, for several years pretty young women should be totally taboo and strictly ignored. That would be the only right thing, the only realistic way out of the whole misery. But unfortunately, unfortunately, I know of course as well as you do that it's not that easy, because the young fellows with their energy can't even help it, they're simply programmed that way by nature, and obviously there's nothing anyone can do to change that, or else all humanity would die out. So what else can be done? Well, not much, but maybe a certain shift could be achieved— hold on, you can protest later, first let me explain what I mean by shift. Okay. I mean that an energetic, lively, sexually active young man—like you—should focus first and foremost on women who are considered not-so-pretty or mediocre, because—hold on, wait, you'll get your turn in a moment—because that way all the women who are pretty as a picture and preferred completely unjustly by all influential men would finally recognize how undeserved their power, how translucent and fragile their dignity, and how empty and boring their oh-so-interesting life really is. Don't get me wrong, I don't want people to make life difficult in any way for other people, whether male or female, to torture them or even treat them condescendingly, no, what matters to me is merely that women who are always regarded as interesting and clever *only* due to their appearance no longer—hold on, hold on, well, all right, all right, I've spoken long enough, now you may speak. Go ahead.

— I just wanted to ask whether you're still eating this here?

— Excuse me?

— Whether I can have the rest of the rice. Or are you still eating it?

— No, no. Of course, young man, please help yourself. Are you really so hungry?

— Yes. I haven't eaten since lunch yesterday.

— Ah, yes, the torments of love . . . It shows, probably . . . Those dark rings under the eyes. And you're so pale that you could easily attend a carnival celebration as a glacier.

Robert, who didn't know how to respond to that stupid joke, began to shovel the rice, which had meanwhile gotten cold, into his mouth. The teacher waited until he was done. Then he stuck a spoon in his mouth and patted his jacket down for a lighter. The gesture looked ridiculous, as always when older people imitate the habits of young people. In the restaurant it was very quiet, they were alone in the large room. Due to the mild temperatures, most of the patrons sat outside in the garden, and their excited voices penetrated inside only dully, like the soft evening music of tropical insects.

Robert regretted having talked about Cordula in the first place. He had actually wanted to speak with Herr Setz about the two folders. But in a subclause he had mentioned that his girlfriend had left him.

— Love is nonsense, said the teacher.

— I wanted to ask, that is, your wi—

— Love! Setz broke in. Love is nothing but a virus, brought into the world by young women who want to have power. You should steer clear of it!

He crossed his arms over his chest and thrust out his lips in an angry way. He looked like a grimly determined frog.

— I'm not planning on it, said Robert. But your wife, how—

— Steer clear of it! You should wait until the feeling that overcomes you is no longer so amorphous. You have to wait until you yourself have matured, have matured inwardly . . . and . . .

He looked up, put a hand on the table. He seemed to have forgotten why he was here and not at home behind his desk.

— Got it, said Robert. But what about your wife? She's pretty and—

— Don't talk! About things you don't understand! the teacher suddenly shouted at him, jumping up. Things you have absolutely no idea about, Robert . . . Herr Tätzel! What do you think, Robert? My wife, that's something entirely different, so, please, Herr Tätzel, don't talk such nonsense! My wife, of course that's love, we've been together for so long, many years, without her, well, without her I would be long—

— I apologize, I didn't mean to—

— Without her I wouldn't even be alive today! Where did you get the idea to compare that with . . . with . . .

He made a peculiar gesture with his hand, as if he were flicking coins across the room.

— I'm sorry.

— Real love, said the teacher. Well, I don't know why you're starting on about that now, but if you really want to know, then I can tell you: You have no idea what that is. You're still very, very far away from it. At least two yards.

Robert looked up in astonishment.

The math teacher was still shaking his head.

— I didn't want to start on about that, said Robert. I actually wanted to ask you about Brussels.

– You know, in my library, the teacher suddenly began. In my library, there's an old lightbulb burning, maybe the last of its kind . . . in any case, an endangered specimen. It looks like a transparent egg with a little twirled wire inside, which is stretched between two poles like a rope that only a spatially distorted tightrope walker could cross.

He moved his forefingers in circles around each other.

Robert tried to picture the bulb.

– And when the power is switched on, this wire glows brightly, the lightbulb immediately becomes burning hot, and this wonderful . . . golden . . . dust-repellent light pours into the room.

Herr Setz sighed in a melodramatic way, as if he were inhaling the light.

– In recent years, he said, pointing with his finger to the ceiling of the restaurant, in recent years, well, actually in recent decades, we've had to witness a really terrible process, a scandal, which is terrible, truly terrible . . . the gradual dying-off of all lightbulbs. And this one, which hangs in my home in the library, is the last one I own. No one knows how long it will hold out. I mean, yes, its light is still strong and unadulterated, it probably regards itself as immortal.

He coughed. It was loud and rattling. He covered his mouth with his sleeve. His face turned red.

– Once, he went on, on a winter day about two and a half years ago, it began to flicker a little . . . and I was already expecting the worst, my God, I didn't even dare to turn the light on, just sat in the dark, for several days. But it was only a loose connection, and I fixed the problem simply by screwing the lightbulb tighter into its socket.

The teacher laughed and took off his glasses to clean them.

Robert asked:

– When exactly were you in Brussels?

– My God, said Herr Setz, what beautiful and comforting inventions they were, those little magic bulbs! Nowadays, these energy-saving and, as if in mockery of all older people, pacifier-shaped lamps hang everywhere with their passionless, harsh, hospital-room-white light! Or those stupid blinking eyes. Ridiculous. You know, in my youth, it was still possible and conceivable that a lonely man in a poorly ventilated room could entrust his distress to a bare lightbulb, which hung radiantly from the end of the electric cord sticking without adornment out of the ceiling. And when he opened the window, then it swung back and forth . . . like this . . .

He demonstrated it.

Robert sighed soundlessly. This here was no conversation.

– Its light plunged everything into a dark golden urban melancholy, a distant atheistic, if you like, hahaha, yes, an atheistic relative of de Chirico's saffron-colored eternal light of Italian plazas and statues, you must know those paintings, right? It's your area of expertise, isn't it?

Robert nodded.

– Even if the light fell on pizza scraps in a box full of star-shaped pizza cutter scratch marks or on a collection of empty whiskey bottles next to a perpetually cold heater or on a few boxes of frozen chocolate cake scraped down to the last bit. Hm . . . yes . . .

– Herr Setz?

The teacher tilted his head a bit, but it wasn't entirely clear whether he had heard the question. Robert wondered where on his strangely unproportioned body he should touch him. Perhaps he would begin screaming loudly, right now—

– No wretchedness in this world, said Herr Setz, was too great for a true lightbulb, no spectacle too unworthy, it bathed everything without exception, gave it reflection and shadow, it was connected with its environment in a way that almost nothing is these days, that little, floating, warmth-giving ball of energy in the middle of the room.

Were there tears in the eyes of the crazy teacher? Robert tried to take a closer look, but Setz turned his face away.

– In contrast, these new lamps, an improved generation of which supposedly comes on the market every year, display a downright absurd indifference. (He blew his nose noisily in a handkerchief.) Their light concerns itself with absolutely nothing! Neither with us nor with other surfaces, nor with the shadows it creates. They're clueless and without sympathy. Ill-bred, inhuman robots! How will the human soul change when in the lamps of the future no incandescent filament will be visible? Soon the last classic lightbulb shape in my vicinity will be the head of that awful man, whose framed portrait hangs over my desk!

— Herr Setz, I'd like to know, in that folder you gave me—

— You know, I was particularly sad recently about the news that the lightbulb that had glowed since 1901 without interruption died. It was, I think, employed in a fire station in California. It . . . it was a gift from the manufacturer to the owner of the fire station at that time. Yes, back then . . . in the year 1901, a lightbulb was still something you could present someone as a precious gift. I think the name of the lamp was Charles. Or George. Something like that. I'm sure lots of people still have some old lightbulbs at home, but how they are taken care of, how their life is extended and their burning-out staved off for as long as possible, is unknown. There must be techniques, I mean . . . it can't be that difficult. Still, these days we stand at a loss before them when they suddenly stop shining, or when they flicker or when they emit a dangerous buzzing as if insects were trapped inside them, the way people used to stand before a syphilitic . . . they couldn't help him, only record the stages of his decline in drawings and descriptions.

— Herr Setz?

— Hm?

Robert cautioned himself, now that he had gained the man's attention for at least a moment, not to speak too fast.

— You gave me your notes on Brussels, remember?

The math teacher nodded in bewilderment. It evidently wasn't clear to him what this question had to do with the subject of lightbulbs.

— When was that? Do you remember?

— What?

— Your trip to Brussels.

— When?

— Ah, said Robert. Forget it. Forget it!

He stood up, held out his hand to the teacher. The man took it, shook it amiably, and patted Robert encouragingly on the shoulder, so that he winced and had to restrain himself from punching the teacher in the face. *You have no idea* came into his mind. He had said the sentence to him once before. A long time ago, telephone card, booth, the system had been unknown to the young tutor. Back then they were all still young, inexperienced. And now this here, this acquitted wreck. With his lightbulbs. He blew his nose again in his handkerchief. Gazed politely, but helplessly. And inhaled and exhaled.

– You don't have to leave yet, the teacher suddenly said.

– That's okay, said Robert.

He buttoned his coat.

– You're safe, Herr Setz said softly.

– Excuse me?

– You're safe. Nothing can happen to you. I made sure of that. A long time ago. Not only for you. Also for other Ind . . . for other Dingo Baits.

He said it in an ironic tone. Robert laughed.

– Did you read everything? asked the teacher.

– No, only the typed notes and the copies, the handwritten pieces of paper interspersed with them, those are hard to decipher.

– Yes, I know, the teacher said dreamily. My block letters.

They were silent for a while. Robert stood there with his coat half buttoned. Then he sat down again.

– I've made sure, said Herr Setz, that things will be quiet for a while. And paid for it, as you can see. But of course it will immediately grow back. The name is always the same, the bearer someone else. They have in common only that lightbulb-like head and the thin stature.

Robert suddenly saw before his eyes the meadow in the Helianau yard where they had played the zone game. Arno Golch with his fingers that smelled like saliva. *Do you know what I wish? That he gets you, the Ference. That he gets his hands on you. What will you dress up as, hm?*

– I inflicted incredible pain on him, the teacher said very softly, even though no one else was in the room. Incredible pain. Are you familiar with those wretched dolls, Herr Tätzel? Those Elis products? They all have a zipper on their back, so that you can turn them inside out. And the inside-out form then has a different character, a different facial expression. They've been making those dolls for more than a century. Some time ago I visited the workshop. Everyone there still works by hand. And they give every single doll a name. They think up the name themselves.

Robert waited for the teacher to go on. But nothing more came. For a while it remained silent.

– You know, I once knew a rooster, Robert began. I gave him a name. Max.

– Max, the rooster, repeated Herr Setz, as if it were a profound philosophical statement.

He tilted his head and repeated the name softly. Robert had for some time been convinced that this man was out of his mind, but he went on anyway:

– I got him out, one evening.

– Yes, said the teacher. Maybe you really did.

He nodded as if he remembered. Robert let out his breath with annoyance, an aggressive sigh, and decided not to say anything else. His former math teacher was useless, there was unfortunately no denying it. Even if his wife pretended not to notice. Well, all right, who knows, maybe every bizarre remark the man murmured, however softly, made perfect sense to her. In that regard, women were equipped with mysterious talents. Lockkeepers of their men who gradually withdrew into nonsense and were in the process of dissolution.

– Max. That's a nice name.

Robert nodded.

– I once took a desensitization course in Vienna. With the money I earned from my second novel. Because of animals and such. The terrible things that happen to them. But it didn't do any good. We all sat in a circle . . . and were supposed to beat stuffed animals. Ridiculous. And then a few videos. Of snakes, rhesus monkeys, guinea pigs, hairless lab mice. I just sat there with my eyes closed. Well, anyway. Wasted money. Really a shame.

Robert waited, but the math teacher didn't go on. Like a car that had only a few drops of gas at its disposal. It drove a few yards and stopped. After a while the waiter came to their table and asked whether there was anything else he could bring the gentlemen.

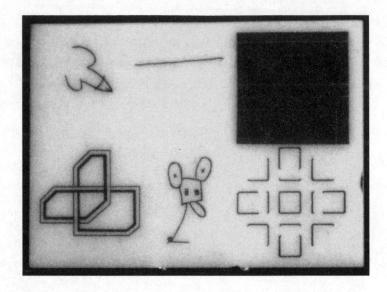

far, far away, on an almost planetary scale, and this was the so-called *Moon Museum*, a small ceramic tile on which six art- ists—Robert Rauschenberg, David Novros, John Chamberlain, Claes Oldenburg, Forrest Myers, and Andy Warhol—each drew a tiny picture. Warhol drew a penis consisting of his ini- tials. This smallest museum in the world was attached to the landing leg of the Apollo 12 lunar module and has remained on the moon ever since. To this day no one has visited the little museum.

HÄUSLER — Z.
THE NATURE OF DISTANCE
P. 77

13. The Letter

On the horizon hung the heavy dark blue of a prestorm sky. The drifting clouds had temporarily cleared and huddled like football players at the beginning of the game, hatching plans beyond the horizon, from where they would soon spread out over the whole land to make everything wet. When we stood outside our front door, a reflection of light trembled on it; the sun, which had grown heavy late in the day, illuminated a window on the opposite side of the street. A jellyfish projected on a wall.

Since my return from Brussels I hadn't been able to touch door handles. They made me think of the widespread theory that every person is no more than six or seven handshakes away from practically every other person on earth. Another reason to keep your hands in your pockets.

– The secretary called from Oeversee High School and asked whether you would be returning to work on Monday, said Julia.

– What did you say?

– I said that you're already feeling better.

– Hm.

– Brussels didn't do you good.

– No. On the last day I should have just locked myself in the hotel room.

– Probably.

– Those people are totally obsessed. One of them they called an *end product*. They were all really in awe of him. An old, withered man who has already been through God knows how many Hollereith treatments.

We climbed the stairs to the third floor. Julia unlocked the door.

I flopped down on a chair in the kitchen. During the days in Brussels I had, strangely enough, found myself constantly thinking of the description of the extermination of the dodos in Thomas Pynchon's *Gravity's Rainbow*, probably because it captures humanity in an incomparably expressive image. A Dutch adventurer named Frans van der Groov at the end of the seventeenth century reaches the island of Mauritius and there kills hundreds of the flightless dodos with a new type of gun, the harquebus. These legendarily trusting animals, named by their discoverers for their unmistakably melodious ducklike call, *doo-doo*, which—if contemporary accounts are to be believed—resounds far across the landscape, naturally put up no resistance. Soon they are all dead, and their rotting carcasses cover wide expanses of the land. Van der Groov ultimately finds one last egg, lying in a little grassy hollow on an abandoned hill. He sits down in front of the egg and waits with leveled gun for the little dodo head to show itself. *There they were, the silent egg and the crazy Dutchman, and the hookgun that linked them forever, framed, brilliantly motionless as any Vermeer.* Now and then van der Groov dozes off, awakes with a start, quickly looks at the egg to check whether anything is stirring. All night long. Finally he walks away without having achieved anything, back into the loneliness of the hunting parties, where everyone gets drunk together and fires at clouds and treetops.

– I remember, said Julia. You read me the passage.

– My absolute favorite book, I said.

– Yeah?

– Absolutely. There's no better image for humanity than that . . .

– Here, a letter for you, said Julia. With a . . . mmh . . . yeah, there's a black border. Oh, no.

The letter was from Frau Stennitzer. I tore open the envelope. On the death announcement was a drawing of a small telescope, above it a black full moon looking down at the earth with a sad face and half-open mouth. Under the moon it said that the funeral would take place next Tuesday. There was even a small section printed from Google Maps, which was meant to facilitate the journey to the cemetery in Gillingen. A little green 3-D pin marked the spot.

PART V

Sturla Sighvatsson told his friend that he had dreamed that he had a sausage in his hand, that he had straightened it out, broken it in half with his hands, and given half to this same friend. Moreover, he knew that the dream was occurring now, in the same moment of time in which he was telling the dream to his friend, holding a sausage in his hand.

—*Eliot Weinberger*

1. Pieces of Paper. Red-Checkered Folder

[HANDWRITTEN PIECE OF PAPER, BACK OF A DEPARTMENT STORE RECEIPT]

Last day. At Getuige X-1 again. A young man named Wilhelm is there. Speaks German with an Austrian tinge. He wears a little silver thing on his chest. When he hits it with his palm, a strange high sound rings out, as if a tiny robot's neck were being broken. Ferenz is totally enthusiastic about the little gimmick, in the end W. gives it to him as a gift. When we are alone for a moment, W. asks me where I'm from. I just shake my head.

Later F. and W. talk about high-speed cam art. It takes me a while to understand what this means. You film a person imprisoned in a room from above with a webcam that shoots a picture only every few seconds or even minutes, these pictures are then made into a time-lapse recording of his movements. The model for this art form is, as they explain to me, the video of a man who was stuck in an elevator for more than twenty-four hours. The video itself is only a few minutes long and readily available on the Internet. The movements of the man in the elevator are hectic and fast, he races through the picture, leans for a second (in reality probably half an hour) against the wall, lies down, rests for a few seconds, stands up again, goes on racing through the narrowly confined space. Finally he is saved, the doors open, and he disappears from the picture. I ask how long a recording like that takes. In general two to three days, they answer. It depends entirely on the person. Some hold out longer than others. W. and F. laugh.

It's a peculiar apparatus. A sort of tank in which the sweating men sit. Many with an eye patch, some also with a snorkel in their mouth, probably a sort of inside joke. I take a seat between a man with side whiskers and a Rumpelstiltskin-like creature giving off a sharp smell of Styrofoam, as refrigerators or other kitchen appliances do, shortly after you've lifted them out of the box in which they were delivered. The geometry of the bodies taking the sweat cure is impressive. All types of head shapes are among them, the most frequent is the lightbulb shape.

Since my childhood, rhomboid figures of all sorts have played a recurring and central role in my dreams. That's why the face of the shriveled creature I sit down next to is so attractive to me, virtually irresistible. I'd like most to measure it, get at it with compass and ruler or subject it to various elementary geometry transformations such as reflection, rotation, and translation. It would fit excellently into the UFA film studio logo. I have fun guessing the occupations of the men sitting in the tank and their positions in the hierarchy of commercial and industrial enterprises, make the man with the striking side whiskers into the head of a many-branched family clan and the shrunken creature into an influential art collector.

After some time a red bulb lights up above us, and the sitting men stir. Those who up to now were holding a book put it down. Some take off their outer garments.

The effects set in after some time. Intense dizziness, accompanied by the feeling of being the only person in the world. Then the desire to quit my job at the high school and become a writer, the most significant in the world . . .

After a while my brain becomes completely empty.

Afterward I talk with the shriveled old man. He turns out to be a hotel owner. Every year he goes at least once to Getuige X-1. It's a rare treat.

I cautiously agree with him.

I imagine that I can detect a relaxation in the flow of my thoughts. Images from my childhood surface in my mind, a bicycle dismantled into its component parts, but maybe I'm confusing things. Confusing things is always a good sign. Mixing up the time periods.

It took him a long time to make it through the entire procedure, says the old man. It took him several attempts, so to speak. But it was worth it, of course.

Of course, I confirm.

Later a tour of the facilities. The courtyard with the identical doors and intercoms. On the doors to the chambers are little stickers with smiley faces. Feeling of another time, another era. At the end of the treatment everyone gets a lollipop. F. refuses it on account of his diabetes. The shriveled man gives me his. Sweets don't do him good either, he says. But he wants to know how it tastes.

Like a Koch snowflake, I reply.

[HANDWRITTEN PIECE OF PAPER, LOOSE, WITH TORN HOLE-PUNCHED EDGE]

Evening of the last day. Together with F. visit a so-called end product. This end product is a man whose age is hard to determine. He looks a little bit like a turtle, his movements are ponderous and clumsy. He walks with a cane. At the same time, he possesses a certain energy, which is conveyed mainly through his eyes and his voice. He has been through more than a thousand sessions and now gives off something like Indigo effects himself. In any case, after a few minutes I feel a slight dizziness. When I inform him of this, he seems to be delighted, he practically begins to glow. How strong is the dizziness, he wants to know. I tell him (exaggerating a bit) that the room is spinning around me. Ah, he says with a nod. He closes his eyes contentedly and seems to be enjoying the effects I've described like the aftertaste of a good wine. So what sort of dizziness is it exactly, he asks, more a spinning sensation or more the lack of an orientation point, that is, more anchorless swaying, or more the feeling of bottomless falling, or maybe more a sort of fear of heights, a terrible, diabolical suction from below? I answer, to test him, that it's a spinning sensation. That does in fact seem to disappoint him a little. He sits there and stirs in his cup.

The cane stands between his knees. He talks about his childhood in the countryside. There was a rooster on a neighboring farm that often crowed, several times a day; the rooster was always crowing loudly. And one day it suddenly stopped crowing. And on that day he himself became ill, a severe fever of unknown origin. He almost died back then, the man says, and shows us a notch on his cane, as if it had to do with the story. Here, he says, and also here. He points to a second indentation, several centimeters below the first. F. changes the subject and wants to know whether he still exposes himself to the sweat cure daily. And how are his hip joints? On the whole, quite good, the man answers. He has the energy of ten jazz musicians, he says. Free jazz, he adds more precisely, and laughs. His laughter is accompanied by the tapping of the cane on the floor. This cup, he suddenly says, pointing to his half-empty café au lait. This cup was safe from him for years, but now those days are over. F. and I exchange a glance. Look, says the man, extending his hand toward the cup. Nothing happens. We watch the cup closely. But it doesn't move. If you tried the coffee now, says the man, you would discover that it's cold. Before it was hot, I burned my lips on it several times. The coffee is always served to me too hot here in the nursing home, the people simply have no feeling for it. We nod. F. takes the coffee cup and examines it. His movements appear as if in a dream, and I have to turn away to keep from losing my mind.

When we leave the man's room, F. stops me, he puts his hand on my shoulder and applies gentle pressure. What you have just seen, he says to me, is a great man. A truly great man. What he was willing to take on—and still takes on—is simply unprecedented. You won't find anything like that again anytime soon, wherever you might look for it, Herr Seyss.

[POSTCARD OF A CHEERFULLY SMILING DOG IN A SPACE CAPSULE. BLOCK WRITING ON THE BACK]

Christmas, heavy whirling snow outside the windows. The attempt to put up the wretched plastic tree. The smell of the wood and the fir needles used to stimulate me, but this odorless plastic piece of shit I'd like more than anything else to throw right back out the window. I break off one of the artificial branches and use it as a cat toy.

[2 PAGES WRITTEN BY HAND]

See article on woman from Great Britain who was convinced that her child was an I-child. Today it has been proven beyond doubt that the child didn't possess the ill effects at all. Nonetheless, it took six whole years for the truth to come to light, beforehand the child was treated as an I-child, was alone most of the time, a doctor came once a week and performed his examinations within a few minutes, literally rushing through them (and complained afterward of a headache). The woman continued to confine the child even beyond the age of six, because she could still feel the effects, the attacks of pain and vertigo were not impressed with the scientific evidence, but instead only worsened, because no one would believe her. She knew, she was firmly convinced that her daughter was an I-child, whose presence was gradually destroying her. She flatly rejected any other explanation of her physical afflictions. Ultimately the youth welfare office had to intervene, and there was a trial, at the end of which the mother was permitted to keep the child but had to undergo therapy and allow regular unannounced inspections by the responsible authorities in her home.

This case had, it turned out, a strange consequence. First it of course sparked debate about whether many Indigo cases might not be based on pure imagination. The unscientific concept of mysterious effects at a distance was again cited, the inadequately performed examinations and experiments, the general suggestibility of people. All old arguments. But then the debate took a surprising turn, a series of articles appeared in the *Guardian* ("Voices from the Void," May 1–11, 2005) in which parents were interviewed who had been convicted of child abuse. And many of them suddenly mentioned reasons for their inexcusable behavior that brought I-symptoms to mind. A thirty-nine-year-old man who had stuffed both of his just one-and-a-half-year-old twin sons in a washing machine and left them confined there for twenty-four hours (though without turning on the machine) claimed he felt inwardly fine when he was at work or out and about, *no problems whatsoever*, but as soon as he had come home and seen his wife there, who spent her time exclusively with the two new housemates, he had become angry, *physically angry*, the anger had struck him like lightning in the sinuses and he hadn't known where he was or what he was doing. A woman from Leeds who had been accused of gross neglect of her daughter and sentenced to two years' probation said that she had had to defend herself against the tinnitus that she got whenever her daughter approached her and asked her for something, such as a pair of socks.

This dark debate soon spilled over into other countries. In September a similar series of interviews with violent and convicted parents appeared in the weekly magazine *Stern*. And suddenly there were apologists of parental violence everywhere, but the truly remarkable thing

[COMPUTER PRINTOUT, FOLDED TWICE]

Bartleby the scrivener—there's not just the one, there are many of his kind, many, many Bartlebys. In the strangest occupations and areas of life. There is, for example, the mysterious case of a torturer in the notorious Kampuchean prison S-21. In that building, which had previously housed a school, tens of thousands of people died at the hands of approximately fifteen hundred torturers. One of them, a man known by the name of Ek, supposedly refused outright one day to perform the torture. He sat next to the prisoner, from whom he was first to extract a confession with electric shocks, immersion for several minutes in ice-cold water, or cruel surgical procedures, and whom he was then to murder, and repeated mechanically one and the same sentence, he would do nothing more, nothing more, never again. Only a few weeks later was this discovered, and he too was imprisoned. But not even that could stop the man from saying the never-changing sentence. It is said that a former colleague ultimately took pity on him and killed him by high-voltage electrocution.

[AN ENVELOPE LABELED *CLARIFICATION*. THE ONLY ONE IN THE FOLDER. CONTENTS: SEVERAL LOOSE SHEETS OF PAPER, CLOSELY WRITTEN]

On the cable car a migraine attack announced itself. Since my childhood I've suffered from such recurring attacks, most of the time they're accompanied by distorted vision, scotomas, and hallucinations. Lights appear at the edge of my visual field and constantly change their form and intensity, or blind spots emerge and swallow objects on the periphery. A vase on a table is invisible from a certain angle, the hole in my visual field is simply painted over the color of the table by my brain: an empty table. Reading and speaking become difficult, words remain recognizable but appear as their internal anagrams, Sunday, for example, looks like Sudnay, even when I examine the word letter by letter, I simply can't find the mistake and suddenly know that I'm inside a migraine aura. It's a strange world, a parallel universe, in which you can go through doors that are afterward no longer in their former place. You pronounce a word, and it's the wrong color. Or you look at a tree and discover geometries in the arrangement of its branches.

– Open it, said the man with the pince-nez on his nose.

I opened the envelope and took out the photo. A shot of an empty room. Only a table stood in it. On it a cactus in a flower pot.

I gave back the picture. My hand had begun to tremble. The wind whistled around the stationary gondola. In the distance the twinkling lights of Gillingen in the evening. In the gondolas in front of and behind us, unreachable, rocked the others.

– We're offering you a trade, Herr Seitz.

A vibration passed through the gondola. Below us trees, a slope.

– You'll get what you've always wanted.

He pulled something out of his backpack and handed it to me. One very thin and one somewhat thicker packet of paper.

– It's not exactly Fontane, but you'll discover that you'd rather take *this* path than waste awa ... waste any more time on the one you're on now. Because this path leads nowhere, Herr Seitz.

— Exactly which path do you mean?

A creak in the massive steel cables from which we hung.

— Here, take a look at this manuscript. Generic stuff, basically. But well done. Really good simulation. What do you think of the title?

— Sounds strange.

—Yeah, doesn't it? That works well, these days. You think of family, the battle of the generations, things like that. It's deceptive packaging, of course, stuck-together pieces that don't really belong together. A jumble, but it's already been accepted. It's yours. If you want it.

— I ... I wrote my thesis in mathematics on a similar topic ...

— Right, yeah, yeah, yeah ...You're a math teacher, yes ... And why aren't you working in your field anymore?

— I broke off my internship.

The wind howled around the gondola. Inside it was as warm as in late summer.

—To devote yourself to other activities?

— Can I leave?

— Of course you can. Anyone can do that. It's like breathing.

Pause.

—That means you're finished?

— No, it doesn't mean that, Herr Seitz. I still have here these two manuscripts. Are you cold? Now, you see, you'll definitely want to begin with this one here. It's shorter and more powerful. This second one here ... well, heavy shit. Two lunatics from Vienna pounded it out in a couple weeks. But quality work nonetheless.

I sighed. The gondola at that moment began moving again.

— Am I boring you, Herr Seitz?

— No. But I'd like to get off. Can I do that?

— Of course you can. You know, Herr Seitz. If someone tells you that you can no longer leave, no longer speak, or no longer breathe ... you understand? Then that someone is not your friend. Then you should avoid him.

2. The Cemetery in Gillingen

In the church everyone stared upward. Their posture was reminiscent of that of a cat sitting under a tree and keeping its eyes on an unreachable bird. A priest had come from the next town, having declared himself willing to bury Christoph Stennitzer, who had died *under such sad circumstances*. Even though Frau Stennitzer's father had paid a special visit to the Gillingen priest, spoken to him for a long time, and even left some bottles of wine with him, the old clergyman had not thought himself capable of celebrating the Mass. A young man who had hanged himself, while all around him the flames of his little house blazed ...

Frau Stennitzer's lower lip hid under her front teeth. She didn't say a word when I greeted her and offered her my condolences. In general she scarcely responded to the chances to interact provided by her environment, only now and then she touched her father's arm, as if she were trying to tell him: *Stop. Stop speaking.* Even though the baldheaded man with the brown gloves wasn't saying anything at all.

Frau Stennitzer's body seemed heavy, as if filled with sand. People needed both hands to shake hers.

When all the mourners had left the church, I introduced myself to Christoph's grandfather. He gave me his hand, without taking off the gloves. Then he nodded and said he understood where I was coming from.

I didn't know what to say, so I nodded too.

Christoph and the family, that had always been a problem, said the old man, taking off his jacket. He was sweating. The day was hot. Once he himself had been threatened by teenagers from the town.

— From a distance, they even shot at us, with blank guns or something like that. Insanely loud, those things. And the one guy was wearing one of those NBC protective suits, so we thought it must actually be Wernreich Benni, from up there. Because his father's in the army.

With that the old man walked away.

Countryside funerals on hot summer days have something particularly intense and distressing about them. People are constantly wiping the sweat from their foreheads and the corners of their eyes, the sleeves of the much-too-warm black mourning clothes are rolled up, but not so far that it would really bring relief and cooling, because that could appear disrespectful. No one wants to signal that his own physical feeling, the heat permeating him, is harder to bear than the pain over the loss of a loved one. The high temperatures make the mourners at once sluggish and impatient; even glances become monosyllabic. The priest in the church speaks with fervor, because here it's still cool, and he savors it for as long as possible. Then, outside, behind the coffin, on the way to the cemetery, the orderly rows of two quickly disperse, the people stay behind, have to retie their shoelaces. Whoever has a hat puts it back on—he won't take it off again until he steps in front of the grave and, as a sign of his reverence, endures the merciless sun bareheaded.

The procession passes hedges and quiet, fenced-in orchards. A sharp smell of charcoal, mixed with something else, possibly incense, is in the air. Insects whir around the cortege, are waved away, buzz sluggishly and stubbornly among the people marching uphill in a stooped posture.

I was sweating all over my body, the dissolution begins in the pores, liquefaction, but I didn't dare to drink from the mineral water bottle I brought along, the gesture could have come across as impious. In the hot season the feeling of literally belonging to the earth, of having been built out of its planetary chemical supplies, is much stronger and more convincing. The winter with its cold, white scalpel severs thoughts like that from the body, the person turns into a ghost drifting through the snowy landscape, hidden under many layers of warm clothing, and I find it hard to imagine what physical sensation I would have if I had to do without this existential cooling that once a year grants me two or three peaceful months.

– Herr Setz, I'd really like to say something to you.

– Of course. Go ahead.

Frau Stennitzer came very close to me. Her eyes avoided mine, she stared at my belly. Then she raised her head for a moment and squinted as if my face were a too-bright lightbulb.

– You have to understand one thing, she said. I'm not sure whether you can really comprehend it. I'm grateful to you. For . . .

She closed her eyes as if it were too painful to utter the word. In its place she made a writing gesture with her hand.

– People here read your articles, of course, she said. Everyone read them. And a few other journalists were here afterward, not only because of the cable car, and . . . well, do you still remember the spot in my yard, Herr Setz?

– In your yard?

– The cone.

– Ah, yes, of course.

– At the time I explained to you how permission for a bur . . . a funer . . .

She couldn't go on. Her lower lip tried to escape from her face.

I reached for her shoulder, but she backed away.

– I'm grateful to you, she said with a cold, deeply hurt voice. You have absolutely no idea how grateful. Your articles . . . even the mayor . . .

Again she went silent. Then she looked to the side, breathed in through her mouth, brushed a strand of hair from the corner of her mouth, and said:

– Everyone came. I didn't even have to send out invitations. Thanks to you, Herr Setz. Thanks to you and your . . . articles.

With that she left me standing there.

A man with an old-fashioned pince-nez on his nose was among the mourners. He had fastened his eyes on me. I returned his gaze, held it for several seconds, and then looked elsewhere. When I looked at him again, his gaze was unchanged. Piercing, intense. Possibly angry.

Then I realized that I still had the white button-shaped iPod head-phones hanging around my neck. I quickly put them away. *Oh, my goodness*, I indicated with an apologetic gesture in the man's direction. That did nothing to change his aggressive staring. At least he raised his forefinger to his temple and saluted. I saluted back.

On the wooden cross on Christoph's grave his initials were larger than the other letters. "C.S."

"Arrived in the Lord," said the inscription underneath.

I staggered backward a few steps and accidentally stepped on some-one's shoe.

After the burial the family and friends dispersed, only a few people gathered around Frau Stennitzer. She eyed me from a distance. I sus-pected that, if I approached her again, she would tear out one of my arms or perhaps an eye.

She gestured toward me, and a man with a strange tall hat who stood in front of her turned around in an inconspicuous way to face me. I raised my hand.

I didn't join any group, but instead went by myself to the tavern across the street from Pension Tachler. The pension itself was closed. I sat down in a dark corner and ordered an orange juice. After several min-utes someone came up to my table. Because the figure stood in front of the bright windows, I made out only a silhouette. A tall hat was put on the table in front of me.

– May I bother you for a moment?

I looked at the stranger, incapable of giving a meaningful reply. What was he planning to do? Was he going to throw me out of the tavern? Or start a fight?

– I just wanted . . . um . . . if you could sign this here . . .

An edition of *National Geographic* joined the hat. The man leaned forward so that I could see his face, moistened his middle finger with his tongue, and opened the magazine. When he had arrived at the article "In the Zone," he pointed to my name and said:

– If it's okay, here . . . please . . .

I made a lost gesture with both arms, a mixture of shrugging and putting my hands up.

– Oh, sorry, of course, the man said, patting his chest down.

He reached into his jacket pocket and pulled out a beautiful old and experienced-looking fountain pen. He pressed it into my hand and pointed again to the same spot.

– Something like this . . . um . . . well, how to phrase it, something like this of course makes the rounds in a relatively small town like this one, hahaha, you understand.

I put the fountain pen to the paper, and under its tip an ink dot emerged, which slowly grew larger and larger.

– It's not every day, said the man in exactly the same tone, that someone does something like this for us, as it were.

My name was there. I had written it automatically. I thought about whether I should tear up the article and the whole issue of *National Geographic* then and there, but the man gently took the magazine and fountain pen out of my hand and bowed.

– Have a nice day. Um . . .

He stopped short, put the open magazine back on the table.

– The middle initial, you forgot it, he said.

He tapped with his forefinger on the author name under the headline.

With trembling fingers I drew a thick umbrella handle between my first and last name. I made it thicker and thicker, until the man took the fountain pen out of my hand with a laugh and carried away the magazine.

– Haha, he said on his way out. Yes, all right. Haha.

A waiter brought me my orange juice. Even though I felt a bit nauseous, I ordered a grilled cheese with it. When I tore at the perforation of the tiny ketchup packet and a thin, red, surprisingly fluid jet squirted onto the plate, I had for a moment the feeling of losing my mind. To fend off the attack, I focused on my knees and touched and patted them, I also wiggled my toes and imagined what they looked like in my shoes.

When I wanted to pay, the waiter bowed to me and said it would not be necessary, of course. The mayor took care of it.

– The mayor, I repeated.

– Yes, just now, as he was leaving. He came back specifically for that. He always makes sure that everything is taken care of.

The waiter clapped me on the shoulder.

– People immediately feel famous, he said. When they appear in an exposé like that. But exposure is necessary, or else the malady won't be recognized.

Scarcely back on the street and in the sunlight, I was approached by another person. Only after a few seconds did I realize that it was a woman. An older woman with a headscarf. I reached into the inside pocket of my jacket and clutched my pencil. Where is the best place to ram a pencil? Into the third eye? Through the lower lip into the gums? Into the temple?

But the woman only wanted to know where the train station was. I pointed in the right direction, and she nodded and thanked me.

Slowly I began to move, heading toward Glockenhofweg. I just wanted to take a look at the burnt little house in the yard and then get out of here.

No one else was out in the town. Frau Stennitzer must have gone with her family to one of the larger restaurants for the funeral meal. I stuck my iPod headphones in my ears and listened, to put myself in a somewhat more respectful mood, to Arvo Pärt's meditative piano piece *Für Alina*.

When I arrived at the house on Glockenhofweg 1, Frau Stennitzer was standing at the gate to the yard, as if she had been expecting me. I was a bit startled and immediately pulled the headphones out of my ears.

– Yes, I . . . I wanted to say goodbye to you, I said.

She opened the gate for me.

— Aren't you spending any time with your family? I asked.

The fact that Frau Stennitzer was standing here in her yard so soon after the funeral struck me as a mysterious doubling of her presence. Déjà vu. A glitch in the Matrix.

— No, she said. Come in.

I followed her into the house.

— You wanted to say goodbye, she said. That's nice of you.

— And I wanted to tell you that if there's anything I can do for you, anything at all, you . . .

— Hm, she said.

It sounded like a very tired, weak cough.

— Why did you come back? she then asked.

— To say goodbye.

— No, no, that's not what I mean, I mean . . . I called you, in your hotel room in Brussels, remember?

— How do you know—

— Oh, please, said Frau Stennitzer. Stop that. Let's talk like reasonable people, all right? During our phone call, you seemed quite changed, Herr Setz. You confirmed Christoph's arrival.

— Excuse me?

— Why did you do that? It confused me.

— I have no idea what you mean.

She sighed.

— I don't want to drive you into a corner, Herr Setz. It wasn't completely obvious. It was very subtle. But still clear.

— What was clear?

Her face contorted in disgust.

— Please, don't be so . . . He told me. He told me everything. Even that you asked him to describe to you what's on such a video! I don't want to judge you, but I find that pretty repugnant, I have to tell you in all honesty.

— What? But no, that wasn't how—

— I find that absolutely voyeuristic and a whole bunch of other things too, which I'd rather not even get into now. Why did you ask him to do that? That's so—

I made a time-out sign with both hands:

– Please, listen to me, that wasn't how it was, okay? I don't know how you know about it, but Herr Ferenz wanted to play the video for me, and I couldn't watch it. So I asked him whether he could describe to me what's on it—

– But why? That's doubly sick! I saw the video too, it's not that bad! No reason to have it recounted to you image by image.

– How are you acquainted with . . . ?

She took a step back, and it looked as if she were quickly casting a glance over her shoulder into the hall of the house to check something. The door there was slightly ajar. I stared at it. But the crack of the door didn't widen by a centimeter.

– I can't trust you anymore, she said. That's all I can say. Herr Ferenz will have to find someone else.

– Someone else?

– Yes. You're not suited to it.

– To what? I don't understand what you mean. Really. And I'm very surprised that you know Herr Ferenz, he didn't tell me anything at all about that, so—

– You didn't notice anything? she asked, in tears.

– No, I—

– You bastard!

Her fist struck my right upper arm.

– Wait! I said, intercepting her hand. Please, just a second! Talk to me. Explain to me what you mean. Are you afraid of something? Is that it? Are you afraid that someone . . .

I didn't know myself how the sentence was supposed to go on.

– Afraid!

Frau Stennitzer spat the word out contemptuously at me.

I lowered my arms. A helpless, flightless animal.

– Haaaaah, Frau Stennitzer uttered, seemingly pressing all the air out of her chest. I have respect for what you did. I mean, I really have respect for . . . for . . . that you went there and so on. But we're different, can't you understand that? We were different. Christoph was . . .

She gestured in the air.

– Christoph was different. Christoph was really ready, you understand? You have no idea. You have absolutely no idea.

The last words got lost in her chest, because she was speaking with her head hanging. Her voice had withdrawn to a warm, familiar place, to the orchard of her childhood perhaps, or into the vivid memory of the innocent past.

C.S., I thought. The initials on the grave.

Arrivé.

The sun began to dance around the house, and I had to put a hand to my temple to keep from falling over then and there.

– You're worthless, said Frau Stennitzer. Come on. I'll show you something.

She walked with me through the house and across the patio into the yard. Surprisingly, the sight of Christoph's little house gutted by fire wasn't at all disturbing. It looked as if the house had been newly painted, with black, bubbly, grainy tar. Because there was danger of collapse, we took only a few steps into the building. I stopped outside the door that led into the boy's bedroom on the right, and looked around. As if it were a sculpture made of matches, said Frau Stennitzer, the little house had gone up in flames.

Outside, in front of the little house, in the grass littered with glass shards, lay the brown air mattress, unscathed.

Frau Stennitzer told me how and where she had found it.

At some distance from the house it had lain, next to it beer cans, cigarette butts, and even a (she needed all her energy to pronounce the word) used condom.

She had picked up the air mattress, warm fabric-like material, not at all smooth, meant for wet, happy bodies that wanted to drift for a while in the water.

Without dealing with the trash lying next to it in the grass, she carried the air-filled thing into the house. It hadn't been at all clear to her what she was doing. In another set of circumstances, she probably wouldn't even have made it into the living room, she most likely would have dropped the air mattress, perhaps even pulled out the plug in shock—and like a mad nightmare giraffe the mattress, snorting and voicelessly whinnying over so much suffering in the human universe, would have let out its air.

Only once the air mattress was lying on the couch did it dawn on her that it was a huge repository of breathing air. The lung contents of her son. Storage spaces connected by small sluices as in an oil tanker, so that a leak wouldn't cause everything to sink immediately. Breathing air. Packaged in brown.

She had left the room and had wondered where you could touch the mattress without suffering any damage.

The world's largest repository of the breathing air of the late Christoph Stennitzer.

She had had to laugh, she told me.

I made a helpless gesture with both arms and tried again to put a comforting hand on Frau Stennitzer's shoulder. But she recoiled from me.

— We're taking a ride on the cable car later, she said. A few friends and I. Perhaps you'd like to join us, Herr Setz?

– Okay, I said.

– Because now you've visited us in Gillingen twice and haven't even seen the cable car up close yet.

And for a moment a strange, almost excited smile flitted across her face.

3.   The Winner

How beautiful it looked when paper burned. You should burn something every day, just as you brush your teeth every day.

The folders might still be usable. Robert put them in his backpack.

The most pleasant aspect of the whole thing was that he couldn't even say why he had done it. *Only villains feel no remorse, Robin.* He smiled, closed his eyes, and leaned back. Burnt-out.

When he stepped out of the narrow side street and wiped his sooty fingers on his pants, he couldn't help thinking of Willi's apartment and of what he had done to it. He imagined Cordula showering four times a day to wash the horrible smell off her body. Eventually they would have children, Willi and Cordula, and they would look exactly like all other couples. No difference.

And for a while everything will go on like this. First distance, then overcoming of distance, then union, and again distance.

On the opposite side of the street walked a woman who looked with the typical expression of young mothers into the stroller in front of her. She followed it with careful steps, as if, like a lawn mower, it had its own will. Most likely she had a headache and would soon vomit on her baby, like so many mothers every day in this country.

After a while Robert recognized the area. Yes, the university hospital, and here the tram stop. Should he ride it, as he had back then? A question you usually asked yourself only at an amusement park, in front of a decrepit roller coaster.

He got on, nodded to the iBall, and sat down on one of the rearmost seats. That way he would have a second longer to see the sign for the pastry shop approaching him.

The tram began to move. Houses rolled past. Parked cars. Soon they would reach the pastry shop . . . He had put the backpack with the empty folders on his knees.

A rattling went through the tram, possibly coins lay in the ruts of the tracks. At least Robert had seen that once on television, many years ago.

Merangasse stop. But there was no sign to catch his eye. Where the pastry shop used to be, there was now a hair salon. Black mannequin heads turned, eyeless, wearing wigs, on rotating posts in the display window.

Noon passed with ringing bells through the district. But that didn't make Robert hungry. He was completely calm. Had he been a cat, he would probably even have forgotten to purr. Between the individual seconds of the day, a pleasant glow became apparent, as in the cracks of escalators. Even when he wasn't paying attention to it, he could sense it. With his eyes closed.

That completely destroyed person, he thought. The math teacher. A miracle that he hadn't long since joined a parade. He was like a heap of ashes with which the wind had already begun to play. Where were they now, all the conic sections and pyramids and tetrahedrons and vector spaces and matrices with which he had spent his life? Would they eventually come to his aid? Would they gather around their old confidant, like a swarm of rational insects? Or would they abandon him, as you—according to Armstrong, Aldrin, and a handful of other participants in later moon missions—were suddenly and inexplicably abandoned by most of your childhood memories after you had returned from the moon? The maiden name of Buzz Aldrin's mother was Moon.

Robert imagined the teacher unscrewing the top of his own skull and reaching with his hand into his head, which was filled with a black, grainy, dry substance. He pulled out a whole fistful and put it in his mouth. Chewed. Swallowed. Shook his head and murmured: Not any better.

Usually Robert would have laughed at a thought like that. And might have felt the desire to draw it.

But now he was completely at peace. He desired nothing. Like ashes in a windless place, say, on the moon. The American flag there after more than fifty years looks like its own photo, it never flutters, stands there like a board.

A few days ago Robert had seen the moon during the day. That regrettable error in the solar system. That confused expression it had. The people on the bridge who paid no attention to it. It was terrible to see it like that. Listing heavily, half capsized in the blue. Bright white and as delicate as the tiny bones in the middle ear. And no responsible authority, no emergency service you could have reported it to, as you report a beached whale or a young cat stuck in a treetop. As if the sky were a glue trap, set thousands of years ago, in which it had gotten caught this morning and from where it now stared down at the daylight versions of people and animals, otherwise unknown to it, with a mixture of bewilderment and fascination, incapable of turning for even a second its face with the half-open crater mouth away from us.

7.2.2007
CALLED FERENZ CELL #
=> COMPUTER VOICE, FEMALE
"DIT NUMBER IS NIET
        IN GEBRUIK"

About the Author

Clemens J. Setz was born in 1982 and lives in Graz, Austria. He has received numerous prizes for his work, including the Leipzig Book Fair Prize 2011, the Literature Prize of the City of Bremen 2010, and the Ernst-Willner-Preis at the Ingeborg Bachmann Competition in 2008. Setz was shortlisted for the German Book Prize for his novels *Die Frequenzen (The Frequencies)* and *Indigo*.

About the Translator

Ross Benjamin is a writer and translator living in Nyack, New York. His translations include Friedrich Hölderlin's *Hyperion*, Kevin Vennemann's *Close to Jedenew*, Joseph Roth's *Job*, and Thomas Pletzinger's *Funeral for a Dog*. He has received the Helen and Kurt Wolff Translator's Prize and a National Endowment for the Arts Translation Fellowship.